SAVING IVAN

SAVING IVAN

Alexander Nekrassov

ATHENA PRESS
LONDON

ISBN 10-digit: 1 84748 061 6
ISBN 13-digit: 978 1 84748 061 3

Second Edition Published 2007
First Published 2002 by
ATHENA PRESS
Queen's House, 2 Holly Road
Twickenham TW1 4EG
United Kingdom

Printed for Athena Press

Foreword to the Second Edition of Saving Ivan

When I first finished writing Saving Ivan in 1999, I could never have imagined that events described in my book would actually happen in real life. As it's never a good idea to give the plot away, I'll just say that readers are bound to recognise similarities between certain dramatic developments in the book and events in the Kremlin seven years ago when Vladimir Putin became acting President of Russia and, more recently, in London when former KGB agent Alexander Litvinenko was murdered by radioactive poison.

I wrote *Saving Ivan* with an idea of combining a fast, pacey thriller with an insight into the Big Con, as I call it, when the world was fooled into believing that communism was finished in Russia once and for all. The sad truth is that it never really went away. Most of the people who were running the Soviet Union, including the bosses of the notorious Committee for State Security, better known as the KGB, stayed in control. They simply rebranded themselves as democrats and liberals and changed the signs on their office doors, but stuck to their old ways of doing things, and even stayed in the same buildings. As a result, a strange new Russia has emerged with democracy and free speech ruthlessly suppressed, the economy in the grip of the so-called oligarchs, corruption even more widespread than in Soviet times and organised crime thriving and reaching out far beyond Russian borders.

This revised and updated second edition of *Saving Ivan* will, hopefully, give readers in the West an idea of how Russia's so-called 'transition to capitalism' went so disastrously wrong. The book also sheds some light on the way the former KGB has mutated into a new, even more sinister force, and explains the origins of some of the alarming events now happening inside Russia and beyond.

Most importantly, however, I hope that *Saving Ivan* will be an entertaining read.

Alexander Nekrassov
London, January 2007

It was snowing in Moscow.

The streets were empty and only an occasional car slowly moved down a dimly lit road, sliding from time to time on icy patches.

It was an early morning in January 1995...

Even the New Russians are keeping quiet these days, police sergeant Pyotr Grushko thought as he sat behind the wheel of the patrol car parked on Lenin Avenue, one of the major routes in the Russian capital that still retained its old Soviet name. Bet the sons of bitches left for the sun with their women.

Pyotr was looking at the neon-lit entrance of a casino that had opened in the area recently. The parking spaces in front of the casino were mostly empty.

Suddenly the tranquillity of the early morning was shattered by a burst of automatic gunfire coming from the grounds of Gorky Park. Several gunshots sounded a moment later.

Pyotr ignored the gunfire. In Moscow it was no big deal. Some heavies were probably having fun after getting drunk in one of the local nightclubs. And even if it was more than just shooting into the air, Pyotr was certainly not going to get involved. He was a simple traffic cop and had other things to worry about.

His partner, Oleg Khanin, came out of the telephone booth, ran to the car, opened the door and got inside.

'It's bloody freezing outside!' he said, slamming the door and rubbing his hands. His bushy black moustache was covered with snowflakes that quickly turned into glistening drops of water.

Pyotr stepped on the accelerator.

'So, did you manage to talk to your brother then?' he said, driving slowly close to the kerb.

'Yeah, yeah, I did,' Oleg said, indicating that he had no desire to discuss the subject. He'd half-turned in his seat and was looking through the rear window.

'What's up with you tonight?' Pyotr said. 'You've been acting weird all evening.'

'Nothing's up with me!' Oleg snapped back. 'You'd better watch the fucking road and stop asking stupid questions!'

Pyotr shook his head but said nothing. He couldn't understand why they had been driving up and down the same stretch of Lenin Avenue for the last two hours with Oleg constantly asking him to stop the car so that he could phone his 'brother'. He had never heard him talk about having a brother before. But then again there were many things that he still didn't know about his partner so he figured there was no point in asking him any more questions. Oleg was the brains in their two-man team. He was born in Moscow and seemed to have friends all over the place. Pyotr, on the other hand, came from a small village near the town of Obninsk, about sixty miles south-west of Moscow. He even looked like a typical country boy with his short blond hair, blue eyes and upturned nose. After serving two years in the army he'd worked for a while as a traffic cop in Obninsk. Later he was transferred to the capital and got a Moscow residency permit. The strict system of permits for anyone who wanted to settle and work in Moscow, introduced in Soviet times, remained intact in capitalist Russia.

When Pyotr teamed up with Oleg he quickly accepted him as the leader. He didn't really mind, since in his eyes his partner was a streetwise big city boy. But most important of all, Oleg knew how to earn some extra cash. Pyotr found it hard to force people to pay to avoid a problem with the law, whereas Oleg was a born operator. He never asked for money directly, but he knew how to put pressure on 'civilians', as he called them, so that they soon reached for their wallets.

'When you force civilians to hand over their cash the law states that you're accepting a bribe,' Oleg would say. 'But if they part with their money willingly, with a smile on their lips, then, in my book at least, it's no more than giving a tip.'

Oleg seemed to know all the rules and regulations and could explain in detail not only how they worked but also how best to find a way round them.

Most of the cops at their station accepted 'tips'. It was deemed normal practice. The salaries were low and, as some of the men used to joke, 'If the people at the top can pretend they're paying us reasonable wages, we may just as well pretend that we're not bending the rules.'

Corruption in capitalist Russia was spreading like the plague. Law and order had practically collapsed and bribery among officials had reached an unprecedented scale. Bureaucrats on every level wouldn't lift a finger without a cash incentive.

The police were no different. The rank and file knew that the top brass in the Interior Ministry were getting huge 'donations' in return for favours. So it was considered no big deal for a cop on the street to earn a grand or two a month on the side to prop up the family budget.

★

It was then that Oleg suddenly yelled, 'Go, go, go!'

A car had passed them doing close to eighty kilometres per hour. Pyotr switched on the siren and stamped on the accelerator.

Oleg grabbed the radio transmitter.

'Calling all cars, calling all cars!' he shouted. 'This is one-four-nine. We're in pursuit of a black BMW. It's moving down Lenin Avenue towards Gagarin Square! Suspected stolen vehicle! Request back-up!'

How the hell did he figure out that it's a BMW? Pyotr wondered. In the falling snow it was difficult even to tell the difference between foreign and Russian-made cars, let alone the exact make.

'Go! Go! Go!' Oleg kept yelling. 'Let's get the bastards!'

The chase ended in a matter of minutes. The BMW skidded on an icy patch turning from Gagarin Square to Kosygin Road, went out of control and smashed into the concrete base of a large vodka advert.

Pyotr and Oleg were first on the scene. The excitement of the chase had not worn off as they approached the BMW from both sides.

'Get out of the car!' Oleg ordered in a loud voice.

A young man in a leather jacket and jeans and a woman in a short fur coat and long skirt, both visibly shaken, got out. They didn't look at all like joyriders.

'Step away from the vehicle!' Oleg said. He turned to Pyotr. 'You watch 'em while I check the car.'

He got into the driver's seat and began to look around. Pyotr noticed a patrol car with flashing lights speeding towards them from the direction of Sparrow Hills, where their station was.

'What have we done?' the young man said. 'Why are you treating us like criminals?'

He was tall, with short fair hair, a thin face and large dark eyes. He turned to the young woman who was shivering in the cold.

'Don't worry, Milla,' he said, 'I'll soon sort this out.'

'Now is that a fact?' Oleg said, getting out of the car. He came up to the young man. 'I need to see your driving licence and passport!'

He was checking the documents when another patrol car pulled up beside the BMW. The two policemen got out and, seeing that the situation was under control, loosened up.

'Nice fucking car,' one of them said, glancing at the BMW. 'Pity about the headlight.'

They stood indecisively, not really knowing what to do.

'Look, guys, give it a quick check while we deal with the paperwork,' Oleg said.

The two policemen started searching the car.

'Ivan Borisovich Ossinski,' Oleg read from the passport. 'And what might you be doing at this time of morning driving at eighty kilometres per hour? Not to mention failing to stop when a police car was in pursuit.'

'We were on our way home,' the young man said. 'I had absolutely no idea that you were pursuing us. As for the speed, well, I'm really sorry, officer. Won't happen again. I'd be very grateful if we could forget about this whole incident.'

He took out his wallet and produced a $100 bill, more than a cop's monthly salary in those days.

Pyotr considered the whole incident to be over and was looking forward to the end of their shift and, maybe, having a couple of drinks with the boys at the station. It was then that one of the two cops who were searching the car shouted, 'You'd better come and see what we've found!'

He got out of the BMW holding a plastic bag with white powder inside.

'Looks like dope to me,' he said.

The young man looked stunned.

'I don't understand,' he said. 'It's absurd; I don't use drugs. I don't even know where to get them.'

He looked helplessly at his girlfriend and then at the cops.

'Sure you don't use drugs!' Oleg said. 'You just carry them around for fun. Well, let me tell you, dope pusher, you're in serious shit now!'

He grabbed the young man by the arm and started dragging him to the patrol car. When he tried to resist, Oleg kicked him in the stomach and he fell to the ground.

'That's for resisting arrest!' Oleg snarled.

He lifted the young man from the ground and pushed him into the back of the police car. The young woman followed quietly, shocked by what she'd just witnessed.

Slamming the door of the car, Oleg turned to Pyotr, winked, and said with a wry smile, 'Life's a bitch for some people, ain't it, partner?'

★

The head of the economic section of the Russian embassy in London, Boris Ossinski, walked into an art gallery in the heart of Mayfair.

On presenting the doorman with an invitation card he glanced at the large mirror on the right and nodded in approval. It was a black-tie occasion and the suit he had hired at Moss Bros on Regent Street was just the right size, unlike the previous time when he went to a diplomatic party at Buckingham Palace and looked ridiculous in his ill-fitting evening attire. This time the suit made him look slimmer.

Boris had a weight problem and was painfully aware of it. He was forty-four years old, but being overweight, of medium height and with grey hair he looked older. He still retained some of the charm that had made him popular with women in his younger days, but the heaviness of his features often made him feel uncomfortable.

Should cut down on bread and potatoes, Boris thought. And

then it struck him that his weight problems paled into insignificance in comparison with the desperate situation that he now found himself in.

It had all started several days earlier…

★

Boris was at his office in the new building of the Russian embassy at 6/7 Kensington Palace Gardens, the private road in the west of London where a square foot was probably more expensive than in any other part of the British capital, or any other capital for that matter. The road was first built in the 1850s and from that time housed mostly embassies and also some of the richest individuals in the world. In the 1930s the Soviet government somehow managed to secure the leaseholds for several properties in Kensington Palace Gardens from the Crown Estate. The ambassador's own residence, the embassy offices, the consulate and the headquarters of the military attaché had all been based there ever since. By the end of the 1960s the embassy in London was bigger than any other Soviet diplomatic mission abroad. And, although in 1971 more than a hundred diplomats were expelled from Britain for spying, the Russian presence at Kensington Palace Gardens remained impressive.

It was only after the break-up of the Soviet Union in 1991 that the Russian embassy in London dwindled in size. As a result of cost-cutting measures, the lease on one of the buildings was sold to an international tycoon for several million dollars. The money was used to run the embassy and pay the rent for the flats of senior diplomats.

Later, the Russians failed to renew two more leases and most of the diplomats found themselves cramped into 6/7 Kensington Palace Gardens, which had stood vacant for several years. But as the financial crisis forced the Russian Ministry of Foreign Affairs to cut ever more of its overseas diplomatic staff, the new building was gradually becoming less and less crowded.

Boris had negotiated the move to the new building. For more than a year he had to combine his diplomatic duties with discussing lease agreements, break clauses, land registry certificates, building alterations, and even compensation claims from the tenants of the neighbouring properties. He had to go through piles of legal documents and technical drawings in order to be able to conduct negotiations with interested parties. Eventually he became something of an expert on the entire infrastructure of Kensington Palace Gardens.

Boris had benefited personally from the move to number 6/7. In the new building he had an office all to himself. It was smaller than his previous one, but at least he didn't have to share it with anyone else.

That day Boris was in his office looking through some economic data. The internal phone rang. The guard at the door informed him that there was a Russian man asking to see him.

Boris wasn't expecting anyone, but still went down to find out who it was. It was not uncommon for some of his friends to come to London from Moscow on business and drop in unexpectedly. He didn't mind these sudden intrusions, as he'd usually be invited to a fancy restaurant for a meal he could never afford on his diplomatic salary.

When he reached the lobby, however, he didn't recognise the man standing there. Must be some friend of Alexander's, he thought.

Alexander Neverov was a former diplomat at the embassy who had since done very well for himself running one of the most successful private banks in Russia. Several diplomats who had worked in the embassy in London had managed, at one time or another, to become successful operators back home and were jokingly referred to by their former colleagues as 'the London mafia'.

Boris approached the stranger.

'I'm Boris Ossinski,' he said. 'How can I help you?'

'Comrade Ossinski, nice to meet you at last!' the stranger said, using the old Soviet-style address 'comrade' that was still quite common in post-communist Russia. He was dressed in an old-fashioned raincoat, buttoned up to the collar, and was holding a black leather folder in his arms. He had a thin face, small dark eyes and his thinning fair hair was parted in the middle.

He looked like some dodgy character from the 1930s.

'My name is Georgi Volkov,' he introduced himself, 'and I've got some news about your son, Ivan.'

Boris's heart started to beat much faster.

'What's wrong?' he said. 'What's happened to Ivan?'

'Nothing that can't be taken care of,' Volkov said. 'Let's take a walk and I'll tell you all about it.'

During the next quarter of an hour Boris learnt that his son had been arrested several days earlier in Moscow for possession of drugs. As they walked slowly in the direction of Kensington Palace Volkov told him that Ivan had been stopped by the police for speeding and that during a routine check of the car a package with cocaine was found in it. As a result he'd been arrested, charged with drug possession and released on bail.

Volkov said that a well-connected friend of his, who'd learnt about Ivan's problem, managed to get him released until the trial. But the charges brought against him were very serious and there was a possibility of a long prison sentence.

'Nowadays the cops in Russia insist on tough sentences for anyone who's caught with drugs,' Volkov said. 'Especially hard drugs.'

Boris couldn't believe what he was hearing. Although it was cold outside and he was only wearing a suit, he didn't feel the chilling wind. That's the end of my career, he thought. He knew only too well that as soon as news of his son's arrest reached the Ministry of Foreign Affairs he'd be recalled to Moscow.

As if guessing what was going through his mind, Volkov said, 'By the way, a friend of mine has managed to keep the news about your son's little problem under wraps. Get my drift?'

Boris stopped and stared at a distance in silence. Volkov gave him a couple of minutes to grasp the situation. Then he cleared his throat to attract his attention.

'I have to fly out to Moscow as soon as possible,' Boris said, snapping out of his thoughts. 'I have to try to save my son.'

Volkov shook his head.

'There ain't nothing you can do to get him out of trouble,' he said. 'You'll only make things worse. But let me tell you something that might work…'

Boris looked at him blankly. He suddenly noticed that two of

Volkov's front teeth were rotten. What the hell is this man talking about? he thought. And how come he knows so much about Ivan? But he did everything to conceal his anxiety.

'Tell me what you have in mind,' he said.

Volkov grinned.

'Well,' he said, 'it's just possible that you might help my friend who got your son out of the slammer. And in return I'm sure he'll do everything he can to resolve the unfortunate incident with your Ivan once and for all.'

He outlined the plan. It appeared that his mysterious 'friend' in Moscow was keen on using Boris's contacts in London. It so happened that he needed help in purchasing several properties in the British capital. He wanted Boris to provide him with as much information as possible about the ones that he was interested in. In return he was prepared to pull the necessary strings and get Ivan out of trouble.

Boris finally got the message. Somebody in Moscow wanted to use his services and was not prepared to take 'no' for an answer. And yet the things he was asking Boris to do for him just didn't make any sense. If he wanted to buy property in Britain he could very easily do it himself. London was awash with estate agents who would be only too happy to find a rich Russian a house – or even a bloody castle. There were no restrictions on property deals for foreigners and no inside knowledge was needed.

The whole thing was absurd.

'But why choose me?' Boris asked, bewildered. He couldn't understand what it was all about. It was as if the mysterious man in Moscow was trying to charge through an open door. 'There are many Russians in London at the moment who can do a much better job than me. I don't have the same contacts in the property market as they have. Some of them have been doing property deals for years.'

Volkov grinned.

'I guess my friend must like you for some reason,' he said, 'otherwise why would I be talking to you at all? Oh, and by the way, Marta sends you her regards.'

Then it hit Boris like a bolt of lightning. Of course – Marta! he thought. That's how the people in Moscow got on to me!

★

Boris had met Marta the year before through a friend of his, Kirill Linko, the host of a popular Russian TV show. At one time they had worked together in the Information and Press Department of the Ministry of Foreign Affairs. Later Kirill left the MFA and went to work in television. It was a time of big changes in broadcasting and he quickly became a celebrity, presenting and producing a hard-hitting current affairs programme.

Kirill called Boris from Moscow and asked him to help a friend of his, a woman who was a producer for central television and owned an advertising company.

'She's got some sort of an ear infection,' he explained on the phone. 'Doesn't know where to find a good doctor. She went to London to visit her son who is studying in Britain. It would be a shame if she couldn't enjoy herself. Please help her if you can.'

Boris got into a swinging mood.

'Is she available by any chance?' he asked.

There was a moment's silence on the other end. Then Kirill said, 'I guess she is now.'

Boris suddenly felt uncomfortable.

'I was only joking,' he said apologetically. 'If she's married or something I'll be on strictly official terms with her.'

Kirill laughed.

'It's okay, don't worry,' he said. 'Just help her if you can. Write down her mobile number.'

Boris called Marta and arranged to meet her at a private walk-in clinic in Harley Street.

When he arrived at the clinic Marta was already in the reception with her teenage son, a plump, mischievous-looking teenager. She had no make-up on and was holding a scarf to her right ear. It was obvious that she was in too much pain to care how she looked. But even then it was apparent that she was a very attractive woman.

'Hi, I'm Marta,' she introduced herself in a low husky voice. 'Sorry for all the hassle. I'm new in London and don't really know my way around here. Not to mention that my English is a bit… rusty.'

'It's no trouble at all,' Boris assured her. 'Let's go and see the doctor.'

★

Three days later Marta called him at his office.

'Hi, it's Marta,' she said. 'I've just taken my son back to his school and thought that maybe we could have dinner tonight. I'm really grateful for your help and would like to treat you to a meal. You choose the place.'

They had dinner at an Italian restaurant in Knightsbridge. Marta looked completely different that evening. She wore a tight-fitting dress that revealed her perfect figure and her unusual haircut resembled that of an Egyptian princess. Her large dark eyes had a mysterious glint in them and her sensuous lips froze in a faint, seductive smile.

She looked stunning.

Boris was initially tense, as most men are in the company of attractive women whom they don't yet know well enough. But Marta proved easy-going and after a couple of glasses of red wine they were chatting as if they'd known each other for ages. She told him about her work and the difficulties she'd encountered establishing herself in the television industry.

'Russian TV is so bloody Soviet,' she was saying. 'The idea that a woman can be a successful producer and a director is still seen as a novelty. The whole industry is run by arrogant bastards who are competing with each other by trying to shag every skirt they meet. You wouldn't believe the things I had to go through in order to get my ideas accepted. On several occasions I had to resort to some very unorthodox methods…'

Boris raised an eyebrow and she quickly added, 'Not the sort of methods you are thinking about.'

They both laughed.

It turned out that Marta was part of the celebrity circuit in Moscow.

'It's one big non-stop party,' she said. 'The Moscow crowd has gone completely mad, blowing money as if there's no tomorrow. And if before they were mostly drinking themselves to death, now they're taking drugs.'

Boris was looking at Marta and couldn't get over the feeling that he'd seen her somewhere before; her face was definitely familiar. But he'd got so out of touch with life in Russia, being cooped up in his embassy most of the time writing reports or going through the business newspapers, that he knew practically nothing about the Moscow celebrity scene.

'I've been avoiding most of the action for the last year,' Marta said. 'At some point I simply lost interest in partying. Making money is much more exciting. I recently bought a restaurant and spent a lot of time trying to get it running.'

It was then that Boris remembered where he'd seen Marta. She had appeared a couple of times on Russian television.

'I'm sorry to ask you this, but what is your full name?' he said.

Marta smiled.

'My friends call me Masha Mogileva, but I prefer to be called Marta,' she said.

Of course, Boris thought. It was the famous Marta Mogileva, one of the first serious businesswomen in Russia, an advertising tycoon. She produced about ten programmes that were running on several Russian TV channels. She was a regular guest on talk shows and on a couple of occasions Boris saw her discussing her new projects and talking about her life. He had also heard rumours that she owed her career in television to some powerful mobsters. But then again, many successful people in Russia were often accused of being friendly with the mob, so few people treated such stories seriously.

It was at that moment that Boris imagined that he was also part of the celebrity circuit. There he was, sitting in one of the best restaurants in London, with Marta Mogileva, a woman who controlled half the advertising on Russian television. The next thing he knew he was pouring wine into her glass and telling her stories about diplomatic cock-ups and his encounters with some very important people.

He got really carried away that evening. He told Marta about his contacts in the City and his friends in the 'British establishment'. He also told her that he'd recently negotiated a 'huge property deal' for the Russian government in one of the most exclusive areas of London – Kensington Palace Gardens, where some of the richest people in the world owned properties.

'I know the place like the back of my hand now,' he boasted. 'It's probably the most expensive road in the whole world.'

Who cares if he was exaggerating, he thought. Marta was obviously interested in his stories. He could see that she was paying attention to what he was saying.

When the waiter brought the bill Boris reached for his wallet, signalling that he would pay. He had got himself wound up by his own stories about the rich and powerful and there was no way he was going to let a beautiful woman pay for the meal. But when he looked at the bill he came crashing down to earth. It was just over £350. Service not included. Boris knew that he didn't have enough on his card. He hesitated for a moment, desperately thinking of a way out of the embarrassing situation. But the expression on his face said it all.

Marta looked at him and smiled. She took out a gold American Express card and, before Boris could open his mouth, said, looking him straight in the eyes, 'I hope we won't start arguing about who's going to pay. I've invited you to dinner, so I pay. And don't give me any of that Russian macho crap about men always paying for women. Don't be a bloody sovok.'

When they were leaving the restaurant Boris felt anger rising in him. He was angry with himself for being such a fool. He was angry at the restaurant for charging too much. He was angry with Marta for having all that money. And he was angry at life for being so bloody unfair!

When they got into the car Marta asked him to show her some of London's night scenery. They drove around the West End and eventually ended up in Marta's hotel room. After several more drinks they were kissing on the big double bed. Boris nearly tore off Marta's expensive dress. She kept smiling, as if teasing him.

Boris got up from the bed and quickly took off all of his clothes. But when he turned around Marta had jumped off the bed, ran to the mini-bar, opened it and took out a bottle of champagne.

She was standing before Boris, completely naked and with a bottle in her hands.

'Look at me,' she said. 'Don't I look like a teenage girl? Look at my body. Look at my breasts.'

Boris dragged her back to the bed. He felt the anger coming back. The embarrassing scene in the restaurant just wouldn't go away. Marta called him a sovok, a nickname usually given to people who were too stupid to break with their old Soviet habits.

I'll show you how to make a fool out of me! he thought. He pinned Marta to the bed and got on top of her. She continued to giggle and was pretending to resist him. But Boris was in no joking mood.

'Help me get in,' he growled. Once inside he started thrusting hard.

The last words he remembered her say that evening were, 'Boris, darling, don't rush things, I want to come with you…'

The next day he took her to the airport. Marta was mostly silent during the journey, only asking a couple of questions about some of the buildings they were driving past. At the airport she kissed him on the cheek and said, 'I'll be in touch.'

Boris felt embarrassed about the previous night.

'Maybe it would be better not to tell Kirill about us,' he said.

Marta looked him in the eyes.

'What's there to tell?' she said. 'These things happen between adults. And besides, he and I are no longer lovers. We are business partners, or, rather, we were partners. He owes money to some people I know and he's been behaving like a shit these last few months. But it really doesn't matter now.'

She did not call.

A couple of weeks later Boris heard that Kirill had been murdered at his flat, gunned down when he opened the front door. His two daughters had witnessed the whole thing. The police said it was a typical mafia contract hit. That usually meant that they wouldn't even bother to look for the killers.

★

Georgi Volkov had been instructed in Moscow not to put too much pressure on Boris during the first meeting.

He was told to approach him, make the offer, and then wait. He was not informed about any specific details of the plan. He only knew that Boris was supposed to help in the purchase of several properties in London, including houses in Kensington Palace Gardens. But he suspected that there was more to it than just buying property. He sensed that something big was in the air.

Several days later Volkov called Boris to arrange another meeting. By the looks of things he was keeping the bad news to himself, although he did call his son on the day of Volkov's first visit. Initially he was planning to keep his cool, but as soon as he heard Ivan's voice on the phone he snapped.

'Why? Why didn't you tell me about your problem with the police?' he yelled. 'Why do I always have to learn about trouble at home from other people?'

Ivan was caught completely off guard. He had kept the bad news to himself and even his closest friends in college knew nothing about the arrest. He was desperately trying to sort out the problem, hoping that his father would only find out about it after it was resolved.

Ivan mumbled something about not wanting to upset anyone and doing everything possible to clear the 'misunderstanding' with the police. But Boris was still on the offensive.

'How could you get yourself in such a mess?' he said. 'I can understand anything: parties, girls, skipping lectures. But drugs? Where the hell did you get the drugs?'

'I don't use drugs or deal drugs,' Ivan replied. 'I was framed by the cops. They planted the drugs on me. Why, I don't know.'

'You all say that,' Boris snapped back. 'Every time somebody gets caught with drugs they pretend to be surprised and say they didn't know they had them.'

'I'm telling you, Dad, I don't use drugs!' Ivan said defiantly. 'You either believe me or you don't. But I'm telling you the truth.'

Boris suddenly realised that he wasn't helping anyone by being hysterical.

'Okay, okay,' he said in a conciliatory tone, 'let me think about everything and I'll get in touch with you later. Meanwhile, please try to act as if nothing's happened. And attend all the lectures at college, and don't say anything to Grandma.'

He put down the phone. If only Marina was alive, he thought, she'd know what to do...

★

All these events flashed through Boris's mind as he walked into a large reception room at the back of the art gallery in Mayfair. The place was packed. He immediately noticed several celebrities walking around. Who on earth is backing this artist? he thought. The reception alone must have cost at least several thousand.

The artist was Yeffim Kaltzman. He specialised in miniature paintings on all sorts of objects, ranging from seashells to lockets and tiny wooden boxes. He'd been living in London for about five years and was rumoured to be making good money selling his miniatures. In reality though, the situation was rather different. Yeffim was involved in the illegal sales of uncut diamonds coming from Siberia via Moscow. Nothing major, but enough to pay the bills and lead a comfortable life in London. He was dealing with people in Russia who were taking on the mighty De Beers cartel and smuggling rough stones to the West. The biggest shipments ended up in Israel and the United States. But Europe was also getting its fair share.

Yeffim had another secret. He was sleeping with the wife of one of the big oil traders from Russia who was his main financial backer. The oil trader, who himself had several girlfriends in Moscow, couldn't find the time to visit London often enough to satisfy his wife and he had no problem with her having a boyfriend. His company was sponsoring Yeffim's exhibitions, allowing him to sell an occasional 'masterpiece', as he referred to his miniatures, and thus create an impression that he was living off the proceeds of his art sales.

Yeffim was moving around the room that evening, smiling at his guests and trying to spot a potential buyer. He had already noticed several people who, in his opinion, could easily part with several grand.

Although looking confident and laid back, Yeffim was still a bit shaken. Only an hour before he had had a blazing row with his wife, Galina, who'd walked in on him and Rita, the oil trader's wife, while they were having a quickie in the small storage room at the rear of the gallery. Rita had raised her miniskirt to her waist, taken off her underwear and was leaning on the table, moaning loudly as she usually did during sex. Yeffim was standing behind her, his trousers and shorts lowered to his knees, thrusting hard.

That was when Galina walked in.

It was an embarrassing scene, made all the more awkward by Rita uttering 'Whoops!' as she saw Yeffim's wife walk in. She made no attempt to cover herself and was looking at Galina defiantly, as if challenging her to say or do something.

There was not much Galina could do. She'd long suspected that her husband was having an affair, but finding him screwing 'that bitch' at the back of the gallery an hour before an important exhibition was a bit too much. So she stormed out without saying a word.

Yeffim thought about it for a moment and then decided that he might as well finish what he started. Later he came face to face with his wife again and they had one of their shouting matches. In the end she slapped him on the face, called him a 'bald prick' and left the gallery.

Yeffim looked in the mirror, checking whether he looked okay after all the shagging and arguing. His left cheek was slightly red from Galina's slap and his ponytail was a bit dishevelled. But otherwise he looked fine.

★

'Boris, my dear chap, I haven't seen you for ages!'

A tall dark-haired man in an expensive tuxedo came up to Boris. He was holding a large glass of red wine.

Boris smiled and nodded.

'It's nice to see you, Jeremy,' he said.

Jeremy Goldberg, a multi-millionaire publisher, had made money all over the world, including Eastern Europe, usually against all odds. Where others failed Jeremy would succeed. For the past four years he'd been involved in several projects in Russia and had somehow managed to avoid any serious problems there.

Like most Russians, Boris was fascinated by wealth. It was difficult for him to contemplate that people could actually earn hundreds of millions. At the same time he respected Jeremy for his wit and seemingly light-hearted approach to life. The new rich in Russia were usually arrogant bastards who imagined them-selves to be tsars and treated other people as if they were their servants. Jeremy, on the other hand, never bragged about his dealings and regarded his success with healthy cynicism.

'Thank goodness most people still believe what they read in the papers and are prepared to pay considerable amounts of money for the printed word,' he would joke. 'Otherwise I would have probably moved into pornography and depended on the really sophisticated customers, otherwise known as wankers.'

Boris found it remarkable that a big businessman could talk this way. Most people he'd met in Britain were very serious when it came to discussing money matters. The obsession with money in the West always amused Boris so it was very unusual for him to hear a real captain of industry crack jokes at his own expense.

He was especially fascinated by one confession Jeremy made to him.

'You know, Boris,' he said once, 'most people think that you have to have talent to get rich. But in my experience I found that it takes determination and a certain level of arrogance to make a lot of money. And luck, obviously. But talent usually has nothing to do with it.'

Boris was very surprised to hear that and even thought at the time that Jeremy must have been going through a bad patch. In turn, Jeremy admired Boris for his intelligence and his ability to explain complicated Russian matters simply and clearly. He also liked the way Boris responded to requests for help. If he said 'yes' he would always keep his word and do as he promised. But if he felt that he couldn't do something, he would say so without wasting other people's time.

'Very un-Russian of you, Boris, to actually have the guts to say "I can't" to people,' Jeremy once said to him. 'Most of your compatriots tend to say "no problem" and then do nothing. Jolly decent of you.'

They had an unusual sort of friendship. Boris was reserved in his approach to Jeremy, as most diplomats are in their dealings with people outside their system, while Jeremy was very casual and open, occasionally making jokes about Boris being a 'KGB super-spy'.

With his permanent bronze tan, the mischievous glint in his dark eyes and a boyish grin Jeremy looked much younger than his forty-eight years. His dark hair was greying at the sides but otherwise his whole appearance, and the energy that he radiated, convinced others that he must be in his late thirties.

Some people stay fit and young-looking without pumping iron or jogging every day. As for Jeremy, he would have laughed at any suggestion of regularly visiting the gym.

'A bottle of good red wine a day will do wonders for one's health,' he would say. 'Personally, I can't stand the smell of gyms. And in any case, it's all about what you inherit from your parents. As my late father used to say, "It's all in the genes, young man, all in the genes." '

Although Jeremy had made his money when he was quite young, his life had been no bed of roses. He was fourteen when his parents died in a plane crash. His uncle Joseph took over and supported him through high school and later university. But once out of university Jeremy stopped accepting money from his uncle and started working as a cub reporter for a press agency.

During the first two years he had to handle mostly boring assignments, run errands, compile internal press reviews and edit, or rather rewrite, reports sent in by the big names in journalism. He would often spend a good hour 'polishing' a story, making it much better than the original. Later the correspondent would send in a cable inquiring 'who the hell ruined my report?' and Jeremy would be warned about 'upsetting distinguished journalists'. He could never really understand how some of the big names made their reputation and, even more amazingly, got away with truly appalling writing. Later in life he was to find out that it was not only in journalism that the mediocre flourish.

Jeremy did well in his first two years and was soon appointed Hong Kong correspondent. After six months of writing reports for the wires he suddenly quit and became a commodity broker with a local company. In three years he made a fortune for the firm and some very serious money for himself.

It was in Hong Kong that Jeremy met Lilley, a young Chinese corporate lawyer. They had a whirlwind romance. When Lilley told him that she was pregnant Jeremy suggested that they move to Europe. But on the day before their departure Lilley was knocked down by a car as she was crossing the street. She was killed instantly.

Jeremy was totally devastated. It was the second time in his life that he had lost someone whom he really cared for, and for the first time he turned to drink to get over his loss.

He moved back to London, but soon got bored with commodity markets. He decided to move into publishing and launched the first quality business magazine dealing with emerging markets. That was followed by several publications devoted to investment, share trading, personal finance and computers. Each one was a success, and Jeremy not only raised capital for each project but exercised direct control over the editorial side.

He realised from the beginning that falling standards of journalism were hitting publishing. Journalistic training at universities and colleges was not effective, if only because good journalists would never turn to lecturing as a career. It became clear to him that in order to improve editorial content, he would have to train young reporters on the job, so to speak. And the only way to put pressure on them to learn their trade properly was to let it be known that the boss himself was reading everything they were writing.

Jeremy would spend whole days reading proofs of stories, making changes in style, putting question marks against what looked like unsubstantiated facts and crossing out phrases and whole paragraphs that sounded banal or made little sense. Soon he became so good at editing that he could skim-read whole pages with his eyes and instantly pick out problems of both style and content.

The knowledge that Jeremy read most of the stuff that was going to print made a difference. His people always tried to come up with good exclusive stories, so his magazines sold well. Readership grew rapidly and after six to ten months each new magazine would usually start to break even – a very rare thing in publishing.

Following his success in the UK, he bought several newspapers across Europe, acquired stakes in TV companies and launched radio stations. Within ten years Jeremy Goldberg had become a publishing tycoon with a vast personal fortune.

★

Jeremy led Boris away from the crowd to an artificial palm tree in the corner of the room. He had noticed earlier that Yeffim was closing in on him and anticipated a 'hostile' attempt to force him into buying a 'masterpiece'. It seemed like a good idea to have a quiet chat with Boris away from the spotlight.

'What's the problem, Boris?' Jeremy asked. 'You look troubled by something.'

Boris sighed.

'Family problems,' he said, 'but I'll cope somehow.'

'Ah, come on, you can tell me,' Jeremy said. 'Is there a woman involved by any chance?'

Boris looked at his friend. Here was a man who had everything, who enjoyed life, made money and looked a million dollars himself. What can he know about ordinary people and their everyday problems?

But at that point Jeremy said, 'Boris, I suggest you lose your diplomatic restraint and open up your heart to your old friend Jeremy. I've made a lot of money in Russia and I wish I could repay your people in some way. I'm ready to start right now and help sort out your problem. Don't ignore such an opportunity.'

He gave Boris a wink and drank the wine from his glass in one go, the Russian way. That was when Boris decided to tell Jeremy about his problem. But as it was not the best place to talk candidly they agreed to meet the next day for lunch.

'I think I'll be making my way out of here,' Jeremy said. 'It looks like the artist is seriously contemplating selling some of his work to me and I'm not really in the mood to buy any of his creations. See you tomorrow.'

And he walked away.

★

They had lunch the following day at Jeremy's Mayfair flat in

Mount Street. It was the place where they had met for the first time several years before, when Jeremy was hosting a party for people with East European connections. By then he was already involved in a number of projects in Russia but was still trying to get the feel of the 'Russkies'.

Boris's name had been suggested to him by the Confederation of British Industry. The CBI was trying to launch a so-called East European Initiative, a project aimed at putting British business-men in touch with potential Russian partners. The initiative failed miserably, but the people behind it claimed that at least it brought some British companies closer to understanding their Russian counterparts. In any case, it enabled Jeremy and Boris to meet and eventually become friends.

They were sitting in the dining room, the windows facing the famous Scott's fish restaurant across the street. They were alone. Although it was a strictly unofficial meeting, Boris, as a typical diplomat, wore a dark suit, white shirt and formal tie. Jeremy was dressed casually, in a blue cotton shirt and jeans.

'It's very serious, Boris,' Jeremy was saying. 'Now let me get this straight: your son has been apparently framed by some people in Moscow who want you to help them buy several properties in London? And they are prepared to put him in jail if you don't do as they say?'

'In short, that's the case,' Boris said. 'What I don't understand is why on earth would they pick me? How can I help them? I'm not an estate agent, and besides, I thought that by now rich Russians had enough people on their payroll in the West to find all the properties they want. It's a complete mystery to me.'

Boris had decided not to mention his one-night stand with Marta Mogileva and her obvious connection with the people in Moscow. He felt bad about their encounter and didn't want to acknowledge that he himself could have been partly to blame for the whole situation.

'Well, at least they gave you time to think about their offer,' Jeremy said.

Boris nodded gloomily.

'You're right, it could have been much worse,' he said. 'Re-cently some thugs kidnapped the son of a Russian businessman I once knew. They demanded a huge ransom. He paid up, but his son's body was dumped outside his dacha several days later.'

Both men were silent for a while, as they tried to appraise the situation. Boris was actually thinking of putting pressure on the mysterious man in Moscow with the help of some of the former KGB people he knew. He still remembered their stories about the KGB carrying all sorts of secret missions, both at home and abroad, that had nothing to do with intelligence gathering. Enemies of the Soviet state were physically eliminated, sometimes by administering undetectable poisons or injecting drug over-doses; people were kidnapped and never heard of again; busi-nesses were bankrupted and sophisticated financial scams were pulled off for the sole purpose of implicating certain individuals.

There was one story that Boris heard from a retired KGB general about an operation to get back the daughter of a very senior Communist Party official who ran off with her lover to the West. The woman was living with her diplomat husband in East Berlin and got involved with a Dutch businessman, fleeing with him to West Berlin. The KGB station chief in East Berlin received a cable from Moscow instructing him to find the woman and bring her back. A team of three people was picked to carry out the assignment. The KGB didn't want the Stasi, the East German secret police, or the Russian embassy people to know anything about it. The three agents slipped into West Berlin and spent two days tracing the pair. Eventually they found them in a small hotel. The man was temporarily immobilised. The woman was not cooperative, so they drugged her, put her in a special container and brought her back to East Berlin. Later she and her husband were quietly moved back to Moscow.

As a last resort Boris was contemplating turning for help to some of the people he knew who worked for the former KGB – now renamed the Federal Security Service, or FSB for short in Russian – and asking them to get his son out of trouble. He was unaware that FSB agents were now charging a lot of money for their services and were themselves often involved in illegal dealings.

As for Jeremy, he knew that it was pointless going to the au-thorities. In fact, he reckoned that it was probably dangerous to do so as there was no guarantee that someone in the police or the FSB wouldn't tip off the very people who were threatening Boris and his son. It was obvious that Ivan had been framed by the cops on somebody's instructions. The question was – who were those people and what would it take to get them to leave Ivan alone?

At that moment Jeremy felt that he himself was entering dangerous waters. It was one thing doing business in Russia and altogether another thing taking on the local mob. There was of course still a chance for him to back out. But when Jeremy looked at Boris, who seemed so vulnerable and helpless, he didn't have the heart to just walk away.

'This is what I want you to do, Boris,' he said. 'When you meet this Georgi Volkov again and he provides you with the questionnaire, tell him you'll need at least three to four weeks to collect all the information about the London property market. Try to convince him that you've decided to cooperate fully. And don't talk to anyone else about what has happened. I'll contact you myself. Whatever happens, don't panic. We'll get you and your son out of this mess.'

★

After Boris had left, Jeremy sat for a while considering his options. It was now clear to him that conventional methods would be useless in trying to resolve the problem. Reasoning with Russian criminals and paying them off was out of the question, as there could be no guarantee that they'd keep their end of the bargain. So someone had to go in and put some serious pressure on them, forcing them to back off. Jeremy could only think of one man for the job. He stood up and walked across the room to the phone.

'Tell George Blunt I'd like to see him as soon as possible,' he said.

An hour later Jeremy was discussing Boris's plight with George, a former Royal Marine who had spent twenty years in the service. Out of these, fifteen years were, in his own words, devoted to carrying out special assignments 'for Queen and country'. George was a typical military man: over six feet tall, short haircut, always clean-shaven, always smartly dressed in suit and tie and always wearing polished black shoes. He had a powerful lower jaw, dark deep-set eyes and a large nose that had been broken on several occasions. George never actually told anyone what he did while he was in the Special Forces, but the scars on his face and hands gave a clear indication that he had had to carry out some pretty rough assignments. It was frightening to think what his large hands could do to a man's throat.

George had been introduced to Jeremy about six years earlier, when the latter had run into problems with some of his publications in Northern Ireland. Local heavies were putting pressure on the printers demanding protection money. George flew to Belfast and sorted out the problem. There were no shootings or beatings, but no pay-outs or concessions either. As George explained afterwards, he used logic and common sense and the people on the other side came to a conclusion that it was best to drop the whole thing.

Jeremy liked that; he despised violence.

Later George helped to solve a number of delicate problems in several countries. Once he even took charge of an operation to release the son of one of Jeremy's friends who had been kidnapped by a group of radicals demanding a huge ransom to finance their 'political struggle'. George and his people managed to find where the 'revolutionaries' were hiding in Italy and freed the youngster. Although he later swore that absolutely no violence was involved, the radical group was never heard of again.

★

'It's going to be tricky, sir,' George was saying to Jeremy after hearing the story of Ivan's arrest and the subsequent meeting in London between Boris and Georgi Volkov. 'We'll have to take on the mob in Moscow and keep the Russian authorities in the dark.'

Jeremy nodded in agreement.

'Is there any information about the criminals in question?' George asked.

'At the moment it's all very confusing,' Jeremy said. 'The man from Moscow only mentioned some mysterious "friend" of his who wants to purchase properties in London. We can, of course, assume that this "friend" is a criminal, otherwise why would he need to frame Ivan Ossinski and blackmail his father. But what puzzles me most of all is why should anyone put pressure on Boris to force him to help buy a house here? It just doesn't make any sense. No sense at all.'

George thought about it for a moment.

'As I understand, sir, Mr Ossinski is bound to be contacted by the envoy from Moscow again,' he said.

Jeremy nodded.

'Yes, he arranged a meeting with Boris for next Friday.'

George smiled.

'Well, at least we know who can help us to identify the gang in Moscow,' he said.

They sat in silence for a while.

'How much do you think it might all cost?' Jeremy asked.

George thought for a while, adding up the sums in his head.

'Well, sir, if things don't get out of hand, I'd say we're probably looking at a million pounds at least.'

Jeremy took it well. It was a lot of money, but he was not going back on his word.

'Now tell me about the unpleasant things,' he said.

George rubbed his chin.

'The worst thing would be, sir, if our men got caught in Moscow blowing somebody's head off,' he said. 'That would mean they'd be handed over to the security people and there might be a big scandal. The Russians might want to make some spy thing out of it.'

Jeremy looked at him.

'Well, we'd better make sure they don't blow anyone's head off, as you say, and stick to the rules.'

George's right eye twitched. He was silent for a moment.

'With all respect, sir, there are no rules in Russia,' he said.

Jeremy grinned.

'Then we'll have to start introducing them to the Russians.'

George nodded to show that he had understood the requirement.

'I expect your men to keep within the boundaries of civilised behaviour and still get the job done,' Jeremy said.

'Yes, sir,' George said. 'How will we code-name the operation?'

Being a former military man he liked things in order. Any job, especially in a place like Russia, had to be conducted like a military operation.

Jeremy thought for a moment.

'We'll call it Operation Saving Ivan. The young man's name is Ivan and it's a name that is usually associated with Russia. So the code name will have a symbolic meaning – by saving Ivan we'll be saving Russia.'

Jeremy realised that he must have sounded like a sentimental fool. But George's face showed no emotion. He was still feeling embarrassed for losing his cool, if only for one brief moment, in front of Jeremy and decided to keep his emotions under wraps. Only when he walked out of the building did he allow himself to adopt a defiant look.

'Civilised behaviour?' he said as if continuing the conversation with Jeremy. 'In Russia? That'll be something of a novelty.'

He started walking down Mount Street.

Now, let's think who I can use…

★

The winter in Yerevan was warm that year. The locals in the capital of Armenia could not remember there being such a winter for many years. Life in the city was gradually getting back to normal. The war with neighbouring Azerbaijan was finally over. No peace treaty had been signed, but at least the fighting had stopped.

The Armenians had managed to secure control over a large chunk of the disputed territory around Nagorny Karabakh. Although Russia always proclaimed a neutral approach to the conflict between the two former Soviet republics, Moscow had been quietly supporting the Armenians. More than a billion dollars' worth of arms were secretly shipped to Armenia on the direct instructions of the Russian Defence Minister. His solidarity with his fellow Christians was generously rewarded. He received a two per cent commission from the sale.

The Azeris were also getting their share of support. Secret

arms shipments had been arriving from the Middle East on a regular basis. But the Armenian army proved too much for the Azeris. Many professional military men were hired to fight on the side of the Armenians. Among them were former Russian officers and mercenaries from several Western countries.

Eventually the Azeris had no choice but to concede defeat. Their leader, Heidar Aliev, former KGB and communist boss of the Azeri republic in the days of the USSR, managed to convince his people that it would be best to stop the war. At least for the time being.

In one of the bars in the centre of Yerevan, at a table in the dimly lit corner, three men were talking quietly. One of them was definitely not a local. With his blue eyes, greying fair hair and pale skin, wearing a leather jacket and jeans, he couldn't look more different from the two other men, both typical Armenians with dark hair, dark eyes and black beards. Both men were dressed in dark blue suits and casual shirts.

'We were very surprised to learn that you're asking for a substantial bonus on top of the amount we've already paid to you, Mr Hunter,' one of the Armenians was saying in broken English. His name was Barsek and he did all the talking, while his companion was watching the foreigner with suspicion. 'You did a fine job on the battlefield. Our people were very impressed. And no one can dispute that since then you've trained our soldiers and officers well. But you were paid generously. And yet you're suddenly asking for more money?'

A faint smile appeared on Hunter's lips.

'I call it a success fee,' he said. 'Considering what I've done for you, it's a very modest sum. Your people would've been in shit if it wasn't for me and my friends. You may be good at selling fruit in Moscow's markets and fucking blond Russian women, but you're hopeless when it comes to fighting.'

Both Armenians did not take it well.

'You are our guest, Mr Hunter,' Barsek said icily, 'but you shouldn't offend your hosts in their own house. You might regret it one day.'

The smile disappeared from Hunter's lips.

'Are you threatening me by any chance?' he said. ''Cos if you are then we'll have to sort our differences elsewhere.'

Barsek shook his head.

'No, I had no desire to threaten you,' he said.

'Good,' Hunter said. 'For a moment there I thought you didn't like me at all. Okay, let's get back to money matters. When we were fighting the Azeris nobody said that it would be a problem. Just tell us what you need, you said then, and we'll provide you with it. Now that we've done everything we promised we'd do you suddenly start counting pennies. And even get upset when I remind you who actually won the war for you.'

There was a moment's silence. Then Barsek said, 'We'll pay you the money you are asking, but first we'd like you to do one more job for us.'

Hunter frowned and shook his head.

'I won't discuss any jobs until I see the money,' he said.

'Don't worry, Mr Hunter, the money is with us,' Barsek said. 'It's in the briefcase under the table. You can have a look at it and then we can discuss business.'

A large briefcase appeared on the table. Hunter opened it, glanced quickly inside, and closed it again.

'There's $100,000 in the case,' Barsek explained. 'You'll get the other half on completion of the mission.'

'Okay, tell me about the job,' Hunter said.

'We would need you to dispose of a man.'

'And who might he be?'

The Armenians looked at each other and then Barsek said, 'The Defence Minister.'

'You mean the Azeri Defence Minister?'

'No, I mean the Armenian Defence Minister.'

Hunter looked at them in bewilderment.

'You have got to be joking?' he said.

But the Armenians didn't seem to be in a joking mood.

'Are you saying that you want me to whack one of your own top guys?' Hunter said.

Both Armenians nodded.

'Yes, that is exactly what we want you to do,' Barsek said.

'And why on earth would you want that?'

'We have our reasons.'

Hunter was sitting, digesting the news. Then he heard the

slight creaking of a chair behind him. He looked at the glass of red wine he was holding in his hand. Like a mirror it reflected the tables behind.

Hunter kept looking at his glass, as if trying to assess the offer. Suddenly he jumped up from his chair, whipped out a gun with a silencer, turned around and shot the man who was sitting behind him. Then he turned back to the two men who were reaching for their guns and shot them both. Grabbing the briefcase he ran out of the bar.

A car pulled up at the kerb and he got into it.

'You were right, Armen,' he said to the man at the wheel. 'They were trying to set us up.'

The car sped away...

★

George tracked Alex Hunter down in Ireland where he was 'recuperating' after an especially difficult job in Afghanistan. It took George three hours, a large bottle of Scotch and a promise of serious money to persuade him to take on the Russian assignment. But he needed more people for the Moscow operation.

★

The cargo ship *Adventurous*, carrying a hundred containers with electrical household appliances, spare car parts and clothing, was approaching the end of its journey. The ship had sailed from Malaysia and, having passed through the Korean Straits, entered the Sea of Japan heading for the Russian port of Vladivostok.

The crew of *Adventurous* consisted mostly of Asians. There were only two Europeans among them and one American. The captain, Jeff Nabisko, was Australian and the ship was registered in Malta.

Adventurous was passing through an area of danger where pirates were known to roam. The captain was on deck. It was getting dark. The sea was calm.

If all goes well, Nabisko thought, this will be my last journey. It's time to settle down.

His thoughts were interrupted by the American. He was one of the three men that had arrived from Hong Kong by plane with papers from the shipping company that owned *Adventurous*. The papers instructed the captain to take the three men on board and use them as ordinary crewmen.

Captain Nabisko didn't like strangers, especially when they got on his ship at the last moment with no prior notice. But the instructions were clear and were signed by the right people. He had no choice and he obeyed.

The three men quickly blended into the crew. The captain kept an eye on them, but there was nothing about them that could give him a reason to feel worried in any way. In his life on the sea he had seen enough of those wise guys who'd board his ship and snoop around only to leave with absolutely nothing to pin on him.

'Cap'n, can I have a word with ya?' the American was saying.

Nabisko didn't like the informal way the American addressed him and the constant chewing of gum irritated him. But he decided not to make a scene and signalled to the American to continue.

'A couple of hours ago I saw a torpedo boat with a heavy machine gun on deck,' the American said.

'It might have been the local navy patrol boat,' Nabisko said.

'Well, in that case how come it didn't have a flag or registration number?'

'So what are you saying?'

'They might be pirates.'

'Pirates?' The captain seemed worried. 'Are you sure you just didn't see the registration?'

'Sure I'm sure,' the American said. 'I just thought I'd warn ya, Cap'n. It's gonna be a quiet cloudy night – just the time to attack a cargo ship.'

Nabisko looked at the horizon. The sun was sinking into the calm sea and there was such tranquillity around that the mere thought of pirates in these waters seemed ridiculous. But there was something in the way the American spoke that convinced the captain that he'd better be doing something in the face of potential danger.

'Okay,' he said. 'I'll tell the men on deck to keep a lookout. And you keep your eyes open too.'

'Yes, Cap'n,' the American said. 'And I'll ask my two buddies to help me.'

Night came and the *Adventurous* was sailing in almost total darkness. The captain left the bridge and went downstairs to his cabin. It was a small cabin with photos of his wife and two daughters, and of some of the places he had visited, stuck to the walls.

Captain Nabisko lay on his bed awake. He was still thinking about the American and his two companions. They wouldn't be able to put up any serious resistance even if the pirates attacked us, he thought. They aren't even armed. At least, nothing had been found in their cabins.

Suddenly he heard several shots. He jumped up from his bunk and ran up on deck. There was panic on the ship. Two torpedo boats were approaching them from starboard. Their powerful floodlights were directed at *Adventurous*, blinding the people on the ship. Machine-gun fire was coming from the boats. Several sailors had been hit and were lying on the deck.

As the captain ran into the control room bullets were smashing into the walls and the sailor at the wheel was crouching on the floor, either wounded or trying to dodge the gunfire. Ducking bullets, Nabisko reached the special frequency radio and sent a distress signal to the headquarters of his company in Malta. It was not supposed to summon help so much as to pinpoint the location of the ship in case it sank so that it would be easier to deal with the insurers. He then got to his internal radio and summoned the crewmen from the lower decks.

Captain Nabisko wasn't planning to put up a fight. He got the loudspeaker and shouted several times in English that he was surrendering the ship.

The shooting gradually died down. Nabisko looked outside and saw one of the torpedo boats approaching *Adventurous*. His crewmen were getting out on deck looking dazed and frightened.

There was no sign of the American or his two friends. Seven pirates, all armed with machine guns, boarded the ship. They signalled to everyone on deck to stay close together. Captain

Nabisko stayed with his sailors. A tall man with a black beard was giving orders; he spoke English with a heavy accent.

'You were wise not to resist,' he said, eyeing each sailor. 'For that you'll be spared.'

His eyes stopped on Nabisko. 'And you must be the captain?' he asked.

Nabisko nodded. 'I'd like to warn you,' he started saying, 'that—'

The bearded man didn't let him finish. The captain fell on deck, hit by several bullets.

'From now on I'm the captain here,' the bearded man announced.

These were the last words he ever said. Out of the darkness three men appeared armed with machine guns. Within seconds all seven pirates lay dead on deck.

'Keep yar heads down, all of ya!' commanded the American. Then he and his two friends started spraying the torpedo boats with bullets.

Both boats turned around and disappeared into the darkness.

'Take the cap down below,' the American said. 'And let's get moving!'

Minutes later he was on the radio.

'Grey Seal calling Fisherman,' he said into the receiver, chewing on his gum. 'Problem dealt with. Repeat, problem dealt with. Over and out.'

He slumped back in the chair. One of the Europeans came into the cabin.

'Nice work, Clay,' he said to the American. 'Pity about the captain.'

Clay didn't turn his head.

'The cap was in on it,' he said, slowly working on the chewing gum with his jaws. 'He just didn't know that they'd decided to cut him out of the deal.'

★

Through his friends George got hold of Clay Jones and invited him to London. Clay had worked for George before and didn't ask any questions. He flew in the next day. At a meeting in a West End pub he agreed to carry out the assignment in Russia.

The money was too good for him to turn the job down.

★

The vast lobby of the Hotel Ukraine, one of the biggest in Moscow, was unusually empty. Apart from several people at the newspaper stand and some children running around chasing each other, there was no one in sight. Even the ever-present local hookers seemed to have taken an extended lunch break and were nowhere to be seen. The lobby, with its high ornamental ceilings and walls covered in granite and marble, looked more like the waiting hall of a railway station.

The Hotel Ukraine was built in the mid-1930s on the bank of the Moscow River and was one of the seven gothic-style 'sky scrapers' that were intended to give the city a majestic socialist skyline. Each of the buildings was decorated with a huge red star at the top that lit up at night to complement the stars on the towers of the Kremlin.

In the bar at the far end of the lobby a man was sitting at a table glancing lazily through a magazine. He was wearing a jacket that had seen better days and a shirt that was fraying at the collar. His dark hair was slightly wet, with an uneven parting, the sort that occurs when people comb their hair without a mirror. He was clean-shaven, but a couple of tiny fresh cuts under the nose and on the chin betrayed a habit of shaving irregularly.

The man looked at his watch from time to time and occasionally shot a quick glance towards the bar with its rows of bottles bearing Western brand names.

His name was Pavel Batalov. He was a former detective from the Moscow central criminal investigation department and he was waiting for 'a Mr George Blunt' to talk about some project he had in mind.

Pavel had absolutely no idea who the man was or how he'd found him. He received a phone call early in the morning, not his favourite time of day. A woman's voice had inquired about the possibility of talking to Mr Batalov. Pavel's throat was so dry that he asked the woman to hold while he 'looked for Mr Batalov'. He then rushed to the kitchen where he drank half a jug of water mixed with bits of lemon. He looked in disgust at the two empty brandy bottles on the table and several paper plates with leftovers stuck to them. The large glass ashtray was full of cigarette butts and stank horribly; some idiot had poured oil from a sardine can into it to extinguish a burning cigarette.

Through the large kitchen window Pavel could see snow falling heavily outside and the children playing snowballs in the courtyard. The temperature had plummeted to $-25\,°C$ the previous night and most of the primary schools cancelled all the lessons for the day, supposedly to allow the youngsters to stay at home and avoid the cold.

Pavel shook his head, imagining spending several hours outside in such freezing weather. He then ran back to the bedroom, wrapped himself in a blanket and sat down on the bed. Clearing his throat he picked up the phone and said, 'Batalov speaking.'

The woman explained to him that she was calling on behalf of Mr Blunt, a businessman from London, and that his – Pavel's, that is – name had been provided by some people whom he had recently consulted on matters of personal security. She mentioned some names, but Pavel could not put a face to any of them, so he just said, 'Of course, of course, I remember them well.'

The woman then asked him whether he would be able to find time to meet Mr Blunt that afternoon. Pavel couldn't help smiling. After they had kicked him out of the CID the one thing he had in abundance was time…

It happened three months earlier. They were ready to bust a big drug dealer. For several months they'd been watching a gang of heroin dealers in the south-west district of Moscow. The man they were after, a Nigerian called Mustafa, was a dropout from Patrice Lumumba International University, who had set up a gang selling heroin. In two years he made a fortune and was running a full-scale operation involving two hundred people. He bought himself a big country house outside Moscow where, as it turned out, he stored some of the drugs delivered from Central Asia.

The cops had a tip-off about it from one of the hookers who took part in an all-night orgy at the house, but did not get paid for her services. 'He forced me to have sex with four of his friends,' she complained. 'I worked hard but all they gave me was a bottle of some cheap wine. Bastards!'

The woman said that she saw Mustafa take out a large plastic bag with white powder from a hidden compartment in the wall behind the sofa in the dining room and pass it to one of the men. She also claimed to have seen them putting similar-looking bags into their sports bags.

It was time to nail the son of a bitch.

The cops waited for several days until Mustafa had got more of some of his people together. Then, without giving them any time to get stoned, thirty men, most of them armed and dressed in body armour, stormed the country house. There was a lot of shouting and swearing, and even some physical resistance offered, but in a matter of minutes all the occupants of the building were overpowered and rounded up.

Pavel was among the team that stormed the house. Once inside, he ran up the stairs leading to the first floor and headed straight for the bedroom. When he got there he pulled out several drawers and swung open the wardrobe doors without even bothering to check what was inside. He then ripped the cover off from the king-size bed and cut into the mattress with a pocket knife. He found several bags with at least a kilo of dope in each and at least a dozen plastic packs with thick piles of hundred-dollar bills in them. But he showed no interest in the dope or the cash. He was looking for something else, and he found it: a black diary, full of names and phone numbers and account details.

He heard footsteps outside the room and quickly hid the diary in the inside pocket of his jacket. Two cops in bullet-proof vests holding machine guns came in. He had first met them only a couple of hours before, so he could not trust them.

'Found the dope and the money,' he said, pointing at the bed.

They eyed him with suspicion.

'I'll leave you boys to it,' Pavel said, moving towards the door.

But one of the cops stood in his way.

'We'd better wait for the chief investigator to arrive,' he said. 'Who knows what he'll want to ask.'

Pavel shrugged his shoulders.

'I have no time to hang around here with you boys,' he said, pushing the cop who was blocking his way aside. 'And besides, the chief investigator knows where to find me.'

Later that evening three men burst into his flat, tied him up and beat him up, demanding to know where the 'little black book' was. He played the hero for about two seconds and then told them it was hidden in the oven. Before leaving, they beat him up some more, obviously enjoying the process.

About ten minutes later – surprise, surprise – the cops arrived, conveniently claiming that one of the neighbours had called them when he supposedly heard suspicious noises in Pavel's flat. They were a bit edgy and tense, those cops, and for some unknown reason began searching Pavel's flat. After the rough treatment he got from his previous guests Pavel was in no shape to protest. His upper lip was swollen and his face was bruised, not to mention the pain in his ribcage. So he just sat on the chair in the dining room and looked in silence at the cops who were ransacking his place.

He knew the whole thing was a farce, and, just like all farces, it had a predictably obvious ending: one of the cops found a plastic pack with $50,000 in it hidden in the wardrobe in the bedroom. It was exactly like the ones found in Mustafa's house earlier that day.

The next day Pavel was suspended and, after a brief internal inquiry, sacked from his job in disgrace...

★

At their meeting in the Hotel Ukraine George explained to Pavel in general terms what he needed from him. Initially he seemed reluctant to take part in the operation, but once George mentioned the amounts of money involved he quickly agreed. He was told to wait for detailed instructions from London.

★

Boris met Volkov for the second time in a bar on the top floor of a hotel, overlooking Kensington Gardens. The Russian embassy often used the hotel to house important guests from Moscow as it was conveniently situated at the entrance to Kensington Palace Gardens.

This time Volkov was a little more specific and sounded less threatening than at their first meeting.

'The guy I told you about is no gangster,' he was reassuring Boris after downing his beer in one go. 'He's straight and he's got a lot of cash. He decided to move to London and he's willing to pay for your help, so don't get any wrong ideas.'

Volkov was obviously experiencing a severe hangover and his whole appearance – he was wearing a dark brown leather jacket, blue jeans and white running shoes – was no longer sinister. But Boris knew his son was in no less danger. The threat of prison was still very real.

He'd already spoken to a lawyer friend in Moscow who told him that Ivan was looking at eight years' hard labour if found guilty. The mere thought of his boy being thrown into jail horrified Boris. He heard about people being tortured and killed by hardened criminals and drunken prison wardens. He also knew what they did to young men in those hellholes.

'I still don't understand what you want me to do,' Boris said, trying to keep his cool. 'You mentioned helping your friend to buy property. What sort of property are you talking about?'

Volkov looked at him and suddenly burped loudly. Boris couldn't help wincing.

'I'll give you all the details when the time is right,' Volkov said, wiping his moist lips with the back of his hand. 'Meanwhile I want you to get me information about the houses in this fancy road where your embassy is. What's it called again?'

'Kensington Palace Gardens,' Boris said. 'But you're wasting your time. It's the most expensive address in the whole of London. The lowest price you'd pay for a house here would be about twenty million dollars and upwards.'

Volkov seemed unimpressed.

'How come you know so much about this area?' he asked.

'I work here,' Boris said with irritation creeping into his voice. 'Many of these buildings were at one time or another occupied by the Russian embassy, and I've been inside the others as a guest. So

I know what I'm talking about.'

Volkov took a handful of salted peanuts and threw them into his mouth.

'Well,' he said, chewing on the peanuts, 'in that case, I guess, you'll have no problem finding out about the houses in the road. And don't forget about the Russian embassy. Who knows, my friend in Moscow might be interested in buying some of these fancy buildings from your people.'

Boris felt that it would be a complete waste of time, but still followed Jeremy's instructions. He promised Volkov that he'd do his best and get all the information he could on every property in Kensington Palace Gardens. But he insisted that he'd need time to get the details together.

Volkov shrugged his shoulders.

'I can wait,' he said. 'I hope your son can wait too…'

They parted company downstairs in the hotel lobby. Volkov walked out of the hotel and turned left, heading in the direction of Knightsbridge. Two men who were standing at a bus stop across from the hotel started walking in the same direction.

★

In a nightclub in West London a Russian-themed evening was in full swing.

A live band was playing Russian pop songs and the barmen were busy serving vodka 'double doubles' to the guests. After several people had too much to drink, the usual fighting broke out. A man was knocked out and had to be taken to the hospital where he was kept until the morning. According to documents found in his wallet, his name was Georgi Volkov and he was visiting London on business. The hospital notified the Russian embassy by fax that they were keeping one of their citizens overnight.

The next day two officials from the Russian embassy came over to see him. After a brief conversation Volkov left with them, as the doctors didn't find anything seriously wrong with him. Some two hours later, a man claiming to be from the Russian consulate appeared at the hospital. He was very surprised to learn that his colleagues had already been there and picked up the patient.

Several days later the Russian consulate received a telex from Moscow requesting help in finding Georgi Volkov, who had failed to contact his Moscow office for several days. The consulate sent back a short cable promising to do everything possible to trace Mr Volkov. But in reality his name was forgotten the minute the message went out. The consulate had more important things to do than waste time searching for some idiot who had gone missing in London.

★

The President of Russia arrived at the Kremlin at 9.30 in the morning, telling his staff that he'd need about half an hour to 'glance through some papers'. Instead, he was sitting in his office staring aimlessly at the wall across.

What the hell are these people trying to do to me? he was thinking. It's like a bloody conspiracy around me. They're all against me. Monitoring my calls, watching me every bloody minute of the day, changing my schedule at the last minute. Probably want me to step aside and leave them to run everything…

He shuffled some papers on the desk, just in case someone was watching him. He had a suspicion that his enemies had installed hidden cameras and bugs in his office to monitor him and record everything he said and did. And although his security people had checked his office and his living quarters for cameras and bugs and found nothing, he remained on guard.

The President didn't trust anyone around him. It was his motto in life, his first rule of political survival. Eighteen months earlier he had orchestrated a palace coup and ousted Boris Yeltsin from power. By all accounts it was a brilliant operation: first Yeltsin was forced to appoint him as vice-president, then the constitution was amended and soon afterwards Yeltsin stood down. And there were still two years of term left so that the new head of state could settle into his job without going to the polls.

The new President had come to power proclaiming an end to political infighting and announced a period of 'national tolerance'.

His first decree was to give full immunity to his predecessor and his immediate family. This was presented as 'the first ever civilised transition of power in the entire history of Russia'.

Behind the scenes though knives were drawn and one by one the top people in the government and the Kremlin administration were replaced. Civilised or not, the new President was not prepared to allow his enemies to stage another coup.

But eighteen months and four government reshuffles later things weren't getting any better in Russia. The economy was in crisis, government finances were in a mess, inflation was going through the roof, corruption continued to flourish and the conflict in Chechnya showed no signs of ending. And, to top it all, the President had suffered a mild stroke during a recent foreign trip.

Once again the Russian people found themselves governed by a man in poor health with no idea of where the country was heading.

The President shook his head confronting his imaginary critics. Well, surprise, surprise, you sons of bitches! he thought. I'm not leaving yet. I'll stay for a while and make you guess who's going to be my successor until the very last minute. Your tiny brains will boil while you're trying to figure out who he is.

He took out a key and opened the lower drawer of his desk.

'Bloody hell!' he exclaimed and glanced around as if someone could have overheard him. There was an opened pack of cigarettes in here, he thought. I distinctly remember putting it there yesterday.

The President liked an occasional cigarette and thought nobody noticed that he smoked. He tried hard to picture himself putting the cigarettes into the drawer. But no picture was emerging.

Or, maybe, I took it with me to the country residence yesterday, he thought. Yes, yes, I must have taken it with me to Gorki. Well, that's a relief. At least I remember things. That idiot doctor was telling me again the other day that he is – how did he put it? – oh yes, concerned about my mental state. Bloody fool! He's probably a good ten or fifteen years younger than I am, and I can still out-drink him any time.

The light on his internal phone started flashing. It meant that his personal assistant, Anatoli, was ready to brief him on the day's schedule.

Anatoli came in with a loud knock. The President watched him closely as he approached his desk. His PA had been with him from day one of his presidency and had grown seriously overweight in recent months. All those chauffeur-driven cars and banquets. Couldn't even be bothered to walk from one building to another inside the Kremlin compound without popping into his official black Audi. Not to mention that he ate like a horse at all those official lunches and dinners and liked his beer with crayfish and shrimps.

But, what was much more important, Anatoli was loyal to him. There was no doubt about that. He'd been tested on several occasions and always came out clean and proper.

The President knew that Anatoli had been approached count-less times by people who wanted him to arrange a meeting with his boss. Big bankers and businessmen were circling round him, offering large sums of money for access to the top man. But Anatoli stood firm, often pretending not to understand what was being asked of him. Sometimes the President even thought that his personal assistant simply didn't have the brains for it.

But on the whole he was okay. He didn't meddle in politics, and he didn't irritate the President. Well, at least not as much as most people on his staff.

'Mr President,' Anatoli announced in a loud voice, 'may I inform you of your official schedule for today…?'

The President rolled his eyes. It was the same question every time, as if he could say 'no'. So he just waved, signalling to Anatoli to go ahead. He started to read from his file, 'At 10.30 you're meeting the chairman of the government to discuss…'

The President wasn't listening. His thoughts had already drifted away. He could hear Anatoli's mumbling, but the meaning of what he was saying passed him by. The President had mastered the trick of absenting himself from reality without showing it outwardly a long time ago. It came from his communist past. There was a joke that Communist Party officials were the only human beings who could sleep with their eyes open. During countless boring party meetings, the President, who was then a senior party boss, had to sit among the honorary guests in front of the rank-and-file members, sometimes for hours on end. So he would often put himself into a trance and then snap out of it the moment the applause began.

The President didn't like his morning briefings. They were part of the boring day-to-day work process that he'd grown to hate. He only liked the award ceremonies. At least then he was mixing with some of the people he really wanted to see. He also enjoyed the small private parties after the official ceremonies where he could talk to anyone he liked, sharing a joke or two. And he could also have a few drinks at those parties without anyone nagging him.

But most important, there was no signing of documents at the award ceremonies. These bloody signing ceremonies were a real pain. His eyesight was failing him and his right hand was not as steady as it used to be. Everyone present would usually be staring at him, watching his every move so that later they could talk about the President being a bit shaky, a bit unstable, losing his grip. Just like Yeltsin in his last year in office.

Idiots! What did they know about power! he thought. What did they know about ruling the country that occupied one-sixth – or was it one-eighth or one-tenth? – of the world's landmass? It really didn't matter. It was a big country, and it took a big man to run it!

The President's thoughts started to drift again. His mind wandered back to the days when he was a young lad in his home town in Siberia. Every morning his mother would give him breakfast, then dress him up like a baby in warm clothes to go to school. He hated all those itchy scarves and thick hand-knitted jumpers. The boys in his class would laugh at him when he took them off before lessons.

And he was always hungry; he was a tall lanky kid, constantly thinking about food. That's why he got involved with some of the boys who decided to raid a military warehouse. They'd heard there was a lot of food there, things like sweets, chocolate, and condensed milk in cans.

The condensed milk was their favourite. It was thick and very sweet. You could open the can, fix it over a fire and watch it turn.

Then you could cut up the sticky brown mass into toffees.

But when they broke into the warehouse, they found not sweets and chocolate but guns, rifles, machine guns and grenades. At first it was a huge disappointment, but then they got excited and pretended to shoot at each other, making all sorts of noises to create a real battle scene.

And then it happened. One of the boys picked up a gun and, taking an aim at another boy, pulled the trigger and shot him. The boy fell to the ground bleeding.

They were all stunned, terrified. And as Leonid, the oldest, shouted, 'Run for it!' they fled from the warehouse and ran away as fast as they could.

The next day news spread that Volodya Kamishin had broken into an arsenal with some boys and somehow a gun had gone off. Volodya had bled to death, as the guards were drunk and only went to check inside about two or three hours too late.

His mother came back with the news from the market.

'Can you imagine,' she was saying unpacking the groceries, 'to leave a boy to die like that. If these boys ever have children of their own they'll pay a heavy price for what they did. There'll be a curse hanging over their children.'

Even now he could hear his mother saying those words. He still remembered them...

'...And at six thirty in the evening both speakers of parliament are meeting you to discuss your annual statement to the nation,' Anatoli ended his report, closing the folder.

He waited for instructions, but the President was not responding. He was staring at the wall opposite. The silence seemed to drag on for ever. Anatoli was getting worried. The President had not yet fully recovered from his last heart attack. God knows what might happen at any moment.

But then the President moved. He looked at Anatoli blankly, as if trying to remember who he was.

'Cancel all my engagements for today,' he said. 'Tell General Kapoustin and Head of Protocol Yashin that I want to see them as soon as possible! And find out where my son Vassili is.'

Not good, not good at all, Anatoli thought. He's depressed again.

★

Terminal two of the Budapest international airport was practically empty.

Sleepy cashiers in the small duty-free shops were gazing lazily at the few passers-by.

Two men were sitting in the small café sipping beer. One of them was a typical-looking American. Square jaw, egg-shaped head, short haircut, big white teeth. His name was Clay Jones and his powerful jaws were moving all the time, chewing on ever-present gum.

The other man was Alex Hunter.

They had arrived in Budapest on a flight from London the previous day. After passing through immigration they had spent a day in the city staying at a private address. The next day they were back at the airport, having passed through immigration with new passports and new identities.

Alex was now a businessman from Birmingham, on his way to Russia. Clay had become a commodity broker from New York travelling with his friend to get a taste of some ecotourism in the former Soviet Union.

Their first names stayed the same, but the surnames were different. Alex was now Mr Macdonald and Clay was getting used to being Mr Tabor.

It was only a few days earlier that both of them were sitting across the table from George Blunt who was telling them about the job in Russia.

'The biggest problem is that we're pressed for time,' George was saying. 'The operation starts immediately. You'd normally expect to be briefed in detail about the assignment. But as I said, time is a luxury we don't have. Your previous experience in Eastern Europe will, hopefully, help you along the way. And as both of you know basic Russian you won't need an interpreter to follow you around. Local back-up will be provided. So if you have any questions turn to your Russian partners. You do not, I repeat, do *not* play smart-arse!'

George's military background was showing.

'The men you'll confront in Moscow are violent and deadly,'

he continued. 'These people are desperate, hardened criminals with no rules. And they are well connected in official circles. But they lack one thing – brains. That's why we're going to beat them at their game.'

'And what happens if the KGB gets on to us?' Alex said.

George looked at him for a moment.

'This whole thing is about avoiding the KGB,' he said. 'And blowing the gang sky-high. And staying alive. And coming back. And getting your money. And, then, maybe, retiring.'

Alex grinned.

'It means we're on our own, doesn't it?' he said.

Clay stopped chewing his gum. George was getting visibly annoyed.

'I wasn't aware that you needed any comfort and support,' he said. 'I thought you liked being on your own.'

Alex nodded. Clay looked at both men and resumed chewing his gum.

'I just wanted to get things clear right from the start,' Alex explained. 'To avoid any disappointment later.'

Not one muscle on George's face moved.

'You'll be paid double your usual fee,' he said. 'So in return you shouldn't expect any special treatment. And if you screw up, well, bad luck for you then…'

Silence fell in the room. For a moment all three men felt uneasy.

'Sounds fair to me,' Clay said finally and roared with laughter.

Both George and Alex smiled. The bottom line was that all three of them were in it for the money. The whole bloody thing was about money. They didn't really care who they were supposed to save or blow away – or why.

'And one more thing,' George said. 'What makes this job especially delicate is that you are not supposed to leave any stiffs behind. I know it might sound crazy to you but on this occasion we're instructed to go strictly by the book and keep our heads down. Do I make myself clear?'

Both Alex and Clay nodded.

★

Alex and Clay were waiting for their flight in Budapest.

'How d'ya say "blow job" in Russian?' Clay asked Alex, who was looking into his glass as if there was something in it that he didn't like.

Alex looked up.

'Shame on you,' he said. 'Didn't they teach you proper Russian before you went to Afghanistan?'

Clay didn't pay any attention to the question. Alex could tell by the unchanged pace of his chewing that his sarcasm had bounced off his partner without causing even a dent.

'I bet ya don't know yarself,' Clay said. 'That's why you fancy-talk yarself out of it.'

Alex felt challenged.

'For your information I learnt basic Russian in six months,' he said. 'And it's a good thing I did. A lot of work came my way thanks to me knowing Russian.'

Clay gave him a sceptical look.

'Okay,' he said, 'so if ya're so damn smart tell me how the Russians say "blow job"?'

'*Minyet*,' Alex said proudly. 'And you'd better write it down along with the other five Russian words you already know.'

Clay looked away and said nothing. He was obviously in no fighting mood.

They sat in silence looking at the people who were passing by. There was an odd couple sitting across the hall. A young woman of about twenty and a man going on sixty. She was dressed in a very tight, revealing white dress and black high-heeled shoes. He was dressed rather shabbily, in an old black suit and a wrinkled white shirt, and looked fidgety. It was the sort of combination where you could immediately guess they were not father and daughter.

'That guy can't wait to get his hands on the broad,' said Clay, getting all wound up all of a sudden. 'Probably stole some money and decided to have one last big fuck. I bet the moment he blows all his money she'll be off sucking some other dick. The bitch!'

Alex look at him.

'I'm sensing some serious hostility here,' he said. 'Have you had any problems with the ladies recently?'

Clay opened his mouth as if to say something, but then appeared to think the better of it and resumed chewing his gum instead. They watched the strange couple for a while.

'So whad'ya think about our contact – this Pavel?' Clay asked finally. 'Sounds like some weird son of a bitch, a cop kicked out for drinking.'

'Most Russians are drinkers,' Alex said. 'There must have been something else apart from the booze. From what George said I gather this Pavel is the son of some important people in Russia. Went to a fancy college and was supposed to be a diplomat or something. But he got into some sort of trouble and ended up working as a cop. And then they kicked him out. I bet you it wasn't the drinking that got him the sack. If they kicked out everyone in Russia who drank too much there would be nobody left…'

'That's just great,' Clay said. 'We've got a bent cop for a partner. I hope George knows what he's doing. Why on earth did he pick him? I don't get it.'

Alex grinned.

'That's why you're still an operational blip and George is riding high up there,' he said. 'He's got connections around the world that few people have. Probably knows half of the bloody Russian government by now. And I'll tell you this – he always picks the best people. And it always works.'

Clay did not seem convinced.

'Take this job, for example,' Alex said. 'He had to find a guy in Moscow who speaks relatively good English, who knows the local underworld and at the same time has good contacts in the police as well. And what do you know? He finds exactly the right man! I only hope that our Russian contact doesn't screw up.'

'I'd be counting on a quick death then,' Clay said gloomily.

'And I'd be counting on him not screwing up,' Alex said.

★

The Moscow Sheremetyevo-2 International Airport, a hideous brownish building that resembled an enormous crematorium, was designed and built by Germans for the Moscow Olympic

Games of 1980. This gateway to Russia was enough to turn most first-time visitors off the moment they arrived.

On the day Alex and Clay flew into Moscow, the airport was very busy with long queues forming at immigration and customs. They'd been instructed by George to wait patiently at the immigration desk. A woman in green military uniform studied both their passports closely but didn't ask any questions.

Once inside the baggage hall they approached one of the luggage handlers who were usually on hand in the area, gave him twenty dollars and let him do all the talking with the customs people. Just like George told them to.

'No fancy stuff,' he had warned them back in London. 'Just tip one of the porters and watch how the gates to Russia will open themselves.'

A middle-aged man in a dark blue uniform led them past the queues of so-called 'shuttle traders' – people bringing in foreign goods pretending they were part of their personal baggage – and straight through customs with no questions asked.

Pavel was waiting for them by the information desk. For some reason Alex disliked him the minute he saw him. He couldn't really explain why but the first time he laid eyes on the man he developed an uneasy feeling about him. In his opinion, he didn't look like a cop at all. And he didn't look like a typical Russian either. More like a Georgian or an Armenian with his dark hair, brown eyes and thin straight nose.

Clay, on the other hand, seemed relaxed and did not show any signs of anxiety.

The three men shook hands and went towards the main entrance.

As they came out of the building, a man in a grey coat put a magazine he had been reading back on the newsagent's stall and moved swiftly across the arrivals hall.

★

On their way from the airport, Pavel, who was driving a battered old Volga, gave Alex and Clay a quick briefing on the situation. He spoke good English, albeit with a heavy Russian accent.

'The people you're after are very dangerous,' he was saying. 'We call them *bespredelshiki*, men with no restraints. I hope you know what you're up against.'

Alex immediately noted that he said 'you' and not 'us'. But he decided not to comment.

A blizzard was blowing outside. The snow on the roads was a strange dark brownish colour. It was a mixture of mud, snow and salt that was used to prevent the snow turning into ice on the roads. Once this mixture got into contact with shoes, they'd usually last for a week or two before losing all shape and form.

Every couple of miles or so they would pass a traffic cop in winter uniform lecturing some unfortunate driver whom he had stopped for some minor traffic violation. At the time the unofficial tariff in Moscow for skipping a kerbside lecture about road safety was a hundred roubles. Most people paid, but for some even that was too expensive and so they had to suffer in the cold, hoping the cop would lose interest in them at some point and go hunting for other victims.

Back in London George had told them there'd be no police involved in the operation.

'Too corrupt, those fellows over there,' he said, puffing on his cigar. 'Not that our boys over here are angels, but the cops in Moscow have gone completely over the top. Can't trust any of them.'

Pavel supported this view.

'When I was in the force we knew that some of our people were passing information to the other side,' he told Alex and Clay. 'When we were only planning our next move the criminals already knew about it. There's no way you can trust the police here, especially when you take on a gang like the Central Brotherhood. These guys have their informers inside the Interior Ministry and can quickly get all the information they need.'

'Sounds very encouraging,' said Alex. Clay laughed nervously.

They were driving down the Leningrad Avenue. It was named after the 'northern capital' of the Soviet Union, Leningrad, which got back its old imperial name of St Petersburg by a majority vote of its inhabitants in the days of Mikhail Gorbachev. And although the name 'Leningrad' no longer existed, the name of the avenue remained the same, just like the name of the motorway linking Moscow and St Petersburg – Leningrad Motorway.

'Why do they call themselves the Central Brotherhood?' Clay asked looking out at the passing cars, all covered in mud so it was practically impossible to see what make and model they were.

'The gang initially consisted of people who all lived in the centre of Moscow,' Pavel explained. 'Many of the Moscow gangs are named after the areas where they first started to operate. In the early days the "central" were involved in burglaries, extortion, the sale of bootleg vodka. Later they moved into gambling, prostitution, money laundering and, recently, into drug trafficking. They even control a couple of banks, construction companies and a food chain.'

'Right,' Clay said acknowledging the information provided. 'So they're powerful mobsters, big guns.'

Pavel nodded.

'They sure are,' he said. 'And they have friends at the very top. Which makes it all very dangerous.'

They passed the grey building of the Supreme School of the KGB, *Vyshaya Shkola Ke-Ge-Be*, and drove into a large square with the famous Belarusski railway station on their right. Here the traffic was really bad and all around them drivers were sounding their horns impatiently as if it could help them move faster.

'We make our first move tonight,' Pavel said as he waited for the cars in front to start moving again. Alex noted that on this occasion he was team spirited. 'There's a meeting planned between the man who runs the Central Brotherhood, Seraphim Voronov, and two Chechen arms dealers. They're meeting at the Oscar Wilde restaurant. I'm going to drive past it so you can take a look at the area, but don't appear too interested – some of Seraphim's hoods might be hanging around the place. He's got more minders than anybody else in the underworld.'

'Don't ya worry,' said Clay. 'If there's one thing we're good at, it's staying unnoticed.'

He turned to Alex for confirmation.

But Alex said nothing. He was feeling uncomfortable. Something was bothering him…

Having had a look at the area around the Oscar Wilde restaurant they finally arrived at a flat found for them by a friend of George's. The owners were some Russians living in America. Their son worked as a translator with the US State Department. For a considerable amount of money the owners allowed the 'two top executives from a multinational company' to stay at their flat for a couple of weeks.

It was a three-bedroom flat in a massive block, built in the style jokingly referred to as 'Stalin's baroque'. The entrance lobby downstairs looked shabby and smelled of boiled cabbage. Both Alex and Clay shuddered at the thought of having to live in such a slum. But the flat itself was not bad at all – large rooms, high ceilings, wall-to-wall carpets, expensive furniture everywhere. The lot.

Crates with equipment had already been delivered, compliments once again of some friends of George's. Alex and Clay took off their coats and started opening the boxes and checking the weapons and equipment. Pavel was helping them.

'By the way, what's the name of that joint again where the bad guys hang out?' Clay asked.

'The place is called Oscar Wilde,' Pavel said. 'And the irony is that it's an Italian restaurant.'

Clay froze for a moment.

'And the irony being?' he said.

Pavel looked at him in bemusement but said nothing.

★

The Oscar Wilde was built on the Moscow Canal, directly across from the building of the British embassy. That might have been one reason why, being an Italian eatery, it was still named after the famous British writer.

The interior of the restaurant was simple, the food was good and the service was extremely good. But what made the place especially attractive was the location: customers could see the towers of the Kremlin from the windows.

On the day Alex and Clay arrived in Moscow, Seraphim Voronov, better known amongst some people as the Crow, was on his way to the Oscar Wilde for one of his business meetings. The chain-smoking underworld boss was escorted, as always, by a team of burly minders and one of his numerous mistresses, all of whom he usually referred to as 'my faithful whores'.

Seraphim had made it big in the 1980s when Mikhail Gorbachev, unable to stop the downfall of communism in Russia, announced his perestroika (rebuilding) – a policy that was supposed to 'rebuild' socialism in the Soviet Union, but in reality brought the country to the brink of economic collapse. A darling of the West, Gorbachev was in fact a true-blooded communist at heart and couldn't force himself to introduce a free market. A communist can never accept economic freedom and true democracy as that would mean an end to the tight state control over the country and, as a result, the eventual loss of influence and power that are allegedly needed to implement the big socialist idea. So Gorbachev opted for a combination of limited political freedoms and some cosmetic changes in the economy that allowed small private businesses, mostly run by criminals, to operate without any control. As a result, in the space of several years they were transformed from small-time crooks and hoodlums into big-time illegal operators.

Seraphim, the son of a KGB thug who took pride in beating 'confessions' out of innocent people, managed to avoid jail for his illegal business dealings thanks to his father's connections. From his father Seraphim inherited a strange obsession with Vladimir Lenin, Joseph Stalin and the whole communist system. He was fascinated by the ruthless discipline that Lenin, and later Stalin, had imposed on the party by mercilessly punishing anyone who disobeyed their orders. He liked Lenin's idea that the leader of any secret organisation – like the Russian Bolshevik party until it seized power in 1917 – had to put all members through a test and force them to 'spill blood' – that is, to prove their loyalty by killing someone. That way the members had no choice but to stay with the group and not get any ideas about betraying others or pulling out.

Seraphim even modelled his gang on the Bolsheviks. He'd often refer to himself as the 'general secretary of the politburo' of the Central Brotherhood, the gang which rose to prominence in the criminal world during the perestroika years.

His father had taught him to be on his guard all the time and never to trust anyone. 'If you ever feel like sharing a secret with your friends,' he used to instruct him, 'go to the loo, take out your dick and squeeze it as hard as you can. Do it every time until you stop getting stupid ideas about telling other people your secrets.'

Seraphim started his career in Soviet days as manager of the meat section in one of the central Moscow supermarkets. In those days it was considered to be a lucrative business, as food shortages, which drastically worsened under Leonid Brezhnev in the mid-1970s, created a huge black market. He made his first money by supplying selected customers with rare delicatessen items 'through the back door', as it was called at the time. He would add his commission to the price and people would gladly pay, as otherwise they'd never have been able to obtain these groceries.

Many of his customers were friendly with him simply because they had no other way of buying decent food for their families. They would occasionally invite Seraphim to their homes for a drink, or pop down to his so-called 'office', a small shabby room at the back of the supermarket, bringing with them all sorts of presents and souvenirs. One of his clients was Konstantin Babich, a diplomat in the Soviet embassy in London. He'd usually come to Moscow for a holiday in the summer and visit Seraphim's office to have a chat and thank him with presents for supplying his mother with delicatessen. He would bring a large bottle of Johnny Walker and they'd finish it in under an hour. Babich would then start telling Seraphim about the 'wonders' of the Western way of life, about the 'palaces', as he called them, which surrounded the several buildings of the Soviet embassy in the famous Kensington Palace Gardens.

'I'll tell you this, Seraphim,' Babich would say, 'if ever there was a place where there were more rich bastards per every square metre than anywhere else, it has to be Kensington Palace Gardens. You should see the cars they drive and the clothes they wear. Filthy rich, that's what they call them over there.'

'Why don't you invite me to London?' Seraphim would ask Babich, who would nod and say, 'We should do something about it.'

And they would drink to that.

Seraphim heard many stories from his other customers, but that tale about a road in the centre of London 'paved with gold' stayed in his mind for good.

Later Seraphim was promoted to deputy manager of the whole supermarket. Gradually he established very powerful connections in the Moscow retail trade. He managed to survive the purges of the early 1980s, initiated by Yuri Andropov, the then head of the KGB, who took over after Leonid Brezhnev died in 1982.

Andropov was a ruthless man. He'd been in charge of the KGB for twenty-five years before becoming General Secretary of the Communist Party and, once in power, he used the same methods as his former subordinates. On Andropov's instructions several managers of the biggest supermarkets in Moscow were put on trial for corruption and sentenced to death.

Seraphim might have been arrested as well, if the purges in the retail trade had continued. But luckily for him Andropov didn't last long and, once he died, the new leader, Konstantin Chernenko, a Brezhnev crony, put an end to the fight against corruption.

Seraphim was in the clear. His influence was now growing by the day and he was getting to know more and more powerful people. Some of his friends were high-ranking officials, top military brass, senior police officers and Communist Party apparatchiks. He had no illusions as to why they were friendly with him. In a country where practically all basic goods were hard to get he was the man who could make things happen. If somebody wanted the best food for their son's or daughter's wedding, he could arrange the delivery in a matter of hours. Need the best booze for a party? No worries, just call Seraphim and everything would be sorted. Problems with the law? Seraphim knew some people in the Interior Ministry who could resolve matters in an instant...

After he set up his company, Moscow House, Seraphim quickly turned into a real criminal godfather. He ruthlessly sidelined anyone who stood in his way and gradually built up his own 'army' of thugs who would threaten and harass his competitors. And if they wouldn't listen to 'reason', his people would beat them up or burn down their businesses.

The Gorbachev years made Seraphim very rich. He became something of a celebrity, collecting art, throwing lavish parties, sponsoring young performers and mingling with the rich and famous. He was gradually turning into a philosopher. 'The meaning of life is to try to escape boredom,' he'd say to some aspiring businessman. 'Everyone dreams of breaking the monotony of life. That's why I do what I do – I run away from boredom.'

By the end of the 1990s Seraphim – now known as the Crow – controlled a wide network of companies. But it was still difficult for him to develop his illegal businesses, since under Gorbachev hundreds of Soviet rules and regulations remained in place.

Then came the failed hard-line communist coup of August 1991, which resulted in the collapse of communism and the disintegration of the Soviet Union. The old rules were swept away in an instant, but none had been created to replace them. No one really knew how to deal with a free market economy and taxation barely existed. In a matter of months Seraphim was running a vast empire.

Soon the whole Russian underworld was turned upside down. The illegal money made by gangsters during the Soviet era now seemed peanuts compared with the vast fortunes made in the days of Gorbachev's perestroika and the capitalist times that followed. The godfathers of the Soviet years found the new breed of criminals hard to cope with, so when the new gangsters moved in on the operations of the 'old guard' a war broke out. The killings started in earnest. People were gunned down on the streets in broad daylight with several shootings a day in Moscow alone.

Ultimately, events in 1993, when President Boris Yeltsin ordered the shelling of the rebellious parliament, established once and for all the status quo in the Russian underworld. In the ensuing confusion, Seraphim, together with other new godfathers, managed to launder millions that helped secure his leading position in the criminal world. From then onwards Seraphim became one of the main power-brokers. He even had a government hotline phone installed in his office, the envy of many people and a symbol of true influence and power. His limousine was equipped with a set of flashing lights and emergency sirens – a 'disco set', as it was called in those days – which were issued only to the most senior-ranking government officials, directors of state-owned companies, military and security chiefs and the police.

Big money was flowing in the direction of the Central Brotherhood. A lot of it came in the form of bank loans and credits that were never repaid.

The set-up was simple: the Central Bank of Russia would allocate money to a private bank for investment purposes at very low interest. The private bank would then lend it to a company to carry out some project and the company would then hide the money or move it abroad and go bankrupt. The loan would eventually be written off as bad debt by the government with all the interested parties getting their commissions.

Seraphim also managed to pull off a huge scam with the so-called 'people's cottage' when several hundred million dollars were allocated to a number of companies to launch the construction of inexpensive summer cottages designed to be affordable to millions of Russians. The idea was that many people would be able to buy a country house with a plot of land for growing fruit and vegetables. The whole thing was presented as a way of taking Russia back to the days of the tsars when most of the population was self-sufficient in basic foodstuffs.

It went down well with everyone, including the foreign economic advisors to the Russian government who were keen to be associated with any plan that would imply some sort of land privatisation.

The project, however, never got off the ground and most of the money mysteriously disappeared. The companies that were supposed to design and build the 'people's cottages' went bankrupt one by one after receiving the funds. Several middle-ranking government officials involved in the project hastily resigned and a private bank that had handled some of the money was very publicly stripped of its licence and closed down.

And that was that. The newspapers wrote about the 'con of the century' and hinted that powerful underworld figures and corrupt officials were responsible for the disappearance of taxpayers' money. But, as on so many other occasions, the Russian press failed to name a single person. The papers wrote about anonymous 'powerful figures', 'influential backers', 'underworld barons', 'shady characters' that were supposedly behind the project. A couple of left-wing commentators even suggested that the whole thing was a 'Western conspiracy to undermine the Russian economy'.

Eventually the whole 'people's cottage' affair was forgotten. The first years of Russian capitalism were marred by so many financial scandals that soon another big story was hitting the headlines and the public switched its attention to new revelations.

Seraphim was very careful to avoid any publicity linking him to the 'people's cottage' scam. He paid off a lot of government officials who lied through their teeth to cover up the whole affair. They knew well that no real harm could come to them. Very few officials were ever held responsible for anything in Russia. They would usually disappear for a while after a scandal broke out, and reappear later in some new capacity.

In a country where tens of millions of innocent people were slaughtered in the name of communism and not a single person was held responsible – the official version was that the political system was to blame – it was not difficult for government officials to literally get away with murder, not to mention fraud and theft.

Seraphim made a lot of money on the 'people's cottage' scam. It was the sort of capitalism that was tailor-made for people like him.

★

Seraphim walked into the restaurant.

He was a tall, heavily built man with curly brown hair and a round plump face. His large swollen hands were covered with yellow stains from constant smoking.

Seraphim was dressed in an expensive tweed jacket, casual trousers and shoes made from the skin of an unborn calf. He ordered all his clothes through a private company in Moscow that imported most of the goods from Western Europe and kept the measurements of all its clients.

A table in the corner of the restaurant was laid for Seraphim and his guests. A large bottle of black label Kristall Stolichnaya vodka, his favourite brand, was taken out of the freezer and put in a silver bucket. Two kilos of the finest black caviar in several silver plates were 'scattered' around the table and a sturgeon was 'smiling' from the centre of the table.

Seraphim was expecting two important people. He was involved in supplying arms to the rebels in the republic of Chechnya who were fighting for independence from Moscow. The two acted as middlemen for the field commanders, leaders of armed groups of insurgents, who masterminded attacks on Russian federal forces. Seraphim was buying the arms through his contact in the Moscow military. The Chechens, of course, would have preferred to deal directly with the suppliers but were unable to establish reliable contacts. Although corruption was widespread among Russian officers, very few of them actually wanted to be directly associated with the Chechens, who had a reputation for being ruthless and violent people.

As for Seraphim, he was prepared to take the risk since the profits from the arms deals were very high. The Chechens paid upfront in cash and it was obvious that they had no problem raising the money. There were persistent rumours that some of the Russian private banks were channelling funds to them in return for protection from other gangs.

Seraphim had no problem with selling arms to the people who were killing young Russian conscripts. For him it was just another business arrangement.

★

Seraphim was sitting with his girlfriend and his head of security, Shark, a huge brute with a cold indifferent stare, at his usual table, waiting for the two guests to arrive. He always picked that particular place so he could see everyone entering the restaurant. Not that many people came in when he was there. Usually, when he was dining at Oscar Wilde, a sign 'Closed for a private function' would appear on the entrance door.

The restaurant was owned by a friend of his, Marta Mogileva.

She was more interested in getting serious customers like Seraphim to visit her establishment than having some drunkards spending all evening there and yet paying no more than the equivalent of a hundred dollars in roubles by choosing the cheapest food and booze.

As he was lighting up his fortieth cigarette of the day, Seraphim noticed two people, a man and a woman, sitting at a table across the room near the window. The man was dressed like a typical Russian: worn-out jacket, creased shirt and casual trousers. The woman, on the other hand, wore an expensive designer dress, but was definitely also Russian, with far too much make-up. Russian women generally tended to overdo cosmetics. Whenever they went out they put on a lot of make-up and they didn't just wear it, they paraded it. No wonder foreigners were always impressed by the number of 'stunning women' on the streets of Moscow.

The woman's face seemed faintly familiar. Seraphim looked at Shark and directed a quick inquiring glance at the couple, as if asking, 'Who the fuck are these two?' Shark, in turn, signalled to the two bodyguards sitting at a table across the room – far enough not to be able to hear what was said, but close enough to deal with any emergency. One of them came over and whispered something to Shark who turned to Seraphim.

'It's the Countess with some friend of hers,' Shark said. 'A former pig kicked out for taking money. You may remember the bitch. She helped us a couple of times in the past. She used your name to get in. The people in the joint thought you okayed it.'

Seraphim felt a pulsating sensation in his left temple. He usually got wound up in a matter of seconds.

'When I give the okay, I do it fucking personally,' he said in a lowered voice, pronouncing every word very clearly. 'And no one, I repeat, no one is allowed in just because they used my name. Is that fucking clear?'

Shark nodded.

'Do you want them kicked out?' he asked.

Seraphim glanced at the couple. The man was actually looking back at him, raising his glass, as if toasting Seraphim. He obviously knew that they were talking about him and the woman who sat beside him.

At first Seraphim felt the urge to order his men to take the arrogant bastard outside and beat him up. But when he looked at him again, he somehow felt that his presence in the restaurant was no coincidence. He suddenly had an instinctive feeling that the man had yet to play an important role in his life.

Seraphim trusted his instincts; he relied on them to survive in the world he operated in. He raised his glass and nodded to the man.

'Leave 'em alone,' he said to Shark, hardly moving his lips. 'But next time I see any unexpected fucking visitors in this place I'm gonna make you all pay for it.'

He then drank his vodka in one go.

★

The two people in the restaurant were Pavel and Lidia, a former hard currency dealer, who was better known around Moscow as the Countess.

Nobody really knew why she was called the Countess. Some people said that she actually came from a noble Russian family, most of whom were wiped out by the communists. Others said that she got her idea for the nickname from some obscure foreign film about a countess who got mixed up with some highway robbers.

Pavel first met Lidia when he joined the central CID of the Moscow police, known by its address as 'Petrovka 38' – that is, 38 Petrovka Street. On a couple of occasions he got her out of serious trouble with the law. In Soviet times all hard currency dealings, no matter how much money was involved, were punishable by long prison sentences. The people who handled foreign currency were perceived not just as criminals, but as 'foreign agents', supposedly undermining the very foundations of the nation's economy.

After Pavel divorced his wife, who was screwing behind his back like mad, he started an affair with Lidia that lasted several months. But after being seen a couple of times in her company by people from the CID, and word going around that he was bonking a hard-currency dealer, Pavel had to end the relationship.

They didn't see each other for about four years. Then, after Pavel got into trouble and was kicked out of the CID, Lidia suddenly called him out of the blue and they met a couple of times. Through her contacts she helped Pavel earn some money as an 'expert in security matters' for foreign businessmen. He was no big expert, but he could speak good English and that seemed more important to the foreigners. It was through one of those businessmen that George Blunt found out about the former cop who was always looking for work.

★

Pavel had introduced Lidia to the guests from London earlier that day at the flat in Tverskaya Street.

She arrived just as they finished unpacking their equipment. Although in her mid-forties, she still retained the stunning looks that fifteen years ago had attracted foreign businessmen in Moscow who sold her hard currency. She was tall, with shoulder-length dark hair and big green eyes. The high cheekbones gave her face that slightly Asian look that is so common amongst Russian women from the eastern parts of the country.

Both Alex and Clay were impressed.

'I'm Alex and this here is my assistant, Clay,' Alex said. 'I hope you realise by looking at us that I'm the one the ladies go for.'

Lidia smiled.

'Do you really think it shows?' she said in her low voice.

Pavel decided to keep the meeting strictly businesslike.

'Gentlemen, how about going through the plan once more?' he said. 'There's not much time left; the operation starts in a couple of hours. And while we're discussing business Lidia here will organise coffee for us.'

The three men went to the dining room where three sets of documents lay on the coffee table. They sat down on the sofa and the two armchairs around the table.

'The people in the photographs are your targets,' Pavel explained as they all opened their respective files. 'The idea is to stage a mock assassination attempt and shoot as close on target as possible, but avoid hitting anyone. The Crow, whom you see here in the photo leaving the Oscar Wilde, is bound to come out of the restaurant with his two guests when they finish their meeting.'

Pavel pointed at several photographs of the Chechens. The photos were crude passport-type shots and the faces on them had vicious expressions.

'Once outside they'll all be standing close to each other so it'll be difficult for them to guess who was the intended target. The Chechens are bound to suspect that Seraphim ordered to whack them.'

He stopped, giving Clay and Alex the opportunity to ask questions. Clay was chewing hard, absorbing the information. He had no questions. But Alex immediately spotted the weakness of the plan.

'What if they don't come out together?' he said. 'What if they fall out during the meeting and the two Chechens leave by themselves?'

Pavel nodded, obviously expecting that.

'You still proceed with the plan,' he said. 'With or without the Crow by their side the Chechens will still think that his people tried to kill them. There's a lot of bad blood between them at the moment and both sides are edgy and suspicious of each other.'

But Alex was still not convinced.

'And what if all of them decide to leave by the back door?' he persisted.

Pavel raised both hands, surrendering to the onslaught of questions.

'That wouldn't be good for us,' he said. 'In that case we'll have to come up with some other idea.'

Alex smiled. At least he'd forced the Russian to accept that his plan was not watertight.

They had another look at the photographs and at the map of the surrounding area. There were also detailed plans of the roof of the building from where Alex and Clay were supposed to open fire on Seraphim and his two guests.

'The two people who'll be meeting the Crow are Chechen gangsters,' Pavel explained as both men studied the documents. 'They are involved in smuggling arms to Chechnya. Recently they fell out with Seraphim over a shipment of outdated arms that he had delivered to them. That works in our favour, as we can cause even more problems for both sides, and, hopefully, spark a serious feud between them.'

Clay looked up at Pavel.

'I have only one question,' he said. 'Why the hell don't we bump off the Crow? Wouldn't it make the whole thing much easier?'

He looked at Alex as if saying, 'Ya didn't expect that from me, did ya?'

Pavel shook his head.

'The whole idea is to make life so difficult for the gang that the only thing on their minds will be how to survive,' he said. 'If you kill the Crow other people in the group will continue to operate. And that would mean that the problem won't go away. Plus, we've got strict instructions to avoid fatalities at all costs.'

At that moment a strange-looking man entered the room. He was short, with curly dark hair, wearing a shabby jumper and worn-out trousers. He had the sort of smile on his face that somehow remained intact even when he spoke.

Pavel introduced the stranger.

'This is Matvei, known as Motya to his friends,' he said. 'He's going to be your guide around Moscow.'

Alex and Clay greeted the man with a nod. Motya suddenly giggled and said, 'So these are the two supermen who are gonna save us and the rest of the world?'

'Mind your manners, comrade,' Alex said in Russian. 'Show some respect for the guests of your sunny country.'

Clay started to move his jaws in a threatening manner.

'Lay off, Motya,' Pavel said. 'The people are here to do a job. Don't piss them off on the first day.'

'I'm terribly sorry,' Motya said with a slight bow of the head. 'I didn't wish to offend anyone. But I thought you'd be… bigger.'

Pavel winced.

'Motya is showing off his profound knowledge of clichés from Western thrillers,' he said. 'He's a big expert on Western cinema. Sold a lot of pirate videos in his younger days.'

Everybody in the room laughed. Motya shrugged his shoulders and raised his hands, pleading guilty to the charge.

'Motya will lead you to the place tonight,' Pavel said. 'If anything goes wrong, he'll be there to help. And he'll take you back to the flat after the job's done. Any questions?'

Clay rubbed his forehead.

'So where will ya be tonight?' he asked.

'I won't be far from you,' Pavel said. 'Now let's go and have some coffee in the kitchen.'

★

'Now that's what I call a real classy broad,' Clay said when Pavel and Lidia had left the flat and Motya went downstairs to check the car. 'What I can't figure is why on earth would she hang out with that guy. I mean, what can an ex-cop with no job and no money offer a classy broad like that?'

'Beats me,' Alex said. 'Everything is strange about this Pavel. And if you ask me, he doesn't look like a cop at all.'

'What d'ya mean?' Clay said, stopping the chewing.

'I mean, I don't trust the guy,' Alex said. 'There's something wrong with him. He's too clean, if you know what I mean.'

Clay thought it over for a moment.

'George would've known if something wasn't right,' he said and resumed chewing. It was obvious from the look on his face that he had buried all doubts about their Russian host once and for all. There was no point in discussing the matter further. Alex decided to lighten up the situation.

'In any case,' he said, as if continuing the conversation, 'Russians do have a way with women. I mean, there is this saying they have: there's no such thing as an ugly woman, there's simply not enough vodka.'

There was a silent pause.

'I don't get it,' Clay said eventually. 'What's vodka got to do with it?'

Alex took a deep breath.

'It's a Russian thing,' he said, 'I don't really get it myself.'

Clay resumed the chewing.

★

They assembled and reassembled two rifles, putting them into two specially designed sports bags. The rifles were custom-made and could only be used by people who wore a special ring on one of their fingers with an encrypted code. The tiny chip in the ring released a signal that activated the trigger.

All firearms delivered to Moscow were programmed with the same code. Only Clay and Alex had the rings that activated the firing mechanisms, so that if the weapons fell into the wrong hands they'd be useless.

In addition there was a set of 'tools' in case they had to break into a house or a flat, two sets of climbing equipment, including specially designed ropes that wouldn't snap in any weather conditions, a digital camera that could take pictures in total darkness and a 'wonder key' that opened most standard door locks. There was also a laptop computer for printing high-quality photographs.

One thing, though, was not included – clothes that could make them inconspicuous in a Moscow crowd. They arrived in casual wear – warm winter jackets, jeans and shoes with thick rubber soles. But even that wasn't suitable for Moscow where most people on the streets looked as if they still got their clothes from some old Soviet stock. So Alex and Clay had to rely on the 'fashion sense' of their Russian host to come up with something that would suit the circumstances. And he lived up to their worst expectations, getting them cheap Turkish sheepskin coats, shapeless rabbit-fur hats and warm Soviet-made trousers. The clothes didn't fit well and were tailored badly, but at least Alex and Clay could now blend into the crowd. As conciliation they were allowed to wear their own shoes.

When Motya came back and saw them all 'dressed up' he nodded with approval and said, 'Now you look like two typical Russians. And if you don't shave for a couple of days and have some cheap liquor to acquire that unmistakable Russian smell on your breath no one will ever suspect you of being foreigners.'

'So that's what turns Russian women on?' Alex asked gloomily.

'I wouldn't know,' Motya said, 'I usually beat them senseless and then have sex with them for as long as I want. Less fun, but no hassle.'

★

Every year since the end of the Second World War, around three hundred influential people from all over the world would gather together in one place, usually a small resort town, to discuss the state of things on the planet. There would be a mix of big businessmen, bankers, former heads of state, retired generals, publishers, rising young politicians and acting cabinet ministers.

None of the guests at these meetings were under any pressure to impress others and no speeches were written in advance. There was no need to talk to the reporters and no one had to worry what the voters might think.

And yet, it was a great opportunity to get together with old friends and discuss serious business in an unofficial environment. Not to mention the chance to eat some really great food, sample some of the best wines in the world and stay at a very good hotel in a remote location, far from the big political capitals.

The agenda of each annual meeting was prepared by a standing committee. The points of discussion were added throughout the year, depending on what had been happening around the world.

There were global issues which were discussed repeatedly year after year. The threat of communism was one such issue. It was constantly included in the agenda, and only after the collapse of the Soviet bloc did other matters receive a higher priority. Privately though, some delegates joked that it was cheaper to have the communists as enemies rather than friends, what with the billions of dollars of aid disappearing each year in Central and Eastern Europe.

Apart from the main agenda, several working groups would debate a number of smaller issues. They were seen as fringe discussions, where certain people could gain access to some of the delegates and talk to them about specific problems.

That year the annual meeting took place in Scotland. One by one political and business heavyweights from around twenty countries descended on a sleepy little seaside town. SAS units and armed police were guarding the event.

Helicopters flew the delegates into a hotel with its own golf course, fishing lakes and hunting grounds.

Jeremy Goldberg was not on the main guest list, but he had pulled some strings to be invited as an observer. He wanted to talk to two people. He was interested to learn a few things about Russia. Not as a place to do business – that subject he knew well. His interest lay elsewhere.

Jeremy noticed several faces he knew as he walked into the lobby of the hotel. He put on his 'official smile' and nodded in different directions. But he didn't stop to talk to anyone. He considered most politicians to be boring and pretentious. So there was no point in wasting any time.

The people he was looking for were far from boring. One of them was a former cabinet minister and an international peace envoy. He was involved in arranging some of the most important international deals in the 1970s, although the official recognition went to the then heads of state and governments. He was an expert on Russia and China and had dealt with some of the top officials from both countries. He was retired, but still kept an ear to the ground. He didn't engage in active politics any more, but many people came to seek his advice.

Jeremy referred to him as the Statesman.

The other one, a woman, was a former Attorney-General and an expert on organised crime.

Jeremy called her the Lawyer.

He found the Statesman in the room where a seafood buffet was laid out. The old man was holding a plastic plate in his hand and eating large prawns. Jeremy quickly picked up a plate and, although he was not hungry, he still helped himself to some seafood so that he could approach the Statesman without seeming to intrude on the great man during a meal.

'Ah, Jeremy, nice to see you,' the old man said when Jeremy came up to him. 'Long time no see. What have you been up to, young man?'

Jeremy smiled.

'It's a great pleasure to see you, sir,' he said. 'I have to be honest, I came here because I wanted to meet with you.'

The Statesman wiggled a finger at him.

'You sly fox,' he said. 'I bet you say that to all the women.'

They both laughed.

The Statesman put down the plate and whispered to Jeremy, 'Let's find a quiet place for our little conversation. I'm afraid there are several people here who are looking for me and if they find me I won't get away easily. Some people, you know, ask me the most extraordinary questions and expect me to come up with solutions as if I am some kind of a magician.'

Jeremy felt slightly embarrassed. He was actually planning to do much the same.

They left the buffet room and found a small study. Jeremy closed the door so that they would not be interrupted. The Statesman sat down on a leather sofa. Jeremy took a chair and sat opposite him.

The old man looked fine, he thought. Considering his age he was in great shape. Sure, the voice was a bit groggy and the movements were slow, but otherwise he was doing great.

Jeremy got straight to the point.

'I wanted to ask you about Russia,' he said. 'I'm still doing some business out there, not a great deal, but enough to be interested in its future.'

The Statesman nodded.

'Russia, Russia,' he said, his eyes closed. 'One of the great mysteries of our time. I still can't figure that country out. Is it a great nation or a tumble of contradictions? Are the Russians destined for greatness in the modern world or are they simply going to fade away? Judging by the last several years the future of Russia looks bleak. But I wouldn't write it off, not yet at least.'

Jeremy nodded.

'I've encountered certain problems in Russia,' he said. 'A friend of mine got into trouble with the locals, so to speak, and in order to help him I'll have to resort to unorthodox ways. The question is, how do I approach the people down there and how can I strike some sort of an arrangement with them?'

The Statesman opened his eyes. He looked bewildered.

'Are you asking me by any chance how to handle Russian gangsters?' he said. 'Because that's not exactly my area of expertise.'

'No, no,' Jeremy shook his head vigorously. 'I'm asking you about dealing with the authorities. It's a strange political culture out there. But I also know that you've managed to find the keys to many doors in Russia's high places.'

The Statesman smiled.

'It's a personal thing,' he said, closing his eyes again. 'You have to approach them on a personal level. Write a letter and you won't get any results. Most of the time you won't even get a reply. But sit down with them for a drink and you might be able to achieve a great deal. Russians attach a lot of importance to the personal touch. But I don't think you needed to hear that from me. You've been dealing in Russia long enough to know how things work there…'

He opened his eyes and looked at Jeremy closely.

Jeremy felt embarrassed again. He shouldn't have tried to mislead the old man.

'Guilty as charged,' he said. 'What I really wanted to know was what the thinking is up there' – he looked at the ceiling – 'about Russia? Are we going to be close friends with Moscow from now on or are we, for example, quietly planning to nuke the Russians or buy up their whole country?'

The Statesman chuckled.

'You sound just like your father,' he said. 'Never beat about the bush. Tell me the meaning of life and tell me now.'

'I'm sorry I sound so straightforward but of all people you surely must know the answers.'

Jeremy knew that flattery might just work. It did.

'There'll be a feeling of mutual suspicion for years to come,' the Statesman said. 'I don't really believe that we can become close allies, not in the foreseeable future at least. The Russians are too unpredictable, too irrational. And they still tend to think that they are destined to teach the whole world a lesson. So they go for public relations stunts and gimmicks, often at the expense of their own national interests.'

Jeremy got the message. At least he wasn't going to be held responsible for causing damage to the blossoming relations between Moscow and the West if the worst came to worst.

'The important thing to understand about Russia is that, to a large extent, it's still a communist country,' the Statesman said after a pause. 'Sure, they've privatised their industry, adopted some sort of democracy and introduced what they call a free market. They think that they've managed to fool everyone around them, but in reality they are only fooling themselves and will eventually pay a high price for delaying the introduction of real economics. They have constructed a neo-communist society with a criminal underbelly. The land still doesn't belong to anyone, and the ruling class, or should I say, the ruling elite, literally gets away with murder, while the government machine is still working against its own people. In essence, that's what communism is all about – when the leadership is waging a constant war against its own people...'

The old man fell silent.

Jeremy had one last question. If things got out of hand, would the Statesman help out?

'You do realise that now I'm thinking that I should have stayed with the seafood?' he said with a smile.

It was a 'yes'.

★

Later Jeremy spoke to the Lawyer. She'd been involved in smashing several organised criminal groups in the 1970s, both in the US and Europe, and had good knowledge of the way the mob operated.

After a quick conversation about mutual friends they got down to the subject of organised crime.

'The only way to restrict the activities of organised gangs is to use economic means to fight them,' the Lawyer said. 'You should look at the mob as a small state within a state. Like any state that assumes the monopoly on violence and punishes its citizens for breaking the laws and rules it imposes, organised crime uses violence to protect its interests. Like any government it collects "taxes", in the form of protection money; it has its own "armed forces" to defend the turf and fight off competition. The mafia creates its own economy and needs to invest, or in their case, launder the proceeds to make new capital for future operations. To create legitimate businesses they have to have a large machine that includes corrupt officials, dishonest lawyers and front men who run the businesses.'

The Lawyer was getting excited. It was clear the subject was close to her heart.

'But the mafia is not as invincible as many people think,' she said. 'The criminals will always have to spend a fortune on so-called "armies" because they can only stamp their authority on the black market with force. They can't go to court – they have to fight it out. So they keep a large force and that force has to be preoccupied with something on a regular basis, otherwise it might start robbing banks and companies that belong to rivals. And then it's war. And one gang might blow the other sky-high. And so it goes on and on, and as a result the mafia has no chance of gaining any serious position in society. Even in Russia it is not as power-ful as it pretends to be.'

Jeremy nodded, showing that he agreed with what he was hearing.

'But let's assume,' he said, 'that we're dealing with a specific matter and we need, for example, to stop a gang threatening a legitimate business?'

'Then you have two options,' the Lawyer explained. 'You can try to cut a deal with the criminals and buy your friends out – I assume you're talking about your friends getting in trouble…?'

Jeremy said nothing.

'…Or you can use an insider and either create an internal conflict within the gang or provoke a major confrontation with another group,' she continued. 'The biggest weakness of any criminal organisation is the total lack of trust between its mem-bers. All those stories about "*omerta*" which are kept alive by Hollywood are pure rubbish. The only thing that binds criminals together is fear. Fear of being caught, fear of being thrown behind bars, fear of being killed.'

Jeremy thought for a moment.

'So you're suggesting that the best way to smash a gang would be to subvert it from the inside?' he said.

'That's exactly what I mean,' the Lawyer said. 'The only way to get to the top people in the mob is to either bribe one of their lieutenants or infiltrate the gang with an informer.'

Jeremy nodded.

'Would it make sense to use a former policeman or former KGB agent?' he asked.

The Lawyer looked at him closely.

'There is no such thing as a former secret service agent or former policeman, especially in Russia. They are always under the umbrella, as they call it there. They can be summoned back at any time.'

★

It was just another morning in the life of Sergei Titov, vice-governor of one of the southern industrial regions of Russia, as he was picked up outside his home by a chauffeur-driven blue Mercedes and taken to work. He was a short, thin-faced man with receding fair hair and delicate hands. He was wearing an expensive dark suit, white shirt and a red tie. As he sat in the back of the car that was speeding down the streets of the city he was thinking about the day ahead and the people he was planning to meet. The day-to-day work routine never bothered him; he got used to it and even liked it. What he didn't like was uncertainty, preferring the comfort of an orderly flow of things. Not that he was lacking in ambition and determination to achieve the goals he had set for himself, but any sudden turn of events usually caught him off guard and confused him.

When he arrived at the office, Yelena, his personal secretary, was not at her desk. That's strange, he thought. What on earth could have happened?

Yelena was always very punctual and would have left some sort of a message to say where she was. He tried calling her at home but there was no answer. He was starting to get really worried.

Sergei was having an affair with his secretary. They'd been lovers for the last two months and although he knew perfectly well that it could harm his position, he felt unable to do anything about it.

Throughout his life he had little success with women, being the short, skinny type, the kind women don't really go for. While in college he was always envious of other students who managed to score with girls and made it look all so easy. Then he met Svetlana, who was a year younger than him. They got on well and she seemed to genuinely like him. She was no beauty – short, plump, with slightly heavy facial features – but she was acceptable by Sergei's standards. And, what was more important, she was the daughter of the managing director of the biggest military factory in the city. They got married when Sergei was in his last year in college.

After graduating, Sergei chose a career in the Communist Party. He joined the Department for Industry in the city's party branch and was hoping that, with luck, in several years' time he could be appointed to a senior position, becoming head of a department and, who knows, maybe even be moved to Moscow to work in the Central Committee of the Communist Party, the ultimate prize for any communist apparatchik.

But then came the turbulent times of Mikhail Gorbachev's perestroika, which ended in a crash for the Communist Party and, later, for the whole Soviet Union. It brought Sergei's party career to an abrupt end, leaving him depressed and confused and not really knowing what to do next. He'd have been in real trouble had it not been for his father-in-law, Vladlen Khodorov, who, despite his fervent past dedication to communist ideals (even his name was a combination of the first letters of the name Vladimir Lenin), turned out to be quite a smart operator in the new 'free market' environment. With his help, Sergei became one of the directors of a newly created private bank called Omega.

Some of the government money earmarked for the military factory where Vladlen was managing director ended up in Omega's accounts. Later the pension fund of all the workers from the factory was put in a supposedly high-interest account in the bank. And two federal interest-free loans granted to the factory were passed over to Omega for 'temporary' management.

Under the guidance of his father-in-law, Sergei was establishing contacts with the new so-called democratic local government officials. He was introduced to the governor of the region, an ambitious young man who had somehow managed to bluff his way to the top of the new political elite in Russia. There was even talk about him becoming the future Russian president.

Sergei's friendship with the governor brought results: Omega was appointed to handle the pension funds of all the local state-owned enterprises in the region. From a small financial company,

Omega grew into one of the biggest regional operators. Sergei was promoted to the position of executive vice-president of the bank.

Vladlen felt that he had managed to pull off an impressive stunt, turning his son-in-law from a frustrated party apparatchik into a powerful financier. But he soon decided that it was time for Sergei to enter politics, being well aware that without political back-up no business in Russia, however big, would survive. And his now privatised factory, where he was one of the major shareholders, needed just that sort of back-up to expand its dealings. He turned to his friends, the founders of Omega bank, who were also – surprise, surprise – the powerful local mobsters and asked them to help his son-in-law achieve success in politics. At their meeting Vladlen managed to hammer out a deal: Sergei was to be given all the backing needed to become vice-governor and in return he was expected to do a few small favours for the mob. Nothing much, as they said, just to ease the restriction on the sale of alcohol and tobacco and help a number of companies receive a licence that would exempt them from paying import duties on goods brought from abroad. Vladlen was to receive a one per cent commission from all future operations.

Sergei's election campaign for the vice-governorship went extremely well. He had the best posters and the local television station proved very cooperative. Donations to his campaign were flowing in nicely and he even appeared on a national TV programme where promising young politicians from the regions discussed the burning issues of the day.

Soon Sergei, occupying the vice-governor's chair, was in charge of the industry of a whole region. He also retained a non-executive position on the board of the Omega bank.

It was several months later that he started the affair with his secretary. When Vladlen found out about it he did not at first consider it a serious threat to his daughter's happiness, hoping that it would soon be over. But when Sergei repeatedly failed to come home for the night, he decided to act. Once again he turned for help to his powerful underworld friends, some of whom had been dealing with well-connected people in Moscow. As a result Sergei's name came up out of nowhere during a discussion in the government about a possible new appointment at the Ministry of

Foreign Affairs. In a matter of days his fate was sealed…

The phone rang in Sergei's office. Thinking that it must be Yelena, he picked up the phone. The call was from Moscow.

A few days later Sergei was in the capital. He'd been appointed Deputy Minister of Foreign Affairs of Russia. His wife arrived with him.

A week later he got a call from his hometown – Yelena, his former secretary, had been found dead at her flat. Police said it was a clear-cut case of suicide.

★

Boris was getting worried. He'd heard nothing from Jeremy following their meeting at Mount Street, and when he tried to get in touch with him his secretary told him that 'Mr Goldberg had left for Europe'. What if Jeremy couldn't come up with a solution? Boris thought. And why should a rich man like him be concerned with the fate of some young man in Moscow?

He suddenly felt the need to do something drastic – like flying to Moscow himself, or talking to the intelligence people at the embassy, even offering them money to get his son out of trouble. When people are under pressure they often tend to wind themselves up, treating any minor incident or development as a sign of serious trouble. In this case Boris got the impression that Jeremy was now avoiding him and that he should turn to someone else for advice. It's all very well for Jeremy to ask me not to talk to anyone, he thought. But what if he fails and I have to live for the rest of my life with the knowledge that I did nothing to save my son?

Finally he decided to discuss the matter with a friend of his, a former diplomat at the Russian embassy in London, who had left the diplomatic service and opened a company. His name was Vadim Mironov, and he was rumoured to have some very powerful connections, both in London and Moscow. No one knew that in fact he was running a small hospitality company that looked after wealthy Russians who were visiting Britain as tourists, organising individual sightseeing and shopping tours for them. He somehow managed to convince his former colleagues in the embassy, including Boris, that he was a 'big-timer', a serious 'capitalist' earning lots of money.

Mironov would often despair that none of the people who used his services saw him as a potential partner or showed any interest in the wonderful projects that he kept trying to sell to them. They loved coming to London, but they did their business elsewhere. And Mironov was getting really annoyed that his attempts to be treated seriously as a businessman were being politely but firmly rejected. He was desperate to find serious players and he did not care how they had become rich.

When Boris arrived at the office of MirVad Ltd, he was greeted warmly by the secretary, a tall, attractive woman with an enormous bust (Vadim liked his women 'big and strong'). She was instructed to treat all the Russian diplomats with the utmost respect, as there was always a chance that they might be helpful. As someone with close access to the ambassador Boris was always welcome at MirVad.

Mironov came out of his office with hands wide open and hugged Boris. He was a tall man with curly brown hair, a round face, large meaty nose and an absolutely huge backside that made him look like a giant pear.

'What important people I see,' he said loudly, 'alone, without the usual bodyguards!'

Boris cringed. It was a greeting from an old gangster film that had long ago become a cliché. But he still forced himself to smile. Mironov was convinced that he had a great sense of humour and expected people to respond to his jokes and puns.

'It's good to see you, Vadim,' Boris said.

For some reason he suddenly got an uneasy feeling that he might be making a mistake by coming to see Mironov. But it was too late to back out without giving at least some sort of explanation why he had asked for a meeting.

They stepped into the office, a large square room with a dark grey desk, a row of black metal filing cabinets along the wall, a black leather sofa, two black leather armchairs and a round coffee table made of glass and metal. Boris sat down in one of the leather armchairs and Mironov placed himself in a huge leather seat behind his desk.

'Tell me what's on your mind, Boris,' he said with a smile. 'I'm all ears. In fact, I'm one big ear that'll only listen to what you're saying. Nothing else in the world matters to me now. It's you and you alone.'

Oh God, Boris thought. He's at it again. Bristling with humour.

Nevertheless he produced a polite smile and nodded a couple of times as if appreciating Mironov's sense of humour.

He then told him about Volkov's visit. He skipped the part about Ivan being arrested for drug possession and simply said that his son got himself in a spot of bother and some people in Moscow, who had helped him out, were now asking to provide them with information about several expensive properties in London.

'They want me to help them and they won't take "no" for an answer,' Boris said.

Mironov was no longer smiling. He looked confused.

'So what did you say to them?' he asked.

'I told them that I'd try to get some information together. But as you know, I'm not a big expert on the property market.'

Mironov was looking at Boris in disbelief.

'Hold it, hold it, hold it!' he said in a loud voice. 'I'm not with you! I'm not on the same frequency! Are you actually telling me that you're wondering whether to earn a lot of money or not?'

Boris frowned.

'It's not as straightforward as you think, Vadim,' he said, lowering his voice. He was worried that the secretary might overhear what they were saying.

Mironov got up from his chair, took off his jacket and started pacing around the room.

'Now let me get this straight,' he said, stopping in front of Boris. 'There are people in Moscow, obviously with big money, who approach you and ask you for assistance in acquiring property in London, right?'

'Right.'

'You say to them that you'll try – and I stress the word "try" – to get some information together about the real estate market, right?'

'Right.'

'You also say that it's not as straightforward as I might think. So let me ask you this – what is there to think when you are offered a chance of a lifetime?'

'These people may not be what they claim to be,' Boris said, choosing his words carefully.

'My dear Boris, who gives a damn who they are! Why should you care? We are talking big money here, very big money. What the hell's wrong with you?'

'They are threatening my son, for God's sake!' Boris said, raising his voice.

Mironov froze for a moment, looking at him in total bewilderment. 'Why the hell should they threaten your son?' he asked.

'Because I suspect they're criminals, Vadim! Because that's how they do things!'

Mironov got back behind his desk. He wiped the surface of the desk with his hands, taking time to control himself.

'So what do you want me to do?' he said.

Boris suddenly felt that he didn't really know what to ask him. It was as if he just needed to talk to somebody about his problem.

'I don't know,' he confessed.

Mironov was looking at him in disgust. Why, why on earth do people with money come to see Boris and not me? he was thinking. What is wrong with this world? Here I am, an expert on the property market in London, an expert on the whole of fucking London. Come to me, people, and I'll arrange the best deals for you! But no, you turn to some pathetic idiot who isn't sure what to bloody do! My dear papa was right: life is shit!

But the next moment it struck him that Boris might get offended and decide to pour his heart out to someone else. He had to act fast. He needed Boris to put him in touch with the people who wanted to buy property. A caring, sympathetic approach was in order.

'Now that I think about it, Boris,' he said, rubbing his forehead as if the thought had just struck him, 'I start to understand why you're worried. If I were still a diplomat and someone tried to force me to work for them I'd probably have second thoughts, just like you. Tell me more about these people. What exactly do they want you to do for them?'

Boris told him that during his second meeting, Volkov expressed interest in properties in Kensington Palace Gardens. Mironov could barely hide his excitement. He knew of several houses up for grabs in the area and also had some information on the last two remaining flats in the luxury block where one of the richest Russian businessmen had already bought a flat.

'I'll have to talk with some of my influential friends in Moscow,' he said, putting on an air of importance, a trick that he had mastered so well. 'But I'll need to meet the man who came to see you. So that I can get an idea where he's coming from.'

He asked Boris to put him in touch with Volkov. Although Boris started to have a really bad feeling about the entire conversation, he nevertheless promised to try to arrange a meeting. When he left, Mironov got back behind his desk and had a 'think-over', as he called it.

His financial position was not good. The income from his company was just enough to pay for the flat, the office and the car. But he wanted more. He wanted a sports car, a yacht, a small plane. He wanted to own a house in the Caribbean, maybe even own a whole island. And all of that could be made possible if he managed to establish contact with the people who had made the stupid mistake of approaching Boris instead of him.

Idiot! Mironov thought of Boris. People are offering him the chance of a lifetime. The commissions alone could run into hundreds of thousands, if the job is done properly. Bloody idiot!

★

The two Chechens arrived at the restaurant an hour late.

Seraphim was furious. He never waited for anyone for more than a few minutes and would probably have left long ago, but for the fact that the matter was of great importance and his relations with the Chechens were not at their best.

There was still an unresolved issue of his people delivering outdated arms in the last shipment worth about $3 million. The money had been paid in full and up front, and the Chechens were still waiting for an explanation, not to mention compensation. Seraphim had promised them to sort the matter out, but in reality did nothing. He had absolutely no desire to return the money to them.

But then things turned nasty. The Chechens made their anger known by killing two of Seraphim's people. The two thugs were on a routine extortion walk-about in one of the central open-air food markets when they were cornered by a group of men and gunned down.

Seraphim did not respond, although some of his people were insisting on a revenge attack. He knew well that an all-out war with the Chechens could finish his gang off. So he pretended to buy the story that his two men had been killed by people hired by the traders at the market who were unhappy with the constant rise in the protection payments. He would still not return any of the money, but, as a goodwill gesture, did pass on some very sensitive information to the Chechens regarding covert activities of Russian counter-intelligence in Chechnya. He was hoping that it would be enough to close the whole matter of compensation once and for all.

But then out of the blue came a freak attack on the offices of one of the companies run by the Central Brotherhood. In broad daylight, three jeeps blocked the entrance to the building. Several armed men came out and started banging on the doors demanding to see the manager. The security people at the entrance bolted up and told the visitors to get lost, but they opened fire, wounding several people behind the doors before driving off.

Seraphim was starting to feel the pressure. He had to do something to stop the conflict escalating into a full-blown gang war, so he invited the two Chechens for a meeting to try to resolve the crisis. He knew that his people had screwed up with the last arms shipment and was prepared to offer a very good deal to the Chechens, expecting them to agree to his terms and pay the money up front as usual. The thing was that he desperately needed to raise a lot of cash for a big operation he'd been planning for some time. And he had to do it in such a way that no one in his own gang would know about it, for he kept all the details of his plan in total secret.

When his two Chechen guests walked in he swallowed his pride and greeted them with a smile, as though they had not made him wait for nearly an hour.

★

It was getting dark very quickly in Moscow. The snow blizzard that had been raging all morning and part of the afternoon had finally subsided, although the wind was picking up again. The city was covered in a thick layer of snow and traffic on the streets was moving slowly.

After crossing the Moscow River over the Crimean Bridge, Motya drove down the embankment, past the dull concrete and modern glass building of the New Tretyakov Gallery, until they reached a large block of flats.

'This marvel of architecture is known as the House on the Embankment,' Motya explained, stopping the car, a rusty old Lada, at the kerb and switching off the engine. 'Stalin ordered it to be built for top party and government officials. It was actually the first luxury block of flats in the whole of Moscow built in Soviet times. The list of people who have lived here would be like a Who's Who in the history of the Soviet Communist Party.'

Alex and Clay looked at the huge grey building with no apparent emotion. It resembled more than slightly the building where they were staying themselves. Uncle Jo, it seemed, was not known to be diverse in his architectural endeavours.

'It looks kinda weird,' Clay said chewing energetically.

'Well it should look weird, considering the sort of people who lived there,' Motya said. 'By the way, the man who was in charge of executing the last Russian royal family in 1918, Yuri Yurkovski, also had a flat there. Wrote his memoirs, but nobody seemed to be interested. The last I heard he went mad and died all alone in his bed.'

'It's all very interesting,' Alex said, 'but when do we make our move?'

'Not just yet,' Motya said. 'We sit and wait for the signal. As soon as I know that the coast is clear and the door to the roof is left open, we move out.'

About fifteen minutes later a man came out of the building and gave a sign to Motya.

'It's time to go,' he said.

They got out of the car and walked briskly towards the inner courtyard of the building, passing the front entrance of the Theatre of Light Entertainment which formed a part of the huge block of flats. They entered the building through the door at the far end of the courtyard and reached the top floor in an old-fashioned creaking lift. They walked up one flight of stairs to a small steel door.

'This is the entrance to the roof,' Motya said. 'I'll be waiting for you here. Once it's over get back as fast as you can.'

When they got out onto the roof a gust of cold wind nearly blew them off their feet. They went slowly to the side of the roof from which the entrance to the Oscar Wilde could be clearly seen. They then opened their bags, assembled the rifles and positioned themselves about thirty feet from each other.

Across the street the glowing neon sign of a Western-type supermarket lit up the skyline. Through their night vision sights they could see a Mercedes parked outside the Oscar Wilde with two men sitting in it. They were Seraphim's bodyguards. Another Mercedes that had brought the two Chechens was parked further from the entrance with only the driver sitting at the wheel.

Alex felt the cold starting to bite at his face. His feet were also getting cold even though he had put on two pairs of thick woollen socks and was wearing warm winter shoes. The icy wind was making things even worse. Alex could see Clay trying to warm himself up by shuffling his feet and constantly rubbing his hands.

After five minutes on the roof it seemed to them that the meeting in the restaurant would never end…

★

The talks between Seraphim and the Chechens did not start well. As soon as he'd sent his girlfriend and Shark away the two men went on the offensive.

'Our people were very disappointed by the last arms shipment,' one of them called Marat said. 'We were not expecting to be so let down. And we were even more surprised when we didn't get our money back.'

Seraphim decided to close the matter once and for all.

'It was all a big misunderstanding,' he said. 'Believe me, the people who were responsible have been punished.'

The two were watching him in silence.

'I think that the next deal will compensate for the unfortunate incident,' Seraphim said. 'The price will be much lower than usual and the quality of arms will be high.'

He could see that his guests were still not impressed. A silence ensued which didn't bode well.

'I think you're missing the point, Crow,' Marat said. 'Our people are fighting a holy war. They are not fighting against the Russian people. They are fighting against the Kremlin rulers who have no respect for their own people. We want to establish our own rules and laws. We want peace, but to achieve peace we will have to fight a bloody war. And for that we need proper weapons.'

Seraphim felt a pulse beating in his left temple. Who was this prick lecturing? he thought. He sold them arms. Without him their bloody people would all be dead!

'Look, I'm no politician, I'm a businessman,' Seraphim said. 'You have your problems, I have mine. I'm not asking you to help me with my problems, am I? You've asked me for rifles and machine guns, I've given you rifles and machine guns. And don't think that it was a fucking joy ride. I lost several of my men delivering the stuff. So don't you forget it!'

Marat and his companion, Timur, showed no emotion.

'These are all words,' Timur said. 'We pay you good money, so don't complain that you have problems. There's no point in arguing. We don't hold any grudges. We have few friends and cannot afford to lose the last ones we have. Also we are very grateful for the information you have provided us with. The scum who betrayed our people have been punished. So we propose to forget all that happened and let's talk business.'

Seraphim nodded. He felt relieved that his guests had not marched out of the restaurant. He had put the pressure on them deliberately to test the mood, and so far it seemed that he'd played his cards right. The peace pipe had been offered to him.

'Our people need surface-to-air rockets,' Timur said. 'They can't fight Russian planes and helicopters with guns and rifles. We've received information that a new offensive is planned by the Russian army in the spring. A lot of planes and helicopters will be used against our people. So they are asking for weapons that can shoot down planes. And they're prepared to pay for them.'

Seraphim was taken aback by the request.

'How on earth do you expect me to get you rockets?' he said. 'It was a hell of a job getting the rifles, mortars and grenades. How can I organise a shipment of rockets? There are hundreds if not thousands of federal agents monitoring the borders. Do you want me to lose all of my men?'

The guests were unimpressed.

'We'll pay you ten million dollars in cash for a hundred and fifty Russian Arrows if you can deliver them by May,' Marat said. 'And don't give us any crap about your problems and your men. When did you start worrying about your people? You must be getting soft, Crow.'

Nobody, but nobody spoke to Seraphim like that! He felt the urge to give a signal to Shark, who sat with them at the table without uttering a word, to get the two arrogant bastards to choke on their own blood. But the ten million dollars in cash sounded too tempting. It would be enough to pull off the big job that he had been planning for so long.

So instead of making an ugly scene Seraphim produced a smile.

'I'll see what I can do,' he said. 'But this time the money should be delivered to me personally. And it must be all in cash.'

Marat nodded.

'Agreed,' he said.

The peace deal was done. The war between the Central Brotherhood and the Chechens was averted.

When they finished their meal and all got up Seraphim accompanied the two Chechens outside. He rarely extended his hospitality to escorting his guests to their cars, but this was a special occasion and as a mark of their new friendship he was making a special effort.

As they walked out and waited for the Mercedes to drive up to the entrance, Seraphim suddenly noticed several red dots dancing on the snow-covered pavement under their feet. One of the dots sneaked up from the pavement to Marat's head. The next moment a bullet went through his eye and he fell to the ground with blood all over his face.

Timur turned to Seraphim. His eyes were full of hatred.

'You son of a bitch!' he shouted. 'You've set us up! You'll…'

But he didn't have a chance to finish. A red dot appeared on his face and a second later he too fell down dead.

Seraphim froze, unable to move. Several more bullets whizzed past, narrowly missing him. The next moment he felt somebody pushing him from behind to the ground. He fell on the pavement as more bullets flew over him. He turned his head and looked at the man who pushed him and was now lying beside him. It was the cop he had seen in the restaurant…

★

General Aleksei Mikhailov, Deputy Director of the Federal Security Service, was looking through a pile of documents on his table. They were reports from local divisions of the FSB concerning recent events in their respective regions.

Several files were related to the activities of organised criminal groups. But the reports in them were mostly about minor things such as the movements of some of the gang members, places where they were hanging out or addresses of the offices that they used. Rubbish! the General thought. Non-essential rubbish! Our people are getting lazy. There's no real substance in any of this so-called information.

He was looking through one of the files concerning a criminal group in the city of Rostov-on-Don. The local FSB agents were monitoring a group that was running the biggest local car repair dealership. There were suspicions that the gang had been stripping stolen cars down for spare parts in the garage and fitting them on vehicles owned by their customers.

On the face of it the efforts of the local FSB division seemed worthwhile. Yet the report contained no information that could have provided grounds for busting the illegal trade. There were photographs of people coming in and out of the garage. Some came once, some came twice. All the licence plates of cars going into the repair shop and coming out were listed. However not a single vehicle was noted as arriving at the garage and not leaving it. What the hell are they up to? the General thought. It's as if they're not investigating but covering up the whole bloody scam!

Rostov-on-Don was known for the unparalleled scale of corruption and collusion between its law-enforcement agencies and the local criminals. In the past two years alone two senior prosecutors, several high-ranking policemen and FSB agents had been arrested and charged with corruption. None were sent to jail though, as the judges were too afraid to hand down custodial sentences: local hoods would have been at their doorsteps the next day.

There were more contract killings in Rostov-on-Don than anywhere else in the whole of Russia. In one year alone, five hundred professional hits were registered there. The local FSB attributed most of them to turf wars between the local heavies. But some of the killings looked very suspicious and General Mikhailov was preparing a memo to the director asking for a group of investigators to be sent from Moscow to look into several of the high profile murders of local criminals, businessmen and politicians.

By all standards the FSB was losing the war against organised crime in the country. Once in a while it would claim a 'big success' and the papers would report how federal agents had smashed a 'criminal network'. But judging by the amounts of money seized and numbers of weapons confiscated it was clear that only small fry were being caught while the big sharks continued to hunt freely in deep waters.

There was one successful operation, though, that few people attributed to the FSB. It had to do with the death of Dzhokhar Dudayev, the hard-line Chechen leader who had rejected outright all offers of dialogue with Moscow to try to settle the issue of Chechen independence. He would accept no less than full and unconditional independence from Russia.

Dudayev was killed by a missile fired from a Russian jet fighter on patrol. He was using his portable satellite telephone at the time of his death. Few people paid attention to that fact, but the phone was the key to the whole thing. It so happened that FSB agents on the ground in Chechnya had managed to lock onto some of the mobile phones used by the Chechens during their raids. They traced the signals to a network run by a company based in London that was providing communications links to firms and individual clients through a satellite network.

The Chechens, as it turned out, were registered in the company files as 'business executives' from several offshore companies. Each one had an individual call code so that the system would recognise them. The Russian army needed to know the codes to program the rockets on the aircraft so that once the call was made, the navigation system on the rockets could lock onto the handset.

The FSB asked the External Intelligence Service, SVR for short in Russian, to get them the codes. For some reason they wouldn't or couldn't do it. So the FSB dispatched its own agent to London. A bit of persuasion and some serious presents were involved and a one-night stand with the company's secretary was also helpful. Eventually the agent got the codes.

Once the Russian military had the necessary information, it was only a matter of time before Dudayev was killed. The Russian Defence Ministry was so surprised that for two days it made no comments about the incident.

Mikhailov opened a file with the tag 'Urgent' on it. It contained documents about an undercover operation launched in order to establish a network of agents in Chechnya. It was a costly and time-consuming exercise, but after months of hard work a network had finally been created. Seven locals, at one time or another connected to the rebels, had been recruited and became informers. For several months all went well and the information they provided helped foil operations by the insurgents. But at some point all contact with them was lost. The security people were completely baffled by this turn of events.

The file contained some of the last reports from the team about movements of armed rebel groups and shipments of arms across the border.

The secretary knocked on the door and entered the room. 'These just came in,' he said. He put two documents on the table and left.

Mikhailov read the first paper.

'Our man has settled in,' it said. 'The party has begun.'

The General smiled. Excellent, he thought. At last we'll be

able to find out what those bastards from the Kremlin's body-guard service are up to.

But as he read the first few sentences of the second report his face became grim. It stated that seven mutilated bodies had been found in Dagestan close to the Chechen border. They all had pieces of cardboard pinned on them, with the words 'traitors' and 'cocksuckers' written in Russian.

Someone had given the Chechens the names of the seven agents...

★

'Personally, I blame the ghastly MTV for the spread of bad taste among young people. The presenters are vulgar and the video clips they show are simply disgusting,' a woman in a long black dress was saying. 'And the lyrics of the songs are not just dis-tasteful – they are offensive, aggressive and downright obscene. No wonder someone called MTV the fifth column of bad taste.'

The woman was standing amongst a group of people who had already discussed the weather and had moved on to criticising the younger generation.

'I think it's the low standards in education,' a tall bearded man standing next to her opined. 'Young people nowadays don't even know who Dickens and Shakespeare are...'

Everyone in the group seemed to agree. Jeremy smiled to himself as he overheard them talking. When will they realise that being young means getting a kick out of everything that irritates the grown-ups? he thought. When will they learn?

He moved on, wandering into the study where some of the men were having cigars. The conversation was about crime and the concept of zero tolerance that seemed to be working in America.

'From what I read in the papers, I can only assume that it's only a matter of time before we have zero-tolerance policing in our own cities,' a grey-haired man was saying. He was sitting in a big armchair smoking a cigar. 'If you ask me, the problem with zero tolerance is that they got the basic concept all wrong. You don't fight crime by pushing it underground. I personally think that the whole crime problem is caused more by corruption in the police...'

The man drew on his cigar and blew out the smoke.

'I don't mean police corruption as in accepting bribes or colluding with the criminals,' he explained. 'I'm talking about corruption as in reluctance to tackle crime. Nowadays the police are either chasing motorists who break the speed limit or running after shoplifters. You won't see them going into a dark alley any more. No, they'd rather be where the lights are bright and the chances of encountering a mugger are low...'

He started to splutter and stopped talking. A man with a large grey moustache who was sitting on the sofa and rolling a cigar with his fingers joined in the conversation.

'I think the government has completely screwed up on the whole crime issue,' he said. 'They got themselves into a corner with this blasted political correctness. So now you can't prosecute somebody because he comes from some minority, or he's too young, or he's the victim of social injustice. What does it mean, social injustice? If one is poor one is allowed to rob other people. Is that what it is? I wouldn't be surprised if we're living in a state of siege soon, just like the Americans.'

'Rubbish!' said a man standing near the fireplace. He looked like a retired military man. 'How can you compare Britain and America? In America...'

Jeremy decided not to listen any further. The only reason he came to the party was because he was planning to meet his friend Ron Baker, former CIA station chief in Moscow, who was running late. Meanwhile he had no choice but to mix with the crowd.

He didn't like parties generally. The majority of them were very boring. The women would usually be showing off their new dresses or jewellery and the men would try to make everyone believe that they made tons of money. Jeremy knew a lot of so-called 'society people' who wouldn't be able to survive a week without going to some party. They usually got up round about noon and then spent hours getting ready for the night out.

'We started at that Italian place in the West End, then moved to Monty's and danced there all night long,' some woman would be telling her friends the next day. 'Did you know that Henry's left Margaret and moved in with Jonathan...?'

On several occasions Jeremy had been lured to a couple of the trendy nightclubs by his friends. He saw old men move around clumsily on the dance floors with their young girlfriends, their bald heads reflecting the disco lights. It was a pathetic sight. On a couple of occasions he bumped into former society beauties who had lost their looks but were still out there trying to prove to the world that they were going strong, hanging onto younger men who were so drunk they would go out with anyone.

★

It was then that Jeremy heard Ron's loud voice in the hall. He hurried to meet him. Ron looked like a typical American, tall and lean, with short grey hair, a set of large milky-white teeth and a powerful lower jaw. He also dressed like an American, preferring flashy jackets, light-coloured slacks and leather shoes with gold buckles. His collection of ties seemed to be enormous and Jeremy never saw him wearing the same tie twice. He also had a weakness for silk cowboy-style scarves that he wore on informal occasions.

And yet, with those eccentricities, Ron was one of the most intelligent people Jeremy had ever met. He had a sharp, calculating mind and he could quickly analyse complicated situations and come up with the most unexpected solutions.

They greeted each other like lifelong friends, although they'd only known each other for about five years. But considering what they'd been through in Russia, it seemed like for ever. Ron had been introduced to Jeremy by a British businessman who hinted that Baker was no ordinary diplomat. Jeremy got the message and was initially careful with what he said to Ron. But by their third meeting they were talking candidly and the sense of having to be on guard evaporated.

Ron knew Russia like few other Westerners. He could speak Russian fluently and most locals felt at ease with him after several minutes of conversation. He once provided Jeremy with the best possible explanation of why Russia would be lagging behind the rest of the world for years to come. They were driving down a motorway to Moscow from a country club and one by one cars started to move into the restricted lane in the middle, narrowly avoiding the vehicles going the opposite way. Soon there were more cars driving down the restricted lane than there were cars on the regular lanes.

'That's why Russia will find it hard to sort itself out,' Ron said, pointing at the cars passing them on the restricted lane. 'In other countries you would get only a few idiots breaking the law. But in Mother Russia, as you can see, for every ten people you get a hundred smart asses prepared to break the rules.'

Later Jeremy found out for himself how true it was.

★

'Jeremy, it's good to see you!' Ron said, smiling broadly. 'How are you, my dear friend?'

Jeremy smiled back.

'I'm fine, Ron, I'm fine. It's really great to see you again. How is Sandra, how are the kids?'

'Oh, they're doing all right. Sandra sends her regards. Unfortunately she couldn't come to London with me. She is a high-flier now. Big-time corporate lawyer – East European connections, you know.'

They both laughed. Jeremy suggested that they go to the winter garden, the pride of the owner of the house, where they could talk in private.

He told Ron about Boris's problem and how he was trying to help him.

Ron looked concerned.

'Don't underestimate the people in Moscow,' he said. 'And don't forget that although there is no more KGB, the people who are now running the new intelligence service are still the same people as before. They can be very professional and cunning. Don't be fooled by all the confusion and chaos in Russia.'

'I know that the risk is high,' Jeremy said. 'But there was no choice. To save my friend and his family I had to act.'

Ron looked at Jeremy.

'The question I would normally ask under such circumstances

is why the hell do you need to get involved? But in your case there is no point in asking that, is there? Knowing you as I do, I would guess that you acted on impulse. And don't get me wrong, I'm not saying that you shouldn't be trying to help your friend. But what if the whole thing backfires?'

Jeremy smiled.

'As I said, I'm well aware of the risks,' he said. 'Don't forget that I've been dealing in Russia myself. So let's just skip the part about the reasons I got involved in helping my friend. The point is that I might need your help. You must still have contacts in Russia. I still remember how you got my people out of trouble when the local hoods went after them in Moscow.'

'That was some stunt we pulled off,' Ron said smiling. 'And to think that the bad guys didn't know up to the very end that we were bluffing all the way and had no real backing from the Russian government.'

'That's the point,' Jeremy said. 'We have a similar situation once again. We have several people on the ground in Moscow but they're up against an army of thugs. Anything can go wrong at any time. What I'm asking you is this – if we get in a tight spot can I count on you and your contacts in Russia?'

Ron looked at Jeremy.

'Sure thing,' he said, 'sure thing.'

★

The man who supplied Seraphim with the arms that were then shipped to the rebels in Chechnya was Colonel Igor Kislov. He ran a network of army officers in Moscow who were involved in illegal sales of arms and military hardware.

Kislov had figured out long ago that the once mighty Soviet Red Army was slowly falling apart. The first signs of decay emerged in the early 1980s during the war in Afghanistan. It was obvious from the humiliating defeats in the battles with the Afghani resistance that the Russian military machine was no longer the force it once was.

The war in Afghanistan was probably the first armed conflict in the history of mankind where one side sold arms to the other.

The Russian officers smuggled arms to the mujahed fighters in exchange for drugs and gold. Some of these same officers, along with thousands of soldiers, were later killed in combat by the very same weapons they had sold to the enemy.

Kislov spent a year in Afghanistan and knew about the illegal arms deals conducted by some of the officers. The drugs and gold that they were getting were smuggled into Russia and sold there.

Morale in the army was low. Many Soviet soldiers could not understand what they were doing in Afghanistan in the first place, especially as the enemy seemed to be everywhere. Both young and old Afghans took up arms to fight the invaders, attacking patrols and firing at convoys from the mountains. Stories about Russian soldiers being lured into traps by children as young as five and then brutally murdered by their relatives were told and retold.

Then came the incident that shocked the whole regiment where Kislov served. Eighteen manned checkpoints down the road from Kabul to the northern border were wiped out in one day. When details of the massacre emerged, no one could believe that over a hundred soldiers could be killed with such ease.

According to a report by Russian military intelligence that Kislov had seen, a peasant cart was used as a decoy to distract the attention of the soldiers. Every time it approached a checkpoint, one of its wheels would fall off. An old man and two young women would then try to mend the wheel without success. The soldiers would then lay down their weapons and try to assist. As they were all attempting to lift the cart and fix the wheel back on, a group of men would appear out of nowhere and kill all the soldiers.

Kislov gradually came to the conclusion that the only way to make some sense out of the 'undeclared war', as it was called in the Soviet newspapers, was to profit from it. His first opportunity came when he was in charge of a mission to destroy a group of armed rebels, *dukhi* as the Russian soldiers nicknamed them, who had attacked a military convoy and had later hidden in a village in the mountains. Four helicopters were provided to carry out the mission.

They attacked the village early in the morning. The helicopters were pounding the ground with machine-gun fire. Kislov wanted to make sure that there would be no surprises once they descended.

When they landed, the village looked like a target practice site: clouds of dust were still hanging in the air and most of the small houses and mud huts were severely damaged. There were dead goats lying all over the place, but there was no sign of people.

Kislov, armed with a machine gun and dressed in a soldier's uniform so that a sniper might not single him out as an officer, ordered his men to be extra careful. They spread out looking for any survivors. Kislov approached a house with one of his men. He signalled to the soldier to enter the house first and check whether any booby traps had been left inside. It was not uncommon for the dukhi to mine homes in villages so that the Russian soldiers were killed or seriously injured when they walked inside.

The soldier came out.

'All clear, Comrade Major!' he reported.

Kislov ordered him to wait outside and went in. He wanted to check whether there was anything of value in the house left. The roof was riddled with bullets and beams of sunlight were coming through the holes, cutting through the thick cloud of dust. In one of the rooms Kislov stumbled upon an old man, who was sitting on the floor in the corner, covered in rags. Instinctively he pointed his machine gun at him. The old man slowly got up from the floor, mumbling something in his native language. He was holding a bag, and, when Kislov approached him, he untied the knot with his trembling hands and showed him the contents. There were gold coins inside, at least twenty, maybe even more. Kislov took the bag from the old man who started to smile and nod his head as if he was happy that the Russian officer had accepted his gift.

Kislov held the bag in his hand: judging by the weight there could have been at least thirty gold coins in it. He looked at the old man who continued to smile. There was no point in sparing his life, Kislov reckoned. He would die in prison of hunger or torture anyway.

He pointed the machine gun at the old man who shut his eyes tight, like children do when they are afraid of something and hope that it will disappear when they open their eyes. Kislov pulled the trigger.

A soldier ran into the room.

'Are you all right, Comrade Major?' he asked, panting.

'I'm fine,' Kislov said, hiding the bag with coins in his pocket. 'Had to finish the old bastard. Tried to take a swipe at me.'

On the way back to base Kislov couldn't help reaching from time to time for the bag with gold coins in his pocket. He was hoping it would be the first of his many 'war trophies'.

Soon he was running his own small operation, smuggling goods taken from villages during seek-and-destroy missions. But all his attempts to get close to any of the serious players failed, as he did not have the right contacts.

After Afghanistan Kislov got a post in the Ministry of Defence in Moscow and was promoted to Lieutenant Colonel, an occasion he celebrated in style with some of his closest friends. For the first time in his life he actually had sufficient money to pay for the booze, the food and the women.

When the Russians started pulling out of Afghanistan he managed to get himself appointed as a member of the team overseeing the withdrawal. Although he didn't manage to make a lot of money at the time, he did establish good links with the veteran groups. Later these contacts proved very handy: he was able to assemble teams of professionals in a matter of days to carry out special jobs for important people.

When Moscow began withdrawing its troops from Eastern Europe, a whole new window of opportunity opened up. By then Kislov had acquired a lot of 'friends' in the military and managed to take part in the sale of stockpiles of arms, equipment, food-stuffs and fuel that had been stored across Eastern Europe for use by the Soviet troops. Kislov was part of a group of former Communist Party officials, ex-KGB agents, military officers and some very suspicious 'civilians' who made several billion dollars' worth of profit from the sales of what was left behind by the western group of the Soviet armed forces. Once again he was not a key player, but this time he did manage to earn good money and widen his contacts.

Later Kislov set up his own operation, organising illegal arms sales. He was introduced to Seraphim by one of the people who was involved in the smuggling of small arms to groups operating in the mountains of Chechnya. By that time he was already a colonel and had a network of connections in the Ministry of Defence. Kislov was recommended to Seraphim as somebody who was capable of providing serious weaponry, not just hand-guns, rifles and the occasional box or two of grenades. Seraphim asked him to get some heavy machine guns and artillery pieces, and Kislov duly obliged. From then onwards they dealt on a regular basis, shipping millions of dollars' worth of arms to the Chechen rebels.

At one of their meetings Seraphim asked Kislov whether he could get special equipment for one of his 'partners'. When Kislov saw the list he was more than impressed: apart from sub-machine guns, handguns and sniper rifles, the list included sophisticated communication equipment, powerful computers and eavesdrop-ping equipment.

'Apart from the stuff mentioned in the list, my friend would also need a team of about a hundred people who are trained in martial arts, can handle different types of weapons and are prepared to travel without asking any questions,' Seraphim said. 'They'll be paid well, very well.'

Kislov was no fool and quickly figured out that there was no 'partner' involved and that Seraphim was planning something himself. He couldn't resist the temptation to find out more.

'Judging by his requirements your partner must be a very serious man,' he said, pretending to buy Seraphim's story. 'I guess the best thing would be for me to meet with him personally and talk over the details.'

Seraphim's eyes narrowed.

'You'll talk only to me,' he said. 'If I need you to know any-thing, I'll tell you about it myself. Is that clear?'

'Yeah, sure, sure,' Kislov said, suddenly feeling very uncomfortable.

★

There was mayhem outside the Oscar Wilde.

Shark was pinning Pavel to the ground and pointing a gun at his head. The other bodyguards formed a human shield around Seraphim to protect him from the snipers.

'Easy, easy, guys, I'm on your side!' Pavel was protesting, but no one was paying any attention to him.

By now Seraphim was on his feet, breathing heavily. He glanced at the two Chechens lying on the pavement. There was blood on the snow all around them. He felt no pity for the two dead men. In his book they were scum and deserved to die anyway, but not on his turf. The Chechens were now bound to suspect that he had lured the two men into a trap in revenge for attacks on his people.

Shark was looking at him, waiting for instructions.

'Send some men to check the area,' Seraphim said, hoping that his voice did not betray any sign of anxiety. 'Just in case anyone has seen anything. And deal with the cops. Pay them off. I don't care how much it costs.'

Shark nodded.

'What do we do with the pig?' he asked, pointing at Pavel who was still lying in the snow.

Seraphim glanced at the cop.

'Take him to the safe house and keep him there,' he said. 'I'll deal with him later.'

Shark got up, gestured to his men to pick Pavel up. Seraphim walked briskly to the limousine and got inside. His girlfriend, who must have been watching the whole thing from the window of the restaurant, dashed out and tried to get into the limousine too. But Shark stood in her way.

'You go home,' he said slipping several hundred-dollar bills into her hand. 'The boss has business to attend to.'

★

It took Alex and Clay under a minute to reach the door that led to the stairs. Motya was waiting for them. They ran down the stairs, disassembling the rifles and packing them into the sports bags. Once outside, the three men walked to the Lada as calmly as they could.

But once they had got into the car and shut the doors Clay exploded.

'What the hell was that?' he yelled. 'Why the hell did ya shoot them in the head? Are ya nuts?'

Alex turned pale.

'Are you telling me that I shot them in the head?' he yelled back at Clay. 'Are you accusing me of killing them?'

It seemed as though Clay had suddenly swallowed his chewing gum in all the excitement. He opened his mouth but couldn't utter a word. There was a strange gurgling sound coming from his throat.

Motya turned round in his seat.

'What the hell is wrong with you people?' he said. 'Do you want us to get arrested? Once we leave the place you can beat the crap out of each other. But not now, not here!'

Both men fell silent.

Motya started the engine and they drove off. They passed under the Big Stone Bridge and were driving along the embankment. Several police cars with their sirens wailing passed them going in the opposite direction.

Alex was thinking hard. He suddenly worked out what had just happened.

'Someone's set us up,' he said. 'Someone else must have been shooting at those guys at the same time as we were.'

Clay looked at him in amazement.

★

The leader of the Russian communists, Gennadi Margalov, harboured a dark secret and no one, not even his closest aides and family, knew anything about it.

Comrade Margalov was the man who, so everyone thought, had a very good chance of winning the next presidential elections in Russia. His popularity rating, according to the polls, was very high compared to the ratings of the President. The communists were enjoying strong support in the rural areas of Russia and in some industrial cities where capitalism had brought mostly misery and despair. Not that the people lived much better in the Soviet times, but at least then they were paid regularly and prices were not spiralling out of control.

The majority of Russians were ready to vote for Margalov. They didn't rate him very highly, but by giving their support to the communist leader they could send a clear message to the Kremlin. What the voters and his supporters didn't know, though, was that the communist leader had a secret pact with the President whereby he would resign if the election went his way.

The deal came about when Gennadi Margalov received a secret invitation from the head of state to meet with him at the Kremlin. His first reaction was to decline the offer but, after some consideration, he changed his mind and decided to go. In his note the President had mentioned some 'important private matter' that he wanted to discuss and Margalov felt that he couldn't simply ignore the invitation.

As agreed, he was picked up from his house outside Moscow late in the evening. A black Mercedes with a private licence plate and darkened windows took him to the Kremlin, passing through the Borovitski Gate without even being stopped and checked by the guards. It eventually brought Margalov to the vast yellow building housing the President and his staff. He got out and walked briskly towards the entrance, hiding his face behind the collar of his coat. He had an uneasy feeling about this visit. What if it's a trap? he thought. What if the press have been informed of my visit? The President's people could invent anything to discredit me.

Margalov tried to dismiss such thoughts from his mind. He even imagined for a moment that the President might have at last decided to set up a cabinet of national unity, as the communists proposed, and to offer him a place in government. But, taking all things into consideration, it seemed highly unlikely, especially as Margalov had recently stepped up his anti-Kremlin campaign, condemning the President and his people for continuing the destruction of the country which was started by Boris Yeltsin when he signed a deal with the leaders of Belarus, Ukraine and Kazakhstan granting independence to former Soviet republics.

'The CIA could only have dreamt of dissolving the former Soviet Union into miniature states that could be dealt with one at a time!' Margalov had said at one of the recent rallies of communist supporters in Moscow. 'Yet, with one signature, Yeltsin did what the Americans were unable to achieve in decades!'

He banged his fist on the podium and the people erupted in loud cheers.

'The current President is no better!' Margalov continued. 'He plans to give away the Kurrill Islands to the Japanese and a large chunk of Siberia to China. This borders on state treason, comrades!'

His speech went down well with the crowd.

★

The President was smiling at Margalov as he walked into his office. He greeted him at the centre of the room, shook his hand, and offered him a chair. He then sat down behind his desk and asked several polite questions about Margalov's wife and their two adult children.

While answering, the leader of the Russian communists suddenly felt total indifference to what was happening and decided to respond to events as they unravelled. When he stopped talking, the President shuffled some of the papers on his desk, as if trying to find the right words to start the meeting in earnest. He then looked at Margalov.

'As you know, Gennadi Petrovich,' he said, 'we are doing our best to sort out the mess in the country. It's a hard job, as we have inherited many problems from the past that we are not responsible for. And at times like these, politicians, and I am talking about *responsible* politicians, should support the head of state.'

Margalov was watching the President closely. I wonder what he's getting at? he thought. He must have some trick up his sleeve.

'As you are well aware, the next presidential election is approaching,' the President was saying. 'It'll be a test for our democracy, a very serious test. The whole world will be watching us. We mustn't let the country become hostage to political ambitions of individuals. All political parties should adopt a constructive stance and stop using unacceptable means of undermining their opponents. For example, your people have recently accused one leading member of the government of links to the CIA. This is not only absurd, it harms our national interests.'

The President stopped. He was looking at Margalov as if expecting him to say something.

'We only reflect what the people feel,' Margalov said gloomily. 'The people are unhappy. They deserve better. They don't want to accept the free market and everything that comes with it.'

The President's face stiffened.

'We are all servants of the people,' he said sternly. 'I suggest you don't imply that only the Communist Party is concerned with national interests. I have become head of state in the first ever civilised transition of power in Russia in the last hundred years. My political mandate is no less democratic than that of the previous president.'

Margalov let it pass. Everyone knew that Yeltsin was pushed out of office, but there was no point in arguing.

'Mr President,' he said, 'I thought that you wanted to discuss some private matter. I'm ready to listen.'

The President nodded, as if recalling why he had invited Margalov in the first place. He pressed the button on his interior phone, and someone entered the room. Margalov had to spin around in his chair to see who it was.

Benedikt Vladimirov, Director of the FSB, walked into the office holding a black leather folder. He was a short stocky man, with thinning blond hair, closely set eyes and a long thin nose. He had the sort of appearance that people usually forget the moment they looked away.

When Vladimirov had been appointed as head of counter-intelligence several months before, there were many eyebrows raised in the Kremlin as he wasn't exactly a typical candidate for the job. He'd worked for about fifteen years in the former KGB, but was primarily involved in foreign intelligence and had no experience of counter-intelligence operations. Later he left the force to pursue a career in Moscow city council. It was from there that he was suddenly plucked from obscurity and appointed, first as an advisor to the head of one of the departments in the Kremlin administration, and then as FSB Director. No one could understand the thinking behind his promotion, but as the decision had been made by the President himself, no one dared ask any questions...

The President nodded to Vladimirov.

'And here's our famous warrior of the invisible front,' he joked.

Margalov automatically got up from his chair and, extending his hand, took the first step in the direction of the FSB Director. Being a true-blooded communist, he always held the 'warriors of the invisible front' in high respect. But Vladimirov's cold, 'this is not the time for niceties' stare made Margalov stop in his tracks and lower his hand. The FSB Director nodded to him and walked noiselessly to the leather couch to the right of the President's desk, sitting down on its edge.

Margalov had no choice but to return to his chair. He was now getting really worried.

'I have invited our distinguished FSB Director to shed light on disturbing facts that have been recently uncovered by our intelligence services,' the President said, looking at Vladimirov closely. 'I think that you, Gennadi Petrovich, will be very interested in what the Director has to say.'

Margalov was now regretting his decision to visit the Kremlin. Things were looking very grim indeed.

Vladimirov opened his folder. He then looked at the President, who gestured to him to begin.

'Our agents,' Vladimirov said in an official tone, 'have uncovered information regarding a group of Russian citizens who have managed to defraud an Austrian bank out of $16 million. These people were posing as managers of a large industrial enterprise in the south of Russia which was looking for an opportunity to convert roubles into US dollars at a good rate. They managed to arrange the deal with the bank but in the end the money destined for the Austrians never got there...'

Vladimirov paused for a moment. The President grinned, watching Margalov closely.

'Can you imagine, Gennadi Petrovich,' he said, 'how some of our compatriots operate on the foreign markets. Not one, not two million, but *sixteen* million US dollars in one go. That's a lot of money, you know.'

Margalov didn't respond. He was waiting for Vladimirov to continue.

'According to our initial information, one man had master-minded the operation to defraud the Austrian bank,' Vladimirov said. 'His name is Grigori Dibrov and he claimed that he was consulted on the matter by Konstantin Margalov, a trade delegation official in Bonn.'

Margalov felt something tightening in his stomach. His son's name had just been mentioned alongside one of the county's top criminals. He didn't know what to say.

The President was watching him. Margalov could feel that Vladimirov was also looking at him although he was facing the President. The silence was becoming unbearable. Then the President spoke.

'I have instructed our people in Germany to conduct a secret investigation,' he said. 'They have established that your son – I assume you know that he was involved with a number of private Russian companies as a consultant – had nothing to do with the scam. Well, not directly at least. There won't be any official inquiry on our side. That is, unless no new facts are uncovered.'

Margalov was so shocked that he could barely understand what the President was saying. How many times did I tell Konstantin that he should be careful in his dealings with those so-called Russian businessmen, he thought. But no, he was too smart, he knew best!

The President made a sign to Vladimirov who then left the room as quietly as he had entered it. Margalov was still reeling in shock, looking down at his clasped hands and breathing heavily. The President gave him some time to think things over and then cleared his throat loudly. Margalov looked up at him.

'I can assure you, Gennadi Petrovich,' the President said, 'that I'll do all in my power to protect your son from any false allegations that might be made against him. Of course I'm not saying that I can give you any definite guarantees, but I'll do my best.'

Margalov knew that he was cornered. There was no way he could shield his son. Even if this whole story was made up, the agents from the External Intelligence could always dig up 'facts' and provide 'witnesses' if needed. He knew that the President's people were ready to use any means at their disposal to neutralise opponents, but was still taken aback. It was classic blackmail and his enemies were hitting him below the belt.

The ghost of Joseph Stalin had returned to haunt the communist leader. The ruthless dictator would often go after the families of his opponents to crush any dissent.

Margalov was waiting for the President to lay down his conditions. But the old man was in no hurry. He liked to keep people guessing. It was at such moments that his enemies would sometimes give away their deepest secrets.

So he waited for his guest to break the silence.

'I suppose,' Margalov said in a lowered voice, 'that in the light of what we have heard from the FSB Director you have some sort of offer for me.'

The President frowned.

'Offer?' he said, looking genuinely surprised. 'No, I have no intention to pressure you into any deals just because your son is in trouble with the law. I have a son myself and I understand perfectly well what you are going through at the moment. I simply wanted you to know about this in case some journalist gets hold of this information. You know how they can be, these hacks.'

Margalov nodded as if he were grateful to the President for telling him the bad news. But inside he knew that he was well and truly boxed in. Half of the people in the Kremlin administration were former reporters or security officers and they could conjure up any story they wished and use it against people in the opposing camps.

'Once again, Gennadi Petrovich, I can assure you that I'll do everything in my power to shield your son,' the President said, rising from his chair. 'And I hope that you'll consider seriously my proposal about the forthcoming elections. We must refrain from mud slinging and unfounded allegations.'

Soon after Margalov had left the President's office, the door leading to the living quarters opened and a man with a crop of ginger hair appeared in the office. His face was covered in freckles and his dark narrow eyes had a mischievous glint in them. He was dressed in a sweater and blue jeans.

He walked to the chair where Margalov had been sitting and slumped down on it. He looked at the President who was sitting behind his desk, lost in thought.

'Well, how did he take it?' he asked.

The President seemed to be far away, as if still going through the brief conversation with the communist leader.

'I said, how did he take it?' the man repeated his question.

The President snapped out of his thoughts.

'He took it well, Valentin,' he said in a lowered voice. 'I only hope he didn't think I was trying to blackmail him.'

Valentin grinned, revealing a gold crown on one of his front teeth.

'And I hope he thought exactly that,' he said. ''Cos if he didn't, you see, you're gonna be invited for a chat to the Prosecutor General's office if you lose the elections! Along with Vassili, your wife and little old me!'

The President grimaced.

'But do you think the people in Germany have actually uncovered something or is it one of those things when we'll have to explain later that it was all a terrible mistake?' he asked.

Valentin shook his head.

'Don't you worry,' he said, 'I'll deal with everything personally.'

He got up from the chair and stretched out his arms.

'I feel like playing some tennis today,' he said and walked out of the office.

Two days later the President received a confidential hand-written letter in which Margalov informed him that should he get more votes than his competitors at the next election he would immediately step down on health grounds.

★

In the course of a normal day hundreds of people pass through Kensington Palace Gardens.

Although a private road, it is only cars that are prevented from driving through by security guards at the two checkpoints at either end. Pedestrians can walk unhindered through the gates and stroll down the road, occasionally stopping to admire the fine buildings. Tourists wander in looking for Kensington Palace, shoppers walk through to get from Bayswater to Kensington High Street and joggers use the road to avoid the crowded pathways of Kensington Gardens.

On one particular sunny day in February two men were slowly walking down Kensington Palace Gardens. One was big and tall, wearing an expensive, long, camel-hair coat with a scarf wrapped around his neck. The other one was of medium height and dressed in jeans and a leather jacket.

'So this is the famous millionaire's row,' the big man said. 'I've heard so much about it that I feel I've been here already. Pity about the roadworks though. They do spoil the whole view.'

The man in the leather jacket nodded in agreement.

'It's not the best time to be here,' he said. 'They are laying down new communication cables and that's why the whole road is dug up. But normally the place looks really grand. Some of these properties are owned by the richest people in the world. It's actually amazing that the Russian embassy occupies several buildings in the road.'

The big man stopped beside a barrier with a roadworks sign on it and looked down into the deep trench that had been dug up. At the bottom of the trench several thick communication cables lay in full view.

'Why would they all need to replace their communication lines?' he asked his companion.

'It's to do with the new phone lines and television cables,' the man in the leather jacket explained. 'Basically they'll be able to have all their communications upgraded in one go.'

The big man nodded, but said nothing. They came up to the Russian ambassador's residence at number 13.

'Looks very impressive,' the big man said, eyeing the building, 'very impressive indeed. If you hadn't told me it was the property of the Russian government I would have assumed that it belonged to some rich Arab sheikh or billionaire banker.'

'It's one of the most beautiful buildings in the road,' his companion said. 'A lot of people would love to get their hands on it.'

The big man grinned.

'I'm sure they would,' he said. 'I'm sure they would.'

The two men continued their walk in the direction of Kensington Palace. It was an unusually warm day for that time of year, sunny with no wind. A group of Japanese tourists passed them by, clicking their cameras constantly.

'For a fancy place like that it is strange that there are no security people around,' the big man said. 'And I don't see cops either. Aren't the locals afraid of burglars?'

The man in the leather jacket laughed.

'No one in his right mind would think of burgling houses here,' he said. 'There are hidden cameras and sophisticated alarm systems installed in every building. Not to mention that all the embassies down the road have their own security people inside.'

The big man smiled.

'You'd be surprised how easy it is to bypass all those security systems and guards,' he said. 'If you put your mind to it, that is.'

'I wouldn't know that, Mr Voronov,' the man in the leather jacket said. 'I'm just a humble journalist and I mostly write about the political life of Great Britain.'

Seraphim, for it was he strolling down the road of his dreams, nodded.

'Well, why don't you tell me about politics in Great Britain then,' he said. 'I have varied interests, you know.'

He didn't want the journalist to get any wrong ideas…

★

Yeffim Kaltzman was growing more desperate by the day. He had run into serious financial problems and needed at least $100,000 to pay off his creditors and some outstanding bills.

His miniatures were not selling well and his girlfriend's husband was, for some unknown reason, staying away from London. Even worse, his contacts in Moscow had stopped sending him uncut diamonds. They'd passed word to him that there were problems in getting the stones out of Siberia. The local authorities had cracked down on the illegal trade and the group had had several of its people arrested. They did promise that the shipments would resume as soon as 'things cooled down'.

But Yeffim needed money now, or risk losing his standing with the people who had been buying the stones from him. The problem was that he had taken several payments up front and now had either to produce the goods or return the cash. And he had no spare cash to return.

It was when Yeffim thought all was lost that he got a phone call from none other than Seraphim Voronov. It was Seraphim's people who supplied Yeffim with uncut diamonds, but he had never met the big man himself and was really surprised to hear that he was in London and asking to see him.

At the meeting Seraphim told Yeffim that he was planning to move some serious items of jewellery from Moscow soon and asked him to get in touch with collectors to prepare the 'sale of the century'.

'We're talking very big money,' Seraphim said. 'Priceless jewellery, gems, the lot. So don't waste time on small clients – I need the top people, the biggest buyers.'

Yeffim knew that Seraphim was a serious player and that if he said that something big was coming up it meant that million-dollar deals were on the cards.

'Your job is to prepare the right buyers,' Seraphim said. 'The ones who don't ask too many questions. I'll be overseeing the whole thing myself, so don't screw up.'

Yeffim assured him that everything would be fine. He knew only too well that you didn't mess around when the Crow himself was involved.

★

After his arrest, Ivan Ossinski was desperately trying to figure out why the cops had framed him. He couldn't think of a single reason for anyone to go to such lengths to set him up.

When Ivan was brought to the police station that night he was still hoping that it was all just a big misunderstanding which would soon be resolved. He was furious at the way he had been treated and wanted to complain about being hit in the stomach by the arresting policemen. But the cops at the station did not even want to listen to his complaints. After the initial paperwork had been filled he was locked up in a cell for the night to 'cool off'.

The cop that brought him in claimed that Ivan resisted arrest and asked to include this point in the charge. That complicated matters even further.

But the worst thing was the way they treated Milla, his girl-friend. Ivan only learnt about it later, after he was released. It was just as well that he didn't know about it at the time as he could have lost control and then they would have piled more charges on him.

Milla told him that the cops insisted on conducting a full body search in order to find out whether she was carrying any drugs on her or, as one of them put it, 'some place inside'. Milla objected to their attempts to search her until a woman police officer could be summoned.

'Now where would we find a woman in a police station at night?' one of the cops said. 'You'll have to trust us.'

Milla begged the cops to leave her alone, but they pushed her into a cell and stripped her naked. They fondled her breasts and even spread her legs wide apart in order, as they explained, to look for possible drugs hidden in her vagina.

After this humiliation she was told to write a statement confirming that she knew about the drugs found in the car. Although she rejected the suggestion, and was kept in the station for several hours, she was eventually allowed to leave.

The next morning Ivan was interrogated by a criminal investigator, a short, blond man with a pointy nose and small beady eyes, who threatened him with a long prison sentence if he did not cooperate. He warned him that he risked being raped repeatedly in prison as he was such a handsome young man. At that point the detective stood up, came from behind his table and started stroking Ivan on the head.

'You're a nice-looking lad, aren't you,' he whispered. 'Go on, give us a kiss.'

Ivan was horrified. He couldn't move a muscle.

But luckily another cop knocked and walked in and the investigator quickly returned to his table. The cop approached the investigator and whispered something in his ear, before walking out. The news must have been important, as the investigator suddenly changed his approach and said that the interrogation was over.

'For the last time I'm asking you to reconsider your position and make a full confession,' he said.

Ivan firmly rejected all charges and insisted that he had been framed by the two traffic cops. He was released from the station but warned that he could not leave Moscow and to report back in three days' time. He was charged with handling hard drugs.

Later Ivan learnt that someone had visited the station and arranged his release.

But he couldn't find out who it was.

The next several days proved very difficult for Ivan. He had to behave as if nothing had happened so as not to make anyone suspicious, and yet report to the police station and live in constant fear that the cops could at any moment arrest him or report him to his college. The thought of calling his father and telling him everything did not cross his mind. He was still hoping to resolve the matter and tell him about it only once the crisis was over.

But having failed to find anyone with the right contacts, Ivan decided to turn for help to the people in a private trading company where he worked part-time as a consultant. The company, with the unusual name of Russian Style, was involved in selling steel and ferrous metals. Ivan was no big expert in metals, but the company nevertheless offered him a part-time job and even hinted that it would be willing to take him on full-time once he had graduated from college.

Ivan reckoned that the company was interested in him primarily because his father was in charge of the economic department at the Russian embassy in London and had extensive connections in the City. He heard that Russian Style was eyeing London as a place to do business in the future.

Ivan went to see the commercial director of the company, Mark Ender. He had heard that he was a man with serious connections. He told Ender about his problem and asked for help. Ender promised to speak to some friends of his in the Interior Ministry.

As soon as Ivan walked out of the door, Ender picked up the phone.

'Young Ossinski has been to see me,' he said. 'He seems to be desperate, wants me to help him with his problem.'

'Watch him closely,' the voice on the other end said. 'Make sure he doesn't run for help to the wrong people.'

Ender nodded.

'Sure thing, Shark,' he said, 'I'll keep a close eye on him.'

★

The shooting of the two Chechens outside the Oscar Wilde was reported in the late editions of the news on several TV channels.

Seraphim's name was never mentioned in any of the bulletins. Shark had a word with some people and the cops on the scene kept their mouths shut. According to the official version, 'two Chechen businessmen' were shot dead by a sniper as they were leaving the restaurant. The police said they were treating the incident as a possible gangland contract killing.

In one of the TV news programmes, a high-ranking cop gave an interview promising that the authorities would do everything to put an end to the rising tide of 'violence for hire', as he called it, and hunt down the thugs responsible for the spate of assassinations in the capital. But few people paid any attention to such promises. After each high-profile contract hit, the police promised to find the criminals but hardly ever made an arrest.

Contract killings in Russia were part of the new way of life. Not a day passed without some businessmen, bankers or criminals being killed by hired assassins in different parts of the country. Gradually the public got so used to hearing about contract murders that they were no longer surprised or shocked to learn that, once again, unknown assailants had blown somebody's brains out and left the weapons at the scene of the crime so there would be no mistake that it was a contract hit. The general feeling was that the bad guys were fighting it out with each other and there was no point in losing sleep over most of the victims.

After each new contract killing the police would launch an investigation that would soon be put on hold indefinitely. And if asked, they would claim that they didn't have enough resources to solve so many crimes.

Strange, considering that Russia had one of the largest police forces in the world and some of the strictest rules regulating residence in big cities.

★

Once inside the flat at Tverskaya Street, Alex and Clay really let their emotions rip.

As soon as the front door closed behind them, Alex pinned Motya to the wall in the hallway.

'Spill it out,' he said. 'Who set us up? And why the hell was your friend out there mixing with the scum?'

Clay was chewing energetically. He had a vicious expression on his face and was ready to kick ass. Anybody's ass.

Motya mumbled something about not knowing anything about anything. He looked stupid with his ever-present grin and that probably saved him from getting roughed up.

'Let's keep him here until the other guy and the broad show up,' Clay said, and slowly licked his lips, as if he had a nasty surprise for their Russian hosts.

Alex eased the pressure on Motya's throat. He put his hand into his pocket and took out the keys to the front door.

'Lock him up in the small bedroom,' he told Clay. 'I need to make a quick call.'

He went into the dining room and took out a laptop from a plastic holder. It had been delivered earlier with the rest of the equipment. He connected to the phone line and sent a coded message to George telling him about what had happened.

They had been instructed to avoid contacting London, as there was always a chance that somebody might intercept the message. But it was an emergency, and George had to know about the two men getting killed and the Russian suddenly showing up out of nowhere beside the Crow and the two Chechens.

It was now clear to Alex that someone had been watching them when they were on the roof of the House on the Embankment. Clay was too good a shot to screw up the job so badly and he could vouch for himself any time. So there must have been a third shooter who was waiting for them to make a move. And that, in turn, meant that the people who monitored them knew about their plan in advance and once they had opened fire the third sniper finished off the two Chechens. The question was – who the hell wanted them killed and why did they go to such lengths to stage the whole thing so that the blame would rest with the London team?

Alex felt like shit. The operation had gone badly wrong from the very start. Two people had been killed and someone was breathing down their necks. And to think that George had told them to keep their heads down in Moscow.

He desperately needed a drink. He searched the dining room and the kitchen but all he found was some Russian bottled beer that tasted like piss. He could have in theory asked Motya whether there was anything stronger than beer in the flat, but after their confrontation he didn't want to be seen as getting friendly again. There were still too many questions left unanswered.

Alex decided to venture out and have a drink. He knew that in Moscow there was no problem finding booze at any time of day or night.

He went to check whether Clay wanted to join him but found the American fast asleep. Clay, it seemed, was keeping his faith in George and leaving all the worrying to others. It was amazing that he could switch off so easily after all the excitement of the evening. Alex walked into the room to switch off the bedside light. It was then that he noticed a small plastic container with white pills. So that's why he sleeps like a baby, he thought, walking out of the room. He put on his sheepskin coat and fur hat and went out.

Although it was not very late there were very few people on the street. It was snowing and the wind was picking up again. Several hookers were standing close to the building, shivering in the freezing cold. One of them started to move towards Alex but he walked quickly up the street in order to avoid her, only to bump into more desperate women offering their services.

Prostitution in Moscow was booming, as thousands of women flocked to the Russian capital from the provinces and from the former republics of the Soviet Union, mostly Ukraine and Belarus. The Moscow authorities did not even bother to pretend that they were dealing with the problem. The police were openly providing back-up and protection to the pimps and their flocks at the so-called 'points', *tochki*, which were scattered all around the city and where customers could pick up a hooker of any age and size during the night. There was talk of senior members of the Moscow government receiving large payments for closing their eyes to the illegal sex trade.

Alex reached a square with a large statue in its centre – a Russian knight on a horse with his hand stretched out, as if inviting someone behind him to appreciate the scenery. It was Prince Yuri Dolgoruki, the founder of Moscow. Across the street from the monument was the mayor's office, a grand red and white building. It was lit by powerful floodlights placed around the square and on the roofs of the surrounding buildings.

Alex turned from Tverskaya Street on to the square and saw a big neon sign above him that simply read 'Restaurant'. He suddenly realised that apart from a cup of coffee with some biscuits he had not eaten anything substantial since getting off the plane and thought it might be a good idea to have some food. He walked up to the entrance and pushed the glass door. It was locked. He could see the doorman, a grey-haired old man, dozing on a chair a couple of yards from the entrance. He knocked on the glass with a coin. The old man opened his eyes and gave him that 'what the hell do you want?' kind of look. He took his time to get up and walk to the door.

'We're closed!' he shouted through the glass. The loud sound of a live band coming somewhere from within the joint strongly contradicted the statement. Alex took out his wallet and flashed some dollar bills at the doorman. That was enough to persuade him to change his mind. Smiling broadly, he opened the door wide and even bowed slightly, welcoming the customer he had just tried to send away. Alex walked into the restaurant. The smell of grilled meat and marinated vegetables hit his nostrils. Loud bursts of laughter were coming from downstairs, amid sounds of live music. It was an oriental restaurant, famous for partying till the early morning hours. Alex slipped a five-dollar bill into the doorman's hand and said in Russian, 'Lead the way, old man. I need a good drink.'

The doorman took his sheepskin coat and fur hat and, with a wave of his hand, invited him to walk down the stairs. A short fat waiter in a worn-out black waistcoat on top of a soiled white shirt and black trousers was standing at the bottom of the stairs smiling at him. Judging by the look in his eyes, he had already had quite a few drinks during his shift.

The restaurant turned out to be half empty but the noise created by the live band and by customers – most of whom were drunk – was deafening. Alex was shown to a table in the corner by the fat waiter who was trying hard to walk straight. The soiled white cloth on the table was covered with breadcrumbs and bits of food. But instead of changing it the waiter simply wiped the cloth with his hand and then produced two large white napkins which he used to cover the surface of the table.

Alex sat down and ordered kebabs, a salad and a bottle of vodka. He was set on getting a good drink to calm his nerves. He wasn't worried about losing control. He could drink as much as he wanted and still be able to find his way back. He called it 'using the auto-pilot mode'.

Several minutes after Alex walked into the restaurant two men came up to the door and knocked on it. The doorman appeared on the other side shaking his head to signal that they couldn't come in. One of the men produced a dark-red leather ID and slapped it on the glass.

The doorman took a quick glance at it and immediately opened up.

★

Alex poured himself half a glass of vodka and drank it straight down. He felt the warmth spreading in his stomach. The stuff they were serving was very strong, he thought. Maybe even too strong.

He looked around him and noticed a large painting depicting Joseph Stalin standing on a mountain top in his military uniform, looking down at the vast valley below. Beneath him were workers and peasants, all smiling and looking adoringly at the great leader. It was really weird to see that relic of communism in a joint like this.

Alex poured himself some more vodka and drank it. He had nearly finished the bottle before the kebabs and the salad arrived and he was getting drunk fast. It seemed strange, as he usually needed much more booze than this to feel any effect.

Then the room started to swirl around him. The voices and the music turned into one irritating noise. He felt dizzy. The bastards must have spiked my drink! he thought, trying to overcome his dizziness.

He suddenly remembered some of the stories he had heard about waiters in Moscow restaurants mixing drinks with drugs in order to get the visitors stoned. Then their buddies would step in, take the victims outside, relieve them of all their money and possessions, and dump them in some alley.

Through the haze he saw a man come up to him.

'Do you need any help?' the man asked him in Russian.

'No, no, I'm fine,' Alex insisted, shaking his head.

He was trying hard to regain his senses. He realised that it had been a crazy idea to go off on his own and get drunk in some dodgy place in Moscow. It was drink that had got him kicked out of the army and it was drink that now got him into another fine mess. The face of his sergeant appeared before him. 'You're a good soldier, Hunter, but you'll end up in the shit one day because of your boozing!' he was saying. 'You'll get fucked up and there'll be no one to blame but yourself!'

He hadn't listened to his sergeant. But then again he had never blamed anyone else for his problems.

The next thing he felt was a burst of cold air in his face. Two men had taken him outside. Alex tried to resist and one of them hit him in the stomach so that he immediately threw up. They were going through his pockets, taking out his wallet, the keys, ripping off his watch. Then there was shouting around him and he fell down on the snow. He didn't see what was happening but he could guess that there was a fight going on. He was lifted from the ground and carried somewhere. It got warmer. He was put on a hard surface.

That was the last thing he could remember. When he woke up later he found himself lying in total darkness. He got up and, with hands stretched out, gradually found his way to the door.

When he opened the door a dim light went on. He looked around. It was an entrance lobby very similar to the one in the building on Tverskaya Street. His sheepskin coat and fur hat were lying on the floor.

Someone had carried him from the street so that he wouldn't freeze to death. Someone had saved him from the thugs.

He picked up his sheepskin coat. His wallet fell out of it. He looked inside. All the money was intact. And the keys to the flat were still in the pocket of his jacket. His watch was still on his wrist.

Things were getting more and more mysterious…

★

In the morning Lidia showed up at the flat. Clay blew his top the moment he saw her.

'What the hell's happenin'?' he yelled. 'What's yar game, lady? And where the hell's yar boyfriend?'

Alex came out of the dining room where he had slept on the sofa. He felt really bad after the adventure of the previous night. But in all the excitement no one was paying any attention to his appearance.

Clay was standing in front of Lidia, looking stupid in a track-suit and slippers. Lidia slowly opened her small black leather handbag and took out a pack of cigarettes. She spent some time taking the wrapping off the pack and getting out a cigarette. Then she reached into the bag once again, took out a gold lighter and lit up. Throughout the whole procedure she was looking at Clay. It was clear that she wanted to annoy him as much as possible. It worked. Clay was chewing very fast.

'Pavel had to infiltrate the gang at the first opportunity,' Lidia said, blowing a puff of smoke directly into Clay's face. 'He probably didn't want you to worry, knowing that he could be close to the people you were supposed to… bump off.'

That did not go down well with the guests.

'Who said anything about bumping off anyone?' Alex said. 'There was no talk about killing anyone.'

Lidia shrugged her shoulders.

'Only Pavel knows about the operation,' she said. 'I haven't been told any details. So I can't help you.'

Clay came up close to Lidia.

'Look, lady,' he said, 'until yar boyfriend shows up ya're staying with us. Get my drift?'

Lidia smiled.

'So, you're going to hold me hostage?'

Clay was struggling to find the right words. Alex came to his rescue.

'You're not a hostage,' he said, 'but we need answers and we need them fast. It's strictly business, you understand.'

Lidia said nothing. There was banging coming from the small bedroom. Motya had obviously been listening to the conversation.

'Can I use the toilet?' he pleaded. 'Otherwise, I'll have to water the flowers!'

Alex signalled to Clay to let Motya out.

'I hope your friend comes back soon,' he said, turning to Lidia.

'He'll be back,' she said.

★

It was late evening. A Jaguar drove slowly down a road in North London. It stopped beneath a street light.

'I'll be here for two hours,' Jeremy told his chauffeur. 'Don't bother to let me out.'

He opened the door and got out. The chauffeur waited until he had entered the house. Once the door closed behind him the Jaguar disappeared into the darkness.

When Jeremy walked through the door of a small room on the left of the hallway he was greeted by an old Chinese man in a wheelchair. Jeremy came up to the man and kissed him on both cheeks.

'Thank you for agreeing to see me at such short notice,' he said.

'You know it's always a pleasure to see you,' the old man replied in a low voice.

Jeremy sat down on a small couch opposite the old man.

'What's on your mind, Jeremy?' the old man said. 'You seem troubled by something.'

Jeremy did not reply for a moment.

'I'm in doubt,' he said at last. 'Once again I am trying to help people who are in trouble. And once again I have a feeling that my actions may backfire on the very people I'm trying to help.'

The old man sat with his eyes closed. It was as though he was locked in his own thoughts, but Jeremy knew that he had heard his every word.

'You're the only one I can talk to about my doubts,' he continued. 'People around me wouldn't understand if I were to tell them that I'm confused. I'm seen as being above doubt. Money is supposed to make me different from others. They would never believe me – even consider me quite mad – if I confessed that I have my own doubts and fears.'

The old man opened his eyes and looked at Jeremy.

'You have to be honest with people and they'll understand,' he said. 'Once you start being insincere they will feel doubts creeping into their hearts.'

Jeremy felt, rather than comprehended, the meaning of the words.

'The answers will come to you,' the old man said. 'Like they did in the past. Remember what I told you about the visions that you were getting? When you thought you could look into the future?'

Jeremy nodded.

'It was a strange feeling,' he said. 'I could actually see the future and the past, as if I were watching a film.'

'You only thought that you could see the future,' the old man said. 'Remember what I told you last time? If you're confused about something and you're not sure where it comes from take a moment and say to yourself, "If what I am experiencing is caused by evil, then I reject it. But if it's good in its essence then let it continue." And as I recall, after you thought about it the visions disappeared.'

Jeremy nodded again. It was a time when he was taking some powerful sleeping pills and drinking quite heavily. This combination seemed to turn his brain into a fast computer supposedly capable of solving problems in a split second. He called it the Sherlock Holmes phenomenon. He sometimes seemed to anticipate what other people would say before they even started talking. At some point he felt he was going mad. He had to find a lot of strength to fight off the visions he was having.

'You were right about that,' Jeremy said. 'And I also remember what you said about the Balance…'

Jeremy was looking at the old man. He had met him several years ago at a charity event. There was something about his face that impressed Jeremy the first time he saw him. They had only had a brief conversation on that day, but afterwards Jeremy visited the old man on many occasions.

They were from completely different backgrounds, but somehow Jeremy felt drawn to him. And later the old man saved his life.

It happened shortly before Christmas. Jeremy was working late and suddenly felt dizzy. He lay down on the couch in his study but the dizziness did not go away. Then his left hand started to get numb and he felt a heaviness build up in his chest around the heart. A burning sensation developed at the back of his head and neck and his feet turned ice-cold.

All were classical symptoms of a heart attack. Jeremy managed to summon his butler and asked him to call an ambulance. He was taken to one of the best private clinics in London where he was put into the emergency cardiology unit.

The blood tests and the ECG showed nothing. The doctors were puzzled and kept him in the emergency unit overnight. But in the morning they still could not say what was wrong with him. Jeremy decided to discharge himself even though he was still very weak and the pain in his chest would not go away.

His chauffeur picked him up from the clinic and took him to his flat in Mount Street. For the first time in his life Jeremy didn't know what to do and whom to turn to. He had always thought that he was not afraid of death, but with each attack of chest pains he became more and more terrified at the thought that this was the end. He was desperately clinging to life; his body was not prepared to give up without a fight.

It was then that the old man phoned him, as if sensing that something was wrong. On hearing that Jeremy was not feeling well he said that he was coming over. Jeremy was too weak to argue and was half-conscious when he finally arrived.

The old man unbuttoned his shirt and started massaging his chest. It was very painful. Jeremy could hardly stand the pain and lost consciousness several times. He then fell asleep. When he woke up he still felt weak, but the pain in his chest had gone.

Within weeks Jeremy had made a full recovery. He returned to work as if nothing had happened. Following this incident the two men grew even closer, and Jeremy stopped visiting his doctor.

'...I always remember about the Balance,' Jeremy said. 'Once you tip life's balance it will restore itself again. You betray someone and soon someone will betray you. Dostoevsky's *Crime and Punishment* sums it up just about right. Punishment starts the moment an evil deed is planned. It makes perfect sense to me. But you also told me that it's dangerous to play God. And yet I see that people want me to be God. They wouldn't believe me if I told them that I make mistakes just like everyone else. And this time I've raised the stakes too high. I've sent men to a faraway land, a hostile land...'

The old man was silent. But Jeremy was feeling some kind of energy reaching him. It was as if the old man was sending him signals. Suddenly his thoughts began to drift in an unexplained pattern. A vision was emerging. It was as if a giant book had opened in front of him and he could read from it.

'Some nations have been living under tyranny for so long that it takes generations for the people to kill the slave inside their souls. Under tyranny most people are equal when it comes to hardships and suffering. When there is no hope of achieving any goal, any ambition, any dream, life is replaced by existence. But once tyranny collapses, a nation finds itself divided. Uncertainty looms, envy spreads. And sometimes it takes an outsider to show the way, to make a difference.'

Jeremy was getting the message. He was the outsider. So he must have been on the right track after all.

'But there are many dangers on the way,' the book was warning him. 'Beware of things that are not what they seem. Beware of people that pretend to be someone else. Beware of hasty decisions...'

Jeremy opened his eyes. The old man was looking at him.

'You must be flexible,' he said to Jeremy, 'because even God is flexible.'

When Jeremy got back home there was a message from George on his computer.

'Russian contact disappeared,' it read. 'Two targets killed.'

Jeremy picked up the phone.

'Find George Blunt and ask him to come to Mount Street,' he said.

★

Pavel was kept overnight in the flat where he had been brought after the shooting of the two Chechens. Three thugs were keeping an eye on him.

Seraphim was too busy to see him. He spent all night and early morning at his headquarters in the heart of Moscow discussing with his 'politburo' ways of preventing an all-out war with the Chechens.

The two arms dealers had been killed at the worst possible moment. Relations were already strained, and now the Chechens were bound to suspect that their people were lured to their deaths in response to the killing of the two hoods at the grocery market and the attack on the company office.

Seraphim was desperately hoping that he could avoid a full-scale war with the Chechens. He also reckoned that the Moscow-based Chechens would not want to be seen as being involved directly in illegal arms sales to the rebels in Chechnya. If word got around that they were helping their brothers in the south, who were killing young Russian soldiers, the authorities in Moscow might just be tempted to close their eyes to other gangs moving in on their turf. The boys from several, mainly Russian, criminal groups were itching to get their hands on some of the operations controlled by the Chechens. They would only need a wink and a nod from the cops to start shooting and bombing.

But there was another thing that really worried Seraphim: who were those mysterious snipers who shot at him and killed the two Chechens? Someone was out to get him and yet he had absolutely no idea who it might be.

★

Pavel was trying to figure out his next move. He had two options – either to make a break and find Seraphim or to sit tight and wait. He was certain that Seraphim's people would check his record and talk to one or two of their contacts in the police to try to establish any link to the incident outside the Oscar Wilde. In that respect he had nothing to worry about – no one could possibly learn about his connection to the shootings. Not for the moment at least.

So the big question was – should he attempt to escape or sit and wait for the Crow? Eventually he decided that he could not waste any time. The operation was moving nowhere while he was held captive.

His chance came early in the morning when his three guards decided to have breakfast. One of them went to the kitchen to prepare the food. The smell coming into the room was horrendous: the idiot was using lard instead of oil to fry the bacon and eggs.

Once breakfast was ready, the 'cook' shouted out to his pals to come and join him. One of the two men in the room immediately got up and went to the kitchen. That was when Pavel decided to make his move. He had noticed when he was brought to the flat the previous evening that the front door had no special locks or bolts on it. So it was a matter of dealing with the one remaining guard and making it to the door and down the stairs. The hope was that the two men in the kitchen would not be able to react quickly enough.

Pavel was pretending to be dozing off on a couch where he had spent an uncomfortable night with his hands tied behind his back. He'd managed to loosen the rope during the night. The guard in the room was not watching him, but looking in the direction of the kitchen. The sound of the clinking beer bottles was attracting his attention.

'I need to go to the toilet,' Pavel said, suddenly rising from the sofa. The rope slipped from his hands to the floor.

'Sit the fuck down!' the hood shouted as he got up from his chair.

Pavel moved swiftly and hit him in the face. He fell back, his head hitting the wall. Pavel ran out of the room and opened the front door. He could hear shouting behind him.

His first reaction was to run out of the flat and head down the stairs. But in a split second he decided to step into the bathroom that was right beside the front door in the hallway.

The two men ran past. Pavel stepped into the hallway and slammed the front door shut. He rushed back into the room where the thug he had hit a few moments ago was getting up from the floor.

There was no time to waste. Pavel ran up to him and hit him in the jaw with all his strength, sending the man crashing down on the floor. He kneeled down and took out a gun from the holster on his trouser belt. He could hear the other two men trying to break down the front door. The obvious choice was to shoot them, but that would have made it much more difficult to convince Seraphim that he was on his side. And Shark would never forgive him for wasting his men.

So there was only one thing left to do. Pavel ran to the front door and, just as the two men were making their final push, opened it, sending them both flying into the hallway and down on the floor. As they were about to get to their feet he pointed the gun at them.

'Freeze!' he yelled. 'One of you moves and you're both dead!'

The two men froze. But Pavel wasn't planning to give them a lecture on the advantages of turning their backs on the life of crime. He hit one of them on the head with the gun and, as the other one tried to snatch the weapon from his hand, he kicked him in the groin.

That was enough to keep them both quiet for a while, so he ran out of the flat and down the stairs to the lobby.

He had to find Seraphim. Fast.

★

Dmitri Sibirski woke up and immediately felt such sharp pain in the left side of his head that he groaned loudly and lay motionless for several minutes, hoping that the headache would go away. When it didn't, he raised his head and looked around him, trying to figure out where he was. The thick curtains were drawn and the room was dark.

Where the hell am I? Dmitri thought. And then slowly it came back to him. He was in London, in his room at the Savoy, the morning after the premiere of the new production of *Eugene Onegin* in Covent Garden. Dmitri sang the part of Onegin and was exhausted after the performance. He generally found performing in operas exhausting, unlike recitals. It was not the singing itself that wore him out, it was the acting. Dmitri was a great singer, but his acting skills left much to be desired and that put a lot of pressure on him on stage and off it.

At the dinner party at the hotel restaurant after the premiere he had drunk two bottles of French red wine, which would have been okay had it not been for the champagne...

Blasted fizz! he thought. How many times have I told myself not to do that! But then every time some idiot comes up with the bright idea of toasting the women with champagne, and I can't bloody resist the temptation. He remembered the loud-mouthed camp-looking music critic who was at their table yesterday. Nobody had invited him, but he somehow managed to squeeze between two guests and stayed till the very end. He even managed to attract the attention of some people at the table with his silly stories about the Three Tenors. Dmitri resented anyone who tried to compete with him for the adoration of others, be it intentionally or unintentionally.

He swore loudly and got out of bed. The air conditioning was on and he shivered from the cold. He picked the robe from the floor and put it on, still trembling. When he switched on the bedside lamp he saw a note on the pillow. He picked it up and opened it. It smelt of perfume. 'Adore you, adore you, adore you. Will call in the evening,' it said.

Who on earth...? he wondered for a moment. And then he remembered. It was that Swedish woman, the one who was at the party yesterday. She was very beautiful and he couldn't resist the temptation.

During dinner Dmitri was looking at her suggestively and, at some point, when everybody got up and started mingling with each other, he managed to slip her the key to his hotel room without anyone noticing. She got the message straight away. She was obviously a wealthy groupie and knew the drill well. Dmitri was always fascinated by those rich married women who followed famous opera singers and musicians around the world, waiting for their chance to add them to their list of trophies. Some of them actually believed that going to bed with famous men somehow rubbed off on them, making them appear sophisticated and even mysterious. In essence, though, they were no different from the groupies that followed footballers or pop stars around.

About half an hour later she made up some excuse and left the party. Dmitri waited for about ten minutes and then simply stood up, bid everyone goodnight and walked out of the restaurant. The door was slightly open when he came up to his room. The woman was already undressed and lying on the bed. He quickly took off his clothes and got in beside her.

They made love, but only once. The drink took its toll...

The phone rang. Dmitri's first reaction was not to answer. But the phone kept on ringing and, thinking that it might be the Swedish woman, he picked up the receiver.

'Dima, good morning,' a man's voice said, 'how are you feeling?'

It was his agent, Francis Morley. He had been at the party and was the one who kept the guests entertained after Dmitri left.

Francis was more than just an agent, he was his friend, his confidant and fixer. He had all the right contacts in the world of opera and had helped Dmitri become a star after spotting him at an international competition for young singers. Dmitri had everything: the looks, the voice, the talent.

Francis was very surprised to learn that he had been rejected by the Bolshoi Theatre on the grounds that he did not have 'classical vocal training'. He signed a deal with him and arranged several recitals in the West.

Dmitri was an instant success, especially in the US. Americans are suckers for talented people with good looks. They went wild about a young Russian singer from Siberia who looked like a movie star with a voice to match. Invitations from different opera houses in the United States and other countries started to flood in and in several years Dmitri became a star. Francis didn't have to help him get bookings any more, although he did arrange the occasional private recital for people who were prepared to pay a lot of money. And as an agent he got ten per cent of everything.

'I feel awful, Fran,' Dmitri said into the phone. 'I really have to stop inviting all those people to parties after premiers. I'm sick of them all.'

'I understand, Dima,' Francis said. 'You know very well that you make me very sad when you drink too much. But I'm not calling to nag you about yesterday. I'd like to have a word with you later, when you have had a shower and got yourself sorted out.'

Dmitri grimaced.

'What's it about?' he said. 'I hope I don't need to meet any of the critics today. I don't feel like talking to any of them.'

'No, no, it has nothing to do with the critics,' Francis said. 'I'll see you downstairs in an hour.'

When they met downstairs in the hotel lobby Francis told Dmitri about an unusual request from a 'very influential agency', as he put it, to sing at one of the private residences on the outskirts of Moscow. And before Dmitri could utter a single word, Francis said, 'They're offering $200,000 for an hour's work.'

Dmitri looked at him in amazement.

★

Pavel got back to the flat at Tverskaya Street in the evening.

'Well, if it ain't our li'l ol' Russian friend!' Clay greeted him with all the sarcasm he could muster. 'And I bet ya've gotta great story to tell!'

Alex said nothing. After his unfortunate experience in the restaurant he was still keeping a low profile. Lidia and Motya were obviously greatly relieved to see Pavel.

'I'll explain everything later,' Pavel said. 'But now we have to prepare for another job. Seraphim is throwing a big party in three days' time and unfortunately none of you are invited. So we need to do some reconnaissance and prepare to gatecrash the occasion.'

Both Alex and Clay stayed silent, looking at him closely.

'I really like the way you skip the formalities,' Alex said finally. 'You don't tell us a bloody thing and then pop up in our rifle sights out of nowhere. Then you disappear for a while and walk in as if nothing's happened. Don't you think you owe us an explanation?'

The tension in the room was building up by the second.

'I had no choice,' Pavel said. 'I was instructed by London to infiltrate the gang at the first opportunity. And the only opportunity I had was when you shot and killed the two Chechens...'

Clay was waiting for that. He lashed forward and hit Pavel on the face, sending him crashing down to the floor. Lidia screamed and rushed along with Motya to help Pavel get up. Alex decided not to interfere in what was turning into a 'domestic dispute'. Clay was watching Pavel, ready to have another go at him if the Russian decided to make any more stupid comments. There was blood oozing from Pavel's lip as he got up from the floor. He was feeling his jaw, trying to establish whether it was broken.

'We killed no one!' Clay screamed. 'We were told to frighten the shit out of the two scumbags and that's exactly what we did. We didn't shoot to kill!'

Pavel was still holding onto his jaw. It was obvious that he was doing his best to control himself.

'So it wasn't you who killed the arms dealers?' he said, scepticism sounding in his voice loud and clear. 'So what happened then?'

'There must have been a third shooter or even several of them in the area at the time,' Alex said. 'He or they opened fire at the same time as we did. The big question is: who the hell could have known that we were on that roof getting ready to start shooting?'

Pavel shook his head. He obviously didn't buy Alex's version of events, especially as it implied that he was to blame for the whole thing, having failed to keep the operation secret.

'It doesn't make any sense,' he said. 'Nobody could have known about you being there. No one. That means that one of you must have screwed up and killed the Chechens.'

That was enough to make Clay hysterical once again.

'One more word out of ya and ya're dead!' he yelled. He was positioning himself to have another go at Pavel.

Alex looked at Clay and for the first time it struck him that his partner was prone to sudden mood swings. One moment he would be calm and placid, and the next he'd lose his temper and get all wound up. It must be those pills, Alex thought. What a team we've got here: two reformed alcoholics, a guy hooked on pills, a crazed midget and an illegal currency dealer. What next? An underworld contract killer or a KGB operative?

Lidia came up to Clay. She looked him straight in the eyes.

'You'd better keep your hands to yourself,' she said, 'or you won't be going back…'

Clay didn't want to hear the rest of the message. He slapped her on the face and Lidia nearly fell over.

Pavel moved fast. With one punch he sent Clay flying. Anticipating a full-blown confrontation, Motya made a quiet exit to the kitchen. Lidia was holding her hand to her face. Her lips were trembling and a single tear was running down her cheek. The situation was turning nasty. Alex had to intervene. He stepped between Pavel and Clay who was getting up with a clear intention to resume the hostilities.

'That's enough!' he yelled. 'Cut it out, both of you!'

He turned to Pavel and signalled to him to move away. He then glanced at Lidia who was rubbing her face and shook his head slightly, indicating to her that he didn't approve of what had just happened.

Clay couldn't see all of the facial signals while he was getting up on his feet. Like a judge in a boxing ring Alex spread his arms wide, keeping both sides apart.

'I'd like to make one thing clear,' he said. 'I really don't think it's a good idea to kill each other right now. Maybe later, maybe in a couple of weeks' time, but not now. I still want to get my money.'

He turned around to face Clay. The American was breathing heavily. His eyes had a strange glare in them.

Maybe he really did bump off the Chechens, Alex thought. He was hoping that the chewing would resume. He did not want another clash.

And then the jaws started to move. Clay was coming back to his senses. Alex turned back to face Pavel who was standing beside Lidia holding a handkerchief to his lip.

'Talk to us,' he said. 'We'd love to know what happened yesterday.'

Pavel frowned.

'I did not tell you about my plan in advance simply because I didn't want to put any more pressure on either of you,' he said. 'Believe me, I didn't have much choice. I had to get inside the gang real fast. The best opportunity for me was to hang around when the shooting started and hope that I could use the situation to my advantage. The Crow couldn't suspect me of being involved in the operation. But things didn't work out as I thought they would. I suggest we go now and I'll tell you the rest in the car.'

Alex looked at Clay. The chewing was in full progress.

'Give us a couple of minutes to freshen up,' he said to Pavel. 'Clay here needs some lipstick and I have to put on my face cream.'

No one responded to the joke, but the tension was definitely disappearing.

Clay followed Alex into the room. When the door closed behind them Alex said in a loud whisper, 'What the hell do you think you're doing? What's wrong with you, mate?'

Clay looked confused.

'I thought ya'd be behind me all the way,' he said. 'I thought we're a team.'

Alex wanted to say something but then thought better of it. He wanted to make a point about hitting women. He had witnessed a lot of that when his father would come home drunk and beat up his mother in front of his younger brother and him. He was always terrified when it happened and his brother would always cry. He would take him upstairs to their room and keep him away from their father. And in the morning their mother would come to their bedroom with bruises on her face and act as if nothing had happened.

Alex took a deep breath. What had just happened out there in the hallway was bound to happen at some point, he reckoned. There had been tension in the air from the moment they met their Russian partners and the situation had to explode at some point. It was better to let the steam out on their own turf, rather than somewhere else. And in any case, the Russians had some explaining to do. There was no way they were getting away with some bullshit like saying that they were worried about them...

Alex decided to make up with Clay.

'We were just pretending out there,' he whispered to him. 'Let 'em think that we're arguing.'

The American smiled and nodded repeatedly to show that he got the message and was ready to play along.

★

Soon they were on their way to the Odintsovo district, an exclusive area outside the Russian capital where Seraphim had a villa.

Motya was at the wheel. He was still a bit shaken after the rough treatment he had received from the guests. This time he was in no joking mood and was watching the road without uttering a word. But the stupid grin on his face would not go away.

Pavel was telling them about his ordeal. He described his escape from the flat and how he managed to track down Seraphim at one of the casinos in the centre of Moscow where he usually played roulette during the day. Despite the possibility of a war with the Chechens he still found time to gamble. His bodyguards, touchy after the incident outside the Oscar Wilde, nearly shot Pavel as he tried to get past them.

Seraphim was surprised to see him. In all the excitement of the previous night he had completely forgotten about the man who saved his life.

'I thought you're spending time with my boys,' he said. 'You know, cards, wine, hookers.'

Pavel shook his head.

'They got bored with me and kicked me out,' he said.

Seraphim put several piles of hundred-rouble chips on the numbers of the first dozen, his usual 'lucky numbers', and looked him in the eyes for several seconds.

Then he suddenly burst into laughter.

'You killed them, didn't you?' he said.

Pavel shook his head.

'I never kill people who haven't been introduced to me properly,' he said. 'Came with my last job.'

Seraphim gestured at a chair beside him at the table while watching the white ball spinning round the roulette wheel.

'So what brings you here, cop?' he asked once the ball stopped in one of the sockets bearing his lucky number.

At that moment everything depended on whether Pavel could convince him that he was of use to the gang.

'I have something important to tell you,' he said. 'I need ten minutes of your time. Alone.'

Seraphim was obviously reluctant to stop playing, especially as he had just won a lot of money. But after a brief hesitation he got up and signalled to Pavel to follow him. They went to a small room with two card tables.

Seraphim lit up a cigarette and looked at Pavel, expecting him to start talking. Pavel told him that he had been trying to establish contact with the Central Brotherhood for some time and that it was pure coincidence that they had met under such dramatic circumstances. He confessed that he was totally broke and needed money desperately. He said he had information that he thought would interest the Crow.

Pavel deliberately did not specify what kind of information he possessed. He kept on repeating that he needed money and that he had no job and that he could be very useful to the Crow.

'Cut the crap!' Seraphim said. 'What the hell are you talking about?'

Pavel made a split second pause.

'I can find out who the traitor in your group is,' he said.

Seraphim showed no emotion. He stayed silent for a while.

'How do you know about it?' he asked finally.

'I've heard things,' Pavel said. 'I don't have a name yet, but I know how to get it. I need time and some back-up.'

Seraphim was studying Pavel closely. What did he have to lose by paying the cop to find the prick who was betraying him? he thought. He could always dispose of him if he was bluffing. And besides, the cop might be useful to him in the future.

'You get me the name of that scumbag,' Seraphim said. 'But if you're trying to set me up, you'll die.'

'I'll find out who it is,' Pavel said, feeling a sense of relief. His plan was working. The Crow had agreed to take him on.

★

It was a cold evening in Moscow, but at least it had stopped snowing for a while. They were driving down the Kutuzov Avenue at high speed. All the cars around them were doing at least a hundred kilometres an hour, moving in a tightly knit formation. It was frightening to think what could happen if anything were to go wrong in this fast-moving stream of cars.

Driving habits in Moscow have always horrified foreigners. Most drivers have a tendency not to let other cars overtake them. Changing lanes is a daunting task, as few cars will let others in. And getting from side roads on to the main routes is a nightmare, as the majority of drivers are not inclined to let anyone get in front of them.

There is no such thing in Moscow as keeping a safe distance from the car in front. Bumper-to-bumper traffic could be moving at any pace, ranging from crawling to breaking the speed limit. Alex felt very uncomfortable seeing how close their Lada was to the truck in front. Not to mention the car behind them that seemed glued to their rear bumper. But Motya seemed to be completely unaware of the dangers of such crazy driving.

They turned from the Kutuzov Avenue passing through the Krylatskoe district, one of the most prestigious residential areas in Moscow. Even the President of Russia had a flat there. Not that he used it very often, preferring to stay at his country retreat. After crossing the Big Moscow Circular they got on the Roublevskoe motorway and after driving for about ten minutes stopped at a roadside supermarket.

'From here we walk,' Pavel explained. 'We don't want to attract any attention by parking too close to the villa.'

Motya stayed in the car. Using small torches, they walked down a path in the snow that ran through the thick pine forest. Pavel was telling Alex and Clay about the plan.

'I'll get you inside the compound in the boot of my car,' Pavel was saying. 'It's big enough to squeeze two people in. But afterwards, guys, you'll be on your own. So you'd better memorise the route.'

Once inside the compound Alex and Clay were supposed to

get into the house unnoticed, reach Seraphim's study on the first floor, photograph the documents that were kept in his personal safe and then leave the same way they got in – unnoticed. Pavel promised to provide them with a plan of the ground floor of the house and the route to the study on the first floor. He also said that he would create a distraction to allow them to escape once the job was done.

The concrete wall that surrounded Seraphim's villa was at least ten feet high, with electrified barbed wire running along the top.

'So when is it you say we're going in?' Alex asked, eyeing the fence.

'The party will take place in three days' time,' Pavel said. 'I've heard that security won't be as tight on that evening.'

Alex nodded, taking that information on board.

'I think we'd better have a quick look around,' he said.

He gave a sign to Clay, who came up to the fence and locked his hands together. Alex put his right foot on the 'step' and Clay lifted him up.

Several cars were parked on the driveway near the house. Two guards holding machine guns were standing near the main entrance. Three armed men were standing beside the entrance gates. Another two armed guards were moving along the fence. Alex jumped back to the ground.

'It's like a bloody Colombian hideout,' he said. 'This Crow sure treats his safety seriously. I'll say this to you: if security isn't relaxed on the night we'll never get out of there alive.'

★

Pavel wasn't lying to Seraphim when he told him at the casino about the traitor in his gang.

From his contacts in the police he learnt that one of the people in the Central Brotherhood had turned informer in exchange for money and full immunity from prosecution. But he couldn't find out who it was specifically. It was the first time ever that Russian police had launched an undercover operation using an informer inside a major gang, and very few people knew the details.

The man in question, one Alexander Bendik, despised Seraphim for the fact that he'd 'never been to see the Master', meaning that he had never served time. He also felt sidelined by the Crow and had been plotting behind his back for quite some time.

The cops approached Bendik's mother and through her passed him a message that they wanted to talk to him. It was a long shot, but to their surprise Bendik responded and at a meeting outside Moscow he agreed to become an informer. He tipped off the police on a number of occasions and several people from the gang were arrested. He also supplied the cops with a couple of names of government officials who were on the gang's payroll. They were arrested too and Bendik got several thousand dollars for each of the men he turned in.

Soon Seraphim began to suspect that something was not right and ordered Shark to investigate. He also tried to use his own contacts in the police to find out who was talking to the law behind his back, but the whole operation was kept under wraps and his people in the Interior Ministry had no knowledge of it.

Seraphim was getting desperate as more and more of his people were going down. That was why when Pavel offered to find the traitor, he agreed to take him on his payroll without much hesitation.

'You'll report to me personally,' he told Pavel at the end of their meeting at the casino. 'From now on you're my security advisor. And if anybody asks you, you tell them that I took you on in gratitude for saving my life. Shark will provide you with a car and five grand for initial expenses.'

Pavel's meteoric rise was met with suspicion in the gang. When Shark learned about the new appointment, he was livid. He didn't trust the cop and decided to nail him at the first opportunity. Most members of the 'politburo' could not understand why the Crow was involving the cop in his affairs. Some even suspected that Pavel might have been chosen as a personal advisor because Seraphim was planning to replace Shark.

Bendik, a member of Seraphim's so-called 'politburo', was terrified at the thought that the cop might find out about his links with the police. He ordered a couple of his men to keep an eye on the cop and to report to him what he was up to.

Pavel knew that after his 'appointment' there would be people in the gang – first and foremost Shark and his men – who'd be watching him closely. He had no idea who the informer was, but could guess that he would be worried. He had to be extra careful in his contacts with the guests from London. But he also had to continue working closely with the team.

The whole idea, worked out by George Blunt, was for Alex and Clay to operate in the background and thus make it extremely difficult for anyone in the gang to pinpoint the enemy. The plan was to have somebody on the inside, backed by a team on the outside with no visible connection to the authorities or the underworld. George accepted there was always a danger that the team might make a mistake and blow its cover. But the odds were still much better with foreigners operating in Moscow.

★

Anyone interested in seeing post-communist wealth in all its glory would be advised to visit the Odintsovo district on the outskirts of Moscow. When driving down the Roublevskoe motorway that passes through the area it is practically impossible to see Russian-made cars on the roads. Most are foreign makes.

The private houses behind the stone walls that can be seen from the motorway look more like castles. The average price tag on properties in the area is a million dollars and rising.

This is the land of the new Russian rich. Top government officials, big businessmen and godfathers of the underworld live side by side in the Odintsovo district. It is an extraordinary mix of wealth – both criminal and legitimate – if such a thing as 'legitimate wealth' exists in capitalist Russia.

The large villa in the Barvikha area that Seraphim owned had been used in the past to accommodate the visiting foreign guests of the Communist Party of the Soviet Union. It was a spacious building with at least a dozen rooms on two floors. A narrow winding road led to the villa from the Roublevskoe motorway. It ran through a thick pine forest and very few people, even among the locals, knew that the 'Party dacha', as it was known in the past, was now private property.

The steel entrance gates were operated by remote control, but there would usually be at least three armed guards in the small hut beside them. At night dogs would roam the territory and any intruder risked being torn to pieces before anyone could get to him.

But on the evening of the party the security was much less visible than usual. Seraphim was hosting the world-famous Russian opera singer, Dmitri Sibirski, who was to give a recital in a huge, specially erected heated marquee delivered from Germany at very short notice, and he did not want crude security measures to spoil the occasion.

The guests were gathering in the large hall on the ground floor of the house. Drinks were served by waiters in white uniforms with gold buttons. Most of the guests were business-men who had had dealings with Seraphim at one time or another. There were also senior government officials present and several military uniforms could be seen in the crowd. Seraphim was known as a big-time operator, a financial tycoon, and many people were grateful to have been invited to his private party. Even those who had reservations about him could not resist the temptation to be present at a recital by the famous Dmitri Sibirski.

At least a dozen celebrities were among the guests: musicians, artists, pop singers, movie stars, 'the usual scum', as Seraphim used to call them. He was standing at the top of the staircase leading to the first floor, watching the guests mingle with each other. He felt a sense of pride that he was hosting a party that would be talked about for months to come. He was hoping that he would be able to outshine his neighbour, the president of a big private bank, who'd managed to get a famous Western pop star to perform for a group of his friends at his house. It was rumoured he had paid $120,000 for a forty-minute concert.

Well, Seraphim reckoned he had already managed to upstage him by paying more for a real performer, a world-famous opera singer.

He then noticed the famous gay pop singer, Phil Lobanov, in the crowd. Phil had risen to stardom solely thanks to 'sponsor-ship' from Seraphim. He was a lousy singer but he had that pretty-boy look that appealed to teenage girls, bored housewives and gays. Seraphim put pressure on several managers of concert halls in Moscow to let him perform there. He also paid for a couple of Phil's songs to stay at the top of the charts for a while and made sure that he was included in several variety shows that were broadcast on TV. Gradually the public got used to Phil and he was even nominated for several awards. But recently he had been overheard complaining about Seraphim being 'a pain in the arse'. He was also telling people that he had grown tired of Seraphim's 'stupidity and ignorance'.

Phil arrived accompanied by several young men, all supposed to be his 'slaves'. They all wore silver collars on their necks with short leather leashes and every time Phil felt like creating a stir he would pull up one of his slaves by the leash and plant a loud kiss on his lips.

Phil looked up and saw Seraphim gazing downstairs. He waved to him. Seraphim gestured to him to come upstairs. Phil nodded and turning to his 'slaves' said something. They all laughed.

Seraphim walked back into his study and went to the window. Although security was relaxed there were still guards all over the place. Why on earth do they have to be an eyesore all the time? Seraphim thought. How many times do I need to tell Shark to move them out of sight? It's a fucking party I'm hosting, not some get-together of the Brotherhood! Let the wolves sit in their cages for a while.

Phil walked into the study. He was tall, with long curly dark hair, dark eyes and a permanent mischievous smile on his face. Seraphim was still standing at the window, his back to the door.

'You wanted to see me?' Phil asked him.

Seraphim turned around. He had a strange glint in his eyes.

'Yes, I did want to see you,' he said. 'I want you to go down on your knees and beg forgiveness for all the shit you've been saying about me!'

Phil's eyes widened. His smile turned into a grimace.

'What are you talking about?' he said. 'I haven't been saying anything about you to anyone.'

Seraphim's face reddened with anger.

'I'm not going to tell you twice,' he said, with steel creeping into his voice. 'Or maybe you would like to spend some time with Shark and his boys?'

He was going to teach the ungrateful prick a lesson. And if needed, he was going to cancel all his shows and scrap all his record deals.

Phil stood in the doorway for a moment, hesitating. Then he closed the door behind him, walked towards Seraphim and slowly got down on his knees.

'Well?' Seraphim said, looking down on him. 'Beg for your life, you piece of shit…'

★

The recital started at eight o'clock.

Before the performance Seraphim spoke briefly to Alla, who was Dmitri's agent in Russia. She was a big woman who kept smiling nervously. She had the type of face that turned red every time she got even mildly anxious or excited. Seraphim thanked her for helping to arrange the recital and handed her an envelope with ten thousand dollars inside. She took the envelope and her face turned dark red.

The guests were slowly filtering into the giant heated marquee where a hundred chairs were assembled. The women were supposed to be seated and the men were supposed to stand. But as it was Russia many male guests immediately occupied many of the chairs, determined to cling to their seats come what may.

Dmitri meanwhile was pacing back and forth in his dressing room in the house, getting ready for the concert. He was always nervous before his performances. He would imagine things going wrong: he might lose his voice on stage, or start singing out of key, or forget the words, or start coughing and sneezing at the most awkward moment.

He tried to combat his usual nervousness by convincing himself that most of the people in the audience knew nothing about classical music and would never even notice if he missed a couple of notes. He'd already been informed by Alla that Seraphim's guests were typical New Russians with plenty of money but with neither taste nor intelligence.

'Mr Voronov wants to talk to you after the recital,' Alla said. 'I suspect he wants to be seen chatting with you as though you've known each other for some time.'

Dmitri looked at her and grimaced.

'I don't care what he wants!' he snapped. 'He should be happy that I've agreed to sing before a bunch of idiots who are more used to listening to pop singers. As soon as this is over I'm off!'

Alla decided not to argue but try to set up a brief meeting between Dmitri and Seraphim immediately after the recital.

The guests had all gathered in the marquee and were waiting for the recital to start. There was an expectant buzz in the air. Dmitri was considered to be one of the best Russian opera singers, but he very rarely performed in his own country. The majority of Russian opera houses could not afford him, so whenever he performed in Russia it was a major event, both musically and socially. That was one of the main reasons why Seraphim had agreed to the proposal of staging Dmitri's recital at such short notice.

He was convinced that it was Alla, Dmitri's agent, who came up with the idea in the first place. He didn't know that in fact Alla had been approached by a mysterious British 'businessman', a tall grey-haired man, who had asked her to organise the private concert at Seraphim's villa. He promised to pay her $25,000 in cash – a fortune by Russian standards – if the plan worked. Alla, who desperately needed the money, decided not to ask any questions. Through her extensive contacts in the music world she managed to find some people who knew Seraphim quite well. She put the idea to them, they liked it, and the whole thing was arranged in a matter of days...

When Dmitri finally appeared on stage, he was met with loud applause. Most of the guests who had been seated stood up. Dmitri bowed his head slightly accepting the applause. He then turned to the accompanist, a bald man with a long ginger beard, and gave him a nod. The applause quickly died down.

Once the recital had begun, Pavel slipped outside. He nodded to the two guards and rolled his eyes, pretending that he couldn't stand all that 'classical crap'. Both men grinned understandingly.

He walked briskly to his car. It was parked at the far end of the driveway, behind some bushes. The security people were nowhere to be seen, just like he was hoping.

Pavel approached his car and, checking that no one was watching, opened the boot.

'What the hell took ya so long?' Clay whispered loudly, getting out. 'It was like a freezer in there.'

Alex said nothing but it was obvious from the expression on his face that he had not enjoyed the ride.

'I couldn't get out earlier,' Pavel explained. 'You'd better hurry, we haven't got much time.'

Alex and Clay ran for the back entrance. They knew their way around well: Pavel had provided them with a detailed plan of the territory and the building. He also managed to photograph the back entrance to the house, the stairs leading to the first floor and even the study itself with a tiny camera that was fitted into the pin he wore on his jacket. He had also found out that Seraphim kept all the important documents in a safe in his study, concealed behind one of the paintings.

Pavel entered the house through the main entrance where two armed men were standing. He had to check whether it was possible for Alex and Clay to reach the study without anyone noticing them. One of the security people was hanging around the ground floor. Pavel asked him to get him a bottle of brandy from the kitchen and several glasses.

'A couple of guests need a warm-up,' he explained. 'It's a bit chilly in the tent. But don't worry, I'll keep an eye on things while you're away.'

The man rushed off to get the brandy from the kitchen in the basement.

Entering from the back, Alex and Clay nearly bumped into the cook who was busy preparing dinner for a small group of select guests who had been invited for a meal after the concert. He was told to prepare something very unusual so as to impress them and was rushing around, terrified at the thought that Seraphim might not be happy with his choice of dishes. It was by pure chance that

Alex heard him approaching and signalled to Clay to hide behind a curtain.

As soon as Pavel saw them entering the downstairs hall, he walked through the door leading to the kitchen so that he could intercept the guard if he came back too early with the brandy. His heart was beating fast. He knew that if someone noticed Alex and Clay going upstairs they would have to shoot their way out.

But everything went according to plan and the two men reached the study undetected. The door to the study was locked but that proved no problem for them: Clay used the 'wonder key' and in a split second they were in.

Pavel returned to the marquee with the bottle of brandy.

Alex found the safe in a matter of seconds. There were several paintings hanging in the room but he somehow guessed that it would be behind the one depicting the military parade on Red Square. The locking mechanism was primitive, but then it had been fitted during Soviet times and nobody could imagine then that thieves would dare rob the villa of the Central Committee of the Communist Party. Seraphim hadn't even bothered to change the safe: security around his house was usually so tight that nobody could get inside anyway.

It took Clay no more than a couple of minutes to open the safe. Alex was ready with a digital camera capable of taking photographs in the dark. The safe contained several thick files. Most of them included financial documents, handwritten notes, signed IOUs and private letters. One of the files contained what appeared to be copies of classified government documents. Another included photographs of luxurious houses and lists of property prices. There were also photographs of people taken at different locations, lists of equipment and technical drawings.

Alex had enough cartridges to photograph every single page, but as he had to finish the job before the recital ended, he started with the documents that seemed more important than the others. He photographed the classified government papers first, then went through the financial documents, the handwritten notes, letters and IOUs.

'You'd better hurry,' Clay whispered. 'I have a feeling that it won't last for long.'

He was standing at the window looking out through the curtains to see whether anyone was leaving the marquee. It was easy to tell that the recital was still going on. Dmitri's powerful voice could be heard even in the house.

Suddenly they heard footsteps down the corridor. Alex stopped photographing and moved closer to the door, so that he might quickly overpower anyone who walked in. They waited till someone went past the study. A moment later Alex resumed photographing the contents of one of the files. A burst of applause from the marquee nearly made him drop the camera.

'That's it, we need to move out,' Clay whispered. 'The gig's over.'

There were still some documents left. Alex was at a loss as to what to do when the applause suddenly died down and Dmitri's singing resumed.

'We still have time,' he whispered to Clay and resumed photographing the documents.

★

Pavel was listening to Dmitri's singing.

His mind was miles away from the recital. He was thinking about the two men in the building and how they were coping. They still had to leave the house undetected. The whole point of the operation was to photograph the documents without raising any suspicion of a break-in. These papers were supposed to play a decisive role in destroying the gang.

From time to time Pavel glanced at Seraphim, who was sitting apart from the others, to the right of the small stage. Occasionally Seraphim would turn his head and look at his guests as if checking whether they were appreciating the great event.

Just like some film, Pavel thought. The music is playing, the villain is basking in glory, and the good guys are at his house going through the paperwork…

Dmitri's voice was getting better with each song. And if at first some people in the audience were openly gazing around, by now their eyes were glued to the stage.

The last number in the recital was *Nochenkya*, a Russian folk song about a young woman who sits in the night holding her baby and praying that her husband will soon return home from the war. It was a beautiful song, performed unaccompanied, with Dmitri radiating his great artistic energy, passing it on to the audience.

When he finished, the audience remained silent. It was obvious that the song made a strong impression. Dmitri knew well that these seconds of silence between the last note and the burst of applause were usually the best indication of the effect he was having – the longer the pause, the stronger the effect.

Seraphim stood up and started clapping. The rest of the audience immediately followed and the burst of applause hit Dmitri like a wave. Seraphim turned his head to the crowd and was looking triumphant. Here he was, having one of the world's greatest singers performing for him and his guests. A world famous singer who performed for royalty and some of the richest people in the world.

He saw Pavel in the crowd. Seraphim looked at him and grinned. Pavel nodded slightly, as if showing his approval of what was happening.

Seraphim nodded back and turned to face the stage. He didn't see Pavel quickly walk out.

As the guests began to leave the marquee, several fireworks lit up the sky with a loud bang. Some people began to applaud and cheer. Several more fireworks followed. The few guards that remained on the territory were also looking upwards: no one had warned them that there would be a fireworks display immediately after the recital. It was supposed to take place much later, for the benefit of the guests who were staying on for dinner.

But Pavel had other ideas. He figured that it would be a good distraction to allow Alex and Clay to leave the compound unnoticed. So he saw to it that the fireworks were launched earlier than planned.

★

They walked back to the Roublevskoe motorway down the same path that Pavel had shown them two days before. Motya was relieved to see them. It was obvious that he had spent several very uncomfortable hours in his Lada and was happy to leave the area.

When they got back to the flat at Tverskaya Street they were in for a shock: George was waiting for them there. He was sitting in the dining room with a glass of whisky in his hand. Lidia was sitting opposite him on the sofa.

Alex and Clay just stood there, numb.

'Nice to see you lads enjoying yourself in Moscow,' George said, greeting them. 'I trust everything went well tonight?'

Clay started to chew his gum a little faster. Alex also felt uncomfortable. The incident in the restaurant flashed before him and he anticipated a very unpleasant conversation with George. But he showed no anxiety and simply said, 'All went well. We've got the stuff.'

George smiled.

'Well done,' he said. 'I see that everything is going according to plan.'

'We did have one problem,' Clay said. 'The men we were supposed to… to intimidate, well two of them are dead.'

Clay was looking at George expecting him to comment. But to his surprise George didn't say anything. In fact, he seemed to ignore the news about the two Chechens getting killed.

'I got word that your Russian partner was having problems,' he said. 'So I decided to fly over here and sort things out. But Lidia here has assured me that everything is fine.'

He looked at Alex and Clay, as if challenging them to contradict him. Both men said nothing. They realised that George probably didn't want to discuss the killing of the two Chechens in front of Lidia.

'Well, that's settled then,' George said. 'And now I'd like you to print the photos and Lidia will help me with the translation so that you can have a rest afterwards.'

Alex and Clay used the laptop to print the photographs. They showed clearly all the dates, names and numbers on the documents. They were passing the photos to Lidia who quickly glanced through them and then translated the parts that in her opinion were the most interesting to George.

One of the documents from Seraphim's safe turned out to be

a copy of a top-secret memo prepared by the FSB, containing details of an undercover operation in Chechnya. It included photographs and names of seven people with their addresses and records of their movements across the republic. When Lidia translated to George the contents of the document he showed no emotion. But in reality he was extremely surprised. Mr Voronov seems to have very diverse interests, he thought. Now why on earth would he need classified information about covert operations of Russian intelligence in Chechnya? I have a feeling we have stumbled on something very big here.

Once they finished printing the photographs Clay went to get changed but Alex stayed behind and studied some of the photos from the 'property file', as he dubbed it. They were mostly of buildings somewhere in central London – very impressive buildings. There were also some photos of people – a smiling young man standing beside a BMW, police mug shots of the very same young man. Then there was an older man, photographed in different locations around London. What can it all mean? Alex thought. I hope George makes sense out of it.

★

Sergei Titov, the newly appointed Deputy Minister of Foreign Affairs, was sitting in his spacious office at Smolenskaya Square overlooking the Moscow River.

As deputy minister he was in charge of management and administration, a powerful position in the Russian bureaucratic hierarchy. In Soviet times the people appointed to oversee the day-to-day running of government departments and agencies were considered extremely important. They acted as 'house managers' to the government, in a country where everything was in short supply. They decided who would be getting which office and who would be provided with chauffeur-driven ministerial cars. But what was even more important – they were in charge of distributing state-owned flats and country houses among senior and middle-ranking staff.

Under capitalism their influence remained largely intact, especially as property prices rocketed and the majority of officials still had to rely on the state to provide them with decent living accommodation.

Sergei had already received several visits from high-ranking diplomats asking about the new country development project in the exclusive area to the north of Moscow. They were mostly interested in the country cottages that were situated close to the local river.

'I need a good view to concentrate when I work,' one of them said. 'I hope that when the cottages are distributed you will take into consideration my work requirements.'

It was obviously total rubbish, but Sergei always promised 'to attend to the matter personally'. He was still new to the job and hadn't yet established whom he had to oblige and whom he could safely ignore. So in his first month on the job he promised everyone who came to his office some sort of help and assistance.

It was after lunch on a Friday afternoon that he got his first call on the hotline telephone, '*vertushka*'. He was informed that one of the senior members of the presidential staff wanted to see him personally. Technically speaking Sergei was not accountable to the people in the Kremlin, but in reality members of the presidential staff yielded a lot of power and no one in his right mind would have ignored their wishes and requests.

Sergei asked his secretary to arrange for his driver to come to the main entrance. On his way to the Kremlin he tried to guess what the meeting would be about, but couldn't think of anything. He decided that it probably had something to do with his recent appointment, a sort of an introduction meeting.

He was driven into the Kremlin through the Borovitski Gate. The guards at the gate saluted the car and Sergei experienced a feeling of 'administrative ecstasy', as one classical Russian writer once described the emotions of government officials who were moving up the bureaucratic ladder. It was the first time that he had come to the Kremlin on official business. He suddenly realised that he was now an integral part of a government machine that was running a vast country. He was on his way to meeting with a senior Kremlin official to discuss some important matters of the state. The lives of thousands if not millions of people could depend on how he copes with the task, he thought.

As the car drove up to the building where members of the presidential staff were housed Sergei got more and more excited. Security in the building was strict. There was a metal detector in the lobby and all bags and briefcases were searched by uniformed guards. As Sergei did not have a Kremlin pass he was accompanied to the second floor by one of the guards.

A young secretary with that Kremlin expression of importance on her face met him at the elevator. She led him down a seemingly endless corridor – oak office doors on each side, with names of occupants written on them – to a large reception room at the end. He was told to wait and sat down on a brown leather sofa.

The secretary took her place across from him at a large desk. There were several phones in front of her, including the one with the Russian two-headed eagle on the dial, the hotline.

Sergei could not help admiring the secretary's legs. They were good, shapely legs in expensive stockings. Sergei suddenly felt a strong feeling of arousal. This place is one power box, he thought. Even a simple secretary radiates all that strange energy.

Sergei had heard a rumour that the Kremlin was haunted by the ghost of Joseph Stalin. According to the story, Stalin's ghost walked along the corridors at night, wearing the uniform of a *Generallissimus* – a military rank he invented for himself – countless medals pinned to his chest. He very rarely showed off any of his honours during his life, preferring the 'modest, down-to-earth' appearance. But after his death, it seems, he decided to show off all of his regalia. As the ghost of Stalin moved, the medals clicked loudly. Several officials claimed to have seen him walking along the corridors. Sergei suddenly felt uneasy at the thought that the ghost of Stalin might suddenly appear in front of him.

A phone on the secretary's table rang and he was shown into the office of Anton Borodin, a senior member of the Strategic Planning Group, who smiled broadly as he welcomed Sergei in his office.

'Congratulations on your move to Moscow, the cradle of political talent,' he said.

They sat down at a small coffee table near the window. After an exchange of the usual bureaucratic niceties Borodin turned to business.

'The reason I've asked to see you, Sergei Vladimirovich,' he said, 'is that I wanted to inform you about a very important project that is going to be launched soon. As you know, the financial situation in the country is desperate. The only way we can tackle the existing crisis is to generate income by any means we can. That's why we've decided to use some of our national treasures for an exhibition that will tour the world and bring in substantial revenues. We've already had several offers from companies that want to take part in the project and they are prepared to pay us a considerable advance fee, plus more than half of the revenues.'

Borodin paused for a moment, giving his visitor the opportunity to ask a question. But Sergei was watching him in silence. His gaze was fixed on the dimple on Borodin's chin. He had always wanted to have a dimpled chin himself. He had heard that women loved men with dimples on their chins.

'As you can understand,' Borodin continued, slightly baffled by his guest's stare, 'we don't want to attract too much attention to the project at the moment. Some people will start jumping to the wrong conclusions and accuse us of selling off the national assets. The idea is to move them to the West quietly and announce the launch of the exhibition later, when everything is properly arranged.'

Sergei nodded, to show that he understood what was being said. In reality he hadn't the slightest idea why he was being told about some exhibition that was supposed to open abroad.

'The national treasures picked for the exhibition will be shipped to London and stored at our embassy until the deal is reached with the Western organisers,' Borodin said. 'I was instructed by the highest authority to brief you on the situation and to ask you to organise the shipment through diplomatic channels. That way, we'll be able to avoid any unnecessary publicity. It's in the interests of national security to keep the whole thing quiet, so we expect you to keep the details of the operation to yourself.'

Sergei finally realised that he had been chosen to take part in a major government operation. Borodin told him that before the diplomatic cargo was dispatched to London, some special equipment, along with a group of experts, had to be sent to Britain, also through diplomatic channels. They would be needed to ensure the security of the national treasures in London, he explained.

'We'll be sending a special envoy who will negotiate with the British the terms of exhibiting the treasures,' Borodin said. 'Until he arrives, it would be best to avoid informing the embassy in London about the real contents of the cargo, for security reasons. In the documents it could be characterised as, say, exhibits intended for an exhibition of Russian folk art.'

Although he didn't really understand most of the details, Sergei felt flattered that he was being brought in on such an important project. He assured Borodin that he would do everything to keep it confidential.

After he had left, Borodin picked up the phone and dialled an internal Kremlin number. He waited patiently for at least a minute until the phone was answered.

'Hello, it's Borodin,' he said. 'I've just spoken to the new Deputy Minister of Foreign Affairs. I've briefed him about the plan, just like you asked me to. He promised to cooperate fully and keep the entire matter confidential. I'll keep you informed.'

When he put the receiver down he sat motionless for a while. I wonder why Vassili takes such a keen interest in this exhibition? he was thinking. As if the President's son has nothing else better do.

★

The moment he received the message about the two Chechens getting killed George knew that he would have to fly out to Moscow. It was clear to him that something had gone terribly wrong. Alex and Clay were too experienced to mess up the job so badly, so there must have been a traitor in their midst. And the first person he suspected was Pavel Batalov.

Not that he was the only suspect. There were obviously others whom Batalov was using as back-up. And George himself had spoken to several people before he got hold of Pavel, so there was always a possibility – however slim – that someone had figured out what was going on. But only Batalov knew all the details of the operation and only he knew about the mock assassination attempt.

George had no choice but to confront him. The operation was nearing its final stage, and it was impossible to change the arrangements. So he was prepared to bargain with Batalov, offer him more money in return for cooperation. And if the Russian would not bargain with him, well, then George had only one option left...

They met at a restaurant off Gogol Boulevard on the day after the concert at Seraphim's villa. They could have obviously had a meeting at the flat, but George didn't want any other people present. So Pavel suggested the family-run eatery as a safe place where they would not be seen by any of Seraphim's people. He was taking precautions after becoming Crow's personal advisor.

On his way to the restaurant George changed taxis to throw off any possible tail. Pavel was waiting for him in the lobby. He had booked a private room for the meeting.

The two men shook hands and proceeded to their room without uttering a word. Once inside they shook hands once again and exchanged greetings in English and took their seats at the table.

Two waiters came into the room bringing the starters, a spicy bean salad known as *lobio*, chicken pieces in rich gravy with crushed walnut, *satsivi*, and red marinated Guriysky cabbage. They also brought two bottles of Hvanchkara, the famous Georgian red wine.

'I must congratulate you on the way you've managed to infiltrate the gang,' George said once the waiters had left. 'I never thought you could do it so quickly.'

Pavel was filling his plate. He hadn't eaten since breakfast and the sight of all that spicy food made his mouth water.

'I had to take a risk,' he said. 'The only opportunity I could think of came up during the operation on the embankment. The Crow could not have suspected me of having anything to do with the people who killed his guests...'

George frowned.

'That's what I wanted to talk to you about,' he said. 'The lads say that someone else was present at the scene. They even think that they might have been monitored by someone who had known about the whole plan and who sent a sniper to the area. What would you say to that?'

Pavel put down his fork and knife. He took his wine glass and drank from it. George was watching him closely, trying to guess whether the Russian, whom he himself had picked for the job, was playing some sort of a double game. In George's opinion the situation was not looking good at all. Pavel was the key player in the whole set-up. He had managed to infiltrate the gang, he knew all the people involved from the other side, including George himself. So if he turned out to be working for someone else the whole operation would be blown sky-high.

Pavel put down his glass.

'Alex and Clay told me about the supposed third shooter,' he said. 'Frankly, I didn't believe them. It all sounded too bizarre. Someone watching them and waiting to start shooting once they opened fire. I thought that they'd simply screwed up and didn't want to accept the blame.'

George said nothing. He was prepared to give the Russian a chance to come up with his version of events.

'I think there are two possible scenarios,' Pavel said, seeing that George was not ready to comment. 'The first involves incompetence on the part of my partners. They had to operate in very difficult conditions, in the darkness, the cold and falling snow.'

'I doubt it,' George said. 'They're used to operating in all conditions.'

'I accept that,' Pavel said. 'But it's still possible that they slipped up and killed the Chechens.'

George nodded, accepting it as a possibility for the sake of argument. He knew that his men could hit a fly half a mile away if needed. The Russian had to come up with something better than that.

'The other scenario would be that someone else knew about the job,' Pavel said. 'Someone you might have spoken to about the operation who then used the information for his own purpose.'

The Russian was actually pointing the finger of blame at

George! Not bad for someone who was the prime suspect! But then again, as George knew well himself, the best form of defence is attack. And the funniest thing of all was that he could have been right. George did speak to other people before he found Pavel. God knows whom they could have been working for. The problem was that George had not had many options at the time. He had had to rely on his instincts and tread carefully, hoping to pick the best people for the job.

George decided to test Pavel. He really didn't have any other choice left open to him. He slipped his hand under the table.

'I'm holding a gun which is pointed at you,' he said, 'and I'm prepared to use it, if necessary.'

Pavel's face turned pale.

'Now I'd like to ask you a question,' George said. 'And believe me, I have my own sources here in Moscow who can provide me with all the information I need. So the question is – are you working for someone else?'

Pavel was looking him straight in the eyes, taken aback by the dramatic turn of events. George really knew how to catch people off guard.

'I'm working only for you,' he said. 'I have no hidden agendas. I need the money.'

If he was lying he was good. George had to hand it to him. It was time to change the line of conversation.

'I'm sorry about this,' George said, taking his hand from under the table, 'but I had to clear the air, especially after what has happened on the embankment. Whether we all like it or not the stakes have risen dramatically. Two men are dead. That means both the criminals and the authorities will be looking for the shooters. We can't have any more slips.'

Pavel was obviously relieved. He knew well that George would use his gun if need be. And he must have been carrying one.

At that moment a waiter knocked on the door and brought in a large plate of Georgian shish kebabs. That helped to ease the tension in the room. Both men tucked into the meat.

'There's one more thing I wanted to ask you,' George said. 'We've received some information that the gang is planning something in London.'

Pavel nodded.

'I've heard some talk about a property deal in London that the Crow was planning,' he said. 'But I'll have to look into it.'

'You do that,' George said.

★

The Crow was having one of his panic attacks.

As usual the first symptoms appeared as he got up in the morning. A trivial worry that he had been harbouring for a couple of days suddenly grew out of all proportion and turned into a full-blown panic. He told his people to find Shark and get him to come to his villa immediately. He desperately needed to have a word with his head of security about one very important matter.

Seraphim had a lot of anxiety in him. He had made most of his money by setting up others and there were many people out there who would like to see him go down. When he started to build his criminal empire he never looked back. He had nothing to lose then. But as his wealth grew and he became accustomed to luxury, he started to worry that 'unforeseen misfortunes' could deprive him of what he had. He would imagine that his people were conspiring against him to get rid of him, or that the authorities were about to arrest him, confiscate all his possessions and throw him into jail to rot. Or he would get it into his head that he might have contracted a terminal disease like AIDS from one of his 'faithful whores' and was going to meet a horrible slow death.

During such panic attacks Seraphim could not bear to be alone. He needed company, any company, to distract himself from his overwhelming fears. So much so that he would some-times summon one of his bodyguards or even servants to his study and talk to them on some irrelevant subject for hours on end.

On that day Seraphim's anxiety was caused by fear that his biggest secret, his plan to pull off a spectacular job in London, was in fact no longer secret. It was supposed to make him so rich that he could retire. He had no illusions about the future of the Central Brotherhood. Unlike other big criminals who thought that their empires would last for ever, he was getting ready to move abroad and disappear without a trace. Russia was too volatile a country to survive in for long. It was best to have a pension plan, and Seraphim had worked one out for himself.

No one in his gang knew anything about the 'London job'. The people who were supposed to carry it out had no direct connection to the Central Brotherhood. Only Shark and a couple of others had a very vague idea of a forthcoming property deal in London and assumed that the boss was planning to buy a couple of houses as an investment.

On Seraphim's instructions Georgi Volkov had flown to London to find out as much as possible about the properties in Kensington Palace Gardens. The Crow needed that information to carry out his plan. On his instructions Volkov contacted Boris Ossinski who was supposed to provide the answers to most of the questions about the area, being an expert on the subject. In order to put pressure on Ossinski Shark's people framed his son, Ivan, planting drugs in his car and fabricating criminal charges against him. Initially all went according to plan and Ossinski agreed to cooperate in return for having his son's charges quashed. But then Volkov disappeared without a trace and all attempts to find him proved in vain.

Seraphim was getting really worried. His plan was in danger of collapsing. And what's more, during a recent drinking binge with Shark, he had boasted to him about a 'huge job' coming up in London that promised to bring him millions. He couldn't remember exactly what he said that night, as he was too drunk, but he had an uneasy feeling that he might have inadvertently given too much away. That was why he was now anxious to check what his chief of security knew about his secret project.

★

When Shark walked into Seraphim's study he could immediately see that the boss was in a bad mood. One of the drivers was sitting in a chair, listening to Seraphim attentively. He's got one of his depressions again, Shark thought. I'd better watch what I say.

The moment Seraphim saw him he signalled to the driver to

leave. Shark took his place and looked at his boss expectantly.

'Have you had any word from Volkov?' Seraphim said, lighting up a cigarette.

'Nothing,' Shark said. 'The son of a bitch vanished without a trace.'

Seraphim grimaced as if that information caused him severe physical pain.

'How much cash did he have with him?' he asked.

'About two hundred grand, but I'd be very surprised if he ran off with it,' Shark said. 'The prick knows that I'll find him and cut him up.'

Seraphim nodded, accepting that Volkov would be crazy to steal from them.

'We can't afford any mistakes,' he said. 'Especially after what happened with the Chechens.'

Shark felt it was a good time to have a go at Pavel.

'What about the pig?' he said. 'I don't trust him.'

Seraphim looked him straight in the eyes.

'Do you really think that I'd put my faith in a cop even if he was kicked out for being a total prick? I suppose you've checked him out?'

Shark nodded gloomily, embarrassed by the fact that nothing had come from his inquiries.

'What about the two Chechens?' Seraphim said. 'I've lost a hell of a lot of money thanks to someone who's fucking me around. What's the news on that?'

'I've heard that the bullets came from some fancy foreign pieces,' Shark said. 'The word on the street is that the cops, or even the Feds themselves, could have been behind it. There's even talk that they wanted to whack you too.'

Seraphim was so stunned by the news that his jaw dropped. He sat motionless for a good half a minute.

'Who told you that?' he said finally, regaining his senses.

Shark realised that he had made a big mistake passing the rumours to his boss, considering the state he was in.

'It was just talk,' he said, trying to backtrack. 'You know, people saying things over a bottle of vodka.'

'And you believe all that shit?' Seraphim yelled. 'Do you really think that the cops or the Feds are up to it? I own the bloody cops and Feds! They'll never dare touch me!'

Shark said nothing. He could see that Seraphim was getting really angry. For the first time in his life someone was challenging him. The Crow was not used to that. He spent hundreds of thousands of dollars each year buying up influence in Moscow, and did not want to hear that there were still people out there who were prepared to stand up to him.

Seraphim extinguished his cigarette in the ashtray and immediately lit up another one.

'Only a few people in our group knew about the meeting with the Chechens,' he said. 'It proves once and for all that one of them is a double-crossing piece of shit. I want you to find him and bring him to me.'

Shark rose to go. But Seraphim signalled to him to sit down again.

'That big job in London I mentioned to you a couple of days ago,' he said. 'You know, moving some stuff over there and that sort of thing?'

He looked in anticipation at Shark, waiting for him to respond. But Shark showed no emotion.

'You were too pissed at the time,' he said. 'I couldn't understand much of what you said then.'

Seraphim grinned.

'I was just bullshitting,' he said. 'There is no London job. We do all our jobs here, at home. Got that?'

'Sure thing, Crow,' Shark said.

Seraphim waved his hand, indicating that he could leave. As it turned out Shark didn't pay attention to what he had said on that evening. The London job was still his personal secret...

★

The moment he approached his front door Pavel could tell that someone had been inside his flat.

The small metal clip he usually inserted between the door and the frame, about half a metre above floor level, was lying on the rug. He had developed a habit of putting in a 'marker' from his

CID days, when on several occasions, during delicate investigations, he had received unexpected visits to his flat in his absence by people looking for documents.

Pavel hesitated for a moment outside the door, going through the possible options. At the first instance he thought that Seraphim might have somehow found out about his link with the people from London and sent his boys to sort him out. But he quickly dismissed that idea, reckoning that Seraphim would have lured him to his villa, had he had found out something about him. He then thought that it could have been George's people. But what would be the point of such a visit? he asked himself. Even if George still suspected him of treachery, there was nothing in his flat that could shed light on anything. Could it be the cops then? But they already had the telephone book he found at Mustafa's house. Or maybe it was Lidia? She still had a spare key to the flat from the old days. But that seemed highly unlikely. Or maybe he simply forgot to insert the clip in the last time he left home? Now that was probably a much fairer assumption.

Pavel inserted the key in the lock, opened the door and stepped in. The moment he switched on the light in the hallway he realised that he *had* remembered to stick the clip in the usual place. Two men were waiting for him. One of them was holding a gun.

'You move, I shoot,' the man with the gun explained.

They pushed him into the dining room and tied him to a chair. Pavel had never seen either of them before, but he could tell that they were not cops. And they couldn't have been sent by George Blunt. So either they were Seraphim's men or someone else in the gang was desperate to find out what he was up to.

'What the hell do you want?' Pavel said.

'We'll be asking the questions, cop!' one of the men, a tall, burly hood with a short haircut and narrow brow, replied.

As soon as he heard the word 'cop' Pavel knew that the visitors were not sent by Seraphim. The Crow was too clever to send two complete idiots to check him out.

At that moment the doorbell rang. The tall man went to open it and a moment later Alexander Bendik walked into the room. Pavel had seen him only a couple of times before, on both occasions at Seraphim's villa, and only spoke to him very briefly.

But he remembered him well, because he was the one member of the 'politburo' who always dressed in designer suits and flashy shirts and ties. He was of medium height, with receding blond hair, thin lips, long nose and a cold indifferent stare in his eyes. This time he was wearing a long black coat with a red scarf wrapped round his neck. He walked slowly to a chair across from where Pavel was sitting, untied the scarf and unbuttoned his coat, revealing an expensive grey suit complemented by a yellow shirt and a wide green tie. He turned the chair the other way around and sat down.

Pavel was watching him closely.

Bendik took out a pack of cigarettes from his pocket, pulled one out of it and lit it up with a gold lighter. All his movements seemed theatrical, as if he was savouring every moment of his own presence.

'I bet you're wondering why I'm here, cop?' he said, releasing a cloud of smoke.

Pavel couldn't help smiling: it was now clear to him why Bendik had come. He must be the informant, he thought. He's probably been shitting himself after he heard that the Crow hired me. But what's his plan? He must be really desperate if he came here. I need to do something fast, or I'm a dead man.

'I guess you came to offer me your undying friendship,' Pavel said finally. 'I'm deeply touched.'

Bendik lost his cool in a split second.

'Stop fucking with me!' he yelled. 'Or my boys here will see to it that you never open your lousy trap again!'

Bendik obviously had no sense of humour so Pavel figured that there was no point in winding him up even more.

'Okay, okay, I get your drift,' he said. 'You probably came here to find out something important, something that's been bugging you for some time.'

Bendik shot a suspicious glance at him. His eyes narrowed.

'And what do you think I want to find out?' he asked.

Pavel drew a sigh. He's so bloody predictable, he thought.

'I guess you want to know who's been talking to the law.'

The chair underneath Bendik creaked. He leaned forward as if trying to get closer to Pavel.

'Are you saying that you know who the traitor is?' Bendik said in a lowered voice.

Pavel deliberately didn't give an answer at once. What would be Bendik's move if he said that he knew the name of the informer? he thought. He might panic and order his men to kill him. On the other hand, if he said that he didn't know who the traitor was Bendik may not believe him and order his execution anyway. So the only way out was to surprise his guests.

'I don't have all the proof at the moment,' Pavel said, 'but according to my information it's Shark who's been sharing secrets with others.'

There was total silence in the room. Bendik was staring at Pavel in amazement. He was expecting anything but that. Then he exploded.

'What the hell are you talking about?' he yelled. 'What are you trying to pull? The next thing you'll be saying that the Crow himself is a police informer!'

It was obvious that Bendik felt relieved and was putting on a show in front of his men, covering his own skinny arse. But it didn't mean that Pavel was off the hook. In fact, he was probably in more danger now than before, as Bendik could have been very tempted to dispose of him there and then.

It was at that moment that he finally managed to loosen the ropes. There was no time to lose. Pavel jumped up from the chair and kicked the man who was closest to him in the groin. The second thug tried to get his gun out from under his jacket but fell down having received a blow on the head.

Bendik seemed to be mesmerised by what had happened, which suited Pavel just fine. He thrust himself forward. Bendik tried to move away but was caught by Pavel. With one single blow he knocked Bendik down, jumping on top of him and pinning him to the floor. He put his hand inside Bendik's jacket and got out a gun with a silencer. The son of a bitch was going to blow my brains out personally, he thought. And then, probably, planned to kill his men and pin the whole thing on me.

Pavel shoved the barrel of the gun into Bendik's mouth.

'I have several choices,' he said. 'I can either kill you right here right now or I can call the Crow and ask him to come over. And guess what he'll do to you once he finds out that you've tried to bump off his personal advisor who's looking for the snitch?'

Bendik was breathing heavily. He was terrified. A gruesome prospect was facing him.

'But I also have a third option,' Pavel said. 'I can let you go so that you disappear from my sight. And if you get any more great ideas about getting rid of me I'll make sure that my people get the message across to the Crow. Do you understand what I'm saying? Do you know what will happen to you if a certain police file gets into the hands of the Crow? They'll torture you till you beg them to kill you.'

Pavel had no choice. He was risking his cover but he had to get Bendik scared. He had to force him out of the way. He knew that Bendik would not rest until he was removed, one way or another. So Pavel had to play for time. The operation was coming to an end anyway and the gang would be destroyed, with or without the help of an informer.

'So, are we clear on everything?' Pavel said.

Bendik nodded.

★

The presidential country retreat outside Moscow was a place where the head of state usually spent his time either plotting against his enemies, or hiding from the rest of the world after each new political blunder or a bout of illness. His health had deteriorated dramatically since he came to power. His wife was begging him to step down and let others fight it out at the next presidential elections.

'You'll run yourself into the grave,' she would say to him. 'And what would be the point? No one will be grateful anyway.'

'Stop nagging me,' he would say. 'I'll step down when the time is right.'

He had no desire to explain to the silly woman that he could not go without creating a 'safety net' to protect his family from possible prosecution. Too many of his enemies were openly saying that they would demand a full investigation into the affairs of the President and his closest relatives and friends once he left office and that they would press for criminal charges to be brought against all of them if any irregularities were uncovered.

Initially, the allegations of corruption had centred on the Kremlin generally and the President didn't pay much attention to them. He treated them as part of the political pressure exerted by the opposition. But gradually the accusations were getting more and more personal.

Then, out of the blue came the story about a villa that his nephew had bought in Italy. Several newspapers even published a photograph of a three-storey house in Milan. The President ordered his people to conduct a secret investigation. They found out that the house had been acquired by a Russian oil company where his nephew was vice-president. The house had been bought for cash and registered in the name of an offshore company where his nephew was one of the directors. It did not sound quite right, but no apparent crime had been committed.

Later his wife's name was dragged through the mud with allegations that, as honorary president of a state-owned television channel dedicated solely to cultural issues, she was paid secret commissions for approving contracts with private firms for the production of documentaries.

The President was furious. His wife was not intelligent enough to be involved in any illegal deals, that he was sure of! Later, however, it turned out that the silly woman had signed some papers without even reading them.

Then came the stories about his son, Vassili. There was talk that he was keeping some very bad company and arranging access to government ministers and Kremlin officials in return for favours. Not to mention the accounts about his wild drinking and womanising.

The President's closest aide, Valentin Ashev, warned him about the dangers of failing to publicly deny corruption allegations. Ashev, who had unlimited and unrivalled access to the President, demanded that countermeasures be taken.

'We have to respond to attacks from our enemies,' he was saying. 'We have to hit back, reject any idea that we're enriching ourselves and accuse them of corruption. We have to use all means at our disposal. Just look how nicely it all turned out with that creep Margalov.'

No one could explain how Ashev, who had arrived in Moscow from a small Siberian town, had grown so close to the President in a matter of months. Everyone was even more puzzled by the enormous influence that the young man, a journalist from a small provincial paper, acquired over the head of state. But then no one knew that Valentin was actually the President's illegitimate son, from a brief affair he had had when he was a Communist Party boss in Siberia. He kept it a secret, even from his wife and son, and only after he got into the Kremlin did he feel secure enough to summon Valentin to Moscow. The official version was that the young man was the son of one of his old friends.

Giving in to Ashev's demands to counter allegations about corruption, the President ordered the chief of his bodyguards, General Andrei Kapoustin, to set up a special unit to monitor all press reports that concerned members of the President's family. A team of ten people filed regular memos on the subject, which were then passed to Valentin who edited them personally and afterwards delivered them to the President. Gradually the old man became paranoid about the subject. His main concern was how to protect his family from his enemies after leaving office.

He suspected that the communists were behind most of the rumours and accusations of corruption. On the face of it he could have easily decreed the Communist Party unconstitutional. After toppling Yeltsin he had the necessary public support to finish them off once and for all. Most of his advisors were telling him to do it, but he was looking further than his people. He knew that the euphoria surrounding his victory over Yeltsin would soon die down, and then the people would start asking questions. Why, for example, couldn't he keep his promises and sort out the mess in the country? Why didn't he put pressure on the oligarchs who were moving their assets abroad? And why was most of the nation still living in poverty?

From the first day in office he knew that he couldn't deliver on his promises. The country was in ruins. Years of mismanagement had left the nation's industry on the verge of collapse. The oligarchs were sucking the blood out of the country's economy and there was nothing he could do about it since they were too strong to be removed. Corruption continued to spread and the welfare system had disintegrated.

So, just like Yeltsin, he had to keep the communists. He had to have someone he could blame for all the troubles. And he also had to have an enemy so that every time a problem arose he could call for support to prevent the return of the 'communist tyranny'. He would usually order new files and archives to be declassified, showing that during the Soviet tyranny the communists had slaughtered millions more than was previously believed.

That always worked. No one wanted a return to the times when a knock on the door could come at any time and people would disappear, never to be seen again. Yeltsin used that to his advantage, and it worked even when his popularity was near zero.

But as the elections were approaching, the President had to come up with some kind of a plan to protect his family. And the only way he could do it was to find a suitable replacement. After an especially long meeting with Valentin Ashev the plan was finally ready.

★

The President was waiting for his closest advisors to arrive. He had sent word to them on the previous day instructing them to come to an urgent meeting at his country retreat.

He wanted them to be guessing, worrying about a possible reshuffle. He had replaced a lot of top officials during his relatively short time in office. But he had no other choice. Most of them were no good at their jobs. Once they were appointed, they would usually get involved in internal politics and devote all their energies to enriching themselves rather than carrying out their duties. Also, regular reshuffles gave him breathing space, as he would usually blame the sacked ministers for most of the problems.

The sound of car engines was coming from the driveway. Black BMWs and Mercs, the favourite car brands of top Russian officials, were pulling up at the main building. The aides and advisors were arriving one after another, having discussed on the phone between themselves the unexpected invitation to see the boss.

The President was ready to meet his team. There was to be

only one item on the agenda – the long-delayed appointment of the vice-president. After the palace coup, the post of vice-president had remained vacant. It was generally assumed that the Prime Minister would be second in line to the throne if something happened to the head of state. But the revised articles of the constitution that had been used to topple Yeltsin clearly stated that it was the vice-president, and not the head of government, who assumed automatic control if the top man resigned or died. He would carry on as the new head of state for the remaining period of the four-year term and could then run for office in an election.

The plan that the President and Valentin had come up with was to appoint as vice-president someone who would never go against his patron, someone who would look after him when he stepped down and even ask him for advice. That someone was supposed to be Valentin himself, the President's illegitimate son. The idea was that the President would appoint him Vice-President, win the next election, and retire a couple of months after the inauguration to let his son run the country for the next four years. He would then be secure in the knowledge that no harm would come to him and his family.

But before making the plan public, the President wanted to make sure there were no other contenders waiting in the wings to take over the vice-presidency. That's why he decided to call the meeting of his advisors and ask them to propose candidates for vice-president. Once they came up with a list of names he would know who his enemies were and would take appropriate steps to neutralise them. He could then appoint Valentin as Vice-President and announce the elections…

They were coming into the room one by one – senior officials from the Kremlin administration, aides and advisors to the President. Valentin Ashev was the last to walk in. He had a patronising air about him that immediately told everyone that something unusual was about to happen.

They all gathered in the President's study, waiting anxiously to find out what the old man had in mind. Rumours of a reshuffle in the top echelons of government were spreading in Moscow and the inner circle was ready to hear who was destined for the chop.

The President walked into the study. He shook hands and hugged each of the people present. He then took his seat behind his vast desk and glanced around at his closest aides.

'Dear friends,' the President said, 'I've asked you all to come here to discuss a very important matter. I would even say, a matter of the utmost urgency.'

He paused and looked around the room. All eyes were on him. They were waiting to hear the names of the people destined to go.

'I am, of course, talking about the appointment of the vice-president in the light of the forthcoming elections.'

There was an initial collective sigh of relief in the room, but then everyone started guessing what this whole thing with the vice-presidency was all about. For the last several months the President had been playing a constant cat-and-mouse game around the succession issue. One day he was saying that he wouldn't be seeking re-election and the next he'd hint that he was still considering running for a second term. Many careers went down the drain when people drew the wrong conclusions from some of his statements.

'What are you getting at?' Nikolai Taranov, a close friend of the President, one of his so-called 'unpaid advisors', said. 'You're not telling us by any chance that you've finally decided to retire, are you?'

The President grinned.

'Do you want me to retire?' he asked, looking closely at Taranov. Everyone in the room also looked at him.

'I'd love to take your place, you know that,' Taranov said and started to roar with laughter.

The President nodded, as if expecting to hear the answer. The rest of the people in the room produced polite smiles and grins.

'My friends,' the President said, 'I'd like you all to go back to your offices after our meeting is over and think about the names of possible candidates for the post of vice-president. Give me several good reasons why you think that the people you suggest are the best candidates for the job. Send me your suggestions and in two weeks we'll all meet again.'

There was uncertainty in the room. The sort of 'do we go

now, or what?' question was hanging in the air.

The President smiled.

'Oh, and by the way, I also wanted to inform you that I won't be running for the second term.'

Everyone in the room was caught off guard completely. It was the first time that the President had told his aides and advisors in a direct way that he would not be running for office. It immediately became clear to everyone present that the whole issue of appointing the new vice-president was getting a completely different meaning in the light of what the old man had just said. The new vice-president would most likely be the next head of state. Suddenly the stakes had risen dramatically.

'And now that business is over, let's have lunch,' the President said, enjoying the stupid expressions on the faces of his advisors. He then turned to Valentin and winked at him, as if to say, 'We got them guessing today, didn't we?'

★

After meeting with Seraphim in London, Yeffim Kaltzman was busy preparing the ground for the sale of precious stones and jewellery. He still had no idea what would be on offer, but he knew that Seraphim was a very serious player and could come up with unique goods. Yeffim got in touch with buyers across Europe and in the US, informing them of a forthcoming 'auction' with only a limited number of bidders allowed to take part. Although he could provide no specific details he hinted that 'very exceptional items' would be on offer.

Yeffim knew a number of dealers who operated on behalf of some very serious buyers and collectors. He had dealt with them in the past and they knew him well enough to expect him to deliver the goods.

Only once did he suffer a serious setback. The incident nearly destroyed his standing in certain London circles. It had to do with the sale of two icons by Andrei Roublev, and the famous *Black Square* by Kazimir Malevich. All three items were smuggled out of the Soviet Union by a businessman who was forced to flee the country after serious criminal charges were brought against him by the prosecutors. He approached Yeffim and asked him to help sell the icons and the painting.

Yeffim agreed and got in touch with some of the dealers he knew. The icons didn't interest any of the big buyers but several people asked about the painting. A price tag of $2,000,000 was put on it by Yeffim. He anticipated a quick deal as the seller had all the relevant documents in place including the certificate from the Tretyakov Gallery in Moscow verifying that the picture was genuine.

But the sale did not take place. The certificate turned out to be a fake. So did the painting.

There was a very unpleasant scene at the home of one of the people who was representing the buyer. He had wisely invited an expert from an auction house to check the painting before parting with the money. Instead of receiving a big commission Yeffim had to search frantically for a bargain deal for the man so that he would keep quiet about the whole embarrassing incident.

He was furious and planned revenge against the businessman who had set him up. But the man had suddenly left London. Fortunately Yeffim was able to find a really good Fabergé item that was obviously stolen and for that reason was being offered for a very good price. As a result the whole incident with the fake Malevich was forgotten.

But now all these past problems could be laid to rest for ever. The forthcoming deal was bound to make Yeffim a millionaire. There'd be no more stupid exhibitions, no more long nights in his studio painting his miniatures. How he hated those miniatures!

And he could dump Rita, the oil trader's wife. The woman was becoming intolerable. Always demanding attention, always horny.

Yeffim was getting ready for a new life.

★

A chartered plane from Moscow landed at Heathrow Airport and was escorted to the cargo area not far from the VIP suite. According to the arrangement between Moscow and London, the diplomatic cargo, all forty crates of it, was to be picked up by the Russian embassy on the plane's arrival.

Boris Ossinski had been overseeing the delivery of the 'communications equipment', as it was described in the coded cable sent by 'hotline' to the embassy from Moscow. It was signed by the recently appointed Deputy Minister of Foreign Affairs, Sergei Titov.

Boris was sitting in his car with the first secretary of the embassy, Nikolai Markovski, a bald yet youngish-looking man in thick-rimmed glasses.

'It's all very odd,' Markovski was saying, 'here we are, getting a ton of equipment and nobody really knows what it is and what it's meant for.'

Boris frowned.

'Well,' he said, 'I'm sure our friends know what it's for.' He tapped himself on the shoulder with his hand when he said the word 'friends', implying that the intelligence people at the embassy must have been informed about the cargo.

'But that's the whole point,' Markovski persisted, 'I spoke to Gennadi and he said that he had absolutely no idea what this whole thing was about. What's more, he doesn't know any of the people who are arriving from Moscow with the cargo. It's all really weird, if you ask me.'

Gennadi, to whom Markovski was referring, was a colonel of the External Intelligence, or SVR as it was known, who was in charge of security at the embassy. He had arrived in another car with one his deputies, but for some reason kept a low profile and stayed in the background. It seemed odd, as he was the man who should have been overseeing the whole operation.

The crates were unloaded from the plane onto the trucks specially hired for the occasion. All of them were driven by embassy staff.

Boris greeted the five men who arrived on the plane. But they didn't even bother to be friendly.

'I presume everything has been arranged for us at the vacant building?' inquired the tall man with dark hair who was obviously in charge of the group. His name was Ruslan Sultanov.

'Yes, everything's ready,' Boris said. 'Temporary living quarters have been provided for you and your colleagues at the vacant building at number 10. A driver will be at your disposal at all times.'

'We don't need the driver, just the car,' Sultanov snapped back.

The five men got into an embassy van and the convoy drove off. On arrival at Kensington Palace Gardens the crates were unloaded and carried into the number 10 building. It was still officially part of the Russian embassy, although it was practically empty, ready to be handed over to the landlords in a few months' time. In order to accommodate the team from Moscow some furniture had been brought back and put into several rooms on the ground floor.

Once all the crates had been carried inside Sultanov came over to Boris.

'I want to see the ambassador,' he demanded.

Boris was getting really annoyed with the man. There was something very unpleasant about his appearance, his unshaven face, cold staring eyes and strong smell of some cheap aftershave. Not to mention the attitude problem.

'I'll inform the ambassador of your request,' Boris said.

Sultanov shook his head.

'I want to see him immediately,' he said. 'We go now!'

★

The ambassador made them wait for a good half an hour. He was from the old guard at the Ministry of Foreign Affairs and looked more like a Communist Party official than a diplomat, with his big round face, heavy jaw, short-cut grey hair and a habit of speaking slowly, pronouncing every word very clearly. He didn't like the fact that Moscow had only informed him at the very last moment that an important cargo was arriving. He was not at all happy with the new informal ways in the ministry. He was from the old school and was proud of it.

The ambassador looked through the letter brought by Sultanov. Having read it, he took his time to remove his reading glasses and put them into a black leather case. He then opened another case, took out his usual gold-rimmed glasses and put them on.

'I don't really understand why you've come to see me,' he said to Sultanov. The tone was cold and official. 'Judging by the nature of your cargo you should deal with our intelligence station chief. I suggest that you talk to the General.'

'But this is a matter of national security and I have instructions from Deputy Minister Sergei Titov to ask you for your full support,' Sultanov protested. 'We need the total cooperation of the embassy and all the back-up we require. Deputy Minister Titov said—'

'Deputy Minister Titov is in charge of administrative affairs, as you know,' the ambassador cut him short, 'and has been in his job barely a month. Are you seriously saying that he wishes me to deal with classified technical information and get involved in some undercover operation of the Russian intelligence?'

Sultanov was obviously furious, but said nothing, as he got up from his chair and walked out of the room. Boris was looking at the ambassador, apparently at a loss what to do.

'Well, Boris Nikolaevich,' the ambassador said, 'don't just sit there, see that our guest doesn't wander into some room he shouldn't be in.'

Boris got up and rushed to catch up with Sultanov.

★

Alex and Clay were awaiting further instructions from London. George had promised them to get in touch as soon as he had sorted out 'some details' in London, but two days later there was still no word from him.

Alex suspected that the mysterious 'property file', not to mention copies of confidential government documents, might have something to do with the delay. It was also possible that George's friends were reviewing their options after the two Chechens got killed. It was still unclear who killed them and why.

But whatever the answer, the job in Moscow was not over yet. The documents that were photographed at Seraphim's villa proved that the gang was earning a lot of money by setting up its rivals. The papers also showed that regular payments had been made to corrupt officials who were supposed to make life difficult for the Central Brotherhood's competitors.

These documents had yet to surface in the most awkward of places so as to cause maximum damage to the Crow and his people. There was also another way of hitting them where it really hurt. The idea was to plant one set of copied papers in Shark's country house along with the camera that was used to make the photos. Pavel would then expose Shark as the 'traitor' and he would have a tough time explaining how the papers got to him in the first place.

It was up to Alex and Clay to plant the documents. But before they could make a move they had to get the plan of Shark's country house. Lidia came up with an idea. She would pass word to Shark that she wanted to meet him to discuss a business matter, something to do with an exchange of roubles into dollars. She was going to suggest that the meeting take place at his country house. She would offer to bring along some of the girls she knew and introduce them to Shark and his friends. During the party she would have a look around and take some photos with a miniature camera, just as Pavel had done in Seraphim's villa.

But Pavel was not at all happy with the arrangement.

'It's too dangerous,' he told Lidia. 'The man's a maniac and a drug addict. He may go berserk at any moment.'

Lidia looked at him and smiled.

'Don't worry about me,' she said. 'I'll see that he gets drunk real fast and I'll slip away an honest girl. And besides, we won't be alone. There'll be other people there.'

Pavel still felt uneasy.

★

In a pub in North London George Blunt was having a pint of Guinness. George liked that pub. It still retained the old traditions and was not filled with noisy tourists all day. And the Guinness seemed especially good, with a thick creamy top and a taste that matched the colour.

George was waiting for Ron Baker. Jeremy had asked Ron to look into the matter of the two Chechens getting killed outside the Oscar Wilde. Ron had travelled to Moscow where he'd spent several days meeting some of the people he knew there. He had returned to London only the day before.

Ron walked into the pub. He immediately recognised George and nodded to him. They had never met before but both were former military men and could distinguish each other from the civilian crowd.

George stood up.

'Pleasure to meet you, sir,' he said.

'I did hope that there would be no need for the "sir",' Ron said.

'I'm sorry, sir,' George said.

'At ease,' Ron said jokingly.

He sat down at the table. George looked at him inquiringly.

'I'll have what you're having,' Ron said.

George signalled to the girl at the bar counter and she took a large glass and slowly started pouring in the Guinness.

'How did you find Moscow, sir?' George said.

Ron grinned.

'Not much change there,' he said. 'Everybody's complaining about the hardships yet everyone manages to live quite well. Nobody gets paid for months but the shops are doing brisk business. The economy is on the verge of collapse and yet industry is still functioning and supermarkets are full. The women look great and the men are not very sober. Just like before the gangsters are driving around in expensive cars during the day and playing at casinos all night. And the police still harass the public and ignore the real criminals. Life goes on.'

The girl brought the Guinness. Once she was gone George got straight down to business.

'Is there any word about the unfortunate incident on the embankment?' he asked.

Ron nodded.

'It has been established that there were three snipers shooting at the time,' he said. 'Two of them were firing from the roof of the House on the Embankment and the third one was positioned on the roof of a house across the Moscow Canal.'

'And what is the official version of the incident?' George said.

'Well, the authorities are saying it was a typical contract killing,' Ron said, 'although they can't understand why so many people were involved in the shooting. They did manage to establish that the two men were killed by a sniper who used an American-made rifle. But they also found other bullets on the scene that came from two weapons that are unknown in Russia.'

'Very interesting,' George said. 'And what might be the outcome of the investigation?'

Ron took a sip of Guinness.

'That's where things get really complicated,' he said. 'It seems that right from the start the Kremlin's secret service or, as they call themselves, the Presidential Protection Service, took a keen interest in this case. The Kremlin security people arrived at the scene of the shooting almost immediately and informed the police that they would be taking over the investigation as the two arms dealers were killed practically outside the Kremlin walls.'

George's right eyebrow went up a bit. Ron noticed it.

'I know, I know,' he said, 'it all sounds very unusual. And believe me, even the Russian police investigators were very surprised. But when they were told to report all their findings to the Kremlin secret service they got really angry. It seems the Kremlin bodyguards have been bossing the police and even the FSB around for some time and the resentment between the sides has been building up recently. It looks like the Kremlin boys are once again trying to get involved in matters that shouldn't really concern them. I suspect they have some sort of an agenda of their own, though only time will tell what they're really up to. But at the moment no one seems to be trying very hard to find the killers of the two arms dealers.'

George frowned and looked at his Guinness for a while.

'So the Russian authorities knew what these two Chechens were up to?' he asked.

'It seems so,' Ron said. 'They must have been under surveillance for some time. Otherwise how would the Kremlin secret service people be on the scene in a matter of minutes and know who they were and what they did?'

George licked his lips.

'It all fits into a pattern,' he said.

'And what pattern might that be?' Ron asked.

'A pattern developing in the fight against organised crime in Russia,' George explained. 'I have a couple of friends, experts on Russia, who have told me about their suspicions that some people at the very top in Russia, maybe even as high as the Kremlin, are involved in staging assassinations of top criminals who are getting too big for their boots. So if we assume for a moment the possibility that someone in Moscow found out about our operation we can see how he might have been tempted to get involved.'

Ron looked surprised.

'Are you implying that someone has hijacked Operation Saving Ivan?' he said.

'I'm afraid that's what it looks like, sir,' George said. 'Care for another Guinness?'

★

The attempted robbery, and especially the mysterious ending to his adventure, were still preoccupying Alex's mind. He felt uneasy, especially as he hadn't told George about the nasty incident outside the restaurant. Somehow he hadn't found the courage to come clean.

He was still unable to figure out what had actually happened on that night. It all seemed weird, surreal even. Someone had interfered and chased his attackers away. Someone had saved him from freezing to death and took the trouble of returning all his possessions and carrying him to a warm place. He wanted to know who that someone was.

On the third day of waiting for word from London Alex decided to investigate. He told Clay and Motya that he wanted to get some fresh air and quickly left the flat before they got any ideas of going out with him.

When he approached the restaurant he immediately recognised the doorman who let him in on the night he was drugged. He must have been the one who informed the two attackers about him. Alex walked past the restaurant's entrance a couple of times thinking how he could lure the old man outside. It made no sense to try and make him talk in front of his mates.

After wandering around the square for about forty minutes Alex was freezing and was thinking about returning to the flat when he saw the doorman come out of the restaurant. He was dressed in a shabby grey coat and a fur hat that had long lost all shape and form. He walked down a narrow pedestrian road leading in the direction of Petrovka Street. Alex followed him at a distance. Soon the old man approached a two-storey building and walked down the stairs to the basement. When Alex reached the spot he saw the sign 'Beer Restaurant'.

He waited for a couple of minutes and then walked down the steps and opened the door. The smell inside was horrendous. It was a combination of stale beer, cheap tobacco, smoked fish and piss. The place was a real dump. It was amazing that the owners had the nerve to call it a 'restaurant'.

It was like a scene from the Soviet days. There were no chairs and the customers stood around plastic tables, sipping beer from cracked glasses and glass jars. They filled their glasses and jars from machines, using tokens they bought from the cashier, a big woman in a soiled apron who was wearing an expensive fur hat and large diamond earrings.

Alex looked around and saw the doorman standing at one of the tables with two men. He got himself a glass of beer and found a place at one of the tables.

The place was packed. Most of the customers were obviously regulars. Some were so drunk they could barely stand. The smoke from the cheap Russian cigarettes was making Alex's eyes itch. He was hoping that the doorman wouldn't stay for too long in that dump. Before coming inside, Alex had spotted a narrow alley beside the pub and was planning to force the doorman into it to have a talk with him.

Alex tasted the beer and immediately spat it out. It was really bad. No wonder some people around him were mixing beer with vodka to kill the taste and get drunk quickly.

The doorman suddenly finished his conversation with the two men and started moving through the crowd towards the exit. Alex put down his nearly full glass and followed him. As soon as he had left a man grabbed his glass and drank the contents in one go.

Alex ran up the stairs and saw the old man making his way back to the restaurant. He caught up with him and grabbed him by the collar of his coat.

Before the doorman could utter a word, he pushed him into the narrow alley. There Alex turned the man around and pressed him against the wall.

'We meet again, old man,' he said in Russian. 'I bet you didn't expect to see me this soon!'

The doorman looked frightened.

'I don't know you,' he mumbled. 'You probably mistake me for someone else. I've never seen you before.'

'Sure you didn't,' Alex said, 'and I bet you don't know the two pricks who tried to rob me two days ago.'

The old man looked closely at Alex.

'Ah yes, now I remember you,' he said, 'you were that customer who got drunk and was taken outside by two men for some fresh air. And then the people from the Kremlin secret service beat the crap out of them.'

Alex was not expecting to hear that. He was ready for anything – Good Samaritans, Salvation Army, concerned citizens coming to his rescue. But the Kremlin secret service? Now *that* was completely unexpected.

He loosened his grip on the doorman.

'How did you know they were the Kremlin boys?' he asked with suspicion.

The old man smiled.

'They showed me an ID when they walked in,' he said. 'I even remember thinking that it was strange to see people from the Ninth Directorate of the FSB, *devyatka*, the ones that are responsible for guarding important people and even the President himself, flashing their ID cards. They usually keep a low profile, these guys. But there they were, out in the street, saving your skin.'

'How come you know so much about those guys?' Alex said.

The old man laughed.

'Well I should, shouldn't I,' he said. 'My son works in the

Ninth Directorate. Comes to see me once in a while with his friends to have lunch or dinner.'

Nice place, Alex thought. Couldn't have picked a better one if I'd tried. He now knew that he had no choice but to tell George about his little adventure. They were under surveillance by the Kremlin secret service and that meant they had to get out of Moscow. The sooner the better.

★

The planned launch of a new national British newspaper, *The Daily News*, was taking up so much of Jeremy's time that for a while he had lost track of all other events in his life. He had invested a lot of his own money in the project and he wanted everything to be exactly right.

Jeremy spent a whole week at his office going over the dummy issue of the first edition of *The Daily News*. He had decided to adopt the tabloid format that had proved so much more successful with readers over the years than the broadsheets. There was of course always a danger that the new paper would be seen as just another tabloid, but Jeremy was prepared to take that risk. He put his faith in the editor of the new paper, a talented journalist and a good administrator.

Jeremy was hoping that the traditional journalistic approach would make his paper a success. He was also quietly talking to some of the best names in the business to persuade them to contribute to his paper regularly. He knew they would not come cheap, but they were worth it.

What he needed now was an exclusive story to put on the front page of the first issue of *The Daily News* that would hit the news stands in several weeks' time…

In the midst of all this came the call from George, asking for a meeting. With all his attention focused on his newspaper, Jeremy had completely lost the Moscow plot.

'We've got a problem, sir,' George said when he had settled down in the chair across from the desk in Jeremy's office. 'Mr Baker came back from Moscow with some very worrying news.'

Jeremy looked at him.

'Tell me all about it,' he said. 'I'm all ears.'

★

It was party time at Shark's country house. There was constant loud laughter coming from downstairs. Someone was telling a joke and everyone was laughing in anticipation of a funny ending.

Shark was upstairs with three of his men.

'Okay, okay,' he was saying to them, 'who of you guys managed to set me up with the pig's bitch?'

Each man had that look on his face that was supposed to imply that he had played a major role in setting up the meeting with the Countess. In reality none of them had had anything to do with it. Lidia had arranged everything herself. She found out where Shark's people usually hung out. It turned out to be the bar on the ground floor of the Intourist Hotel, a hideous-looking glass and concrete building in the centre of Moscow. She dressed up for the occasion – leather skirt and jacket, high-heeled shoes, fishnet stockings – and went to the bar. She gave the waiter ten dollars and told him that she'd like a table near the entrance all to herself.

It didn't take long for Shark's boys to notice a stunning woman sitting all alone. If they had any brains they would have stayed away from her. The bar at Intourist Hotel was not a good place to approach lonely beautiful women, unless you were looking for trouble that is.

Soon they were sitting with her and buying her drinks. Lidia skilfully steered the conversation into areas that were bound to bring up the name of Shark. And after twenty minutes or so of seemingly innocent exchanges she managed to pass on a message to Shark about a possible business meeting. She gave her phone number to one of the three men whom she thought smart enough to understand what was needed of him. He passed the word to Shark, who got interested and called Lidia. The meeting was set up at his country house for the following evening.

★

Shark was grinning.

He was going to teach Batalov a lesson. While he was searching for the informer in their gang, Shark was going to screw his girlfriend. He still couldn't understand why Seraphim not only let the cop live but took him on as his personal advisor. Shark didn't trust Pavel: the way he got into the restaurant that evening, the way he sneaked outside when the shooting started. He had ordered his men to dig up anything they could on the cop. They already had a word with some of their contacts in the police, but no one could tell them anything of any interest.

Shark quietly put a reward on the cop's head. Anyone who got any information was promised ten grand. He wasn't prepared to allow some prick to simply jump on board. He didn't know what Seraphim's plans were, but he had ideas of his own. He had to protect his boss against people like that cop.

Shark had known Seraphim since they were both kids. They were of the same age and grew up together in a rough neighbourhood in Begovaya Street, close to the famous Moscow racetrack. They lived in a grim block of flats built by German war prisoners in the 1940s.

They became friends after one particular incident. That day there was a big fight outside the Tempo cinema on Begovaya Street between the locals and some hoodlums from the Sokol district. They'd been feuding for years and occasionally would battle it out in some prearranged place. This fight broke out after nearly half an hour of both sides hurling abuse at each other. Seraphim, Shark and several other kids were watching from behind an ice cream kiosk. They were frightened and yet could not force themselves to leave. It was the same strange feeling that they had experienced when they witnessed funeral processions.

After a while the fight turned nasty. Someone took out a knife and stabbed one of the locals with it. The guy with the knife started to run away but bumped into Shark who had come out from behind the kiosk to get a better view of the fight. The man tripped over him and fell to the ground.

All the boys immediately disappeared. But Seraphim was paralysed with fear and could not move. The guy with the knife got up, looking at Shark with his bloodshot eyes.

'You little shit!' he growled. 'I'm gonna cut your heart out!'

Seraphim wanted to call for help but his throat produced only some strange gurgling noises as if something had got stuck there.

His whole body was trembling and he felt warm urine run down his left leg. He was hoping that the man with the knife wouldn't notice him. But he did.

'What are you staring at?' he shouted, turning to Seraphim. 'You'll be next after I deal with this—'

He didn't have the chance to finish. While he was looking at Seraphim, Shark jumped to his feet, grabbed a stone from the ground, and hit him on the head with all his strength. The man dropped the knife and fell down.

'Run for it!' Shark yelled. But Seraphim did not follow him. He went up to the man lying on the ground. He looked at him and then started kicking him as hard as he could. His fear had turned into uncontrollable rage.

Shark had covered a good hundred metres before he turned around. He saw Seraphim kick the man on the ground several times and then run off in the opposite direction.

They met the next day outside their school. Seraphim was really worried that Shark noticed how frightened he had been of the man with the knife and how he'd wet his pants. If word got round about it he would have been branded a coward and a 'pissing baby' for years to come. But for some reason the dumb bastard seemed to have got a different impression.

'You did that piece of shit well yesterday,' Shark said to him. 'He was squealing like a pig when you kicked 'im. You was a real hero.'

From that moment they became friends.

Years later their paths crossed again. By that time Shark had been in jail twice already and was involved in extortion and peddling counterfeit booze. Seraphim needed someone with criminal authority to help him deal with stubborn competitors. Shark was perfect for the job. He did all the dirty work for Seraphim and killed at least a dozen people who were causing problems for his boss. Seraphim pretended not to notice the disappearance of his enemies. He never actually asked Shark directly to kill anyone. He'd just tell him to 'deal with the problem' and the problem would soon be resolved, simply because the people who were causing it would vanish.

Although Shark was a cold-blooded killer he had a strange

obsession with Seraphim. The image of him kicking the man on the ground had imprinted itself in his brain and from that moment he thought of himself as for ever connected to the Crow. Like a big bully who goes all soft when his kid brother runs to him for help, Shark protected his friend from the outside world. And if he thought that anyone was planning to hurt his friend he would act swiftly and ruthlessly.

And Pavel, in his opinion, was someone who posed a danger to the Crow.

★

The laughter downstairs died down. Judging by the sound of a car pulling up outside, the guests had arrived.

The Countess said she wanted to discuss business. Something about changing dollars for roubles or the other way round. But Shark was more interested in other things. He had heard that some foreigners paid up to five grand for a night with the Countess in the old days. So she must have been good considering that the top hookers were charging no more than a thousand a night in those times.

Shark was planning to try her out himself. He pulled out the top drawer of the table and took out a small plastic bag with white powder.

'I think we need an injection of strength,' he said. 'Man's sort of strength.'

The three men in the room roared with laughter.

★

Out of the blue George appeared in Moscow.

He called from Sheremetyevo-2 Airport and said that he'd be at the flat in about an hour. Alex was dreading the moment he would have to tell him about his unfortunate adventure. The only conciliation was that, had he not ventured out that night he would have never found out that the Kremlin people were watching them.

When George finally arrived, the three of them gathered in the dining room.

'The situation has changed,' George told Alex and Clay. 'We'll have to finish the job even faster than we'd planned. And we have to be extra careful and watch our backs all the time.'

It was then that Alex suddenly realised that George probably knew about them being monitored by the Russians. Otherwise, he reckoned, why would he come to Moscow and warn them to be extra vigilant?

When George went to the kitchen to fix himself a drink, Alex quickly followed him to have a word in private. While Alex was telling him about the events of that night George was sipping whisky and making no comments. Not once did he look up, preferring to study the ice cubes in his glass. When Alex finished his story, George drank his whisky and put the glass on the table.

'So, what do you make of it all?' he asked looking at Alex.

There was no hint of anger or irritation in his voice. Alex was now completely certain that George knew about the surveillance.

'I guess someone tipped the Russians about us coming here,' he said. 'And if the two guys in the restaurant were really from the Kremlin secret service, as the old man said, then it means that they must be watching our every move. The only thing that puzzles me is why on earth would the presidential bodyguards be interested in us? I can understand the cops or the KGB – although these guys as I understand are part of the KGB – but why the hell should the Kremlin secret service be involved at all?'

George did not respond for a while. He seemed to be lost in his thoughts. Alex felt that the situation was not looking good at all. By his reckoning the best thing to do was to get the hell out of Russia as soon as possible.

But George seemed to have other ideas.

'We continue as if nothing's happened,' he said. 'Under no circumstances do we show the people who are watching us that we know that they know that we know.'

★

Against George's advice Jeremy arrived in Moscow.

It was the first time he had ignored George's opinion, but he felt that he had no other choice but to travel to Russia. He had initiated the operation, and now that the people he had hired for the job were in trouble, he felt obliged to protect them. In his business dealings he always took personal responsibility for his actions. When he offered to help Boris he knew there and then that the buck would stop with him. In the long run he had enough contacts around the world to avoid a political scandal. And he was prepared to use his chequebook if the need arose to bail out the team in Moscow.

There was also the matter of the strange file found in Seraphim's villa that contained information about Boris and his son, and about properties in London. It seemed to indicate that the gang was actually planning to buy up real estate in the British capital. But why choose houses on Kensington Palace Gardens only? And why go to all that trouble by setting up Ivan and demanding that his father provide information about the property market in London? It all just didn't make sense and had to be investigated.

Jeremy booked into the Metropole, a five-star hotel in the centre of Moscow that had been recently refurbished at a cost of several million dollars. The next day he took a taxi to the International Trade Centre where a meeting had been arranged with one of Ron Baker's contacts, Daniel Liberman, an American businessman of Russian origin. He was an oil trader with wide connections in Moscow. The Russian oil industry at the time was mostly run by two kinds of people – retired or active intelligence officers, or gangsters – so Liberman had to tread a fine line. He kept his ear to the ground and knew of many things outside the oil sector. He was a short, bald, energetic man who spoke four languages and spent most of his time travelling across the former Soviet Union pitching for business.

They met at a restaurant called China Garden. The owner of the place was an old friend of George's, a businessman from India who owned several restaurants in the Russian capital. Liberman told Jeremy that the gang headed by the Crow was close to some very important people at the top and had managed to avoid problems with the law by using their contacts in the government.

'So whom do you suggest we approach to get things moving?' Jeremy said. 'Who will act on the information that we have and go after the Crow and his people?'

Liberman frowned and scratched his forehead.

'It's a difficult question,' he said. 'Corruption in Russia is so widespread that you never know who might be linked to some criminal group. But if I had to make a choice I'd probably take my chances with General Aleksei Mikhailov. He is Deputy Director of the Federal Security Service and is one of the people who would continue to investigate a case even if top names came up.'

'How do you suggest we do it?' Jeremy said.

'You give me the documents and I'll make sure that they get to the General,' Liberman said.

They agreed that George would pass him the documents as soon as possible.

★

The next day Jeremy met with George and told him about his conversation with Liberman.

They were walking slowly through Red Square, passing the famous St Basil Cathedral, one of the most beautiful and original cathedrals in the world. According to legend, when it was built the tsar ordered the two craftsmen who designed the cathedral to be blinded so that they would never create anything as beautiful again.

'So, as I understand, someone in the Russian intelligence service knows about our operation,' Jeremy said. He was covering his mouth with his scarf against the windy gusts coming from the Moscow River. 'So there must have been a leak somewhere right from the very start.'

'I believe so, sir,' George said, holding his hand in front of his mouth.

'Can they be watching us now?' Jeremy said turning round suddenly as if to check his theory.

George nodded.

'They might be,' he said. 'We're on their turf so they can do as they please.'

Jeremy looked at the people around them. They seemed to be ordinary people enjoying themselves. No suspicious characters in the vicinity. The KGB must have polished its act. He turned back to George.

'So where do we stand then?'

George hesitated for a second.

'Well,' he said, 'the Russians obviously know most of the details, but up to now they didn't seem to mind. The Crow is a dangerous man and many people would love to see him removed. And I guess in their view it might just as well be us. The only problem is, what happens after we bring the Central Brotherhood down? Will they let us disappear or will they go after us?'

Jeremy stopped opposite Lenin's mausoleum. Despite the cold and the wind there was a queue of people waiting to see the mummified remains of the communist leader. These people probably had no idea that Lenin was a paid agent of German intelligence and officially approved the creation of the first ever labour camps in 1918. Millions of Russians later perished in these vast prisons where people were used as slave labourers under communist rule. The Nazis copied and developed Lenin with their concentration camps. But even the Nazis proved to be less efficient than the monsters they were inspired by. There were thousands of cases when prisoners had managed to escape from the German concentration camps. But there were very few, if any, escapes from the Russian labour camps in all the time of their existence.

Jeremy looked at the slow-moving queue for a moment and then turned to George.

'Who do you think the traitor is?' he asked. 'Is it our Russian contact, Pavel Batalov?'

'I don't think so,' George said. 'I had a word with him and, in my opinion, he's in the clear. But the most important thing is that the gang still doesn't know about our operation. So my guess is that the KGB is keeping quiet about us. I suspect they want to use us as a weapon against the Crow and his men. But as I said, I fear that once we have dealt with the gang they might be tempted to go after us…'

George stopped and looked at Jeremy, leaving him the option of spelling out the final decision.

'Operation Saving Ivan will continue,' Jeremy said. 'I'm going back to London and I'll have a talk with Ron Baker and some other people who might be able to help us find out how long the

Russians would be prepared to tolerate us. They'll also know what to do if things get out of control.'

They parted at the Revolution Square underground station, three hundred yards from the Metropole hotel.

Two men in sheepskin jackets followed George at a distance and another two went after Jeremy.

★

Early in the morning a convoy of five trucks left the warehouse area of Boutovo outside Moscow and travelled under heavy guard down the Big Moscow Circular Motorway to the Sheremetyevo-1 Airport. Until 1980 it was the main international airport in the Russian capital. But following construction of the Sheremetyevo-2 International Terminal for the Moscow Olympic Games it was mostly used for domestic travel, with only occasional flights abroad.

The trucks were accompanied by five police cars with their lights flashing on and a company of Interior Ministry troops in several vans. The convoy started its journey while it was still dark and covered the whole distance in less than two hours.

On arrival at the airport the trucks were allowed to drive on to the airfield. A specially chartered cargo plane was waiting for them at the far end of the runway. The trucks were unloaded and the crates carried on board the plane. They were all different shapes and sizes and were marked 'Diplomatic Cargo, Handle With Care'. After the trucks had left the airfield, soldiers armed with sub-machine guns formed a ring around the plane. They had orders to shoot anyone attempting to approach the aircraft without giving the password.

Later in the day a coach brought the plane crew and four other people who were to accompany the cargo abroad. One of them carried a letter signed by Deputy Foreign Minister Sergei Titov authorising the delivery of the special cargo to the Russian embassy in London. It was destined to be stored at 13 Kensington Palace Gardens, in the underground garages of the Russian ambassador's residency.

The ambassador was informed that the sealed crates contained items for an exhibition of Russian folk art that would be shown at a later date across Western Europe, the United States and Asia. He was also told that a special government envoy would be arriving soon to hold discussions with British officials and businessmen about organising the world-wide exhibition.

★

The plan to exhibit priceless national treasures abroad was the brainchild of a group of officials in the Kremlin. They were desperately looking for ways to raise money in order to solve the financial crisis in the country. The funds were needed to pay pensioners and officers in the armed forces, civil servants, miners and oil workers. As the elections were approaching, the Kremlin needed to boost the President's standing in the public opinion polls which was declining as more and more people realised that the new head of state was no different from the previous one.

The Kremlin aides tried everything. There was even talk about the possible sale of nuclear technology to developing nations.

It was then that an idea of using Russia's national treasures as collateral for a massive short-term loan came seemingly out of nowhere. No one seemed to remember how it was actually raised during the discussions conducted behind the Kremlin walls. It just sort of appeared and landed as a proposal on several tables. It was as if some invisible hand was pushing through the idea, which at first sounded absolutely crazy, even bordering on treason. But the more the Kremlin aides looked into it, the less unacceptable it seemed. And considering the desperate situation the country was in, it gradually started to look very attractive indeed.

The collection of national treasures would be taken out of the country to be shown around the world as a long-running exhibition to raise funds for social programmes. Once the Russian public had grown used to the idea that the treasures were destined to 'tour abroad' to raise money for the state, a secret deal would be struck with a group of banks for a loan that would be used to pay the bills and finance the next election. The confidential agreement would state that until the loan was repaid the collection would not return to Russia. A special protocol would confirm that in case of non-payment the treasures would become the property of the group of lenders.

That was the worst possible scenario. But the Kremlin aides believed that once oil prices recovered the situation would improve, the loan would be repaid, and the treasures would return safely to Russia.

The only question was, should the President, who was at the time recovering from a mild heart attack, be informed of the plan? At a meeting of the closest aides it was decided that the head of state should be spared and kept unaware of the scheme. For the time being at least.

Preparations for the exhibition started in January. The biggest problem, as it turned out, was to persuade the directors of various museums, including the Kremlin's Armoury, to let go of their priceless treasures. That proved very difficult and it took a lot of effort to force them to agree. But eventually the precious collection was put together. A cautious approach was made to a group of Western banks. They responded well to the idea of releasing a substantial loan secured by the national treasures of Russia that would be kept in the West and supported by the relevant documents.

The stage was set for a major loan agreement that would help bail Russia out in time for the presidential elections.

★

The annual Oil Week opened in London in March.

These conferences first began in 1992 and proved very popular with oil traders and businessmen from Russia and other former republics of the Soviet Union. For them it was a good opportunity to meet not only with executives from the Western big oil companies, but to mix with each other. In Moscow everyone was always too busy to find time for a meeting and it sometimes took days and even weeks to get through to some top executives on the phone, not to mention meeting them in person. But in London things were different. During Oil Week you could easily walk up to a president or chairman of a major company and talk to them over a drink without having to make appointments or wait for hours outside their offices. Russian businessmen abroad tended to unwind and shed that silly air of importance that makes them elusive and unapproachable back home.

Two days before the start of Oil Week Boris got a phone call from a Russian man who told him that he'd arrived to take part in the conference together with a colleague and wanted to meet him to discuss one 'pressing matter'. The man who introduced himself only as Glyeb said that he got Boris's phone number from a mutual friend in the Ministry of Foreign Affairs.

There was nothing unusual about the call, especially as the name of his close college friend had been mentioned, so Boris had no reservations about agreeing to see the two visitors. They met in a pub, not far from the Russian embassy. It was an Irish pub which the diplomats frequently visited as food was served all day and the Guinness was always extremely good.

After getting the drinks and settling down at a table, one of the two men who had earlier called Boris, told him that they were both from the SVR, the Russian External Intelligence, posing as oil experts. Glyeb, who looked more like a convict with his broken nose and a scar on his left cheek, suddenly asked, 'Comrade Ossinski, do you by any chance know a man by the name of Georgi Volkov?'

Boris nearly choked on his Guinness.

'What about him?' he said.

'We were informed that he had contacted you here in London,' said Glyeb. 'We'd like to know what he wanted from you and where he is now.'

Boris knew that he had no choice but to tell the two SVR officers about Volkov. Especially as it was obvious that they knew about him anyway.

'He came to see me about three weeks ago. He told me that my son was in trouble and offered to help. We met once again afterwards, but I haven't heard from him since.'

Glyeb nodded as if what he heard was correct.

'So, what was the problem with your son?' the second man asked. His name was Shamil. He had dark hair and a dark beard and looked like a Chechen warlord.

Boris hesitated for a moment. He was talking to people who he did not really know and they were asking about things that he hadn't told anyone at the embassy. As if guessing what was going through his mind, Glyeb assured him that everything they were talking about would be kept strictly in confidence.

'My son was accused of drug possession,' Boris said, anxiety showing on his face. 'But I can assure you it was a mistake! My boy would never be involved with drugs! He was framed!'

The two men seemed unmoved by the outburst.

'For the moment we'd prefer not to discuss the matter,' Glyeb said. 'We do know about your son's problems and understand that something was not right. I can promise you that once our operation is over we'll clear your son's name. I only hope that you didn't tell anyone else about your problem, especially the locals.'

Glyeb looked at Boris, who shook his head implying that he had spoken to no one.

'At the moment we are conducting an investigation and are trying to track down a group of people. We suspect that these people are using your son to blackmail you,' Glyeb said.

'But why should they blackmail me?' Boris said. He was getting more and more nervous.

'That's exactly what we wanted to find out from you,' Glyeb said. 'What did Volkov ask you to do for him?'

Boris took a deep breath.

'Volkov asked me to provide him with information about the properties in Kensington Palace Gardens,' he said. 'I personally thought it sounded very strange. I mean, what sort of Russian could afford houses in that road? You have to have many millions to buy a place there.'

Glyeb nodded understandingly.

'And did you get him that information?' he asked.

Boris frowned.

'I did start to get some documents together,' he said, 'but Volkov never showed up again. He was supposed to stay in touch with me but never called since our last meeting.'

Glyeb nodded again.

'We would need to see these documents,' he said. 'To evaluate what it was that the criminals were trying to find out.'

Boris promised to pass the files to him. He was getting more and more upset. Glyeb looked inquiringly at his partner and the man nodded to him as if giving him the go-ahead for something.

'Comrade Ossinski,' Glyeb said in an official voice, 'what I'm about to tell you is a matter of national security.'

In the next ten minutes Boris learnt about a joint covert operation by the Russian and British intelligence services to stop illegal transferrals of large amounts of Russian federal budget money to the West. Top Russian government officials were suspected of being involved in the scheme. The losses to the Russian state amounted to several billion US dollars a year. The latest illegal transfer of funds was destined for London. Volkov was suspected of links to the group that was behind it and Boris was probably targeted as one of the people who could have provided important information to the gang. He'd been in Britain for nearly five years; he was in charge of the economic group in the embassy and obviously had contacts in the business community.

A whole new picture was emerging. Instead of flying to Moscow and meeting the appropriate people Boris made a crucial mistake and had turned for help to Jeremy. But how could he have known?

He was completely overwhelmed by this new information. He was trying to assess the situation and his thoughts had drifted away so that he did not even hear the question addressed to him.

'So are you sure that nobody else knows about Volkov?' Glyeb was asking.

Boris looked at him, trying to understand what the question was.

'I did mention him in passing to one Russian who is based here,' he said. 'But it was in very general terms, without giving his name or anything, and I only discussed it in the context of the London property market. He is a big expert on property you see.'

'What is his name?' Glyeb said, his face suddenly turning serious.

Boris felt that no harm could come to Mironov if he gave the two agents his details.

'His name is Vadim Mironov,' he said. 'He's a former diplomat who is now a businessman in London. I thought that with his help I could gather all the relevant information about properties in Kensington Palace Gardens.'

Both Glyeb and Shamil watched him in silence for a while. Boris suddenly felt very uncomfortable. He was beginning to think that this whole affair might still backfire on him.

'That was not very wise of you,' Glyeb said finally, breaking the unpleasant silence. 'What if this Mironov is connected to the criminals in Russia? Give us his number and we'll talk to him. And I hope that this time you will keep our conversation to yourself. You should realise that any disclosure can undermine our whole operation.'

Boris nodded, scribbling down Mironov's phone number on a piece of paper.

'And one more thing,' Glyeb said, taking the paper from him. 'Recently your embassy received a cargo of communications equipment that was stored in the number 10 building. As I understand, there were questions raised about the delivery and the people who came over. I want you to know that the equipment has been sent with the approval of the highest authority in Moscow to help carry out the undercover operation.'

Glyeb looked hard at Boris, who swallowed nervously a couple of times.

'I hope that you'll be able to stop any unnecessary rumours spreading in the embassy and inform us about any inquiries being made,' Glyeb said. 'We suspect that some diplomats in your embassy might be linked to the gang so it would be important to keep them unaware of the operation.'

Boris was nodding, realising at that moment that he had made a terrible blunder by sharing his secret with Jeremy. He would have to get in touch with him as soon as possible to explain himself, he thought.

★

In Soviet times the ruling Politburo of the Communist Party of the Soviet Union gathered every week. For most people, the whole process of decision making in the USSR was shrouded in mystery. Newspaper reports presented a picture of a group of wise elderly statesmen meeting on a regular basis to discuss matters of internal and international policy. Statements condemning 'international imperialist forces' for committing some new crime would be approved. Reports on the successful development of some sectors of the Soviet economy would be adopted.

In reality, though, the Politburo members were rubber-stamping decisions already made by the general secretary of the Communist Party and his closest aides and advisors. The only reason why these weekly meetings took place at all was dictated by the need to have 'collective responsibility of the leadership'. Since Vladimir Lenin's time, this arrangement had been considered sacred by the leaders of the Soviet Union. The collective responsibility principle meant that all the Politburo members unanimously approved all decisions, and later, when things went horribly wrong, as they usually did, no one was held personally responsible for anything.

Seraphim inadvertently copied the communist system and set up his own 'politburo', as he called the circle of his closest people who helped him run his empire. Although he had no inside knowledge of how things were run in communist times, his 'collective leadership' in practice worked pretty much along the same lines as in Soviet days. He came up with decisions, discussed them with Shark or some other close confidants, and they were later approved without any resistance. And if things went badly wrong, well, there was no one to blame. Just like in the good old Soviet times.

An emergency meeting of the 'politburo' was being held in Seraphim's villa.

Twenty 'members' were present. Once everyone calmed down Seraphim said, 'Brothers, I've invited you today to tell you that I'm stepping down as leader of our organisation. I propose that you nominate two people, one of whom will replace me, and that we hold a vote in one month's time to elect the new head of the group.'

His words had the effect of a bombshell. No one could have expected the announcement. Only Shark seemed indifferent, although it was news to him just like for everyone else present.

For a while there was total silence. The first to break it was Scarface. He didn't actually have any scars on his face, but he'd been such a big fan of the movie *Scarface* with Al Pacino that he couldn't resist the temptation to name himself after the main character in the film. Especially as his previous nickname was much less attractive, being derived from his Ukrainian surname Kozyel (Goat). Russian criminals generally had a weird habit of modelling themselves on characters from Western gangster movies. There were hundreds of copycat gangland murders in Russia, when people would be tortured and then killed in the exact brutal manner portrayed by Hollywood.

'Why the hell are you stepping down?' Scarface asked.

Seraphim did not answer immediately. He looked around the room, trying to guess by the reaction on the faces who could be the traitor. But all he could see was amazement and bewilderment.

'I feel it's time to bring in new blood,' he said, barely hiding a faint smile. 'I'm getting too old for this.'

Everyone in the room knew that age could not be the reason for his decision. But no one challenged him.

'I bet you know something that we don't,' Scarface said. And for once in his life he was closer to the truth than anyone could guess.

Seraphim smiled. Scarface was an idiot, but he usually got away with questions that others wouldn't dream of asking.

'I want to leave peacefully and avoid any conflicts amongst us,' Seraphim said, turning serious. 'You can elect anyone you want to run the Brotherhood. I'm giving you the chance of a lifetime, so don't fucking blow it!'

He looked around the table again. He could see that already people were getting ideas and thinking about taking over from him. He knew that once the meeting was over they would split up into groups and stay up all night plotting against each other. And that's exactly what he wanted them to do: to get at each other's throats and fight like mad while he pulled off the crime of the century. He also wanted to confuse the traitor, who would now be more interested in finding out who the next boss of the Central Brotherhood would be, rather than checking on Seraphim and his plans. Plans that remained totally secret.

★

Georgi Volkov, known in the Moscow underworld as Wolf, was confused.

For several weeks he'd been held prisoner in a remote house somewhere outside London. He was taken there by three people who grabbed him outside the hospital the day he was discharged after that fight in a nightclub.

It had all happened very quickly. When the two 'embassy officials' collected him from the ward he was ready to escape from them the minute they left the hospital. But as they came out, three men approached them, nodded to the 'embassy officials' and, having surrounded Volkov, escorted him to a car parked across the street. He tried to protest, but the mysterious men paid no attention to what he was saying. In fact, it was obvious that they didn't even understand Russian.

The car took them outside London. They drove down a motorway, then turned off on to a two-lane road and eventually ended up driving down a country lane with tree branches occasionally brushing their windscreen.

It was obvious that the route was not used often.

The car pulled up at a large country house. Volkov was brought to the front door, which opened as soon as they approached. A man with ginger hair and a ginger beard was standing in the doorway, looking sternly at the visitors. He then stepped aside and gestured for them to come in. Volkov was taken into the house, up the stairs and into a large bedroom. The door closed behind him and he could hear the turning of the key.

He was terrified. Who were these men? he thought. What did they want from him? And what would Shark think about his disappearance?

And then it hit him – the money! The two hundred grand hidden in his suitcase in the hotel room. He was supposed to pass it over to some people in London. What happens if the hotel staff start going through his things once they realise that he has vanished? Oh shit! he thought. They'll steal the money and Shark will think that I've blown it on booze and hookers.

He knew of cases when people had been wasted for stealing

much less money than he had with him. Shark would give a signal to his hoods and, just as some poor bastard thought that he'd got away with it, he'd be dragged to the basement to meet some horrible death.

Volkov ran up to the window to see if he could get out and climb down. But there were steel bars on all the windows. He started banging on the door.

'I need to tell you something!' he shouted in Russian. 'I need to go to my hotel room! Oh please, please, let me go to my hotel!'

After a while he got tired and sat on the floor near the door. I'm a dead man, he thought. Shark will kill me. How the hell did I land in such a mess? I need to do something. I need to get out of here.

In desperation Volkov looked around the room for an object that he could use as a weapon. He noticed a marble-based bedside lamp. He pulled the plug out, picked the lamp and removed the shade. He tied the electric cord around the base, which was heavy enough to knock anyone out. He took off his jacket so that it would be easier for him to swing the heavy object.

There was only one thing left to do – sit tight and wait. Volkov was ready to jump anybody who walked in.

After about half an hour, when he was getting impatient, he suddenly heard footsteps. Someone was approaching his room. He got up and ran to the bathroom. He opened the door, switched on the light, and turned on one of the taps in the basin so there would be a sound of running water. He was hoping that the noise would convince anyone walking into the room that he was in the bathroom. He got back into the room and positioned himself beside the door, so that when it opened whoever walked in wouldn't be able to see him.

The key in the door turned, the handle moved down and the door slowly opened. Volkov lifted the lamp base, ready to bring it down on the heads of his captors. But to his surprise no one came in. He stood there for a good minute and yet there was no movement behind the door.

Slowly he looked around the door. There was nobody in the doorway. Volkov looked out of the room and before he could do anything the big ginger man, whom he'd seen when they entered the house, hit him in the face with his giant fist, knocking him out cold.

When he regained his senses he was lying on the bed. There were several people in the room. One of them, a grey-haired man, was sitting on the chair to the right side of the bed. The others were standing.

'Mr Volkov, how are you feeling?' the grey-haired man in the chair said. 'I hope Tom here didn't cause you any serious injury.'

Volkov did not speak much English, but could understand a bit when other people were talking.

'I Russian citizen,' he said in broken English. 'I demand Russian consul.'

The man in the chair smiled. He signalled to one of the people in the room who approached Wolf.

'Mr Volkov, you've been detained on suspicion of money laundering and blackmail,' he said in Russian. 'Two hundred thousand dollars have been found in your room. Also, you have tried to force a Russian diplomat to take part in an illegal deal. Please remember, anything you say might be used against you.'

Volkov was stunned. These people knew everything. But how? Who could have tipped them off?

The man in the chair started asking him questions through the interpreter.

Who sent him? Why did he meet a diplomat from the Russian embassy? What did they talk about?

Volkov guessed that the people who had detained him were not the police. He had had a lot of experience dealing with the cops back in Russia. He knew them well.

The thought that the people were not cops was a relief. So what if they found the money, he thought. It's not a crime to have dollars in the West. And even if he told them about the houses that his friends in Moscow were planning to buy there was nothing illegal in that either. No, these people must be interested in something else. Why on earth would they go to all the trouble of taking him to a country villa in order to find out things about some company in Moscow?

He decided to cooperate with his captors. Sort of cooperate. He said he represented a group in Moscow that was looking to expand abroad. He described the group as a perfectly legitimate company run by Mr Seraphim Voronov, a respected businessman, well connected, with friends in very high places. His instructions were to approach a Boris Ossinski in London and to ask him to help the group set up a business abroad.

Asked about Mr Ossinski's son Ivan, Volkov could only say that the young man had got himself into trouble with the law and his friends were trying to help him out. He didn't know of any threats to the young man or his father. And yes, he did say to Mr Ossinski that in exchange for the assistance to be given to his son the people in Moscow were expecting some token of gratitude. The man in the chair asked him several times what sort of gratitude he was talking about. But Volkov could only say that it was something to do with buying property in London.

After about two hours of interrogation the man in the chair suddenly got up and walked out of the room. The interpreter and two other men followed him. The door closed and the key was turned.

Volkov was left wondering what would happen next. Strange thoughts started to creep into his mind. What if the people in the room were friends of the Crow? What if they were testing him? He would be dead as soon as they got in touch with Moscow.

Suddenly he felt sick. He ran to the bathroom and threw up.

★

Volkov lost count of the days he had spent in captivity. He grew a beard and piled on weight. The only human being he saw throughout all that time was the ginger-haired man who brought him his food.

On a couple of occasions Volkov tried to strike up a conversation with his guard but got nowhere. The stubborn bastard just wouldn't talk to him. So he spent most of his time watching television. There were about thirty channels to choose from and in the evenings there were even some soft porn programmes. Volkov would lie on his bed and watch the naked men and women moaning and kissing each other.

One day he had a visitor. It was morning and he was finishing his breakfast when he heard footsteps. He no longer had any stupid ideas about escaping or hiding in the room. He continued to sit behind the table by the window.

The door opened and a man walked in. He looked familiar.

'Good morning Mr Volkov,' the man said in Russian. Georgi recognised the translator from the previous visit.

'How are you doing?' the man asked.

'How do you think I'm doing?' Volkov said. 'I'm kept in solitary confinement with not a soul to talk to and no idea what happens next!'

'Don't worry, you'll be released as soon as it's safe for you,' the man said.

'Safe? What do you mean safe?' Volkov asked getting nervous.

'Don't worry, Mr Volkov, I can assure you no harm will come to you. What I want you to do now is to look at some photographs and perhaps you'll be able to recognise some of the people in them.'

The man laid several photographs in front of Volkov. A man was walking down some London road. Two men were standing outside a pub. The same two were entering a hotel.

Volkov pointed to two people in the photographs.

'I know these guys,' he said. 'They work for Mr Voronov.'

The interpreter smiled.

'Here's a pen,' he said. 'Please write down their names on the back of the photograph.'

★

After the meeting with the two SVR agents Boris rushed to his office and tried to get in touch with Jeremy.

Oh my God! he was thinking. What have I done? I've interfered with a secret operation of the Russian and British intelligence! What the hell can I say to Jeremy now? But when he got through to Jeremy's secretary, she told him that her boss was abroad and would only be back the next day. Boris asked her to tell Jeremy that he needed to speak to him very urgently.

The next day he was sitting in his office in the embassy, imagining all sorts of terrible things that could happen just because he could not keep his big mouth shut. In order to distract himself, he collected together all the documents that he had previously gathered for Volkov concerning the properties at Kensington Palace Gardens. He had promised to leave the file in a large sealed envelope at the embassy's reception for Glyeb or Shamil to pick up.

Then, around five o'clock in the afternoon, Jeremy called him at last.

'Thank God you're back, Jeremy!' Boris said in a loud voice that betrayed his anxiety. 'We need to meet as soon as possible. Something's come up and I really need to talk to you.'

'Is it about Ivan?' Jeremy asked. 'Is he in danger?'

'No, Ivan is fine, he's fine,' Boris said. 'But we need to talk.'

They met for dinner at a restaurant in Mayfair. Boris was fidgeting with the napkin, not knowing where to start.

'I've been a fool, Jeremy,' he said finally. 'I made a mistake telling you about what happened to Ivan. But believe me, I had absolutely no idea what was really going on!'

Jeremy looked bewildered.

'I don't understand, Boris,' he said. 'What has actually changed? Your son is still in trouble, right? And the people in Moscow are still expecting you to do certain things for them, is that not correct?'

Boris shook his head.

'Yes, yes, it's correct, but the overall situation has changed,' he said. 'First of all, I've been told that an undercover operation is being conducted by the Russian and British governments and that my son's innocence will be confirmed once it's over. Secondly, it turns out that Volkov had been monitored by certain people and I wouldn't be at all surprised if he's already locked up in some prison in Moscow. You see…' he hesitated for a moment, '…I've been contacted by two Russian officials and they briefed me on the whole thing…'

Jeremy was silent for a while. Boris thought that he must have managed to persuade his friend that everything was now under control. But although Jeremy kept his cool outwardly, he was not at all impressed by what he had just heard. In fact, inwardly he was getting more worried by the minute.

'I'm so sorry, Jeremy,' Boris continued. 'I'm afraid it was all a waste of time and money for you. And it was all my fault.'

Jeremy nodded several times, as if he accepted Boris's explanation. The waiter brought the main course and he watched him as he placed the plates on the table and poured some wine and water into their glasses. Something is definitely not right here, Jeremy was thinking. I wonder where Boris got all this information? In any case, I'd better play along for a while and act as if I bought the story. No point in upsetting him.

'You acted as any father would have done,' Jeremy said once the waiter had left. 'How on earth could you have known that the Russian authorities were monitoring the situation? Frankly, I'm very surprised that they approached you at all.'

Boris was relieved that Jeremy was not asking too many questions. He hated the idea of being forced to explain that he had made a mistake by sharing his problem with a 'local', as Glyeb had put it.

'Still, I am very, very grateful to you, Jeremy, for your help,' Boris said. 'I really appreciate you trying to help my son.'

When Boris had left, Jeremy took out a mobile phone and dialled a number.

'Is it you Phillip?' he said. 'I'm okay, thank you. I want to ask you something. Are you aware of any joint intelligence operations involving the Russians?'

The man on the other end of the phone laughed.

'I can tell you right now that there's no joint intelligence operation going on in Britain or anywhere else for that matter with the Russians. We might be friendly with them, but not that friendly.'

'You're sure?'

'Positive. I would have known from my sources.'

Then Jeremy made another call. It was to one of George's people who had been instructed to keep an eye on Boris all the time. He reported that Boris had been in contact that day with two Russians, both of whom had been photographed and later identified by Georgi Volkov as being linked to the Crow.

It was clear that Boris had been set up. Operation Saving Ivan was still on.

★

Bloody bastard! If he thinks he can treat me like some stupid cadet he's got another thing coming!

Lara Davidovitch, senior investigator of the Odintsovo district criminal division, slammed her office door and slumped down on a chair behind her desk. Her hands were trembling as she pulled a pack of Russian cigarettes from the drawer and lit up.

She had just stormed out of a meeting with her boss who had told her that her request for transfer to the Moscow central CID had been rejected on the grounds that she didn't have enough 'operational experience'. After six bloody years of hard work in this shit hole they say I don't have enough experience! she thought. Well, if I don't have experience then who the hell has?

She drew on the cigarette and nearly choked. Russian cigarettes had withstood the test of time and the challenges of capitalism to remain some of the worst in the world: the paper was lousy and the tobacco was mixed with some unbelievable rubbish. Lara would have gladly switched to foreign cigarettes but her salary was too low to allow herself such a luxury. On a thousand roubles a month she could only afford the cheapest fags she could get.

Lara was one of the few criminal investigators in the whole of her division, if not the whole district, who did not accept bribes. She had an ambition to become a member of the elite squad at Petrovka 38 and didn't want to screw her clean record by getting involved with lowlife. It was not that she planned to stay whiter than white all her life. You could never be sure about police work. There would always be someone out there who could offer you an amount you would find hard to resist. Like a million dollars for example.

But in the meantime she was prepared to suffer quietly and wait for the right time to put through a transfer application. That was, until the moment she was summoned 'upstairs' and the captain told her that she'd have to wait another year.

Lara lost her cool and stormed out of the captain's office. She was so angry that she decided to quit right there and then. All her friends from the Law Faculty at the Moscow State University had made their careers as criminal or civil lawyers and most already had good flats or even houses, a car, a husband, a couple of kids. They were always making fun of her when they got together for their annual institute reunions. Some of them even suspected that Lara was a closet lesbian and chose to be in the police to have a macho image. She was a big woman with a low voice and large powerful hands. She always cut her hair short and dressed in clothes that lacked any femininity.

Lara would listen to her friends' jokes without responding. She was secretly hoping that one day they would all envy her when she'd be interviewed on national television after solving a sensational case for the Moscow central CID.

She had a friend at Petrovka 38, an investigator who promised to help her get her request approved. But recently he had got into some sort of trouble and she was mostly relying on her own good work and honest record to get promoted. Until her meeting with the captain, that is.

She took a sheet of white paper out of a drawer and started to write a formal letter of resignation. She wanted to make it as brief as possible, so that she'd be able to catch the captain before he left the office. But she had barely written the full name and rank of her chief in the top right corner of the letter when the phone on her desk rang.

'Investigator Davidovitch,' a man's stern voice said, 'there has been a homicide in the area, please come down. The group is leaving in five minutes.'

Lara threw down the receiver and sat motionless for a moment. Ah, what the hell! she thought. I can always resign tomorrow.

She put on her coat and ran downstairs.

★

About forty minutes later they finally arrived at the scene where the body was found. Before getting there the driver had to find petrol for their car. He'd used it all up while delivering several boxes of vodka for a police party at the local stadium.

The semi-naked body of a woman had been discovered in the

woods by a group of children. She was hidden under piles of branches and would have remained unnoticed for some time if the kids, who were playing cops and robbers, had not crawled under the branches and stumbled on a human hand sticking from the snow.

The woman, it seemed, had been dumped in the forest while still alive and had eventually died of her wounds and hypothermia. No documents were found on her.

Lara could immediately tell by looking at the underwear alone that the woman was a pro. She earned less in a month than the price of the lingerie on the dead woman. Then she saw a ring on one of her fingers that looked sort of familiar. She came closer and knelt down beside the body. It was an unusual ring: a gold bumblebee on a black onyx foundation. Lara studied the face of the dead woman. Bloody hell! she thought. It's Lidia, Pavel's former girlfriend.

When they came back to the office Lara called Pavel's flat a several times, but always got the answering machine. Eventually she left a message, asking him to call her as soon as possible. She decided to keep quiet about Lidia's identity until she had talked to Pavel.

The body was brought into the morgue and a missing person's alert with the general description of the woman was put into the police computer system.

Pavel called about two hours later.

'So, what's all the fuss about?' he said jokingly. 'I hope you're going to tell me that you're getting married at last.'

On hearing his voice Lara found it hard to tell him the news. She hesitated for a moment.

'It's Lidia,' she said finally. 'She's dead. Someone's killed her.'

There was a long silence on the other end. And then Pavel hung up.

Several hours later, out of nowhere, three agents of the Kremlin secret service arrived in a black Volga at the Odintsovo CID. They took a quick look at the dead woman and ordered her to be brought to the special morgue in the Yasenevo district of Moscow.

The cops were really surprised that the Kremlin's bodyguards had reacted so swiftly. But they were relieved that a nasty homicide case had been taken off their hands.

★

The Crow summoned Pavel to his villa.

When he arrived he looked pale and seemed uptight. It was as if he'd been drinking hard the previous night.

'I thought you were busy finding out who's been talking to your friends in the police,' Seraphim said. 'And I see you're keeping a busy social schedule, sucking vodka.'

'I've made some progress,' Pavel said gloomily.

'What do you mean "you've made progress", eh?' Seraphim screamed. 'What the hell is "progress"? I want a name from you! I want to have a name as soon as bloody possible. Things are happening that I don't like! So don't give me all that progress shit!'

Pavel stood in silence. His face turned from pale to white. Seraphim looked hard at him for a moment.

'What's the hell's wrong with you?' he said. 'Are you on dope or what?'

Pavel glanced at him. He wanted to lock his hands around his fat neck and squeeze until the son of a bitch choked to death. They'd killed Lidia. The bloody bastards had tortured her and then left her in the cold to die! They were going to pay, all the bloody lot of them!

It took him an enormous effort to control himself in front of the Crow.

'I'll find out the name,' he said. 'I need two more days to finish the job.'

★

When Pavel broke the news about Lidia's death to Clay, the American started to sob like a small boy. In a way he was a child, a big child who had killed a lot of people in his life. And if it had not been for the medication prescribed to him several years ago he would probably have blown his brains out in some remote motel, like several of his buddies from the airborne forces had done.

Alex, on the other hand, showed little emotion on hearing about Lidia, while Motya was obviously shocked and kept taking off his glasses and wiping them with a handkerchief.

Pavel came to the flat at Tverskaya Street without even checking whether he was being followed by Seraphim's men or by anyone else. He was like a zombie. He had to talk to someone after he had learnt from Lara Davidovitch that Lidia had been found dead in a forest off the Roublevskoe motorway. He couldn't stay around Seraphim's people. He might have lost control and said or did something that would have blown his cover.

They were sitting in the kitchen drinking vodka.

'We're going to set up Shark and we won't be needing any plans of his country house,' Pavel told them. 'I've brought you the address of Shark's flat in Moscow and all the particulars of the location: security arrangements, fire escape routes, plan of the roof. Motya will take you to the place. Here's a set of documents from Seraphim's safe. Plant them anywhere you want. It doesn't really matter where they're hidden, as long as you don't leave any signs of a break-in. Once they find the documents the bastard is as good as dead.'

Pavel left them to get ready for the operation. He was on his way to see some of the people from the central CID to arrange a small matter of a backdated file being opened with information from a 'mole' in the Central Brotherhood. This file was crucial for setting up Shark as the fall guy. In fact, once it appeared in the central CID's computerised file, Shark was as good as dead.

Motya took the two men to the Frunzenskaya embankment where Shark had a flat on the seventh floor of a vast apartment block. As there was always a concierge present in the lobby downstairs they couldn't simply walk in, take the elevator and get to the seventh floor. Having had a look around the area, they decided to get into the flat through one of the windows facing the inside courtyard. A steel fire escape ladder led to the roof from the courtyard so they could get up there with no problem.

They went back to collect the equipment for the break-in from Tverskaya Street and were back at the embankment by midnight. Motya stood on the lookout as they climbed up the fire escape and positioned themselves on the roof, directly above Shark's flat. Having secured the ropes on the roof, they lowered themselves to the rear windows. It was windy that night, which made their job even more difficult.

Clay cut out one section of the window, big enough for him to squeeze through. Alex held the glass while Clay eased himself inside.

As he dangled on the rope Alex started to get all kinds of stupid ideas. Like dropping the pane of glass and waking up the whole bloody neighbourhood. Or falling down himself. I guess that would constitute a failed mission, Alex thought gloomily. The cold was really getting to him.

Several moments later Clay got out. They fixed the panel of glass back in the window, securing it with special glue, and then climbed up the ropes to the roof. They managed to get down the fire escape without anyone seeing them and got back safely to the flat at Tverskaya Street.

Over the following few days copies of documents from Seraphim's safe began to surface all around Moscow. It was only a matter of time before the Central Brotherhood would begin feeling the pressure.

★

The first bad news came on Sunday. Shark arrived at Seraphim's villa around lunchtime and rushed in to see the boss.

'We've got a problem,' he said, walking into the study.

Seraphim looked up at him.

'The Tatars hit two of our gambling joints early this morning,' he said. 'In one place they killed five people.'

For a moment Seraphim remained speechless, trying to digest the news. Then, having realised what had happened, he got up from his chair behind the desk.

'How the hell do you know it's the Tatars?' he said, looking closely at Shark. 'I thought we had a deal with them – they don't touch our gambling operations and we don't interfere with their grocery markets. So, what happened? Who pissed them off?'

Shark seemed to be uneasy with the question.

'Well?' Seraphim said. 'What the hell's gone wrong now?'

'They found out we're dealing with the Uzbekis behind their backs,' Shark said gloomily. 'They say that we took over some of their markets. And paid the tax people and the cops to put pressure on them.'

Seraphim could not believe what he was hearing. He prided himself on being the only serious player in Moscow who had managed to keep the peace with the Tatars. He despised them at heart and would have moved in on their turf openly a long time ago, but the Tatars were a tightly knit group who had been in the business longer than anyone else.

So Seraphim was moving in on them quietly instead. He was talking to people behind their backs, forging alliances with the Uzbekis, with the Armenians and the Georgians who controlled a lot of trade in the capital, bribing officials to cause problems for the Tatars. But all his dealings and double-dealings were always done in total secrecy. There were only a few people who knew about his operations.

'How the hell did they find out about our deals with the Uzbekis?' Seraphim said. He was getting angry.

Shark shook his head and sighed. He hated giving the Crow bad news.

'The word is that someone gave them some papers or something that proved that we were dealing with the Uzbekis.'

Seraphim looked at him in amazement.

'What the fuck are you talking about?' he roared. 'What papers? There are only three people on our side who know about the set-up: you, me and our accountant. And as for Mirza, I can vouch for him. He'd rather die than talk to others about our arrangement.'

Shark shrugged his shoulders and frowned, signalling that he had absolutely no idea how word about the deal had reached the Tatars.

Seraphim walked to the safe and opened it. The papers were all there. He turned around.

'Find the accountant,' he said. 'Make him talk.'

'Sure thing, Crow,' Shark said, 'I guess we'll need a new accountant?'

'Don't guess, just do what you need to do.'

★

The next day brought more bad news for the Central Brotherhood.

Two of Seraphim's people were shot and killed outside a restaurant by the boys from the Taganskaya gang. As it turned out, Slava the Satan, the head of the Taganskaya group, found out that his arch-enemies had been supplied with weapons by the Central Brotherhood. For many months Satan had been desperately trying to find out who was arming the Zarechni boys, but all in vain. Then out of the blue came the information he was looking for. Copies of documents revealing the sales of arms were found by Satan's people by pure chance. He made several phone calls and soon all the pieces of the puzzle were in place.

Satan declared war on Seraphim and his men.

That very day the cops got a package with documents from an anonymous source showing that the 'brothers' were paying off several high-ranking government officials through the roulette table. These people were regularly getting 'lucky' at the casinos belonging to the Central Brotherhood. They were some of the best contacts Seraphim had inside the government and they were all arrested and charged with accepting bribes.

To make matters worse, several of the Central Brotherhood's companies based in Moscow were suddenly raided by the police and closed down pending further investigation. They were all charged with tax evasion and VAT fraud.

And to top it all an article appeared on the front page of a leading Russian newspaper alleging corruption in high places and links between government officials and criminal groups. A state-of-the-art military factory was mentioned in the newspaper story that had been privatised and sold off for practically nothing to a suspicious Moscow company. Seraphim owned the company in question and the newspaper called upon the authorities to investigate the way the factory was privatised and find out who was behind it. The article also mentioned a private bank – again owned by Seraphim – that had been involved in laundering money.

Seraphim was really starting to feel the pressure. Someone was spreading sensitive information about his operations, causing him maximum damage.

And just when he thought that things could not get any worse someone tried to kill him. It happened as he was coming out of a restaurant after a meeting with one of his partners. A car roared past and several shots were fired at him. Two of his bodyguards were wounded. Seraphim himself was not hurt but only because one of his guards managed to push him to the ground before the shooting started.

All that made him even more determined to carry out the London operation without a hitch. The problem was that he had to raise cash to finance the job. Any new arms deal with the Chechens was out of the question. The revenues from his illegal operations in Moscow were disrupted by the recent attacks and crackdown by the authorities.

So the only way was to get a loan. From Big Brother himself...

★

Everything was set for the final showdown between Pavel and Seraphim.

Apart from the incriminating documents that had been planted at Shark's apartment by Alex and Clay, a backdated 'file' was opened in the police records. It contained statements from a certain Semyen Akulov concerning some of the activities of the Central Brotherhood. It took a lot of persuasion on Pavel's part to open that file. The archive people were very reluctant to tamper with the files of the CID, but an offer of ten grand in cash eventually did the trick.

Pavel called Seraphim and asked for a meeting.

'I've got the name, I'm on my way to see you,' he said and put the phone down.

When he walked into the study Seraphim was standing by the window with his back to the door. He turned around to face Pavel. He was wearing a single-breasted black suit, a black waistcoat, a white shirt and a black tie. It was as if he was all dressed up for a 'funeral' – a sort of burial of trust, getting ready to find out the name of the scumbag who betrayed him. A faint smile touched Pavel's lips. The Crow was sure prone to stupid gimmicks.

'Well?' Seraphim said in a coarse voice.

Pavel took a deep breath.

'I've known who the traitor was for some time,' he said. 'The only reason I didn't give you the name earlier was because I had to make double sure my information was correct.'

Seraphim's eyes narrowed.

'You knew the name of the prick who was selling me out and yet you kept it to yourself?' he shouted, his face getting red with rage. 'Do you know what I do to people who fuck with me? Do you know how many people I've punished for lesser things?'

Pavel remained calm. He was actually surprised himself at how calm he was. This was the most important part of the whole operation, and yet he was not even nervous.

'It's Shark,' Pavel said. 'He's been passing information to the cops for the last year at least.'

Seraphim felt an explosion of pain in his temples. For a moment he could not breathe and was opening his mouth like a fish out of water. He couldn't even understand whether it was anger or shock that he was experiencing. It was as if the room had suddenly got dark.

Pavel knew that it would take much more to convince Seraphim that Shark was the traitor than just telling him about it. He also knew that he was stepping into a potential minefield. It was quite possible that Seraphim might decide to arrange a face-to-face confrontation and let them battle it out. But Pavel also knew that Shark would have a hell of a time explaining the presence of the documents at his flat and especially the existence of the police file.

But things turned out not at all as he expected. After the initial shock Seraphim quickly calmed down. A strange smile settled on his face, more a grimace than a smile.

'How do I know you aren't lying?' he said in a strange, creepy voice. 'What if you're playing a game with me?'

'Well, then you won't reward me, will you?' Pavel said.

Seraphim stayed silent for some time. Pavel decided it was time to put on some more pressure on the fat bastard.

'I have information that'll prove that Shark has been double-dealing behind your back,' Pavel said. 'And there's one more thing. He's been bragging about a London job a lot.'

He remembered George's request to find out about some plan to buy up property in London and decided to test Seraphim, hoping that he would break under pressure and reveal some details. The mere mention of London had the effect of a cold shower on Seraphim. Shark doesn't know about the London job, he thought. He only knows about the property deals, and that means nothing to him.

And yet the mere idea that Shark might have somehow found out about his secret plan filled Seraphim with horror. All of a sudden his pension plan was in danger. He pretended not to pay attention to Pavel's words, but in his mind he was set on finding out as soon as possible what Shark knew. The idea of staging a meeting between Pavel and Shark that he was contemplating just a moment ago became irrelevant.

'Tell me everything you've got,' Seraphim said. 'The whole lot…'

★

An hour later, when Pavel had left, Seraphim called two of his bodyguards and ordered them to search Shark's flat in Moscow and his country home.

'As soon as you find anything suspicious, you call me at once,' he told them.

Then he got in touch with Shark and asked him to come over to his villa.

Shark arrived late in the evening. Seraphim behaved as if nothing had happened. Like a snake he was preparing to play with his victim before devouring it. He was all politeness.

They sat in the dining room drinking. Seraphim was talking about loyalty.

'You know what I've always admired in you?' he was saying. 'I've always admired you for your loyalty. You were the only one I could trust. You knew all my secrets and kept them to yourself.'

Shark kept silent. He was sensing some sort of danger and was trying hard to guess where it was coming from.

'Times are hard,' Seraphim continued, pouring vodka into their glasses on the table. 'You can't even trust your own family nowadays.'

'What trust?' Shark said. 'What are you talking about?'

'Nothing, nothing,' Seraphim said. 'I simply called you here to talk about business. Business has been bad recently. And I'm just wondering why the hell it's getting worse every day. Don't you think that something is very wrong?'

Shark loosened up a bit. At least he knew what was going on.

'We've dealt with the accountant as you ordered,' he said. 'I personally spoke to him. He didn't say anything of interest.'

Seraphim shot a suspicious glance at him.

'As I've heard, he couldn't say very much,' he said. 'You beat him up so bad before he could even start to talk. And wasn't it a bit hasty drowning him in a tub? Shouldn't you have waited a day or two?'

Seraphim was getting wound up. Then the phone rang. He picked it up and listened for a while, occasionally saying, 'Oh, is that a fact?' At the end of that mostly one-sided conversation he said into the phone, 'Bring me everything you found. Every bloody page.'

When he put the phone down his face was pale.

'What's wrong?' said Shark. 'What's happened?'

Seraphim looked at him blankly. For a while he was silent.

'It seems we have a small problem,' he said finally. 'But I think everything's going to be resolved soon. Let's have a drink and forget all about our worries. Oh, and by the way, I'd like you to stay here for the night. I feel I want to have somebody beside me whom I can really *trust*.'

Although Shark had a bad feeling about it, he did not dare to disobey the Crow and stayed overnight at his villa.

★

The next morning, as Shark got up, he did what he usually did every day in the last month: he went to the window to see whether his car was okay. It was instinctive. He really liked the new Mercedes that he had bought recently. He couldn't get enough of it.

Shark parted the curtains and was surprised to see several cars parked outside the house. All the cars were his people's. As far as he could remember he did not authorise anyone to be there.

Something's up, he thought. Must be the Chechens or the Tatars again.

Shark got dressed quickly. He opened the drawer where he had put his gun last night but it was empty. He looked under the bed, in the bathroom, but could not find it anywhere.

That's weird, he thought. I remember clearly that I put the shooter in the drawer.

He decided that he'd look for his gun later and went downstairs.

Seraphim was in the dining room. He was having breakfast. He looked up at Shark and smiled. The smile did not bear well. Shark knew that smile. Something was definitely up.

'Join me, please,' Seraphim said.

Shark sat opposite him.

But before he had a chance to pour juice into his glass, three men walked in and quickly approached him. They grabbed him by the arms, twisted them back and handcuffed him. It all happened in a matter of seconds. Shark was so surprised that for a moment he couldn't utter a single word.

'What the fuck is happening?' he growled finally. 'What's your game?'

Seraphim bit off a piece from a small sandwich and was chewing it as if nothing much was happening.

Shark was looking at him, waiting for an answer.

'Strange, isn't it?' Seraphim said at last. 'Strange how people manage to imitate surprise and bewilderment when they are caught red-handed?'

'What the hell are you talking about, Crow?' Shark yelled. 'What's going on? Why are you cuffing me?'

'Questions, question, questions,' Seraphim said as he got up from the table. 'I think that I should be asking the questions, not you. Now tell me about the documents. Why on earth would you need to copy all the documents I keep in my safe?'

'What documents? What the fuck are you talking about?'

Seraphim looked at him for a moment.

'I see that you've been developing artistic talents while you were betraying me,' he said. 'It looks like you have chosen the slow and painful way.'

He turned to the men standing at the door.

'Take him away and make him talk,' he ordered. 'But don't kill him. If he dies all three of you die, understood?'

The three hoods nodded. Shark was taken to a room in the basement of the villa. It was mostly used for storage but on several occasions people were interrogated in that room. Shark conducted the interrogations and after every such experience the people would never be seen again, regardless of whether they talked or not.

The three men started beating Shark as soon as they all entered the room. At first he tried to resist, but they quickly overpowered him and punched him with their fists. Soon there was blood all over his face.

He did not plead for mercy. He had trained these people himself. He had handpicked them so that they would never feel sympathy for any of their victims.

Shark wanted his men to derive pleasure from other people's pain. Just like he had near-orgasms when he was torturing his victims. Occasionally he would stop beating them, go to the toilet and have one great big wank there.

He started getting these weird sexual arousals when he was a kid. Along with some other boys from his neighbourhood he would catch stray cats and dogs, tie them to a tree or a fence, and torture them. They would burn them, pierce them with knives, stick burning cigarette butts into their eyes, pour acid over them. The poor animals would howl and squeal and make all sorts of terrible noises. They would eventually get stiff which meant that they were dead. And when Shark went to sleep that night he would get a strange sense of pleasure from picturing those terrified creatures writhing with pain.

But once he found himself on the receiving end there was no pleasure in it. He had often wondered how he would cope with the pain. And it turned out that he was no masochist.

Shark lost consciousness after about forty minutes of beatings. The three men tied him up and went for a smoke.

★

Seraphim's authority in his gang, and in the Moscow underworld as a whole, had been greatly undermined by the announcement of his imminent 'retirement'. And once word got around that it was Shark – one of his closest lieutenants – who did all the talking to the cops behind his back, the Crow's position weakened even further.

Desperate to win more time to finish the final preparations for the big job in London, he decided that the best way to cause a distraction and take the heat off himself was to provoke a major gangland war in Moscow. The Chechens were breathing down his neck, planning revenge for the death of their two people outside the Oscar Wilde, so it seemed like a good idea to Seraphim to drag them into a feud with some other powerful criminal group and hope that the conflict would eventually spread to other gangs. He reckoned that in all the confusion he would be able to pull off his disappearing act and take personal control of the operation in London.

He had just the man to help him out – his friend and drinking buddy Vassili, the son of the President of Russia. In the past, Vassili, who held the post of special advisor to the President, let it slip in a drunken conversation with Seraphim that he knew some people in the intelligence network who could organise anything, including professional hits.

'There are guys,' Vassili said, 'trained killers, former special forces and all that. They can whack anyone, all nice and clean and quiet. And I know how to get to them.'

Seraphim took note of his words then; he always remembered important things. And now he was going to ask his powerful friend for a favour.

Through the usual channels, he passed word to Vassili asking for a meeting. It was arranged outside Moscow, in a private room at the famous restaurant The King's Retreat, where the main course cost half of an average Russian monthly salary. It was a favourite spot for rich businessmen and powerful officials to mix together and hammer out deals. The place was built in the old Russian tradition, like a huge *izba*, a village house, with a chimney stove in the middle and walls made out of logs. The waiters were all dressed in Russian folk costumes and the restaurant served mostly Russian food, offering about a hundred different brands of vodka.

Vassili arrived at the restaurant in a brand new Mercedes with his three bodyguards who were also his drinking companions. Like his father, who had been known throughout his political career to socialise with members of his household staff, like drivers and cleaners, Vassili chose to befriend his loyal minders. He always preferred to spend time with those he could patronise and mock and who would still praise and flatter him.

The President's son looked like a typical Russian peasant: short, with crooked legs, badly cut blond hair, a round red face and an up-turned nose. The flashy designer clothes he wore did nothing to improve his common appearance. But despite resembling a village idiot, he was quite a cunning character. When it came to money, he had an impressive ability to get the best possible deal for himself.

Seraphim arrived at the restaurant a quarter of an hour later, giving his friend some time to consume a couple of large drinks and achieve some sort of mental stability. He walked into the room just as Vassili had drunk a third large vodka, and was trying to figure out what he should put into his mouth to help the drink 'settle down'.

Seraphim stopped at the door. He knew that the presidential special advisor treated his drinking very seriously and didn't like others to interrupt the three-stage process of consumption – 'pour, drink, nibble'. Seraphim waited while a salted gherkin disappeared into Vassili's mouth. He then walked in and announced his presence.

'Vassya, my dear friend, I'm so glad to see you!' he said in a loud voice, walking up to the table, getting ready for the Russian-style hug with three pecks on the cheeks. But Vassili didn't even bother to stand up, and only raised his right hand as a greeting gesture.

Seraphim immediately felt the anger in him grow. The pulse in his left temple began to throb, but he kept his cool. It was not a good time to fall out with Vassili.

Seraphim sat down at the table and put down the large brief-case he was holding beside his chair. He had expected Vassili to send his bodyguards out of the room, but he showed no desire to part with his buddies. Instead, the three brain-dead burly lookalikes remained sitting beside him at the long wooden table. He even poured some more vodka into their glasses, as if teasing Seraphim.

'What's up, Vassya?' Seraphim said, trying hard to conceal his fury. 'Is there a problem?'

Vassili looked at him, but instead of answering took another drink from his glass. He then picked a large gherkin from the plate and bit off half of it. He was sure taking his time in replying to the question.

'I'm very disappointed in you, Seraphim,' he said finally, still chewing on the gherkin. 'I didn't expect to be treated like some traffic cop who's happy when he's given a hundred roubles.'

His three minders giggled in unison at his words. They were obviously used to reacting with laughter to any stupid comment Vassili made, eager to please him.

'I don't understand,' Seraphim said. 'What are you on about?'

Vassili's face reddened with anger.

'I'm on about the last payment I've received for my consultancy services to you and your people,' he said. 'Do you really expect me to be happy with fifty thousand dollars? Fifty measly grand for getting that idiot Titov, the Deputy Foreign Minister, to help you move all that stuff of yours to London. Not to mention pushing through that crazy idea to stage an exhibition of the Kremlin jewellery collection abroad.'

Vassili shook his head slowly, as if expressing his own disbelief at the way he had been treated. Seraphim watched him in silence, waiting to hear more of his whining.

'And how about the information on Chechnya I got for you?' Vassili said. 'Now that was one hell of a job! It was classified stuff, you know! Top secret material! And in the end what do I get for all that? Small change! I think that you're forgetting who you're dealing with, Seraphim! I'm the special fucking advisor to the President of Russia! Get it? The top man in the country!'

Seraphim was drumming the table with his fingers, listening to Vassili. The meeting had definitely not got off to a good start. The son of a bitch was playing hard to get.

But all was not lost. Once Vassili stopped talking, Seraphim got up from his chair, picked up the briefcase that stood beside it, and threw it on the table smashing some of the glasses and plates. Vassili and his three minders looked startled, not knowing what to expect next.

'Who says I'm not grateful to my friends!' Seraphim shouted, his eyes bulging and his face becoming almost purple. 'Who says I don't look after my partners...?' He raised a glass of vodka and drank the whole contents in one go. Then he threw it on the floor with such strength that it shattered into a hundred pieces.

For a moment Vassili sobered up. He pulled the briefcase across the table to his side and opened it with a loud clicking sound. It was full of cash. He looked up at Seraphim as if asking, 'so what are we talking about here?'

Seraphim grinned and rubbed his puffy hands.

'Feast your eyes, dear Vassya, on three hundred thousand American dollars,' he said. 'All in crisp new notes, ready to spend on anything you want!'

Vassili glanced at the money and then looked up at Seraphim. Finally the news sank in – he was getting three hundred big ones, in cash, tax-free. His small eyes lit up like two tiny light bulbs. He wiped his lips with the top of his hand. He had a habit of wiping his mouth when he got excited.

'Let's have some more vodka!' he yelled all of a sudden. 'Let's party all night! Let's screw all the local hookers!'

He shut the briefcase and slumped back in his chair, exhausted by all that burst of emotion.

Seraphim sat down on his chair too. He felt relieved. His theatrics had paid off. The meeting was now back on track. All that remained was to sort out the business side of things before Vassili got completely drunk and passed out. He started with the money he needed for the London job.

'First of all, Vassya, I need to talk to you about a deal I'm arranging,' he said. 'I need a quick loan, fifteen mil to be exact, to start the whole thing rolling and I promise to include you in the profits. I'm opening a betting chain in Moscow and need the money real quick. I'll explain the details to you later, but you know me – I've never let you down on a deal before, have I?'

Vassili was slowly slipping back into his drunken state. He raised a glass of vodka and said, 'Fifteen mil is a lot of money but I'll see what I can do.' He finished the vodka and swallowed a piece of salmon.

Seraphim kept up the pressure. 'Oh, and there's one other thing I wanted to ask you to do for me,' he said. He could see that his friend had softened up and that the sight of money had lifted his spirits.

'Talk to me,' Vassili said, 'I'm in a good mood tonight.'

Seraphim glanced at the three bodyguards. This time Vassili got the message and signalled to his boys to take a walk. Once they were gone Seraphim poured more vodka into their glasses and they both downed the contents.

As soon as Vassili had 'polished' the drink with a piece of herring, Seraphim said, 'I need your help in sorting out some very nasty people. Two nasty ones, to be exact: Mussa Bartaev and Slava the Satan.'

Vassili raised his head. For a moment he sobered up again. It was amazing how he could slip in and out of his drunken states, depending on the situation.

'The Chechen gangster and the madman from Taganka?' he said slowly. 'You want me to sort out the head of the Chechen gangsters in Moscow and that psycho who runs the Taganka mob? Are you fucking crazy?'

Seraphim kept his cool.

'I'm not crazy, Vassya,' he said calmly. 'You heard me right. I want you to sort out Mussa Bartaev and Slava the Satan for me. I'm not asking you to whack a policeman or something, am I? All I'm asking you is to get rid of two scumbags. You told me yourself you know people in the system who can organise a hit any time. Well, now I'm asking you to do me a favour and get rid of these two pricks. And as a token of my gratitude' – he paused for a second, looking at Vassili – 'I'll give you three hundred thousand dollars. In addition to the money I've already given you.'

The pause seemed to add more value to the amount mentioned. Seraphim had learnt to pause at crucial moments. It helped to stress the point he was making.

Vassili watched him for several seconds. It was obvious that two feelings, greed and doubt, were battling inside of him. Eventually greed gained the upper hand.

'I want to see the money,' he said, his throat turning dry.

'I knew you would,' Seraphim said with a wry smile.

He stood up and went to the door. As he opened it one of his bodyguards passed him a briefcase. Seraphim walked back to his chair and put the briefcase on the table. Vassili pulled it to himself, opened it and looked inside.

'You're one crazy son of a bitch!' he said after a while, looking up at Seraphim. 'But how can I refuse to help an old friend.'

'Bless you, Vassya,' Seraphim said. 'Where would I be without you?'

★

After exposing Shark as the 'traitor' Pavel was lying low.

There was no telling what Seraphim might do after one of his most trusted people turned out to be a police informer. There was always a risk that he could turn nasty and order his men to dispose of him.

But there was another reason for Pavel to be extra careful. He now knew that it was Lidia who had tipped off the Russian intelligence about Operation Saving Ivan. After George confronted him head-on about his possible double-dealing, Pavel quietly began his own investigation. Using his contacts in the police and elsewhere, he eventually managed to piece the puzzle together. Lidia knew about the forthcoming meeting between the Crow and the two Chechen arms dealers and the 'assassination attempt' planned by the London team and passed the information to her controllers. Someone then must have decided to prevent the rocket deal between the Crow and the Chechens going through. So they bumped off the two arms dealers and would have probably killed the Crow, were it not for Pavel's intervention. The hit was timed perfectly, as the murders could always be pinned on Alex and Clay, two 'foreign mercenaries'.

Pavel tried to find out who Lidia's contacts in the intelligence were, but no one could tell him anything specific. One of his sources did say that he had heard something about the Countess being linked to the Kremlin's secret service in the last couple of years and later Pavel learnt that the presidential bodyguards were quick to collect her body from the morgue in Odintsovo's criminal division and move it to the special clinic in Yasenevo. But it still didn't make much sense. Why would the Kremlin agents monitor the London team and even involve themselves in Operation Saving Ivan?

Pavel decided not to tell George anything about his findings. He knew that he would probably have to come clean at some point in the future, but figured that it could wait, as it was too late to do anything about it anyway: Lidia was now dead, killed trying to help them bring down the Central Brotherhood, and it didn't really matter which branch of the Russian intelligence was breathing down their backs. Especially as George knew that his team had been under surveillance from day one and yet no one tried to prevent them from going after the gang.

It was all part and parcel of the life Pavel had chosen to lead. He himself had worked as an undercover agent for a special department in the Moscow's central CID, infiltrating gangs and collecting information about their operations, including their links with officials from law enforcement agencies. Posing as a 'bent cop' he had managed to dig up facts that eventually resulted in arrests and prosecutions of corrupt policemen. It was during one of his undercover operations that he had found out about the connection between Mustafa's gang of drug dealers and some senior officials in the Interior Ministry and even in the FSB. His investigation eventually led him to that little black book in Mustafa's house, containing names of all the people on the gang's payroll and details of the payments they had received for their 'assistance'. The book also contained information about other gangs and their links to corrupt officials. By pure luck Pavel not only managed to get hold of the book before anyone else could get to it, but had enough time to copy it. What the thugs who burst into his flat that evening to recover the book didn't know was that he had already passed its contents to his contacts in the Prosecutor General's office. The only reason that Pavel was still alive was because no one from the Interior Ministry and other law enforcement agencies, linked to Mustafa's gang, had been arrested yet. Mustafa himself, helped by his powerful allies, was out on bail and was even quietly peddling drugs again. The prosecutors let him walk free for a while, gathering information and preparing to nail – for the first time ever – a whole network of corrupt senior cops.

Pavel's dismissal from the force took the heat off him. But his friend at the Prosecutor General's office was frank with him.

'You'd have no chance of getting away from these guys once they start going down,' he said to him. 'Your best bet is to disappear for a while. Otherwise you might end up feeding the fishes in Moscow River, once they finally figure out who was the first to point the finger of blame at them.'

It was then that George Blunt had approached Pavel and he agreed to take part in the operation. The money he was promised was enough for him to disappear for a long time, until things settled…

From a flat belonging to one of his friends Pavel sent a coded fax message to George in London, asking him what his next move should be. He was primarily interested in finding out when he could get some money.

When he called his friend later in the day Pavel was surprised to learn that a reply had come back from London within a couple of hours. He rushed over to read it as it was in code.

'Congratulations on the job well done,' it went. 'Will require your assistance in London. Please travel to St Petersburg and go to the British consulate. A man by the name of John Roberts will assist you in getting a visa. Hope to see you in London soon. We'll sort out the finances over here. George.'

Pavel was invited to London to collect his payment. He was given a chance to disappear from Moscow. Considering the situation, this suited him just fine.

★

The Central Moscow Baths, better known as *Sandyunni*, had been built in the middle of the nineteenth century as a place where the hard-drinking Russian city folk could rejuvenate themselves. It became a 'temple of personal hygiene' for the working masses during Soviet times. The idea was that whole families could come to *Sandyunni* to bathe, sweat in steam saunas and swim in the pools. But from day one, and even in Soviet times, it was mostly famous for heavy drinking, wild orgies in private rooms, and meetings between criminals.

Mussa Bartaev, the bushy-browed black-bearded head of one of the biggest criminal groups in Moscow, was a regular at the *Sandyunni* baths. He would usually come on Wednesday after-noons, when the general public was barred from the place, accompanied by at least five bodyguards.

Not that Mussa was afraid of anyone. It was more of a status thing. The presence of bodyguards was proof that he was an important man, a well-respected and serious player in the Moscow underworld. Mussa knew well that no matter how many bodyguards you have there is always someone out there who has enough determination and experience to dispose of you. He himself had ordered the elimination of well over two dozen people, respectable people like himself, who had many body-guards and who carried guns themselves. Yet they could not escape from Mussa's hired killers.

On one occasion, just to prove his point that no protection was foolproof, he hired two junkies. They were promised a grand each if they hurt a 'nasty man' who, as they were told, was actually planning to put them away where they wouldn't be able to get any more of that shit that they pumped into their veins. The two idiots got so wound up that they clubbed him to death with baseball bats right in front of his four bodyguards. After the initial shock had worn off, the four minders pulled their guns out and filled the two crazy bastards with lead. Not that it made any difference to their dead boss.

Like no one else, Mussa knew well that bodyguards were just a fashion accessory in the world where he operated. And he was always ready for the worst, because in his world people rarely had the chance to retire.

The minders who usually accompanied Mussa to *Sandyunni* saw to it that their boss enjoyed himself to the full, had a long undisturbed steam session and a good beating at the steamer with dried birch branches. One of his men would attend to the temperature in the big Russian sauna. The second one would provide a good heap of birch branches and hit him hard on his big hairy back and fat buttocks while he lay on the top shelf where the temperature would rise to 100 °C. Later another of his people would give him a massage, a really painful one, and afterwards they would all have refreshments and drink a lot of tea.

On that Wednesday Mussa arrived at *Sandyunni* for a quick sauna rather than the full steam treatment. He was attending a big party at the Savoy hotel and wanted to freshen up a bit, as he was expecting to be introduced to a famous young film actress. He once mentioned to one of his friends that he would like to screw her and, would you know it, she was going to meet him in a hotel room after the party.

When Mussa was leaving the baths, surrounded by five of his people, a loud bang sounded from across the street, as if a car had backfired. The bodyguards immediately assumed threatening positions, ready to pull out their guns from their shoulder holsters. But it was too late. Mussa Bartaev had been hit with one bullet. It went straight between his eyes and he was dead before he hit the ground.

Later that evening an anonymous caller told Mussa's younger brother that he was killed on the orders of Slava the Satan who had decided to move in on his turf.

★

Slava the Satan, the head of the Taganskaya gang, collected cars. He had more than thirty, including a 1918 Rolls Royce that had been used by Felix Dzerzhinsky, the founder and spiritual father of the Soviet secret police. He also had a Mercedes that had been supposedly used by Joseph Stalin. All the rest were brand-new Western models, bought for cash through a dealer in Moscow who took orders several months in advance and demanded full payment up front.

Slava also kept another 'car' in a vast garage on one of his estates outside Moscow. The garage was built on the site of a huge cow barn that had been used by a collective farm in the Soviet times. It could have easily housed fifty or more vehicles, so Slava still had a long way to go before he ran out of space.

The special 'car' was a replica model of an old Moskvitch that sold in the 1960s. It was leg powered and big enough for children aged between five and seven. Slava saw a car like that for the first time when he was a kid himself. Their neighbour's son was given one as a birthday present. The lucky boy's father was the managing director of a confectionery factory and, according to some rumours, earned a lot of money by selling sweets and chocolates 'from the back entrance'. He could easily afford to pay forty roubles – an absolute fortune in those days – for the replica car and his son immediately took it outside to show it off in front of his friends.

Slava was mesmerised by the car. It was light blue in colour, all shiny and had headlights that could be switched on and off. Slava begged the owner to let him go for a ride in the car but he knew well that he wouldn't get a chance. If it was his car he wouldn't have allowed anyone to even come close to it. He stood watching as the boy drove around their courtyard, pressing the horn and switching the headlights on and off.

Many years later, when Slava was running the biggest car operation in Moscow, selling stolen vehicles in their thousands across Russia, he'd often remember that day when he saw the toy car. It was as if a sign had been given to him then that cars would play a major role in his life. Once he unexpectedly came across a toy Moskvitch, exactly the same colour as the one he saw all those years ago, when his men were smashing up a warehouse belonging to some people who refused to pay protection money. Slava ordered the car to be 'serviced' and since then it was kept in the garage along with all the rest of his prized possessions.

One sunny afternoon in April Slava decided to test-drive a new Aston Martin that had arrived a few days before. He called the garage and told the mechanic to prepare the car for a drive. He didn't recognise the voice on the phone.

'Where's Borya?' he said. 'And who the fuck are you?'

'I'm Mitya,' the man on the other end said. 'Borya's ill. Went to a funeral yesterday and got poisoned by some home-made shit. Couldn't make it today.'

Slava felt a tingle of suspicion.

'Do you know anything about Aston Martins?' he asked.

'Sure,' Mitya said. 'I've been handling foreign cars for the last twenty-five years. Worked in a garage that fixed cars for foreign embassies in Moscow.'

Slava was still not satisfied.

'And who brought you in?' he said.

'The Owl called me and told me to come over,' the man said.

The Owl was Slava's right-hand man. It was okay. The man was in the clear.

'Get the car ready for me for four o'clock sharp,' Slava said. 'I'll be driving myself.'

When he arrived at the garage the Aston Martin was parked outside the garage. It was washed and waxed and was gleaming in the sun. But there was no sign of the mechanic. Slava told his driver to check inside but there was no one there either.

Slava felt uneasy. Something was not right. The sudden change of mechanics, the absence of people at the garage. He looked at the car. It was begging him to have a drive. But Slava was no fool.

'Get into the car and do a couple of circles in the yard,' he told his driver.

'Sure thing, boss,' the man said. He too appreciated the car and didn't need to be asked twice to have a drive. He quickly got behind the wheel. Slava moved back to the entrance gates. Just in case.

The engine started and the car did two full circles around the garage yard.

The man at the wheel was clearly impressed by the car's performance.

Slava signalled to the driver to pull up. He stopped the engine, got out and Slava took his place behind the wheel.

'Wait for me here,' Slava said to the driver. He was getting really excited. The new leather upholstery smelt great. He was going to enjoy himself.

He pressed the accelerator and drove through the open gates on to the open road. Some two hundred metres on the car exploded.

The next day word spread around Moscow that it was a revenge attack by Mussa's people for the killing of their boss...

★

All hell broke loose in Moscow after the shooting of Mussa Bartaev outside the Central Moscow Baths and the murder of Satan during a test drive of his brand new Aston Martin. Their deaths immediately sparked a wave of revenge attacks across the city.

The Chechens hit several car showrooms controlled by the Taganskaya gang. During one of the attacks two cars stopped across from the showroom and the men in the cars kept firing machine guns for a good couple of minutes non-stop. Seven people in the showrooms were killed.

The Taganskaya boys retaliated by attacking a grocery market controlled by the Chechens and burning down several big stalls. Later the same day, unknown assailants shot four people outside a casino in the south of Moscow known to be under Chechen control. In the evening and during the night sporadic gunfire could be heard in different parts of the city. By morning several more gangs had been sucked into the conflict.

The resentment against the thugs who were turning the streets of Moscow into battlefields, and against the authorities who were helpless to stop the killings, was growing. Several sporadic demonstrations took place outside police stations. People were accusing the cops of corruption and incompetence. The protesters were quickly dispersed, but the atmosphere in Moscow remained tense. Interior Ministry troops were ordered onto the streets and after nine o'clock in the evening documents were regularly checked.

Seraphim had achieved what he wanted. He also took care of two of his enemies in his 'politburo' who, as he found out, were plotting to speed up his resignation. Through some people he passed word to the Chechens that the two men were involved in the attack on one of their businesses. Both men were gunned down the next day.

Seraphim pretended to be furious and vowed to find the killers of his 'loyal friends'. He also sent flowers to the families of the dead men.

The Crow was prepared to sacrifice as many people as necessary in order to win time and carry out his secret plan to become super rich.

★

General Aleksei Mikhailov was getting more and more confused: strange things were happening in Moscow and beyond and, for some unknown reason, the Kremlin's secret service was bang in the middle of it all...

First there was the shooting of the two Chechen arms dealers outside the Oscar Wilde restaurant. The Kremlin's bodyguards appeared on the scene of the crime minutes later and even claimed that they had been monitoring the two arms dealers for some time and knew about their attempts to negotiate a sale of Red Arrow anti-aircraft rockets for the Chechen rebels. If that was not enough, the Kremlin secret service involved itself in the investigation of the killings and even hinted that it had uncovered a connection between the death of the two arms dealers and the presence of a 'group of foreign mercenaries' in Moscow.

General Mikhailov could not understand why the presidential security team was allowed to operate outside its jurisdiction and meddle in the affairs of other law-enforcement agencies, including the FSB. But it seemed that someone at the very top was turning a blind eye, allowing the President's bodyguards to run loose.

Then a major disaster struck: an entire network of agents, recruited by the FSB in Chechnya, was lost in a matter of days. It was clear to General Mikhailov that someone had revealed their identities to the Chechen rebels. That someone had to be in a very senior position in order to have access to such sensitive information. The General's inquiries revealed, to his amazement, that copies of reports from Chechnya had somehow found their way to the so-called anti-terrorist division of the Kremlin's secret service. It was unclear why it had asked for that information in the first place and how it had been used.

And then came the shooting of Mussa Bartaev and the car bomb murder of Slava the Satan. The first took place in broad daylight, in the centre of Moscow, barely a stone's throw away from the Lubyanka, as if someone had made a point of showing the FSB who was running the show in the capital. The second was a much more complicated hit involving a sophisticated time bomb that had been planted in one of Satan's cars and operated by remote control.

On both occasions the hits were professional – too professional for the General's liking. He was aware of rumours about a secret 'hit squad' operating from within the intelligence service. And if there was any substance to these rumours then the two killings of known gangsters proved that there were some highly trained individuals running loose in Moscow.

But what was bothering General Mikhailov even more was that the Kremlin's secret service was once again meddling in the investigation of both gangland killings. Its people were demanding to see the police reports relating to both crimes and even tried, for some unknown reason, to get access to the forensic evidence.

As more and more people were openly showing their discontent with the way the authorities were handling crime, General Mikhailov was asked by the FSB Director to go on television and reassure the public that the intelligence service, along with the police, would not allow the criminals to get the upper hand. In his interview the General sounded sincere and honest in his promise to bring the criminals to book. He also acknowledged that corruption in the police and the FSB was undermining efforts to win the war against crime and assured the public that drastic steps were needed to root it out.

'It's time to turn our law-enforcement agencies into teams of "untouchables", people who won't give in to any pressure from anyone,' he said. 'The war against crime has to be fought like a real war. It's no longer just a social problem. It's a threat to our national security.'

The interview went down well with most people. General

Mikhailov looked very impressive on screen. His steely grey hair combed back in a 1950s style, his powerful chin, his deeply set dark eyes and his calm and reserved manner of delivery appealed to many. The General became an instant hit with the public, and his idea about a force of 'untouchables' who would fight crime caused a real stir in the media.

The following day he received a call from one of the presidential aides, who congratulated him on his appearance but warned against 'over-passionate' addresses to the public that might inflame the situation even more. 'It sounded a bit too political,' he said. 'It was as if you were thinking of running for some high office.'

The General despised the Kremlin crowd. He knew that they were all terrified of any competition to their boss and kept a close eye on anyone who could be perceived as potential rivals or contenders. Most of the people working in the Kremlin administration were bleak, grey men hired because of their family connections or links to aides.

'I'm a military man and I say what I believe in,' the General retorted. 'I don't have any hidden agendas, apart from my desire to do my job as best as I can.'

The Kremlin aide laughed nervously and bade him farewell.

★

After his TV appearance General Mikhailov launched his own investigation into the murder of the Russian agents in Chechnya, the shooting of the two Chechen arms dealers outside the Oscar Wilde and the high-profile killings of Mussa Bartaev and Slava the Satan. He felt that a strange connection had emerged between these three sinister developments – in all three cases the President's Protection Service had shown an unhealthy interest and even demanded to be kept informed about the ongoing investigations. Not to mention that in the case of the two arms dealers who got killed by a sniper outside the restaurant the Kremlin secret service had even started its own investigation.

General Mikhailov decided to have a word with the head of the Kremlin's security, General Andrei Kapoustin.

The President's Protection Service was a powerful force within the intelligence. Although officially it was part of the Federal Protection Service of the FSB, in reality it had more power and influence than any other division being close to the top leadership of the country. One of Kapoustin's predecessors, the all-powerful General Alexander Korzhakov, who was a long-term friend and drinking partner of Boris Yeltsin, had created a vast network that eventually either duplicated or even took over some of the responsibilities of the presidential staff. The Kremlin's bodyguards even had their own press office and constantly meddled in the affairs of government departments and agencies.

General Mikhailov knew how meet with the chief of the President's security in private, without going through the official channels. He phoned an old friend of his, the managing director of a special health club for senior government officials outside Moscow, and found out when General Kapoustin would be having his next sauna session. He then asked the director to include him in the list of people who would be visiting the health club that day.

The club had everything: a gym, a big swimming pool, a billiard room, and an excellent steam sauna. There was also a dining room with a widescreen TV and a stereo system with speakers in every corner.

On the day when General Kapoustin was having his steam session General Mikhailov arrived at the health club. Kapoustin was not surprised to see him. Saunas were places where government officials would meet each other and exchange the latest gossip.

They went into the steam room and settled down on the upper shelves. Kapoustin threw some water mixed with menthol and eucalyptus leaves over the stones and the steam room quickly got very hot. They had to wait for the temperature to fall a little before they could talk to each other.

Finally Mikhailov broke the silence.

'What have you been up to, Andrei? I haven't seen you for ages.'

'Well, well, look who's asking the questions,' Kapoustin replied sarcastically. 'I thought your people were informed about everything. Listening to our telephone conversations and planting bugs in our cars and offices.'

'You know we don't do it any more,' Mikhailov said with a faint smile.

They sat in silence for a while.

'So how is the old man doing?' Mikhailov said.

'That is a state secret,' Kapoustin said jokingly. 'I'm not allowed to discuss it.'

Mikhailov nodded. He knew that the President's state of health had become a sensitive issue, especially after his recent heart attack. It reminded him of the times when the state of health of Soviet leaders was one of the biggest secrets.

They waited till the sand clock showed that they'd spent a full fifteen minutes in the steam room and then moved to the dining area. There was a bottle of vodka on the table along with two bowls of fresh vegetables and a large plate of sizzling kebabs. Warm Lavash bread was cut up in big slices and lay in a pile on a wooden plate. In Russia most health clubs served alcohol on their premises. No one saw the irony in the fact that many members got drunk instead of working out.

After having several drinks and discussing what their mutual friends and acquaintances were up the two men gradually moved to internal politics.

'There's too much confusion everywhere nowadays,' Mikhailov was complaining. 'Contradictory orders coming from the top, inexperienced people being appointed to run huge ministries and departments, sensitive information being passed to anyone who asks for it. I wish someone would tell me what the hell's going on. There's no longer any system in place.'

'You worry too much, Aleksei,' Kapoustin said, chewing on a kebab. 'It was as bad before. Remember the South Korean passenger plane that was shot down over Siberia? Where was the system then? At first no one wanted to take responsibility for giving an order to force the plane down or destroy it. For several hours they were passing the buck to each other while the plane was flying over our territory without permission. Top people were not answering their phones at the time just because they didn't want to make a decision.'

'And do you remember that stupid first official statement published by TASS? It actually claimed that the plane had left Soviet air space in the direction of the Sea of Japan. What bloody Sea of Japan? By then everyone knew that it had already been blown to pieces with all the passengers on it!'

Kapoustin poured some more vodka into the two glasses in front of them.

'And at the time of the incident with the South Korean plane we supposedly had the most effective government machine on earth.'

They toasted each other in silence and drank the vodka.

'And don't forget Afghanistan,' Kapoustin continued. 'If anyone needed proof that our whole system had gone rotten, that was it. It was probably the first time in history that a full-scale war was started simply because some people in the leadership had decided to conduct an ideological experiment and prove to the whole bloody world that socialism can emerge from the Stone Age—'

Mikhailov interrupted him.

'Okay, okay, I get your message,' he said. 'You're saying that things are as bad now as they were then. But even with all the mess we had in the past there was still some sort of chain of command, some kind of order. Good or bad, but that system worked!'

Kapoustin wiped the sweat off his face with a towel.

'I'm surprised at you, Aleksei,' he said. 'Are you naive or just pretending not to see things the way they are? Years ago I too was under the impression that we had a "system", as you call it. I thought that whatever was happening, somewhere in the depths of the Central Committee of our beloved Party there were people who were preserving the national interests, who were ready to act in time of national crisis. But when Konstantin Chernenko, that walking corpse, was elected by his Politburo chums as General Secretary of the Communist Party I finally realised that there was no one up there. Just a bunch of apparatchiks worried only about their jobs.'

Kapoustin put some more kebabs on his plate and looked at the empty bottle of vodka as if asking himself whether he had drunk enough or whether he should call the waiter to bring another bottle.

'So then I decided to stop worrying,' he said. 'What was the point of getting disappointed all the time? But you are still at it, aren't you? Still trying to analyse everything, always the wise guy. Beware, it's not a good time for wise guys in Russia. Do you really think that nobody else can see that many things aren't right? What do you expect from the people at the top? They have inherited this mess from Gorbachev and Yeltsin. They need time to sort it out.'

General Mikhailov decided that it was time to skip the philosophy and get down to business.

'I want to ask you about the Chechen network,' he said.

Kapoustin gave him a surprised look.

'I thought you were the main expert on that subject,' he said. 'If I'm not mistaken this whole idea of creating a secret network of spies in Chechnya was your doing?'

'The idea was mine,' Mikhailov confirmed gloomily, 'but it turned out that too many people knew about the network…'

Kapoustin grinned.

'Are you by any chance suspecting someone in government of betraying your agents?'

Mikhailov nodded.

'That's exactly what I think happened. And I won't rest until I find out who did it. You know everything that's going on behind the Kremlin walls. Can you tell me who apart from your anti-terrorist team knew about the operation in Chechnya?'

Kapoustin put some more kebabs on his plate, as if he was counting them.

'I think some of the advisors to the President had received that information,' he said.

Mikhailov was not satisfied with the answer.

'The President has many advisors. Which ones specifically?'

Kapoustin looked at the empty bottle of vodka once again. He was starting to become irritated with the direction the conversation was taking.

'Look, Aleksei,' he said, looking Mikhailov straight in the eyes, 'I've known you for many years and I've always tried to help when I could. But this time I suggest that you stay away from this whole matter. It's in your interest to do so.'

But Mikhailov was not prepared to give up.

'I know that there are some things that should be left alone,' he said. 'But this time I need to know. Think of it as a matter of stupid pride. I've spent a lot of time creating the network in Chechnya. We were getting proper intelligence for the first time in the whole campaign. And then someone simply gave all the names to the rebels. I need to know what happened, if only to avoid the same mistake in the future.'

Kapoustin was looking at his plate while Mikhailov was talking. He was visibly irritated now.

'If it's any consolation to you,' he said, 'the information was requested by the special advisor to the President.'

'You mean Vassili?'

'Yes.'

That was what General Mikhailov needed to know. The pieces of the jigsaw puzzle had finally fallen into a pattern. And the President's son was smack in the middle of it all.

When he arrived home that evening he discovered a thick envelope in his letterbox. When he opened it, he found documents inside along with a cover note saying: 'These are the papers of the Central Brotherhood. They may interest you.'

★

After the meeting at The King's Retreat things moved fast. It was always a mystery to Seraphim how an idiot like Vassili could set the wheels in motion so quickly.

The elimination of both Mussa Bartaev and Slava the Satan was done very professionally. As a result the whole of Moscow's underworld was in complete disarray with most of the major gangs sucked into the conflict.

The loan issue was also resolved very quickly. One of Seraphim's companies, which had earlier applied to the Central Bank for a loan of fifteen million dollars to start the construction of a chain of betting shops in Moscow, was suddenly given the green light. The idea was to create a chain which would receive bets on sports events outside Russia, like football and racing in Britain, baseball and basketball in America and boxing world-wide. The licence had already been issued by the gaming commission of the Moscow government.

On paper, the project looked very impressive. A betting chain would open in Moscow providing much-needed taxes for the local budget, which was being constantly drained by huge construction contracts awarded to the close friends of Moscow's mayor.

The money was available immediately, so Seraphim wasted no time transferring it to the accounts of his company. The next day it was sent to an account in Hungary and from there to an off-shore account. This was illegal, of course, but Seraphim was not planning to remain in Russia for long, so he did not care what anyone might think.

★

Vadim Mironov was growing impatient. More than two weeks had passed since his meeting with Boris, who had told him about the people from Moscow who were interested in buying properties in Kensington Palace Gardens. But as yet there were no signs that Boris had actually pointed anyone in his direction. He was getting worried that someone else might barge in and take over the lucrative job.

Vadim had been waiting for an opportunity like this for a long time. His hospitality company was not doing well and he was under serious financial pressure. And yet he didn't even think of changing his lifestyle; he was dating several women at once and treating them to some serious wining and dining in London. He was driving a brand new BMW and had recently moved into a luxury rented apartment in Chelsea.

He was enjoying life and was not prepared to sacrifice any of his pleasures.

Then at last came the phone call he was waiting for. The man introduced himself simply as 'Glyeb' and said that he wanted to talk about some of the things that Boris Ossinski had mentioned to him.

'You have a great Russian name,' Vadim said. 'These days people tend to go for foreign-sounding names and ignore the great Russian heritage.'

The caller didn't seem impressed.

'I suggest that we meet tomorrow at three o'clock,' he said dryly. 'At the Embassy Hotel.'

'That suits me just fine,' Mironov said. He was prepared to meet these people any time and any place. 'I'll be wearing a brown suit and a gorgeous yellow tie.'

After he put the phone down he felt that he shouldn't have said 'a gorgeous yellow tie'. It made him sound like an idiot, he thought. But he so wanted them to know that he was a man of good taste and that he could find the best houses in London for them!

They met at the bar of the hotel on the ground floor. Glyeb arrived with a man who introduced himself only as Shamil. He was holding a black leather folder in his hand. The place was crowded and noisy and they had to look for a table so that they could hear each other. Once they settled down Glyeb got straight to the point.

'I gather Boris Ossinski has already spoken to you about the matter of finding good properties in London?' he said.

Mironov scratched his forehead, as if trying to recall their conversation.

'He didn't really go into any specific details,' he said. 'He simply told me that someone had approached him asking for information about properties in Kensington Palace Gardens and that he was thinking whether he should take on the job or not.'

Glyeb was watching him closely.

'Anything else he told you?' he said.

Mironov was desperately trying to recall his conversation with Boris.

'No, that's about it,' he said. 'He did mention something about his son being in some sort of trouble, but I couldn't really understand what he was bragging on about. Boris can be a bit weird at times, you know. One thing I can tell you straight away: he's definitely not the man for the job. He's got no experience, no sense of style, no class. If you want to buy property in London, I'm your man.'

Glyeb nodded.

'Tell me, Comrade Mironov,' he said, 'are you a patriot of your country?'

Vadim was taken aback by the question. He was getting ready to discuss properties and prices and all of a sudden he was asked about his feelings towards the country he was only happy to leave behind.

'I guess I am,' he said slowly, 'but what does it have to do with our meeting?'

Glyeb smiled.

'I just thought I'd better find out what sort of man I'm dealing with,' he said.

'We meet a lot of Russian people during our travels and some of them have only one thing on their minds: money and more money. No sense of national pride, no understanding of the relevance of some things, no integrity.'

Vadim could not understand what the man was getting at. But he decided to play along.

'Yes, come to think of it, I'm a patriot of my country,' he said. 'I may live abroad, but I still care deeply what happens at home.'

'Good,' Glyeb said with a wry smile. 'Now is your chance to help your country. You see we work for a leading financial group which has been appointed by the government to invest serious amounts of money into properties abroad. The returns from such investments are potentially enormous and the group has decided to start with London, the world's leading property market. So how about providing us with information about the houses in Kensington Palace Gardens?'

Mironov smiled broadly.

'Just tell me what you want to know and I'll get you all the information you need,' he said.

Without uttering a word Shamil handed Mironov a leather folder.

'You might find some of the things we want to know a bit strange,' Glyeb said. 'But we need to know everything about the properties as some of them may later be sold to Russian businessmen and bankers. And you know how these people are. They worry about their personal security, insist on total privacy, and want to keep their valuables protected. So don't be surprised by some of the questions posed.'

Vadim took the file, opened it, glanced at a couple of pages and then closed it again.

'I don't really care what my clients do in their spare time,' he said. 'As long as we agree on the price I'm willing to provide you with anything you want, including the plans of the Crown Jewels in the Tower of London. How much time do I have?'

'Not a lot, I'm afraid,' Glyeb said. 'We need everything in less than a week. But we'll pay you $500,000 in cash for the urgency.'

Mironov smiled nervously. It seemed that he was about to ask a question.

'We'll only pay on delivery,' Glyeb said, anticipating the question. 'But we'll pay the full amount and, as I said, in cash.'

Mironov licked his dry lips. He always got that dryness of the lips when he was discussing money matters. The temptation to ask for a prepayment was great. But there was something about Glyeb and his companion that put him off making any demands.

'One more thing,' Glyeb said. 'I would ask you not to breathe a word about what we've discussed today to anyone. Not to your friends, not to your relatives. And I also suggest that you keep this secret from you friend, Boris Ossinski. There's no point him knowing about our little arrangement. Okay?'

Mironov nodded.

'We were never close friends anyway,' he said. 'So I have no desire to involve him in my affairs.'

On his way back to the office Mironov was cursing himself. I should have asked for at least ten per cent deposit! he thought. Never work without a deposit. Idiot! Idiot! Idiot!

★

Flying into London, Pavel was lost deep in his memories.

How strange it was, he thought, that he was going to a place where he had spent most of his childhood, a place he had never imagined that he would ever go back to.

It was more than thirty years ago that Pavel had first come to Britain with his mother to join his stepfather, a senior diplomat at the Soviet embassy in London. His stepfather, Viktor Samarin, was only in his late twenties and already First Secretary, a very senior diplomatic rank for a man of his age. Viktor was the son of a big party boss and his career in the Ministry of Foreign Affairs made many people envious.

Viktor started travelling abroad when he was only twenty-three years old. In Soviet times he was part of a select circle whose members visited other countries and were considered celebrities simply because they were able to cross the borders of the USSR.

Pavel's mother could not resist the dashing young diplomat she met at a party at the home of one of her friends. She had left her husband when Pavel was only two years old and she married Viktor as soon as her divorce came through. Not only was Pavel officially adopted, but his mother somehow managed to get a new birth certificate issued which stated that he was born Pavel Viktorovich Samarin. He did not know about the existence of his biological father until he was in his early twenties, by which time he had already died of cancer. But Pavel still restored his name back to Pavel Aleksandrovich Batalov.

The rift with his stepfather happened when Pavel declined to be recruited to the KGB during his last year in college. He had other plans. He wanted to become a journalist and not spend another three years in the KGB academy supposedly mastering the art of the cloak and dagger. He had little respect for the so-called 'warriors of the invisible front'. Many of them were arrogant people who used their position to harass others. Pavel couldn't stand those thugs and often said so publicly. So he was very surprised when he was invited for a 'chat' with the KGB recruitment officers. He told his stepfather about the forthcoming meeting and his decision to say 'no' to the KGB.

Viktor was furious.

'You stupid idiot!' he yelled, his face turning red. 'It's your only chance to work abroad! I've done everything humanly possible to get you into college and now you want to screw up such a chance! Don't you realise that they'll blacklist you and you'll never get a decent job?'

Pavel still said 'no' to the KGB and very soon found out that his stepfather's prediction was correct. Two months before graduation, when all of his college chums were getting 'recruitment requests' from different ministries and departments, he received no job offers. The only possible choice open to him was to become a customs inspector at Sheremetyevo International Airport.

It was then that Pavel surprised everyone. He applied to the Moscow central CID and joined the division investigating crimes committed by foreigners living in the Soviet Union. He was accepted immediately, as the Moscow central CID could not normally even hope to get recruits who spoke English fluently and had spent time in the West.

★

Pavel sat glued to the window as the plane began its descent.

Flying over the centre of London in the direction of Heathrow Airport he could see the Houses of Parliament, Trafalgar Square, Buckingham Palace. His heart was beating faster as he anticipated stepping down from the plane in the country which he always considered to be his second home. He also had a feeling that he might not be returning to Russia soon, as the Prosecutor General's office had began issuing arrest warrants against high-ranking policemen and Interior Ministry officials. The little black book that Pavel had found during that drug bust was coming back to haunt the corrupt cops.

As the plane was making its descent, scenes from Pavel's childhood days flashed through his mind. He remembered how he had arrived in London for the first time more than thirty years ago and his stepfather had met them at Heathrow. They drove from the airport in a strange-looking car called a Rover. Everything about it was unusual, especially the steering wheel being on the 'wrong' side. And he was fascinated by the red double-decker buses, the black cabs, and the many makes and models of cars on the roads. Back in Moscow there were only three types of mass-produced cars on the roads – Volga, Moskvitch and Zaporozhets. And there were so few of them there compared to the constant flow of traffic on the streets of London.

Pavel couldn't help smiling as he remembered his first visit to a supermarket with his mother. He was amazed to discover so many types of chocolates and sweets on display. And chewing gum – so popular and so scarce in the Soviet Union that children used to pass it around to their friends even when they had already chewed it – was sold in so many different varieties. He was also fascinated by the selection of exotic fruit and vegetables in the store. In Moscow the shops sold only basic fruit and vegetables and things like bananas and pineapples were unheard of.

The first year was difficult for Pavel, as he didn't speak or understand English and had to learn the language quickly. His stepfather tried to speed up the process and gave him a few lessons, but it all ended in tears as Viktor could not understand why his stepson could not grasp what he was told.

What else was it that he still remembered about those distant times spent in Britain? he thought. Ah yes, the music. His parents played tapes with songs of the Beatles. He remembered the Beatles. It was a strange kind of music, nothing like the songs he was used to in Russia. It was loud, it was aggressive, it was pleasant, and it was melodic and catchy. The lyrics were very simple, even primitive, but everyone seemed to like them. The Brits were always very good at selling their musical talent to the whole world.

He also remembered the TV programmes. *Danger Man*, *Dr Who*, *The Avengers*... Ah, *The Avengers*! Now that was something! Like a fairy tale, with people driving strange-looking cars and chasing weird-looking criminals.

And then there was the dreadful *Coronation Street*. He could still hear the opening music and the credits with hundreds of rooftops, all with chimneys. Pavel hated *Coronation Street*, because when it came on his mother would usually walk into the dining room where the television was and would say, 'Now Pavel, go to your room and read a book or a comic while I enjoy half an hour of peace...'

Then there was the football. His favourite team was Chelsea. He loved to watch them play. And the World Cup of 1966. His stepfather arranged some tickets and took him to Wembley. And what a final it was. England versus Germany. All the Russians in London were of course supporting England. And they clinched the title. Pavel so exhausted himself supporting England that day that afterwards he fell ill.

He also remembered his parents arguing about money, about his poor marks at school, about his stepfather coming home late from work. And he also recalled overhearing his mother and stepfather discussing Britain with their friends. They would both say that London was the best city in the world, the 'cradle of tradition', as his stepfather described it.

For Russians there was so much to see in London. You simply must go and see the Tower, his mother would say to visitors from Moscow. And don't forget Piccadilly Circus, the National Gallery, Madame Tussauds. And if you go shopping don't miss Selfridges and Marks and Spencer.

There were very few bad things in Britain, as Pavel could gather from what he heard the adults say. The women were 'too thin', no one seemed to have a proper haircut and it rained a lot. They were also complaining about the taps in the sinks being split into 'hot' and 'cold', making it difficult to wash their hands and faces thoroughly, especially in winter, and about the food being unseasoned and generally 'dull'.

Once, the Soviet military attaché, a general, came to their house with his wife for a drink. He walked into Pavel's room when he was sitting on the floor playing with his toy soldiers.

'I bet you want to be a soldier when you grow up,' he said looking at the battle raging on the carpet.

'Nah, I want to be a secret agent like James Bond,' Pavel said. He got up from the floor and took out his James Bond kit, a toy gun with a silencer and a telescopic sight.

The general smiled.

'That's a mighty impressive-looking gun you have there, young man,' he said. 'I hope you know how to use it.'

Later when the adults were having drinks in the dining room he heard the general say, 'The British have one thing in common with us Russians. Just like us they're as stubborn as mules. That's why when the Nazis started the Second World War, we were the only two nations stubborn enough not to give in. We both lost a lot of people, got into debt, but we didn't give in…'

Pavel's stepfather laughed.

'You're such a philosopher, Evgeni,' he said. 'But don't forget what the Party teaches us – it was the Soviet Union that broke the back of the Nazis.'

Then everybody started talking at the same time and Pavel could no longer follow what they were saying.

When he returned to Russia for good, Pavel sensed that he was being treated like someone special. Grown-ups would come up to him and say, 'You lucky boy, you've been to England. Tell me all about it. Is it true that it always rains there and the fog is so thick that you can't see your outstretched hand?'

He would start explaining about the rain and the fog but they would cut him short and pat him on the head. 'You lucky boy,' they would say, staring at him as if he was some unusual creature.

He also remembered that look in the eyes of the KGB officer who tried to recruit him at his last year in college. He had received a phone call from the faculty director, who told him that he was going to have an interview at a police station, of all places. Pavel arrived there and was shown to a small office that had only one desk and two chairs in it.

A man was sitting at the desk. He looked up at Pavel when he walked in and signalled to him to sit down.

'I can see, Comrade Samarin, that you've lived in England for many years,' he said without introducing himself. 'Tell me about England. I always wanted to go there.'

It all seemed like a dream. And yet here he was, about to touch down in London.

★

Seraphim gathered his 'politburo' for the last time.

Not that his people knew it was their last ever meeting. They were still coming to terms with the loss of their 'brothers' in the war that was sparked by the murders of Mussa Bartaev and Slava the Satan. Many of the businesses controlled by the Central Brotherhood had been paralysed and some had been completely destroyed by competitors. The documents that had surfaced all over Moscow did a lot of damage to the gang. In effect it was falling apart with many of the 'brothers' switching sides or simply going into hiding to avoid being shot by rivals.

Many of the 'politburo' members were blaming the Crow for the disaster. Seraphim knew that he would have to leave the country as soon as possible. His gang was no longer of any importance to him.

The job in London was supposed to make him millions. He decided that he would then move to America and settle down somewhere on the West Coast. He would buy a new identity and nobody would ever find him. And to hell with his people! They would have to look after themselves. No big deal, as most of them had been stealing from him for years anyway. They must still have some money hidden under their mattresses – enough to live on after they came out of jail.

For Seraphim was actually planning to betray most of his 'brothers' by providing the police with enough evidence to send them all away for many years. He reckoned as he was no longer going to run the Central Brotherhood, it was just as well that it did not exist at all. The people he had hired for the London operation were completely unknown to his gang. He always remembered his late father's advice about keeping his secrets to himself. That's why even Shark didn't know anything about the London job.

At the meeting Seraphim proposed to elect a new head of the gang in three weeks' time. Everyone agreed.

And that was the end of the Central Brotherhood.

★

Access to the President of Russia was always extremely difficult.

The entire Kremlin administration seemed to be involved in an obscure game of trying to prevent anyone whom they perceived as an 'outsider' from gaining, as it was jokingly called, 'access to the body'.

The Kremlin staff seemed to be obsessed with the idea that the top man should have as little exposure to the outside world as possible. Many senior officials would be denied the chance of meeting the President simply because they were deemed to be an unnecessary risk to the stability of the presidential office, whatever that meant. Work schedules would be changed unexpectedly so that the President would be unable to meet with people who might voice concern about any of the Kremlin's policies. Visitors would be briefed and instructed what to say and what not to say to the President when they met him. It was a remarkable situation: the leader of a nuclear power was denied access to a lot of information simply because the people around him were too scared to let him learn the truth.

The Kremlin administration consisted of groups of officials linked to different business empires. Money was paid to them in ways that would not compromise them directly. A low-interest loan would be given to the wife of a head of department, and would be later written off with no fuss. A book would be commissioned for a lot of money about some obscure country that no one would read. A consultancy fee for allegedly 'precious advice' would be paid to the son or a nephew of some senior aide. A holiday abroad would be arranged for a fraction of the price, a refurbishment would be done in a flat or a country house for virtually nothing, a close relative would be provided with a highly paid job.

It did not cost much to buy information about the situation in the Kremlin. And in Russia, where the economy was always highly politicised, it was crucial to have someone on the inside who could inform in advance about certain decisions.

As the health of the President deteriorated, meetings with officials and politicians became less frequent. The Kremlin aides now had a new and very effective way of blocking any attempts to contact the head of state. The President is being monitored by doctors, they would say. Or, the President is having a check-up. Or, the President has been strongly advised by medics to rest.

There was nothing much anyone could say to that.

Most visitors were required to explain what sort of subjects they were planning to raise during the meeting with the head of state. If they were going to ask for any favours, like, for example, a promotion, they had to tell the aides about it in advance. On some occasions a request to meet the head of state would be denied simply because the Kremlin aides deemed the answers to their questions 'evasive'.

The only people with unrestricted access to the President, apart from the Prime Minister, were the so-called *siloviki*, the heads of the security services, the defence and interior ministers and, in their absence, their deputies. There were also several close friends of the First Family who were able to put through a request and sometimes get to see the President in a matter of days. Sometimes a name would drop out from the list of close friends and another would replace it. And sometimes the old names managed to creep back in again. No one really knew exactly how it all worked.

General Mikhailov had no problem arranging a private meeting with the President, especially as the FSB Director was away at the time. It was not uncommon for the deputies of security chiefs to talk to the head of state in private. In fact, the President encouraged these meetings; it gave him the opportunity to pretend that he knew certain things that were unavailable even to members of his inner circle. That is why, when stating their reasons to see the President, the heads of the intelligence services and their deputies would write down something like, 'To inform the head of state of matters relating to national security.'

But on this particular occasion General Mikhailov was going in knowing that he was about to drop a bombshell. He had collected evidence pointing to the involvement of the President's son, Vassili, in some very suspicious activities. The files that the General had received from an anonymous source proved that Vassili had received large amounts of money from the Central Brotherhood run by a criminal known as the Crow. There was also proof of his involvement in appointing several high-ranking government officials, possibly in return for substantial payments. And there was the evidence that Vassili had been connected with some of the members of the Kremlin's secret service, who had been regularly requesting confidential information from the FSB.

But the most sinister revelation of all concerned his involvement in the leaking of information about the undercover network in Chechnya to the rebels. Copies of confidential documents about the activities of the Russian agents in the republic had found their way to Vassili's office and soon afterwards they mysteriously fell into the hands of the Central Brotherhood, resulting in the entire network being wiped out. This was treason, an offence that still carried the death penalty in Russia.

When General Mikhailov walked into the President's office, the head of state was sitting at his desk, perusing a file. The General stopped about two metres from the desk and cleared his throat twice before the President looked up at him. He smiled and gestured to the leather chair in front of the desk.

'How are you, Aleksei Gavrilovich?' he inquired once the General was seated. 'How is Galina Grigorievna; how are the children?'

Must have been reading my file just now, the General thought. He would never have known my wife's name otherwise. I hope they didn't put in the file that I have gout. It will take us ages to get down to business if he starts asking questions about my health.

But the President was satisfied with the short answers that the General gave.

'All is fine... Family fine... Wife fine... Children fine.'

Once all the niceties had been dealt with the President turned to business.

'So, how are things on the invisible front?' he asked, using the old phrase about the so-called secret war being constantly fought by the intelligence service with the enemies of Russia.

'The battles rage on, sir,' the General replied.

The President nodded in agreement.

'I know exactly what you mean,' he said. 'We're surrounded by enemies, just like in the old days. Only now it's much more difficult to tell who is who.'

The President was convinced that most of Russia's problems were caused by the outside world. He refused to accept the fact that it was his administration's policy that was to blame for the mess in the country.

'So what's your opinion on the Chechen situation?' the President said. 'That is what you wanted to talk to me about, isn't it?'

General Mikhailov gave a brief overview of the overall situation in the republic.

'According to our sources, sir, the Chechen bandits are getting a lot of funding from abroad,' he said. That played along with the President's assumption that all bad things had a foreign cause. 'Our people are reporting an increase in arms shipments to the insurgents. The fighting has intensified in several mountainous regions and our forces have suffered heavy casualties...'

The President immediately got restless. He didn't like to be reminded about military disasters. He remembered well the damage caused to Yeltsin by the Chechen campaign when it went horribly wrong and 100,000 people died.

'I'm aware of the overall situation in Chechnya, General,' he said. 'I know about the problems in the area. Tell me about the loss of the network. What could have gone wrong? I heard that the initial results were excellent.'

General Mikhailov took a deep breath.

'Sir, the information about the undercover network that took us nearly a year to create was passed over to our enemies by someone in our government,' he said. 'The agents were killed as soon as the information reached the bandits. It's a very disturbing development. Before this happened we had succeeded in preventing several major operations by the field commanders because we had been informed in advance by our people on the ground. But now we no longer get any reliable information from the republic...'

The General had to stop to catch his breath. The President was looking at the papers in front of him on the desk.

'The sad fact is,' the General continued, 'that there are officials in Moscow who are prepared to betray their country for money. And if our enemies abroad find out about it they can use the information to blackmail these corrupt officials...'

The President looked up at him. His face darkened.

'What are you getting at, General?' he said. 'I'm not getting your message.'

He knows something, Mikhailov thought. He must have been warned by Kapoustin. The son of a bitch has betrayed me.

But he still decided to go on.

'I'm sorry to inform you, sir,' the General said, 'but I have reasons to believe that your son, Vassili, is involved with a criminal group and is assisting them in providing information to the Chechen bandits. Also, possibly unintentionally, he might have been involved in passing the details about our network to the other side.'

He stopped. He could hear the President's heavy breathing.

'You can go now, General,' he said. 'This meeting is over.'

Mikhailov stood up, saluted the head of state, and walked out of the office.

The President pushed the button on the selector and asked to summon General Kapoustin. Then he called Anatoli, his personal assistant, and asked him to find his son and bring him to the Kremlin.

The security people spent a good two hours searching for Vassili all over Moscow. At last they tracked him down to a massage parlour where he was having a good time with several hookers. His three bodyguards were with him.

A group of gypsies had been summoned to the sauna earlier. They were singing and dancing in a large room where a billiard table would usually have stood. A Siberian bear on a chain was made to 'dance' in front of Vassili.

He had been drinking since early morning and turned nasty when the security people approached him. A jug of ice-cold water and several empty beer bottles were hurled at them when they suggested a trip to the Kremlin. Eventually they managed to persuade Vassili to come with them. He got dressed and left the sauna accompanied by both his own and the Kremlin's minders. All his attempts to find out why he was summoned at such short notice were in vain. The security people were instructed not to say anything, not that they knew anything anyway.

When Vassili walked into his father's office he could immediately tell that something was wrong. The head of the Kremlin secret service, General Kapoustin, was present. He was discussing something with his father and once he appeared in the doorway they stopped talking and looked at him.

Vassili quickly sobered up. He had an amazing ability to get his act together at a moment's notice if the need arose.

'Hi, Dad,' he said, adopting the informal approach. He was family with the President of Russia, and General Kapoustin, as he saw it, was just a piece of shit.

But his father was obviously not in the mood for informality.

'Sit down,' he said, gesturing at the chair in front of his desk.

Vassili obeyed. He sat down on the very edge of the chair, assuming the look of repentance. He could see that his father was trembling with fury.

'What sort of company have you been keeping lately? Vassili,' the President said, his voice shaking with anger, 'I've been hearing things about you, very unpleasant things.'

Vassili shrugged his shoulders. 'I don't know what you are talking about, Dad,' he said.

'Cut the crap!' the President banged his fist on the desk. 'You got mixed up with criminals, you bloody idiot! Do you know what can happen to you if the word gets out that you're involved with people who are connected to the Chechen bandits? Do you realise what you've done?'

At this point Vassili sobered up completely. He was terrified of his father. He always pictured the painting that he had once seen with his class on a tour of the Tretyakov Gallery. It was called *Tsar Ivan the Terrible Kills his Son*. Ivan the Terrible was depicted kneeling on the floor, holding his son whom he had just killed in a fit of rage by hurling a heavy silver candlestick at him. Vassili could still recall the horrified look on the Tsar's face and the bleeding wound on the left temple of the young prince.

He decided that it was time to play the role of the helpless victim.

'It's the curse, Dad,' he sobbed. 'You know, it's the curse.'

The President turned pale. He started to breathe heavily. Sweat appeared on his brow. General Kapoustin signalled to Vassili to leave the room.

Once again the trick had worked, and it'll work again and again, Vassili thought as he walked out of the room. The President looked at the General.

'What do I do now, Andrei?' he said in a tired voice. 'Why are they out to get me? Is it because I wasn't elected through a national poll? But I have taken over legitimately from the first democratically elected president of Russia in a thousand years. And I will prove that I have every right to be here when I win the next election...'

General Kapoustin looked at the President in surprise. Just a few days earlier, at the meeting at his country retreat, he had told all of them about his decision not to run for office. So the plan must have changed in recent days.

'Why are they trying to get rid of me?' the President continued, ignoring Kapoustin's surprised expression. 'I'm an honest man. I've never accepted anything, even small gifts, from anyone. So they get to me through my son. They trick him and get him drunk all the time. They get him into all sorts of trouble. But in reality they're after me. They want to destroy me. Their President.'

Kapoustin felt the anger grow in him. He was getting really annoyed with Mikhailov.

What the hell did he want to achieve? he thought. Some stupid undercover operation that he'd started had not gone as planned. Seven Chechens had died. But we've been losing hundreds of Russian soldiers every month, and that didn't seem to worry the General. And now he wants the truth to come out. As if he didn't know that the army, the Interior Ministry and his treasured FSB were corrupt through and through. That was why I had to beef up the President's Protection Service. We were becoming the untouchables that the General had spoken about so passionately on television. We are the very last echelons of law enforcement and in our book any means are acceptable in the fight against crime. Even physical elimination of the enemies of the state.

Kapoustin looked at the President who suddenly seemed much older than his years.

Mikhailov claims that he wants to know the truth, he thought. Well, the truth is that we've lost the country to the bloody liberals. The Chinese had the guts to stand up to the scum that threatened the future of their country. Had those young thugs at Tiananmen Square triumphed, China would have fallen apart, just like the Soviet Union. But the Chinese were wise, they sent in tanks. Several hundred were killed, but the country was saved. And what did they do in Russia? Gave everything away to the liberals and the criminals. And what is the result? The bloody bastards are pulling the country apart!

Kapoustin straightened in his chair. He looked at the President once again.

'Don't worry, sir,' he said. 'I'll deal with this matter personally.'

He then stood up and marched out of the room. This was his Tiananmen Square. And he was not going to give up without a fight.

★

The team hired by Seraphim to carry out the job in London had been split into several groups, each one travelling by a separate route.

The largest group, consisting of forty men, reached London using the so-called 'hooker's route', via Dublin and Belfast. Russian prostitutes would usually enter Britain this way, hence the nickname. They would obtain tourist visas to the Republic of Ireland and, once in Dublin, would travel by train to Belfast and then take an internal flight to the British capital or any other mainland city. After earning enough to last them several months in Russia they would simply fly home and return with a new passport once the money dried up.

The second party of thirty men travelled to London in several groups from Paris as tourists. They used the Eurostar express having obtained British single-entry tourist visas in Moscow.

The twenty-strong third group had been smuggled into Britain by Spanish fisherman who were paid to take them on board in Spain as sailors and then land them on the south coast of England.

Members of the fifth group arrived in London one by one from different countries and gradually assembled in a small hotel not far from Kensington Palace Gardens. There were twenty highly trained men in the group and they were headed by Colonel Igor Kislov.

That group did not establish any links with the others. They had a separate mission from the rest.

★

The Vice-Premier of the Russian government, Vitalli Tenko, was getting ready to fly to London and then to the US.

He was being sent on an important mission: to hold talks about the launch of a world-wide exhibition of the Kremlin's treasures. Tenko had never before been involved in business negotiations, but he was assured in Moscow that his job was to start the whole thing rolling and a team of experts would then take over from him and deal with the matter.

Vice-Premier Tenko was a great survivor. He started his career under Leonid Brezhnev in the 1970s and from that time onwards managed to stay afloat in political waters, whatever the weather. There were of course ups and downs in his life, but the ability to be liked by his superiors, and his mastery of presenting himself as a simple-minded man with no serious ambitions, helped him greatly.

When communism collapsed and a strange sort of democracy started to blossom in Russia, Tenko was one of the first to transform himself into a fervent democrat, pledging allegiance to Boris Yeltsin and his team of so-called young reformers, ambitious thugs who mishandled everything they touched. After Yeltsin, Tenko skilfully manoeuvred in the stormy political waters, getting appointed Minister for Information, and along the way managing to establish friendly relations with Vassili, the son of the new President, and later with the powerful Kremlin aide, Valentin Ashev. He regularly went to see them both and briefed them on the situation around the Kremlin: who said what about the President, about the government, about the President's aides. No one asked or forced him to do that, but Tenko knew that such services would be greatly appreciated and that he would be able to survive even if he failed every job he was given. Which, in fact, he did. Later he was promoted to the post of Vice-Premier, in charge of all media.

When Tenko was told by the Kremlin to go to London, he immediately agreed. He never said 'no' to any assignment, no matter how unpleasant or inconvenient it was. But on this occasion he was especially unhappy with the idea of flying to London to discuss some stupid exhibition, as he was worried that he'd be away from Moscow at a crucial time when there was talk of an impending reshuffle.

He was well aware that in the past several months the President got into the habit of forgetting the names of some of his aides and ministers. On many occasions there would be very embarrassing scenes at the Kremlin, when the head of state would clearly not recognise some high-ranking official who had actually been around for quite a long time. So the President had to be gently reminded that so-and-so was still in the team and that he was doing a good job. The President would look unsure, realising that once again his memory had failed him. And his aides would feel annoyed at some people's habits of disappearing from sight or travelling abroad too often. One thing could lead to another and at some point a certain minister, whose existence had slipped the President's memory on a couple of occasions, would find himself out of his cushy job.

The one consolation Tenko had was that Vassili, the President's son, had promised him personally that he was going to talk to members of his father's inner circle and lobby on his behalf to keep him as Vice-Premier after the approaching reshuffle.

Tenko was pondering his future in his office when he received a phone call from Vassili.

'Vitalli, how are you?' he inquired.

Tenko pretended to be very happy to hear his voice.

'Vassili, how good of you to call!' he said, as though they hadn't spoken for ages.

'I bet you've already packed your bags and can't wait to get the hell out of Moscow,' Vassili said and roared with laughter, convinced that he had said something very funny.

Tenko knew well that most government phone lines were tapped, so he pretended that he was not at all happy with the forthcoming trip. Throughout his whole political career Tenko was always very careful what he said on the phone and even how he said it. This time he pretended that he was not very keen on going away. Just in case.

'Oh, I've got mixed feelings,' he said. 'On the one hand I should be happy that I'm flying out to London, but on the other hand I'm reluctant to leave Russia. I've got so much work to do here and I promised my wife that we were going to spend a week with her mother in Yalta and now she feels let down.'

'Cut the bullshit!' Vassili said. 'You're going to Britain, not to bloody Mongolia, so you should be jumping with joy. And besides, what's there to do in your bloody Yalta. Don't give me that crap about feeling sorry.'

Tenko giggled to show that he appreciated Vassili's sense of humour.

'I'd like to ask you for a small favour,' Vassili said, changing the subject. 'I hope you won't refuse the request of the special advisor to the President?'

'Vassili, how could you say such a thing,' Tenko said. 'You know me. I'm a big fan of the President and his family.'

Vassili laughed. That always worked on people. They could never refuse him a favour. Even if they didn't like what they were asked to do.

'I want you to take a passenger on board with you,' he said. 'A fellow traveller. He's a friend of mine and I'm sure you'll get on just fine with one another. His name is Voronov, Seraphim Voronov.'

Tenko bit his lip. He knew the name well. In fact he had, at one time, tried to establish some sort of an 'understanding' with Seraphim and possibly earn some money along the way. But later he changed his mind when he heard rumours about Seraphim and his people. Vice-Premier Tenko was always prepared to bend the rules a little, but he was cautious and careful enough not to deal openly with people who were too well known for all the wrong reasons.

Yet he couldn't say 'no' to Vassili.

'I'll be delighted to take him with me,' he said cheerfully. 'How can I refuse to help anyone who is friendly with the First Family?'

Tenko stressed every word in his last sentence, hoping that the people who were tapping their conversation got everything right.

★

It was time for Alex and Clay to leave Moscow.

The only problem was that they could not simply board a plane and fly out of Russia or hop on a train and travel abroad. They were bound to be detained at the immigration desk or at the border control. The people who were monitoring them were obviously not prepared to let them leave the country.

Jeremy decided to turn for help to the Statesman. He traced him to Paris, where he was on a lecture tour. When they met, Jeremy told him about the situation. The old man was not at all happy.

'You do come up with the most awkward of requests sometimes,' he said. 'Just like your late father. And I must be a madman to agree to help you.'

But he did. He called a friend in Moscow from the hotel room and hinted that there was a delicate matter in respect of which he needed his help. Jeremy suddenly realised that it was probably not the first time that the Statesman had called his mysterious Moscow friend to request help in a 'delicate matter'.

'How can he contact your people in Moscow?' he whispered to Jeremy, covering the receiver.

Jeremy gave him the phone number of Liberman who was informed about the situation and could pass word to Alex and Clay without the Russian intelligence finding out about it.

'Oh, and just to let you know,' the Statesman said, having given the man the number, 'the people in question might be experiencing a certain breach of their privacy at the moment, if you know what I mean.'

★

They were all gathering at Mount Street…

Both Alex and Clay had safely returned from Moscow, flown out of Russia on a chartered plane destined for Budapest with new passports. Everything had been arranged by a Russian whom the Statesman had contacted from Paris. Pavel came to London on a regular flight from St Petersburg.

Their mission in Russia was accomplished. The Central Brotherhood had fallen apart. The authorities were moving in on the gang, weakened by infighting and pressure from other groups, who received documents showing that the Brotherhood was double-crossing them behind their backs. Pavel's contacts in the central CID and in the Prosecutor General's office were looking into the matter of Ivan Ossinski's arrest. The two traffic cops who 'busted' Ivan were about to be arrested.

The documents incriminating the Crow and his friends at the top had also been passed to the FSB and to the Prosecutor General's office through Liberman. Seraphim's days were obviously numbered and there was no sign of Shark after he had been exposed as the 'traitor'.

And yet some important questions still remained unanswered. The file found at Seraphim's villa indicated that something sinister was about to happen in London. The Central Brotherhood may have been destroyed in Moscow, but there remained a possibility that the criminals might yet strike in the British capital.

Suddenly the spotlight was on London...

★

The meeting at Mount Street was due to start soon. Pavel had arrived at the flat where Alex and Clay had already spent an hour talking to Jeremy. They were expecting George and Ron to come any minute. Earlier, George had telephoned and said that he was paying a visit to 'some Russian friends' with Ron. It sounded strange, but George promised to explain everything on his arrival.

They appeared half an hour later and the meeting started. Everyone gathered in the dining room. George and Ron were looking strangely calm. They were sitting at the table sipping tea.

Jeremy stood up.

'Gentlemen,' he said, 'I'm happy to announce that the Moscow phase of Operation Saving Ivan has been successfully completed. We've managed to smash the gang that was putting unnecessary pressure on my friends. I'd like to thank all of you for your part in that operation.'

Jeremy pointed to several thick briefcases. They contained the payment for each member of the team.

'And now Mr Blunt will brief us on the current situation.'

Jeremy sat down. George remained seated. He got out a small notebook and put it in front of him.

'Before we proceed any further,' he said, 'I'd like to make it clear that the money you've been paid today only covers the Moscow stage of the operation. As for your services over here, there'll be additional funds provided to you on completion. Any objections to that?'

There were obviously no objections.

'And now that we've cleared the financial side of things let's get back to business,' George said. 'It seems, gentlemen, that we may soon find ourselves confronted by a group of highly trained individuals who have recently arrived in London. We have reason to believe that they have set up their base at number 10 Kensington Palace Gardens. There's some very unusual activity taking place in the building that has been recently vacated by the Russian diplomats. Technically, it still belongs to the Russian embassy. Until the lease expires, that is. But at the moment it's being used by a team from Moscow that seems to have acquired a lot of friends in London in the past couple of weeks. I'd say about a hundred or so friends.'

George glanced at the notebook and continued.

'There are also two men claiming to be Russian intelligence officers who've been meeting a lot of people recently and asking all sorts of questions about Kensington Palace Gardens,' he said. 'We've managed to check their identities and found out that they once worked for the KGB. However, that was a good while ago. Since then they've been linked with several organised criminal groups in Moscow, including, surprise, surprise, the late Central Brotherhood.'

George just couldn't resist the temptation to pronounce the Brotherhood dead.

'That means,' he said, 'that the two so-called agents have come to London to assist the criminals in carrying out their plans. Having evaluated the situation, we've come to the conclusion that the criminals are planning a robbery at one or several addresses in Kensington Palace Gardens. It's quite possible that they're targeting the Russian ambassador's residence where some very valuable paintings are on display in the halls on the ground floor. Also, we've learned that a cargo of items for an exhibition of Russian folk art has arrived at the embassy recently and is being stored at the compound...'

George closed the notebook and looked around the room.

'The situation,' he said, 'is complicated by the fact that we have no definite proof of anything illegal being planned and therefore can't go to the authorities. Another problem is that we are greatly outnumbered by the possible enemy and will need some back-up to offer resistance. That's why Mr Baker and I paid a visit to the Russian ambassador. We told him about our suspicions and asked him for assistance...'

Jeremy looked up at George and his left eyebrow rose slowly upwards. Clay stopped chewing his gum, a sign of great surprise. Alex looked completely bewildered and Pavel thought that he must have misheard the last sentence.

George was waiting for the initial shock to pass. Ron was watching everyone with interest.

'I can see by your reaction, gentlemen, that you anticipated such a move,' George concluded jokingly.

Clay was the first to get over his surprise and start chewing again.

'I guess it's the only way out,' he said matter-of-factly. 'If we're up against an army we'll need some help. So why not pick the Russkies?'

'Beautifully put, Mr Jones,' George said. He turned to Pavel. 'We've arranged with the Russian ambassador to have a liaison officer to help us communicate with the embassy,' he said. 'I hope that you, Mr Batalov, will take up the position with immediate effect.'

Pavel nodded.

'I'm ready to go there straight away,' he said.

'In that case,' George said, 'I'll arrange for the transport to take you to Kensington Palace Gardens and for me and Mr Hunter and Mr Jones to go get some equipment we might need. Meanwhile,' he turned to Jeremy, 'I hope that Mr Baker will be able to fill you in, sir, on the details of our very useful visit to the Russian embassy.'

George signalled to Alex, Clay and Pavel to follow him. When they had all left, Jeremy walked over to the bar and filled two glasses with Scotch. He then sat across the table from Ron and said, 'I would love to hear your story.'

Ron smiled. 'Well, it was like this, old boy…'

★

The chartered plane carrying Vice-Premier Tenko had landed in London.

The Vice-Premier was carrying a letter to the Russian ambassador informing him about the real nature of the cargo that had been delivered earlier and was being kept in his residence. In the letter the ambassador was instructed to give all support necessary to the Vice-Premier in arranging sponsorship for the Unseen Kremlin Treasures exhibition. The letter said nothing about plans to raise credits secured on the treasures and Tenko himself had no more than a very vague idea about the plan.

Seraphim Voronov arrived on the same plane.

The Vice-Premier was met at the airport by Boris Ossinski, who was standing in for the ambassador. Tenko was visibly annoyed by the ambassador's absence, although he tried very hard not to show it. He came up to Boris and hugged him as if they were old friends.

'I hope that my dear friend Yuri is well,' he said, as if hoping to hear that the ambassador was indisposed, which would explain his absence.

Boris had been instructed by the ambassador to say that he was preoccupied with unexpected urgent diplomatic work. Tenko was not at all happy to hear that.

A vice-premier of the government is coming to London and the ambassador can't find the time to greet him at the airport! he thought angrily. I'll need to have a word with Vassili in Moscow and tell him how I was treated.

It was then that Seraphim approached them. Boris had not been told about anyone else coming with the Vice-Premier and thought that he must be an interpreter, although he didn't look like one at all, with his expensive coat worn over a smart Italian suit.

Tenko hesitated for a moment, obviously unsure what to say.

'I'd like to introduce Mr Seraphim Voronov who is accompanying me on this trip,' he said finally. 'He is a close friend of the First Family.'

Being a careful man, Tenko decided to present Seraphim as somebody else's friend. He'd heard a few things about Seraphim, some of them very unpleasant things, and he didn't want to be seen as being too close to Mr Voronov.

Boris looked at the stranger. The name had been mentioned that same morning during the bizarre meeting at the embassy between the ambassador and George Blunt and Ron Baker.

George had said that the people who were planning a major crime in London were controlled by Seraphim Voronov, also known as the Crow.

Was it just a coincidence that a man travelling with the Vice-Premier of Russia had the same name and surname? Boris thought. He decided that it must have been a coincidence, as it was impossible to imagine that he was meeting the man who had ordered his son to be framed by the police. He did sense, however, that the Vice-Premier was not exactly enthusiastic about his companion.

Boris shook hands with Seraphim.

'Welcome to London; my name is Boris Ossinski,' he greeted him.

Voronov gave him a strange, slightly startled look.

'I hope London will be good to me,' he said. 'I have a feeling that this city will bring me luck.'

They walked to the Jaguar with its RUS 1 licence plates. The ambassador had sent his official car to pick up the Vice-Premier at the airport. Boris opened the back door for Tenko, but Seraphim pushed him aside and got in first. Tenko had to walk around the car to get in from the other side.

On their way to the embassy they stopped at the Park Lane Hilton where, as Seraphim explained, he had a room booked for him. When the car stopped and he got out, two men who were standing outside the hotel entrance rushed to him. Seraphim walked towards them. He didn't even bother to say goodbye to anyone in the car.

What a strange character, Boris thought. Behaves like a typical rich Russian thug.

He turned around and looked at the Vice-Premier as if inviting him to make a comment of some sort. But Tenko remained silent.

★

Russian traffic cops are a unique breed.

They had developed a sixth sense that enabled them to pick out the one car out of a stream of vehicles whose driver would be willing to settle a dispute by paying them a backhander to get them off his back. Very rarely did they make a mistake and encounter a driver who would prefer to go by the book and pay the official fine.

That day promised no surprises for Lieutenant Oleg Khanin and Sergeant Pyotr Grushko of the Moscow traffic police as they patrolled the area of Lenin Avenue.

They drove up and down the avenue, stopping occasionally to monitor the traffic flow. From time to time they would pick out a speeding car and pass the licence number and brief description – model and colour – to the next patrol further down the avenue. Then they in turn would get a message about some 'speeding son of a bitch' and start the pursuit, lights flashing and siren blasting. The car would stop, a conversation would start and the driver, sensing that a heavy fine was looming, would slip a hundred roubles or more to one of the traffic cops. The cops would then get back into their car and drive for a while looking for the next victim.

Oleg and Pyotr were parked opposite the Fifth Moscow City Hospital when a brand-new BMW 5-series whizzed past them doing at least a hundred kilometres an hour. Oleg could not resist the temptation.

'We're looking here at least at a hundred dollars,' he said to Pyotr. 'Hit the accelerator and let's nail the rich bastard.'

They caught up with the BMW at the next set of traffic lights just before October Square. Oleg gestured to the driver and he pulled up at the kerb. The two cops got out of their Volga and approached the BMW.

'Good day, driver,' Oleg said through the open window. 'That was some pretty fast driving back there. Can I see your documents, please.'

The man got out of the car. He was short, with curly hair, wearing a shabby leather jacket and worn-out jeans. By any standard, he didn't look like the owner of an expensive foreign vehicle. But then the 'common' look was popular that season among the Russian rich, and Oleg had seen worse-looking drivers who sometimes paid several hundred dollars to settle a problem. So he wasn't paying much attention to what the man was wearing. Rather, it was the 'screw you' attitude written all over his face that

272

convinced Oleg that it was safe to make a move.

'You're probably wondering why we've stopped you, driver,' Oleg said. 'The fact of the matter is that you've exceeded the speed limit on a major route of the capital. I hope you haven't been drinking.'

Oleg stretched out his hand expecting to receive documents. The man hesitated for a moment.

'I only have my passport with me,' he said. He took out the passport and gave it to Oleg. It was a serious offence not to carry a valid driving licence and a registration certificate for the car.

Oleg took the passport and opened it. There were five hundred-dollar bills inside. He turned to Pyotr who was standing several metres away.

'Go back to the car and wait for me,' he told him. Once Pyotr was gone he turned back to the driver.

'It's very unfortunate,' he said, 'that you don't have your driving licence and the registration certificate for the car. You do realise that under the regulations I shall have to detain you until we establish whether the car belongs to you and whether you actually have a valid licence...'

He paused for a moment, assessing the reaction on the man's face. But there was no sign of anxiety. The expression was still one of 'go and screw yourself, for all I care'.

Oleg smiled.

'But then again I might make an exception and let you off with a warning on this occasion,' he said. 'I'm really at a loss what to do here.'

The driver conveniently looked away. Oleg took the money and slipped it into his trouser pocket. He then returned the passport and saluted the man.

'Have a safe journey, driver,' he said. 'Consider yourself lucky today.'

The man nodded indifferently and got back into his car. He started the engine, but didn't drive off. Oleg walked back to the patrol car, got inside and closed the door.

'Well?' Pyotr asked impatiently. 'How much did he give you?'

'Gave me two hundred dollars,' Oleg said. 'Not bad for five minutes' work.'

He handed a hundred-dollar bill to Pyotr.

At that moment a black Volga pulled up behind them. Two men stepped out of it. Suddenly the BMW, instead of driving away, reversed and stopped right in front of the police Volga so that it was boxed in between the two cars. The driver of the BMW got out. He approached the police car.

'Get out!' he ordered the two cops. They got out.

'Lieutenant Khanin and Sergeant Grushko,' the man said, 'you are under arrest for accepting a large bribe in the line of duty.'

Oleg and Pyotr were both speechless. It was the sort of thing they could only imagine in their worst nightmares – getting caught in a sting operation. The men from the black Volga acted swiftly and took their guns away.

The driver of the BMW came up close to Oleg.

'You're in serious trouble, you son of a bitch,' he said. 'We've been watching you for some time. You're a disgrace to the force. I'll see that they throw the book at you.'

They were handcuffed and escorted to the black Volga. By then a crowd of onlookers gathered on the pavement, whistling and jeering as the two cops were handcuffed and bundled into the car. Muscovites despised their traffic cops and enjoyed seeing them getting a dose of their own medicine.

'What do we do with the patrol car, sir?' one of the two men asked the driver of the BMW.

Senior investigator of the Moscow's Prosecutor Office, Matvei Zakharov, known to his friends as Motya, was looking at the police car. Who could have imagined only a couple of months ago, he was thinking, that he would be involved in smashing one of the most powerful gangs in Moscow and rescuing the son of a diplomat? It was he who helped his friend Pavel Batalov to carry out the operation against the Central Brotherhood. And it was he who persuaded Pavel in the first place to accept the assignment proposed to him by George Blunt.

Motya had figured out then that, whatever motives those foreigners may have had for going after the Crow and his people, it was the best chance possible for nailing a whole criminal syndicate. No one in Moscow would have dared to take on the Central Brotherhood. The authorities would only act if they felt that the gang had lost its grip, and now it was time for revenge.

'Just leave the car here,' Motya said.

The radio transmitter in his car started to buzz. Motya rushed to the BMW.

'Zakharov here,' he said.

His assistant informed him that Ivan Ossinski, who had been kept under surveillance for his own protection, had suddenly disappeared.

'I'm on my way,' Motya said and switched on the ignition.

★

If anyone had told Ivan Ossinski about how an international operation had been launched to get him out of trouble he would have thought they were crazy. A millionaire businessman from Britain financing a daring mission to destroy one of the most powerful gangs in Moscow? And all to save a young man he had never seen in his life?

'Nah, get real,' he'd have said. 'Not a chance.'

Having told Mark Ender, one of the directors of Russian Style, the company where he worked part-time, about his problem, Ivan was hoping it would soon be resolved. He had absolutely no idea that Ender was one of the people who had framed him in the first place, on the orders of the Crow. And he could have never imagined that he was about to play a major role in one of the biggest crimes ever.

It was while he was planning his disappearance from Moscow that Seraphim suddenly came up with the idea of moving Ivan to London. He thought that his presence there could help keep up the pressure on his father. As Ivan had visited London on many occasions in the past and held a multiple-entry visa to the UK, it was only a matter of buying him an airline ticket. Once the job was done, Seraphim thought, the young man would lose his value and could easily be disposed of. Along with his father.

Seraphim ordered his people to dispatch Ivan to London as soon as possible. He was summoned by Mark Ender, who told him that the company had 'pulled some strings' and that the charges against him would soon be dropped.

Ivan couldn't believe his luck. He was ready to do anything to repay the people who had saved him. When Ender told him that he would need to travel to London to help with one of the company's projects, young Ossinski got even more excited: instead of having to return the favour he was actually getting a free trip to London!

Ender instructed Ivan not to breathe a word to anyone about going to Britain until charges against him were officially dropped. He also told him not to say anything to his father, as he was still bound by the terms of his bail and could not leave the country.

'Once you're in London you'll be able to get in touch with your father,' he said. 'But don't even think of calling him from Moscow. You know how these phone lines always have more than two people on them.'

And he roared with laughter.

Ivan was too overwhelmed by the good news to suspect anything. The only problem was that he had to invent some sort of reason to go away for several days so that his grandmother would not be worried. He decided to tell her that he was going to St Petersburg on business.

In the evening he got a call from his company telling him that his ticket was ready and that he would be leaving the next day. He was told that a car would pick him up to take him to the airport and the driver would give him the ticket.

The next day Ivan was taken to the airport in a company Mercedes. He felt on top of the world. He was going to London. His problems would soon be over and his father would be proud of him.

Little did he know that his life was in even greater danger than before.

★

Jeremy was listening in amazement as Ron told him about the visit that he and George had paid to the Russian embassy.

Before they got the idea of striking a deal with the Russians, both Ron and George did some investigating. They found out that the two so-called 'intelligence officers' from Moscow who had approached Boris were definitely acting on behalf of the Central Brotherhood. Georgi Volkov provided their names – Glyeb Gorshkov and Shamil Taraev – and, after Ron pulled some strings, the whole picture finally emerged.

The two men turned out to be former agents of the First Directorate of the KGB who had left the force about five years before and since then were known to have been mixed up with some very nasty people. It was also established that the two men had met with members of the team that had arrived at the embassy escorting a cargo of communications equipment.

According to some people Ron knew from his days in the CIA, the activities of the inhabitants of number 10 Kensington Palace Gardens were highly suspicious and unusual. For example, each member of the group took turns jogging down Kensington Palace Gardens. They would occasionally stop at the gates of some of the buildings and examine the entrances and the security arrangements. There were suspicions that some of the 'joggers' were taking pictures of the buildings using miniature cameras. They also regularly stopped at sites where cable engineers had earlier dug up the road and pavement and were laying new communication lines.

The most intriguing thing about the inhabitants of 10 Kensington Palace Gardens was that they seemed to be growing in numbers by the day. Initially there were only five men in the building, but later many other people were seen coming in and staying for long periods of time and the overall number swelled to at least eighty.

Several days after the first cargo had arrived, a large shipment of crates was brought in and stored at the ambassador's residence. According to the official papers from Moscow, the cargo included 'items of contemporary Russian folk art' that were intended for an exhibition to be opened in London later in the year. The people who accompanied the second cargo did not establish any contact with the team that had arrived with the first shipment.

Having exchanged information, George and Ron both came to the conclusion that the inhabitants of 10 Kensington Palace Gardens were definitely up to no good. As there were no grounds to alert the British authorities they decided to pay a visit to the Russian ambassador.

They got in touch with Boris Ossinski, explaining to him that they were working for Jeremy Goldberg and needed to see the Russian ambassador as soon as possible. Boris thought that George and Ron must have been business associates of Jeremy and persuaded the ambassador to squeeze then into his busy schedule. Boris called George back in a matter of minutes saying that he and Ron should come to the embassy immediately.

By then they were already on their way to Mount Street to meet with Jeremy and the Moscow team, and had to turn around and rush to the ambassador's residence. Boris met them in the entrance lobby. Ron had to explain the situation to him very quickly. Boris was shocked to hear about the two phoney 'intelligence officers' and about a bizarre plan by Russian criminals to stage a robbery in London.

Still reeling from the news, he led the two men upstairs to see the ambassador. It all seemed so bizarre to him: Russian gangsters targeting the embassy in London. But the most worrying thing was that if the two 'agents' were in reality working for the gang in Moscow that meant that his son Ivan was still in serious trouble…

★

The Russian ambassador spoke good English and there was no need for an interpreter. George did not beat about the bush. He told the ambassador that he had reason to believe that a group of Russian criminals was plotting a robbery and that their target might be the Russian embassy itself.

The ambassador looked at Boris in amazement. He was expecting to meet two businessmen and instead he was sitting with two men who looked more like intelligence people and were telling him that his embassy was facing an attack. Boris didn't even try to explain anything. The thought that his son was still in grave danger suddenly sank in and he was trying to come to terms with the new situation.

Ron took the initiative from George.

'You may not take our warning seriously at the moment, Mr Ambassador,' he said, 'but we suspect that some very unusual activity has been taking place in recent days around your embassy.

A lot of people have arrived from Moscow and are taking a close interest in this area. Unhealthy interest, I might add.'

The ambassador seemed unconvinced.

'This is the most remarkable situation I have ever found myself in during the entire thirty years that I've been a diplomat,' he said. 'One of my own staff arranges a business meeting under false pretences with two complete strangers who seem to know more about my embassy than I do. Remarkable, absolutely remarkable. I really don't know how to react to this.'

Ron made a desperate attempt to turn the meeting around.

'Mr Ambassador,' he said, getting up from his chair, 'I'm not at all surprised at your initial reaction. But I've heard that you are a reasonable man. You say that Mr Ossinski here has tricked you into having a meeting with us. Well, let me tell you this, Mr Ambassador. Mr Ossinski has proved himself to be an honourable man. He's been under enormous pressure in the last few weeks. His son's life has been in danger, and yet he has been doing his job as usual. He held on and held on well. Knowing, let me add, that he could lose his son at any moment.'

Ron looked hard at the ambassador.

'You know, sir, what it means to lose a son,' he said. 'You know how it feels because you yourself went through that tragic experience. Well, let me ask you this: are you prepared to see other young men who work in your embassy die just because you did not wish to believe us? It's your call now, Mr Ambassador.'

Ron looked exhausted by his emotional outburst and sat down. He took out a handkerchief and wiped his forehead. There was silence in the room. Then the secretary knocked on the door to inquire whether everything was all right. She had heard loud voices and didn't know what to make of it.

The ambassador signalled to her that everything was under control. He looked at his guests one at a time and then stood up.

'Gentlemen,' he said, 'I'll leave you for a moment.'

And he walked out of the room.

George and Ron both looked at Boris. They were expecting him to indicate what to expect. But Boris merely shrugged his shoulders, not really knowing what to say.

George got up.

'Do I sense that we've blown our chance?' he asked.

'You sense wrong,' Ron replied. 'He'll be back. He's a reasonable man, he'll be back.'

George gave him an inquiring look, questioning why he was so certain that the ambassador would return, but Ron just sat there saying nothing.

The ambassador did return, about ten minutes later. He was accompanied by Colonel Gennadi Kotov, chief security officer at the embassy. Boris's pulse began to race. The ambassador walked around his desk and sat down.

'I know I'll probably regret this for the rest of my life,' he said, 'but I have decided to act on your advice. Can I introduce to you, gentlemen, our head of security, Colonel Gennadi Kotov. He'll be in charge of introducing new security arrangements at the embassy.'

Colonel Kotov was a typical KGB type. Medium height, thin-faced, with a short haircut and eyes that seemed to penetrate everyone he met. He was wearing a grey tweed jacket, black trousers, white shirt and a dark blue tie. He was under the impression that a tweed jacket could be part of a formal dress code, a view that was shared by many Russian diplomats who wore tweed jackets to work practically all the time.

Boris introduced Ron and George to Kotov, who responded with a nod to each of them.

In the next fifteen minutes a plan was drawn up. Kotov was instructed by the ambassador to summon all the diplomats who were fit enough to offer resistance to any possible attack and assemble them in the underground conference bunker that had been used in the past for holding regular meetings of the embassy's Communist Party branch and was considered impregnable to any eavesdropping equipment. Security at the embassy was to be tightened and nobody was to be allowed into the building without prior notification.

Gennadi was given three hours to assemble the men.

George and Ron left for Mount Street but promised to send a Russian-speaking man to establish a line of communications between them. They agreed to hold another meeting later in the afternoon.

★

Deputy Minister of Foreign Affairs Sergei Titov was basking in his new-found glory.

He was now hot property. Important people sought his company. He was receiving invitations to state banquets and corporate parties.

In his own ministry, senior officials would come up to him in the corridors, shake his hand and laugh at his jokes. Many people in the Ministry of Foreign Affairs wanted to improve their living accommodation. Many of them had recently moved to Moscow from the provincial towns and cities, and Sergei was the man who could help them. He had already signed several papers allocating large flats to very influential people. Some of them were even saying that he was still young and should be getting ready, perhaps in a couple of years, to take over a whole ministry.

Sergei was also proud of the fact that he was involved in a secret project concerning the movement of the national treasures to London that would help sort out the economic crisis in the country. He knew that the cargo had been safely delivered to London and was stored in the embassy compound. He was still a bit confused by the other shipment. Some sort of 'communications equipment' which was apparently needed by the embassy. Quite a lot of it, actually. But as the request to send it over to London came from the Kremlin itself and there had been no complaints from the embassy he reckoned it was routine stuff.

Sergei was planning to visit London soon. He thought that his first trip abroad should be to Britain. His wife had heard so many stories about wonderful shopping trips to London and was anxious to go. As he still felt a bit embarrassed about his affair, he reckoned it would be a good idea to travel to some nice place abroad together, to patch things up.

Sergei decided to have a short day. He called the garage and asked his driver to bring the car round to the number one entrance. As he came out of the main building, the weather was changing and clouds were starting to gather. Gusts of cold wind were blowing from the Moscow River. But although the weather was not looking good, Sergei still felt a surge of happiness. He breathed the cold Moscow air into his lungs. It's good to be alive, he thought.

The car pulled up at the entrance. The driver, a young man from a small town outside Moscow, was smiling broadly at his boss.

Life was beautiful for Sergei Titov. And if someone had told him there and then that his battered body would be lying on the roadside about twenty minutes later after a head-on collision with a truck on the Uspenskoe motorway he would have laughed at the suggestion. 'That could not happen to me,' he would have said. 'I'm too young to die.'

Unfortunately for Sergei, there were people who didn't share that view. In their opinion he had fulfilled his role. It was time for him to go.

The driver of the truck was later interrogated by the police, but couldn't recall a thing, as he was too drunk. He vaguely remembered two guys in a café where he was having lunch. They were friendly people. Offered him a drink, then another one. And another. How on earth he got drunk, he couldn't quite remember. Then the strangers asked him to give them a lift. Naturally he agreed.

He came to his senses only after the collision. His truck had somehow swerved and veered into the opposite lane, hitting the black Volvo. Both people in the car died on impact.

And his two new friends disappeared without trace.

★

Vadim Mironov had a hell of a time getting all the information together for Glyeb and Shamil.

When he read the lists of questions from the file they had given him he was very impressed. These guys wanted to know everything possible about the properties in Kensington Palace Gardens. They seemed to be very interested in the Russian ambassador's residence and requested the full layout of the building and of the surrounding grounds. A lot of questions were related to several other buildings down the road and to the overall security arrangements in the area.

Vadim knew well that for $500,000 in cash he had to produce something substantial. So he dug up all the information he could think of. He managed to find detailed plans of the ambassador's residence at 13 Kensington Palace Gardens, as he had kept them since the days when he took part in overseeing the refurbishment work there. He also found the layout of the building that was sold, and decided that, although it no longer belonged to the Russian government, it might still be of interest to potential buyers. And he managed to get some plans of other buildings in the area.

Vadim was under the impression that the people in Moscow were planning to buy mostly the buildings occupied by the Russian embassy. In all the chaos in Russia it was quite conceivable that someone might have been able to approach the right people and get hold of a juicy bit of government property abroad. And with the right money, he reckoned, they might be able to buy some of the other properties in the road as well. For instance, the embassy next door to the Russian ambassador's residence was definitely too big for the small Asian country which was currently using it. But with proper investment, and after refurbishment, it could look grand and might be worth an absolute fortune.

The two residences of ambassadors from African countries located on either side of the now vacant number 10 building were probably out of reach of the people in Moscow. But Mironov did manage to get the layouts of both buildings, just in case.

A private block of flats next to the Russian embassy building at number 6/7 might be interesting for the buyers from Moscow, Vadim thought. So he got the plans of that building as well.

The information about the security arrangements for the whole of Kensington Palace Gardens proved to be extremely difficult to obtain, but he did manage to get some details about the telephone cables, CCTV cameras and the street lighting arrangements.

After getting all the paperwork together, Vadim called Glyeb late in the evening on the mobile number that he had been given at their meeting. Glyeb sounded very upbeat on the phone and suggested that they meet outside 10 Kensington Palace Gardens at eleven o'clock the following morning.

Vadim wanted to ask about his payment, but Glyeb anticipated the question.

'Don't worry about the money,' he said cheerfully. 'The cash is ready, just like I promised.'

The next day Vadim took a taxi and arrived at 10 Kensington Palace Gardens. He walked through one of the two front gates. He'd heard that the building was now being used to store some communications equipment that had been delivered recently, and that there were several people from Moscow in the building looking after it.

Glyeb greeted him at the main entrance. Smiling broadly with a briefcase in hand, Vadim walked inside the building. Glyeb led him up the stairs to the first floor and into a small room that had been used in the past by the embassy's dentist. The room still had a dentist's chair in it and an old desk. Vadim shuddered, remembering how he had had dental treatment in that very room when he was a diplomat. It had hurt like hell because the dentist was somebody's son or nephew who had been sent to London because of his family's connections.

Glyeb sat on the edge of the desk. There was nowhere else to sit, so Vadim was left standing in front of him like a schoolboy facing his teacher.

'Show me what you've got for me,' Glyeb said.

Vadim suddenly turned possessive.

'I'd love to see the money first,' he said licking his dry lips.

Glyeb grinned.

'Don't you trust me?' he said. 'Do you really think that I'd be sitting in this building, still belonging to the Russian embassy by the way, trying to con you?'

Vadim thought about it for a moment and decided he would show the papers to Glyeb. One by one he took out the files and briefly explained what each of them contained. Glyeb was listening with interest.

When the last file was on the desk, Glyeb stood up.

'The papers cover only some of the buildings that we're interested in, not all of them,' he said rather sternly. 'You promised to get us all the information that we wanted, didn't you?'

Vadim felt that his lips had turned so dry that they started to hurt. The money was slipping away from him.

'I've brought you all the papers concerning the properties belonging to the Russian government,' he said. 'There are also documents covering the properties next to the buildings of the Russian embassy.'

Glyeb seemed unimpressed. Vadim was getting desperate.

'The rest of the information is still in here,' he said, tapping himself on the temple. 'That's where it stays until I get paid.'

Glyeb roared with laughter.

'I get the message,' he said. 'I can take a hint, you know. Wait for me while I fetch the money.'

He walked out of the room and closed the door behind him. Vadim felt a sense of relief. He'd managed to convince the stupid son of a bitch that he knew much more about the properties in the area. And come to think of it, he did know quite a lot about them. Just like Boris Ossinski did. Both of them had visited most of the embassies down the road for diplomatic parties and both had been involved in the selling and buying of properties, and moving from one building to another. At that moment Vadim even thought that he knew his way around Kensington Palace Gardens so well that he could have easily pulled off a daring robbery and become a very rich man. Yes, he thought, some robbery that would be!

And then it suddenly hit him: these people were interested in the layouts of the properties at Kensington Palace Gardens and they wanted to know the security arrangements – but they never even asked about prices.

Bloody hell! he thought. These guys must be planning to rob all of these buildings!

He remembered his conversation with Boris when he had come for advice to his office. Boris did warn him then that these people were threatening his son if he did not do as they said.

Of course! he thought. They want to get all the details together so that they can plan their move.

He was suddenly very frightened. Money was no longer of interest to him. He wanted to get away as soon as possible.

The door flung open and Glyeb came in. He was accompanied by two men.

'Comrades,' Glyeb said, 'this is our guest, Vadim Mironov, and he seems to have a lot of information in his head which is of great interest to us. I think we should persuade him to share it.'

Three hours later Vadim's battered body was carried down to the basement and thrown into a freshly dug grave in the storage room. He was still breathing, but the two men who beat the information out of him didn't care. They buried him alive and went upstairs to have some beers.

★

Pavel approached the Russian ambassador's residence and hesitated for a moment.

What am I going to say to the people inside? he thought. That I'm a former cop from the Moscow central CID and that I now work for an English millionaire?

He was hoping that George and Ron had told the ambassador about the situation and that he wouldn't need to go into any details.

Pavel pushed the button at the entrance gate and a voice from the loudspeaker inquired who he was.

'I've come to see Boris Ossinski,' he said. 'My name is Pavel Batalov.'

The gate slowly opened in front of him. He walked up the driveway and entered the building. A guard was sitting on the right behind a counter.

'Boris Nikolaevich will be down shortly,' he said. 'Please wait for him in the next room.'

Pavel walked through to the reception hall. He recognised the paintings on the wall on the right-hand side of the hall. One was a portrait of a Russian peasant woman in a red scarf and next to it was a painting depicting the Red Square. They were both worth a lot of money.

He looked at the staircase on the left that led to the first floor. Up there were the ambassador's living quarters, his office and the offices of his personal secretaries and assistants.

Little had changed since the last time Pavel was here. When he lived in Britain with his mother and stepfather he was in the same class at the embassy's school as the ambassador's son, Fedyor, and they became friends. Pavel would often come to the embassy with Fedyor after school, and they would play football in the garden or watch television together. They would run around the building and no one would dare stop them. They would wander into the Winter Garden and then go outside and drink tea with the drivers in the building beside the garages.

Boris interrupted his thoughts, coming out from behind a curtain that covered the entrance to some of the offices on the ground floor.

'I am Boris Ossinski,' he introduced himself.

Pavel extended his hand.

'My name is Pavel Batalov and I work for Jeremy Goldberg,' he said. 'I suggest we skip the formalities and get down to business. We don't have much time left.'

★

Shark had no idea how long he'd been held in the basement of Seraphim's villa. Two hours, five hours, a day, two days? Time had stopped for him, interrupted only by pangs of pain inflicted on him with ruthless regularity by his tormentors.

The pricks couldn't get a single word out of him. They kept asking him about some papers they said had been found in his Moscow flat. He never took any bloody papers! He couldn't even read properly. But why should he tell them anything!

They were also saying something about him talking to the cops about the Central Brotherhood. Now that was total bullshit! He would never go to the pigs. He'd personally killed four cops in his time, so the last place he would go would be the law.

But then one of the pricks said something about a 'file' in his name being kept in police records with his 'reports' in it. At first Shark couldn't understand what the hell he was talking about. What file? What reports? But then it hit him: it must have been that bastard Batalov! Only somebody like him could arrange for a backdated file to appear in the police archives.

When Shark finally realised what had happened he started to groan. Right from the start it was all a set-up! Batalov must have known that there was a sniper out there on the roof, waiting for the Chechens to come out. So he managed to fool the Crow into believing that he had saved his life! Well, Seraphim will find that out soon enough. The stupid bastard will learn the hard way. And he'll only have himself to blame.

Seraphim came down to the basement at the end of the second day of the interrogation. He walked in and sat on a small chair, looking at Shark who was lying on the floor with his hands tied behind his back.

For a brief moment Shark thought that he actually noticed a trace of pity in his boss's eyes. But when Seraphim started to talk, he realised that he was mistaken.

'So, you decided to take the hard way and say nothing,' he said. 'You arrogant son of a bitch! Do you think I'll just order them to kill you and all your sufferings will be over? Well, I've got news for you! You'll rot in this hole until you become a pile of bones. You'll be begging to be killed, but we'll keep you alive for as long as possible.'

Seraphim stood up. Shark was lying on the floor showing no emotion. He knew that there was no point in trying to convince the Crow that he was not the traitor. He even thought that this whole bloody charade suited him just fine. He had long suspected that Seraphim was planning to pull off some big job and then just disappear. His only hope now was that if his men found out that he was being kept prisoner at Seraphim's villa they might try to free him. It was a slim chance, but still a chance.

Seraphim came up to him.

'You might pretend that you don't hear me,' he said. 'But I know you heard what I said. I know you inside out. You managed to fool me once before, but then who wouldn't have fallen for a tricky bastard like you? Killing your own kid brother when I suspected him of treachery. You really impressed me then. But to think that you did it to cover you own double-dealing. You'll rot here till you die.'

He walked out of the room. The next day he was on his way to London.

★

The head of the Presidential Protection Service General Kapoustin decided to have a last talk with General Mikhailov.

He wanted to warn the FSB Deputy Director of the danger of his political games. Mikhailov, in his opinion, was playing with fire by coming up with accusations against the President's son. In effect he was undermining the whole institution of the presidency in Russia.

Kapoustin's people had also gathered a lot of compromising material on many politicians and senior officials. The list of their misdeeds was endless: embezzling government funds, abusing their official position to enrich themselves, accepting bribes, evading taxes, having sex with underage children. But no one made a big deal of it; no one was rushing to silly conclusions. In politics there was a right time for everything, and on most occasions the right time just never came. In Russia, just like in most other counties, no one was prepared to rock the boat so hard it could sink. There were different rules for the people at the top. Otherwise the whole bloody system would have collapsed ages ago.

Kapoustin was hoping to persuade Mikhailov to back off. In a friendly way. What was he trying to achieve? he was going to ask him. He would never be able to change anything anyway. Even if Vassili were sacked, he'd be back in another cosy government job in a matter of months, if not weeks. Would Aleksei never learn? The people who were behind the hard-line communist coup in 1991 and the attempted coup in 1993 were already holding high official posts or running big companies. The Russian establishment never punished its own.

Kapoustin had no desire to meet Mikhailov at the FSB head-quarters. It was not safe to talk there. Mikhailov, he thought, might be tempted to record their conversation and afterwards use it against him. He was now probably licking his wounds after the meeting with the President, thinking he should have never got himself in such a mess. He must have guessed that Kapoustin had warned his boss about the possible contents of the report that the FSB Deputy Director might come with.

In fact, he should be grateful to him, Kapoustin thought. If it were not for him the President might have become so upset that he could have sacked Mikhailov on the spot. Or even worse – sent him to Chechnya.

Through his contacts in the FSB, Kapoustin managed to find out that Mikhailov was planning to visit the Interior Ministry that afternoon and meet with some of the top policemen to discuss the situation on the southern borders of Russia. That suited Kapoustin just fine. The Interior Ministry was about five minutes' drive from the Kremlin, so he figured they could talk outside and no one would be able to hear them.

He went to the Interior Ministry roughly two hours after the meeting between General Mikhailov and the officials was supposed to start. But he still had to wait for another hour until Mikhailov finished and came out of the building.

Kapoustin came up to him.

'Hello, Aleksei!' he said. 'I'd like to have a quick word with you.'

Mikhailov was clearly not very happy to see him. He even glanced at his watch purposefully, demonstrating that he was pressed for time.

'It won't take long,' Kapoustin assured him. 'Let's have a stroll down Ogarev Street.'

General Mikhailov signalled to the driver of his black Mercedes to switch off the engine and wait. They started to walk slowly in the direction of Gertsen Street.

'I hope you're not drawing any wrong conclusions from the meeting you had with the President,' Kapoustin said. 'He had a very serious talk with his son after you left and I was instructed by him to conduct a full investigation and report to him as soon as possible on my findings.'

Mikhailov stopped and turned to face Kapoustin.

'Well, if you're going to investigate the matter then I suggest that you come to see me at my office and I'll present you with several files regarding the activities of the special advisor to the President. It's all in there.'

Kapoustin ignored the invitation.

'What are you trying to prove, Aleksei?' he asked. 'That the world is not a perfect place? That people are corrupted by power and money? That the son of the President is a money-grabbing creep? We all know that. But why do you have to go against the first ever Russian leader who has been above corruption all the time he's been in office? All the previous people in his position either stole like mad themselves or allowed others to do it for them. Remember Yeltsin? His relatives and friends robbed the country blind. And now when at last we have a decent man at the top you go after him. What would we all gain by his downfall?'

Mikhailov shook his head.

'You don't get it, do you?' he said. 'This is not some personal vendetta. I have nothing against the President. But if he is presiding over serious crimes like treason, then I have to respond. There are limits, even for a Russian head of state. Even Lenin and Stalin were eventually sidelined and neutralised by their own people for getting corrupted by power. And they were considered by many to be above all laws. But now, when we have democracy, whatever that means in our case, the head of state must not be allowed to destroy the whole country.'

The man's obsessed, Kapoustin thought. There's absolutely no point in this conversation.

He forced himself to smile.

'Okay, Aleksei, I get your point,' he said. 'You're on a mission to save Russia. All I can say is good luck to you. But remember what I've said to you: it's a bad time in Russia for wise guys.'

General Mikhailov nodded without saying anything. He was expecting another meeting with the head of the Kremlin's secret service quite soon. An undercover operation had just been completed. A special agent of the FSB had managed to infiltrate a secret squad of professional hit men who had been carrying out assassinations of major criminals and corrupt businessmen.

The agent had uncovered a direct link between the hit squad and the head of the Kremlin's secret service, who had personally ordered many of the killings. The agent also found out that Vassili, the President's son, had been in close contact with several members of the hit squad who were suspected of carrying out the assassinations of Mussa Bartaev and Slava the Satan.

As Kapoustin was walking back to his car Mikhailov felt an overwhelming desire to tell him that he knew about the hit squad.

'Andrei!' he called out to Kapoustin. 'I know about your secret squad!'

Kapoustin stopped and turned round slowly.

'What squad?' he said. 'What on earth are you talking about?'

General Mikhailov said nothing. He suddenly realised that he had probably made a big mistake. He'd acted like a foolish teenager boasting that he knew somebody else's secret.

But it was too late. At that moment his fate was sealed.

★

The meeting in the basement of the Russian ambassador's residence at 13 Kensington Palace Gardens started in a tense atmosphere.

Colonel Gennadi Kotov, the embassy's head of security, rejected outright any arrangement that would allow outsiders access to office premises on the ground and first floors, not to mention the ambassador's quarters and *referentura*, the communications room. 'Over my dead body will any foreigner run around the premises,' he was overheard saying to one of the diplomats before the meeting.

Anyone in his place would probably have been worried, seeing that the ambassador was allowing former Western intelligence people not only to enter his official residence but also to take part in a meeting in the basement that had always been off-limits to any outsider. And it was his bad luck that the SVR station chief had left for Moscow on holiday two days before, so any decision Kotov took regarding security would be his and his alone.

But the ambassador was thinking along different lines. Russian embassies across the world did not have teams of marines, as many American diplomatic missions did, to protect their premises in case of emergencies. And turning for help to the British authorities was out of the question, as that would have meant officially acknowledging that the embassy was providing assistance to criminals, by allowing them to use one of its buildings with the approval of the Deputy Minister of Foreign Affairs in Moscow.

The only way they could defend themselves was to seek outside help. The ambassador was not planning to let the foreigners in on any secrets, but he was ready to find a compromise solution to prevent a possible massacre of his men. He trusted Boris Ossinski's judgement. He knew him well enough to realise that only in extreme circumstances would he bring Ron and George to see him. And he also knew what it meant to lose a son. He had been through the trauma and the guilt of knowing that he could have done something to help his boy, who was killed by thugs because he owed money to a local drug dealer.

George, Ron, Clay and Alex were brought to the ambassador's residence in a diplomatic minibus with darkened windows. They entered the premises from the back garden, so that anyone who might have been watching the front driveway would see no suspicious activity. Several diplomats escorted them to the conference hall, a large room with walls made of solid concrete to prevent any possible eavesdropping, where they assembled with the Russian diplomats who, as the guests were told, had 'volunteered to help'.

For the first few minutes both sides viewed each other with suspicion. The Russian diplomats could have never imagined that they would be meeting with foreigners to discuss ways of defending their own embassy, in the heart of London, from Russian gangsters, of all people. It all sounded absurd and surreal. And yet it was happening.

The guests, on the other hand, were thinking that they had a real problem on their hands, trying to take on the Russian mob with the help of a bunch of people who had probably never held a weapon in their hands before, apart from the two men from the military attaché's office.

Pavel came to the meeting with Boris. Earlier he had explained to him a little of his background. He mentioned that his stepfather was a diplomat and that he spent half of his life under the name of Pavel Viktorovich Samarin. He skipped the part about being kicked out of the police and simply said that he had left the force to pursue a 'business career'.

'Samarin, Samarin,' Boris repeated several times, trying to remember something. 'There was a diplomat, Viktor Samarin, stationed here in the late 1960s,' he said. 'Was he your stepfather by any chance?'

Pavel nodded. Boris looked at him in amazement.

'You are the stepson of the legendary Viktor Samarin? The first man in all of the Ministry of Foreign Affairs to become ambassador at the tender age of thirty-five? And you of all people ended up working in the Moscow central CID? What college did you graduate from?'

Pavel was starting to get annoyed with this line of questioning. What business was it of anyone's where he had studied and where he ended up? It was his life. He'd screwed it up himself – he was not asking for anyone's sympathy.

'It's a long story,' Pavel said, 'and some day I'll tell you all about it.'

Then, changing the subject, he asked Boris to help persuade the ambassador and especially Colonel Kotov to allow Ron, George and others to help set up the defences in the embassy.

'I know the bastards who are planning to hit you,' he said. 'They won't hesitate to kill anyone who gets in their way. I've dealt with their boss, Seraphim Voronov, and I can tell you that he is one cunning bloodthirsty son of a bitch.'

Boris reacted to that name immediately.

'You probably won't believe this,' he said, 'but when I went to the airport to meet Vice-Premier Tenko earlier today he introduced me to a man who had arrived with him on the plane. His name was also Seraphim Voronov. Strange coincidence, isn't it?'

Pavel stared at him in disbelief.

'What did he look like, the man at the airport?' he asked anxiously.

'He was tall, close to six feet, overweight, curly hair, large hands—'

'Bloody hell, that's him!' Pavel cried out. 'That's the Crow! So he's in London! That means they could strike at any moment. But how on earth did he manage to get on the government plane?'

Boris was taken aback by his reaction.

'The Vice-Premier introduced him as a close friend of the First Family,' he said, suddenly realising that he'd actually shaken hands with the man who was threatening his son. 'As far as I could understand he flew in with Tenko officially.'

Pavel shook his head, trying to work out what to do.

'I have to tell George about the Crow as soon as possible,' he said. 'Find me a private mobile phone so I can call him. I don't want to use the embassy line. They might be listening.'

Boris brought him his own mobile phone from the office.

'I'll keep the phone for a while,' Pavel said, 'so that you can find me at any time.'

Pavel went into the back garden to talk to George. Boris visualised the scene at the airport in his mind. He had actually greeted the man who was attempting to destroy him and Ivan! How could he be so blind? No wonder the Vice-Premier had been acting so strangely, trying to distance himself from his companion.

When the meeting in the basement eventually started, Ron Baker was the first to speak.

'Before we go into any details,' he said, 'I'd like to say this: I'm well aware that some of you guys here don't really like the idea of cooperating with us. But let me remind you that our nations have been united in the past against a common enemy. My father fought against the Nazis in the last war and he was one of the American GIs who met with the Russians in Berlin. The British soldiers were also there and there was no hostility then. So just let us assume that we're all once again fighting a common enemy. And just like then, let's kick ass!'

His last words were met with cheers from several men. Ron knew how to patch up the differences between people.

Then George spelled out the rough plan. There was a suspicion that the criminals would attempt to burgle the properties in Kensington Palace Gardens, including the Russian ambassador's residence. There were enough paintings and other valuable items in the building to make a small fortune on the black market. The combined team would provide protection and defence against a possible attack. George's people would be on the outside, armed with their own weapons. The only problem was that they could not give the Russians any of their weapons, as it could result in a serious diplomatic row. So the big question was, were there any weapons kept inside the Russian embassy?

George glanced inquiringly at Colonel Kotov, who'd been looking very uncomfortable from the moment the meeting started. He knew that allowing foreigners inside the embassy was bad enough in itself, but confirming the presence of firearms on the premises of a Russian diplomatic mission would be even worse. Next, he thought, they would be asking for the codes to the hotline.

Kotov cursed his bad luck for working with an ambassador who seemed to be willing to believe any story foreigners told him. He was also very unhappy that he had to take all the decisions by himself, as the SVR station chief was away. But as the ambassador had instructed him to comply with all reasonable requests, he had to give some sort of an answer to the question just raised. The eyes of all present in the room were fixed on him.

Kotov cleared his throat and assumed an expression that was supposed to demonstrate to the people in the room that he was reluctant to give out the information, but was in effect obliged to do so.

'We have ten Makarov handguns, five Kalashnikov automatic rifles and five Uzi sub-machine guns,' he said.

There was a surprised murmur among the Russian diplomats, who were impressed by the size of the arsenal in the embassy and by the choice of weapons. The Makarov handguns were useless, everyone knew that. But the Uzis were undoubtedly the best in close combat.

The Kalashnikovs were good weapons too. The Americans had learned the hard way what it meant to be on the receiving end of those rifles in Vietnam. But an AK-47 is at its best on the battlefield, in extreme weather conditions, when you need reliable weapons that can withstand rain, snow and dust. In a restricted urban combat situation the Uzis were best.

George was relieved to hear that the Russians kept some weapons at the embassy. At least they stood a chance of fighting off the attackers.

'Gentlemen,' he announced, 'I suggest that we all wear blue ribbons on our left arms so that we know who is who and avoid shooting each other. Also, Colonel Kotov, as I understand, is going to show all of you where you'll be positioned in the building. We assemble in two hours. It's quite possible that the attack will take place in the next two days.'

He turned to Kotov.

'I hope that Mr Batalov will be allowed to take up a position in the entrance lobby,' he said.

Kotov nodded and got up from his chair, showing that he had had enough of making concessions that day.

The Russian diplomats left to get ready for the operation. They were instructed by Kotov not to breathe a word about the matter to anyone.

The four foreign guests left the building by the back entrance and were driven away in the same van that had brought them there. It was arranged that Alex and Clay would be picked up at an agreed location two hours later and brought back.

Pavel remained in the building. The ambassador allowed him to use the guest quarters to take a shower and rest.

It was strange for him to find himself in a room where he had spent countless nights as a boy thirty-odd years earlier. Fedyor, the ambassador's son, would invite him to stay overnight in the small bedroom facing Kensington Gardens. The room had its own shower and toilet, and even a small fridge, so that he had no need to wander around the embassy looking for a toilet or a drink of water.

Pavel lay on the bed, remembering how he used to play with Fedyor in the garden outside, how they would have dinner with the ambassador and his wife, a large, strict-looking woman who always dressed formally for every occasion. The ambassador, a tall, thin man with a long nose and a sorry smile, seemed to be afraid of her. He was always saying 'yes dear' or 'as you say, dear' whenever she spoke to him.

When in 1971 the British government expelled more than a hundred Russian diplomats for spying, Pavel was staying over at the ambassador's residence, having spent the whole evening playing football with Fedyor. They were told by the cook that dinner would be served soon and they had better go and wash their hands.

Just as they sat down for dinner with Fedyor's parents there came a knock on the door. The ambassador's wife seemed genuinely surprised. She looked at her husband sternly, as if expecting an explanation.

'It must be Moscow, dear,' he said apologetically getting up from the table. 'I won't be a moment.'

And he quickly walked out of the dining room. He came back several minutes later, looking pale.

'What is it, dear?' his wife asked him.

The ambassador didn't respond immediately. He was holding some papers in his hands.

'It seems that the British authorities are going to announce the expulsion of a hundred and four of our diplomats tomorrow,' he said, looking in bewilderment through the papers. 'One of our trade delegation officials defected two days ago and provided the British with a list of names of people who are involved in espionage. All of them will be declared *persona non grata* and given twenty-four hours to leave the country. This is a disaster.'

Pavel and Fedyor continued eating but were listening to every word. When the ambassador stopped there was silence in the room. And then Pavel asked, 'Does it mean we'll go to war with Britain?'

The ambassador's wife suddenly realised that there were children in the room who were hearing things that should not concern them.

'Take your plates and finish your dinner in the small dining room,' she said. 'Quick – the adults have to discuss some things that won't interest you.'

They left the big dining room. But through the door they could still hear what the ambassador and his wife were saying.

'You don't understand, darling,' the ambassador was saying, 'I can be recalled to Moscow for allowing a crisis like this to happen. It took Moscow twenty years to build a network in Britain. It's going to be the worst diplomatic crisis we've ever had in our history.'

'You shouldn't panic, dear, and think that you're to blame for this,' his wife said. 'No one's going to blame you for a provocation against our country. You warned Moscow on several occasions that there were too many diplomats based in London who were doing too many things. They knew the risks. So don't worry and let's see what happens tomorrow. Now go and change and let's have an early night.'

Pavel phoned his stepfather and told him that a lot of people were being kicked out of Britain. His stepfather ignored his words.

'Behave yourself there,' he said and put down the phone.

The next day the British government announced the expulsion of more than a hundred Soviet diplomats and very soon the embassy became unusually empty.

Pavel's stepfather was not included in the list of spies, and they remained in Britain for another year.

★

General Aleksei Mikhailov finished work late that evening and phoned his driver to pick him up at entrance number three of the main building of the FSB at Lubyanka.

When he came outside, the car was already waiting for him at the kerb. It was a warm April night. The General took a deep breath and thought that if he lived nearer the office he would have probably chosen to walk home that night. I really need to exercise more, he thought. I'll get fat if I continue to sit at my desk all the time and use the car whenever I need to get somewhere.

He decided that from the following week he would start working out and, with a clean conscience, got into the back seat of his black Mercedes.

'Let's go home, Zhenya,' he told the driver.

As soon as the Mercedes pulled off the kerb another car that was parked about a hundred metres down the road also started moving. It kept following the Mercedes at a distance.

The General arrived at the apartment block he lived in at about 11.25. He told the driver to pick him up the next day at eight in the morning, got out of the car and stood for a while outside the entrance, smoking. When he extinguished his cigarette and started walking towards the door he suddenly heard someone calling out his name. He turned around. A man was standing about fifty metres away from him.

'General Mikhailov, I've got a message for you,' the man said. He took out a gun with a silencer and shot the General three times, killing him instantly before running off into the night.

One of the neighbours heard a voice outside and looked out of the window. He saw somebody lying on the ground outside the entrance. The police and ambulance arrived a quarter of an hour after the shooting. The block of flats was known to have some very high-ranking government officials living there. It was always assumed that the place was monitored day and night and that FSB agents were patrolling the area. But no one was at the scene when the shooting took place.

When General Kapoustin was told about the murder the following day, he broke down in front of his assistant. Twenty minutes later he called the President and told him about the 'huge loss' the country had suffered. He asked his permission to organise a funeral with full military honours. The President agreed and Kapoustin started making phone calls in order to speed up the preparations.

★

After the meeting in the basement of the Russian ambassador's residence Ron and George went to Mount Street to discuss the situation with Jeremy.

Alex and Clay were told to prepare for a possible confrontation with the criminals. So they went to an address in East London where Alex knew a couple of people who could provide them with weapons.

When George and Ron arrived at the flat, the butler told them that Jeremy was on the telephone in his study and would join them as soon as he finished the conversation. He led them to the dining room.

When Jeremy walked into the room ten minutes later the two men could immediately tell by looking at him that something had happened. Jeremy walked to the centre of the room and stood there facing his guests.

'My friends,' he said, 'complacency has let us down. While we've been praising ourselves for saving the young man, he has vanished and no one in Moscow knows his whereabouts.'

Both men were stunned to hear that. They had both felt that Operation Saving Ivan had entered a completely new phase where the two words 'Saving Ivan' related more to helping the Russians sort out a crisis situation than just rescuing one young man.

'Sir, I thought that the case against the young lad was going to be closed and the charges dropped,' George said.

'Dropped they will be,' Jeremy said, starting to pace up and down the room, 'but who could have expected the enemy to make such a move.'

He was thinking hard.

'This whole thing couldn't have come at a worse time,' George said. 'We've pulled all our men out of Moscow and we can't turn to anyone out there. And what's more, we learned today that the Crow has arrived in London, courtesy of the Russian government, no less.'

Jeremy froze in his tracks and looked at George.

'What are you talking about, my dear fellow?' he said.

'It turns out, sir, that the Crow flew in, if you'll pardon the expression, together with the Vice-Premier, a certain Vitalli Tenko,' George said, looking up the name from his notebook. 'Mr Ossinski met them at the airport and even shook hands with this man, without realising who he was, of course.'

'How on earth did he get onto a plane carrying a member of the Russian government?' Jeremy said.

'Well, as we were told, the Vice-Premier introduced his companion to Mr Ossinski as a friend of the Russian First Family,' George said. 'That, as I understand, means the family of the President of Russia.'

There was silence in the room. The three men were trying to come to terms with the new situation. Jeremy was the first to speak. He turned to Ron.

'Can you run a check on this Vice-Premier, whatever his name is?' he said.

'I'll make a few phone calls and ask some people,' Ron said. 'I've met the guy a couple of times and if you ever wanted to meet the biggest ass-licker in Moscow then I would strongly recommend him.'

'Can he be part of the Crow's operation?' George asked.

'I doubt it,' Ron said. 'He is too much of a coward to raise the stakes that high. I suspect he's acting on someone else's instructions.'

Jeremy was pacing around the room again, trying to assess the new facts. Then he stopped abruptly.

'If the man you call the Crow is here,' he said, 'then might we not assume that young Ivan may also have been brought to

London? His value here would be much greater than in Moscow, wouldn't it?'

George and Ron both nodded. Jeremy continued.

'And that would mean, gentlemen, that he is probably somewhere in London now, kept as a hostage.'

Both men agreed with that assumption too, without comment.

'And if that is the case than the young's man life is in even greater danger than it was before,' Jeremy concluded gloomily. 'Which means that Operation Saving Ivan is back to square one.'

★

Boris returned to his flat at 43 Holland Park Road, rushed to the telephone and dialled his Moscow number.

He desperately needed to talk to Ivan and find out what was happening. It was clear to him that the situation remained unresolved. The two phoney agents had lied to him and he was now completely baffled as to what he should do next. But in Moscow no one was answering.

He decided to take a quick shower before calling Ivan again. Events were unravelling at such a pace that he barely had any time to stop and think. Normally at this time of the year the embassy would have been going through a quiet period. It was the start of the spring holiday break, which began just before May Day and lasted till Victory Day, which the Russians celebrated on 9 May. Many of the diplomats were away and Moscow was not exactly expecting any flurry of activity in the embassy.

And yet, something absolutely extraordinary was happening. The ambassador's residence was being turned into a fortress while 10 Kensington Palace Gardens had been taken over by people who were suspected of planning a robbery. And if that was not enough, the Americans and the Brits were helping Russian diplomats protect their embassy from the Russian mafia.

To top it all, the Vice-Premier Tenko was in London and the ambassador had still not met him. It was bound to end in a scandal.

Boris got out of the shower and, drying himself with a large towel, went to the bedroom to call Moscow and talk to Ivan. But before he could pick up the receiver the phone started ringing. Suddenly, for no apparent reason, he had a bad feeling about that call.

'Boris Ossinski speaking,' he said in Russian into the phone.

'Comrade Ossinski, nice to hear your voice again,' the caller said.

Boris recognised the man immediately. It was one of the two 'agents' who had approached him and tricked him into believing that Ivan was safe.

'Whom am I speaking to?' he asked, desperately trying to figure out what to say.

'Oh, I'm sorry, I should have introduced myself,' the caller said. 'It's Glyeb; we met recently, remember?'

Boris decided to end the conversation as quickly as possible. He was afraid that he would not be able to keep up the pretence of not knowing who Glyeb really was.

'Look, Glyeb,' he said, 'I don't really have the time to talk to you now as I am rushing off to the embassy. We have a very busy period and an important delegation has arrived from Moscow.'

Glyeb laughed.

'Of course, I understand,' he said. 'But I still think that you'd be interested to know that your son, Ivan, is here in Britain and is helping us conduct our investigation.'

Boris's heart missed a beat.

'Where is my son?' he cried out. 'What have you done to him?'

Glyeb was silent for a moment, as if taken aback by Boris's response to the news that Ivan was in London.

'You offend me,' he said finally. 'You talk as if I was some sort of criminal. You know what I do and you know that in my line of work we don't endanger the lives of other people. We protect them.'

Boris was thinking hard, knowing that he mustn't show that he knew who Glyeb really was. So the only way out was to play along and try to find out more about Ivan.

'I'm sorry,' he said. 'My nerves are playing up. What was it that you wanted?'

'That's better,' Glyeb said. 'Now here's what I want you to do...'

★

On the day General Aleksei Mikhailov was buried Moscow was awash with rumours about a conspiracy at the very top to remove him.

Although no one had organised anything, about ten thousand people gathered outside the central entrance to the Novokuntsevskoe cemetery where the General had been buried earlier in the day.

The burial had taken place with full military honours, including a rifle salute by a squad of FSB troops. A cabinet minister led the mourners. A letter from the Prime Minister was read out and the FSB Director Benedikt Vladimirov spoke about the 'terrible loss to the nation'. But the whole ceremony was unusually brief and very few journalists were allowed to be present. The only photographer permitted to have access was from the official ITAR-TASS news agency.

The people who gathered at the gates of the cemetery didn't know the General. But they still came to mourn a man who, as they concluded, died because he was not afraid to uncover the truth about corruption at the top levels of power. Word spread that the General had fallen out of favour with the First Family and that he had been punished for refusing to stop several potentially explosive investigations.

As usual, Communist supporters were trying to hijack the occasion to promote their discredited slogans and ideas. They were trying to fuel 'spontaneous' protests, hoping to ignite the crowd. It was their usual tactic – to provoke unrest, force the cops to disperse the crowds and then claim that their supporters were once again denied the chance of expressing their views.

No big conflict erupted though. A few scuffles did break out in several places but these were quickly brought under control by the police. It was clear that the demonstrators had no desire for a confrontation.

But just when it seemed that the demonstration was winding down an incident happened that led to on of the worst days of rioting in Moscow's history.

As people were leaving the area, a crowd of about three hundred remained outside the gates of the cemetery. They were being addressed by a man who had jumped on an empty wooden crate and who spoke passionately about the forces of evil taking over the country and destroying everyone who attempted to oppose them.

'In the past the communists arrested their enemies and threw them into jails and labour camps,' he said. 'Now the new rulers don't pay people wages for months or throw them out of work. And the ones who are openly opposed to them are killed and later it's claimed that the gangsters did it! And this is called democracy!'

Emotions in the crowd were starting to run high. The speaker had hit a raw nerve.

'Citizens,' he continued, 'our new rulers are neo-communists. They are even worse than the previous lot. They're stealing billions and hiding them abroad. It's time to stop them!'

Suddenly a man dressed in a black leather jacket and jeans got a gun out of a sports bag he was holding and shot at the speaker several times. The man fell down. The gunman then shot randomly at people in the crowd, dropped the weapon, and ran off. No one tried to apprehend him.

There was panic. People standing near the gates made desperate attempts to get through the crowd. Others started pushing and shoving and falling over each other. Instead of trying to prevent people being trampled the police used batons to establish 'control' of the situation.

The news about the shooting spread quickly across Moscow and, as usual, was grossly exaggerated. According to rumours at least a hundred people were killed and many hundreds injured. Several hours later a large crowd gathered outside the Moscow mayor's office, demanding the resignation of the President and the government.

'Crooks! Crooks! Crooks!' they were shouting. 'Down with the criminals in the Kremlin! Put an end to corruption!'

As darkness fell, the crowd grew in numbers. By about seven o'clock there were at least ten thousand people gathered on Tverskaya Street. More and more police and Interior Ministry troops were gathering around the area outside the mayor's office. On several occasions the demonstrators openly challenged the police and a violent confrontation looked inevitable.

The Interior Ministry troops arrived in riot gear, with shields and batons. No firearms were issued, as there were worries that the demonstrators might attack the soldiers and get hold of some of their weapons. Eventually a mob of about two hundred people started pelting the troops with stones and empty bottles. Several soldiers were injured.

The violence was escalating and the crowd of protesters grew in numbers. A car was overturned and set alight and several shop windows were smashed.

The troops were poised to make a baton charge to try and disperse the crowd. And it was then that several shots were fired. Two soldiers and one policeman were killed.

The soldiers attacked the demonstrators without waiting for the order. Fighting broke out on Tverskaya Street. People started running away through the side streets. A stampede followed and several demonstrators were trampled to death.

At the entrance to Ogarev Street, which was cordoned off by the police to prevent access to the headquarters of the Interior Ministry, fighting broke out between the cops and protesters who were trying to get through. Several shots were fired into the air by the police, but that only made things worse, as the people behind thought that they had fired on the demonstrators.

More panic ensued. More demonstrators were wounded in the confusion. Additional Interior Ministry troops were brought in and eventually all the protesters dispersed.

The next day Moscow woke up to an eerie calm on its streets. But it was clear to everyone that it was not over…

★

General Kapoustin had been present at the funeral of General Mikhailov, but left before everyone else.

The next morning he received a copy of the report about the disturbances, which had been prepared by the FSB for heads of all intelligence services, but remained indifferent to the news that more than twenty people had died and hundreds were injured. These scum deserved what they got, he thought. Next time others will think twice before attacking the police. And to think that they conjured up this whole thing days before May Day holiday!

The report about the demonstration in the centre of Moscow was written in the old Soviet style. Phrases like 'anti-social elements', 'unruly gatherings', 'unacceptable behaviour' and others were scattered throughout the document. It also stated that steps had been taken to conceal the number of people killed and wounded in order, as it was termed, 'to prevent anti-government elements from using the situation to stir up more hooliganism and dissent'.

General Kapoustin closed the folder and started drumming the desktop with his fingers. The death of General Mikhailov had started a chain reaction that he had not anticipated. He blamed himself for not stopping that madman earlier, when he had started collecting information about the President's son. He had had his own suspicions about Vassili's 'indiscretions', as he called them, for quite some time. He knew that the special advisor was mixing with the wrong crowd. There were numerous incidents when he went on drinking binges with total strangers, and later it turned out that he owed these people a lot of money. And the only way he could repay them was to do them a favour.

General Kapoustin had long ago concluded that the state of things in the heart of the government machine was getting out of control. He knew that many senior officials were colluding with known criminals who were buying influence at all levels of power. So he decided to act and ordered his top people to set up a team of professionals, ex-military men, who would act as a deterrent against the criminals who were penetrating the very core of political power in Russia. In a matter of weeks a team of about fifty former members of the special forces were brought from all over the country and assembled together. Kapoustin met them at a secret location outside Moscow.

The meeting was brief. He told them that from that moment they were all back in Spetsnaz and all their missions would be classified as top secret. They would be paid $4,000 a month and housed at a former military base outside Moscow where they would undergo additional training and be taught special skills. No one was to be allowed to leave the base without his authorisation.

He warned them that failure to comply with the rules carried a fifteen-year sentence in a high security jail, which in Russian terms meant the death sentence.

All the men who were brought into the squad had experience of Afghanistan and Chechnya behind them. None of them had been able to adapt to civilian life and they all hated the new capitalist ways. They despised the people around them for not showing proper gratitude for their past heroic deeds, but they possessed enough integrity not to turn to crime like many of their former comrades.

Several weeks after that meeting the first criminal godfather was shot outside a restaurant in Moscow. Later, one by one, some of the most notorious gangsters in the capital met their deaths under different circumstances. All these criminals were known to meddle in politics and control politicians. Every hit was carried out so professionally that the cops had no leads and no witnesses.

The newspapers then wrote about a new gangland war breaking out in the Russian capital. Which suited General Kapoustin and his people just fine.

The hit squad quickly grew in strength. Within a few months they had their own intelligence group collecting information about the movements of known criminals. They knew where these guys wined, dined and gambled. They obtained information about their day-to-day routines, who their friends and girlfriends were and who in the government was linked to them.

It was only a matter of time before the hit squad got involved in politics and several high-profile politicians linked to organised crime died as a result. Soon the hit squad was 'touring' all over Russia eliminating local gangsters, corrupt officials, terrorists and leaders of extreme nationalistic groups. In the city of Rostov-on-Don alone the team eliminated nearly a hundred targets.

General Kapoustin had no reservations about giving orders to kill people. He saw himself as a 'lone warrior' protecting Russia from the scum that threatened to destroy the country. Political stability in his book was much more important than the lives of a few hundred 'greedy bastards' who put money or personal ambition before their country's national interests. He had learned his lessons the hard way, first in Afghanistan, and later in Chechnya…

★

Colonel Andrei Kapoustin had been in charge of an armoured regiment, reinforced with infantry, with orders to wipe out a group of armed insurgents operating in the north of Chechnya. The rebels had crossed the border with the neighbouring Dagestan several times, inflicting casualties on the Russian troops stationed along the Caspian coastline. They also attacked towns and outposts deep inside Dagestan, causing panic among the locals. After their latest raid the commander of the Russian forces in Chechnya ordered his troops to track the rebels down and destroy them.

Colonel Kapoustin and his men were hot on their tracks. Kapoustin was at the head of the column in an armoured personnel carrier. On the way he had presided over two very brief 'tribunals' and had ordered five policemen executed for corruption and siding with the enemy. One village whose inhabitants were suspected of giving shelter to the rebels had been burnt down completely on Kapoustin's orders. The locals begged him not to destroy their homes but he was firm and told them that they should be grateful that their lives were being spared.

The rebels, who were trying to escape from the Russian troops, were being forced to flee over harsh terrain as word about the approaching 'mad Russian colonel' had made the policemen at the roadblocks reluctant to take money and let the Chechen fighters through, as they had been doing before.

On the second day of the chase, when the regiment crossed into Chechnya from Dagestan, the Russian troops closed in on the rebels and a fierce battle broke out. Although casualties were high on both sides, Kapoustin was adamant – the rebels had to be destroyed, down to the very last man. It was a matter of revenge for the lives of the Russian officers and soldiers.

Suddenly the gunfire started to subside. Kapoustin got out of his armoured personnel carrier and looked around. He had not given any orders to stop the offensive.

A young lieutenant with a bandaged arm approached him.

'Comrade Colonel,' he said, 'there are civilians in the field. They have formed a human shield and are protecting the rebels from our fire.'

Kapoustin took off his helmet and wiped his face with a dirty cloth. He looked around. Although it was cold, the weather was fine. The sun had come out from behind the clouds. The snow patches on the ground were turning black at the edges, a sign of spring coming.

Kapoustin looked at the lieutenant. He was too young to understand what war was all about. There were no civilians in a war. There was the enemy and there was the side you were on. And once one side went soft the other would usually take the upper hand.

'Blast them to kingdom come, son,' Kapoustin said to the lieutenant. 'Just remember what they did to our people.'

In half an hour it was all over. The rebels were all wiped out. Along with the civilians.

Kapoustin got drunk that night, but slept well.

★

Only once in his life did General Kapoustin give an order with a heavy heart – to eliminate General Mikhailov, a man he had known for over twenty years. But in his opinion there was no other option. He had to protect the presidency and save Russia.

At the end of their last meeting General Mikhailov had mentioned the hit squad. He was probably bluffing, repeating some of the rumours that had been circulating around Moscow. But that made General Kapoustin even more determined to remove the FSB Deputy Director. By going to see the President and confronting him with his stupid evidence, General Mikhailov, in Kapoustin's view, was breaking the most important rule of politics – never, under any circumstances, undermine the leadership. Whatever evidence you get, whoever from the inner circle is involved in dirty dealings, you do not drag the top man into the mess. General Mikhailov was not just rocking the boat, he was trying to smash the hull and take the whole bloody thing to the bottom of the ocean. The stakes were too high to let him continue his investigation. He had to go.

But General Kapoustin was unaware of several important developments. He didn't know that before his death General

Mikhailov had received documents from the London team via Liberman with details of the operations of the Central Brotherhood and its links with some top government officials, including the special advisor to the President. Kapoustin also didn't know that an FSB undercover agent had managed to infiltrate his hit squad and report to General Mikhailov about its operations. All this information had already been passed on to the FSB Director, along with preliminary conclusions.

This time the hit squad had acted too late.

★

The day after the rioting in Moscow, General Kapoustin paid a visit to the FSB Director Benedikt Vladimirov.

It was a hastily arranged appointment. General Kapoustin called Vladimirov and asked whether he could see him within the next hour.

'I won't take a lot of your time,' Kapoustin said. 'There's one urgent matter I need to discuss with you.'

Although the FSB Director had a very busy schedule, he still agreed to see General Kapoustin. After all, it was not every day that the man in charge of Kremlin's security and a close confidant of the President was asking him for a meeting.

Thirty minutes later General Kapoustin walked into Vladimirov's office at the Lubyanka. A large portrait of Felix Dzerzhinsky, the founder of the notorious All-Russian Emergency Committee that was eventually re-named the KGB, was hanging behind the desk. Although the statue of Iron Felix – as Dzerzhinsky was known in the dark days that followed the October coup of 1917 – was dragged away from the square outside the main office of the former KGB by the crowds in August of 1991, his portraits still hung in the headquarters of the Federal Security Service.

'I'm honoured to see you, General,' Vladimirov said, greeting him at the door of his office.

Kapoustin knew that he was taking a risk by coming to see Vladimirov. Especially as he was planning to tell the FSB Director that some things were better left untouched, whatever the temptation to act on them. Having removed General Mikhailov,

Kapoustin was now prepared to order more executions to protect the First Family. He was even ready to go as far as sacrificing the life of the FSB Director himself, unless he listened to reason. But for now he was smiling broadly and shaking his hand.

Vladimirov was expecting a visit from Kapoustin, although not quite so soon after the funeral of General Mikhailov. The FSB Director had already read the documents that Mikhailov had passed to him and knew of the existence of the hit squad and the President's son's connection to the Central Brotherhood. His dilemma was how to respond to all that. Should he go to the President and tell all or should he wait? Kapoustin's visit promised to provide him with an answer…

'Benedikt Vladimirovich, I've come to see you about General Mikhailov,' Kapoustin said, having settled down in a leather armchair across from Vladimirov's vast desk with its numerous telephones and piles of documents.

'Tragic, very tragic,' Vladimirov said, shaking his head. 'The country has suffered a great loss. As you know, I've ordered an investigation into the killing and I won't rest until we find the murderers. You need have no worries in that respect. Especially as you were so close to the General.'

Vladimirov looked inquiringly at his guest, waiting for his reaction.

'Oh, I'm not worried about your determination to find the killers,' Kapoustin said. 'I have absolutely no doubt that the FSB will do its best to solve the murder of one of its best people.'

Vladimirov nodded, accepting the General's assurance.

'I'm also not planning to intervene in the investigation in any way,' Kapoustin went on, 'but I wanted to suggest that you take a sensible approach and not rush to any hasty conclusions.'

Vladimirov's eyebrows shot up. If that was not intervening, then what was?

'What sort of hasty conclusions are you talking about, General?' he asked.

Kapoustin felt that it was time to give his host a hint.

'I'm talking about all those silly rumours that General Mikhailov was supposedly investigating corruption at the highest level and even falling out with the…' and he pointed a finger at the ceiling without finishing the sentence… 'President himself.'

Vladimirov's eyes widened.

'I was not aware,' he said in a lowered voice, 'that my deputy had a problem with the head of state.'

Kapoustin nodded slightly.

'General Mikhailov,' he said, leaning forward as if he wanted his host to hear him better, 'went to see the President some time ago and had a nervous breakdown right in front of him. I don't know whether he told you about that. The President was very upset, but asked me not to say anything about it to anyone. It seems the General came across some information concerning people who are close' – and he again pointed his finger at the ceiling – 'to the top leadership. I suspect he may have reached a hasty, irrational conclusion. He may have put two and two together and got five or even six. He was confused, I can tell you that. He was having doubts about the present system of government, about the overall state of things, about his...'

The FSB Director was nodding his head. It was then that Kapoustin suddenly realised that Vladimirov had the face of a rodent: small, closely set colourless eyes, thin, long nose, small ears. This is ridiculous, he thought. Just when I need to concentrate stupid things start coming into my head.

'Is anything wrong?' Vladimirov said. It seemed strange to him that the General suddenly stopped in mid-sentence and was looking at him with an odd smile on his lips.

'No, no, forgive me, it's just something I suddenly remembered,' Kapoustin said. 'It has absolutely nothing to do with what we're discussing.'

Vladimirov eyed him with suspicion. It was not the first time that he found people smiling at him for no apparent reason and he could never understand what it was that amused them. He considered himself to be an intelligent and serious-looking person and the thought that he might be likened to a small animal never crossed his mind.

'So, as you were saying, Andrei Petrovich...' he invited Kapoustin to continue.

'I think that General Mikhailov,' Kapoustin said, 'was under enormous psychological pressure in the days before his unfortunate death. I met him two days before the tragic incident and he looked very tense and nervous. He said some very strange things and I was even under the impression that he was mentally unstable. So it would be wise to keep all of this in mind during the investigation into General Mikhailov's death.'

Vladimirov was now staring at him saying nothing. The silence lasted for a good half minute. Kapoustin was getting rattled. I wish he'd say something, he thought. God knows what goes on in that tiny head of his.

Vladimirov moved at last.

'General,' he said, 'I'm very grateful for your thoughts. The problem is that General Mikhailov didn't leave us any clues regarding the investigations he was involved in. As you know, in our system we don't go around telling each other about our investigations. And with all the recent leaks of information my own deputies and assistants sometimes don't even inform me of some of their undercover operations until they are concluded.'

Kapoustin nodded.

'I just wanted you to know that, whatever facts come to light in the future, our first duty is to protect the interests of the state and not those of individuals,' he said looking Vladimirov straight in the eyes. 'Just like you, I'm totally devoted to our head of state and, just like you, I'll be ready to take *any* measures needed to safeguard him…'

Kapoustin fell silent. It was then that Vladimirov suddenly realised that the head of the Kremlin's secret service must have been himself involved in the killing of Mikhailov and that he was actually threatening him now.

'I'll look into the matter once more and then report my findings to you,' Vladimirov said. 'But I can tell you now that there are no definite clues in the paperwork he left behind.'

Kapoustin stood up. He was satisfied. General Mikhailov had left nothing of substance and, what was even more important, Vladimirov was demonstrating his willingness to take his advice.

He shook hands with the FSB Director and left. Vladimirov returned to his desk and sat motionless for a few minutes. He then picked up the phone.

'I want round-the-clock surveillance put on General Kapoustin,' he said. 'Yes, you heard me right – General Andrei Kapoustin.'

★

Boris could not believe what was happening.

It was like a bad dream. He had just been instructed to go to the Embassy Hotel in Notting Hill Gate where Glyeb, the so-called 'SVR agent', was waiting for him. Ivan must be held hostage in the hotel, he was thinking. They must have brought him here so that they could get me to do anything they want. Bastards!

And yet when he thought about it again it all seemed so absurd, so unreal. In the heart of London the son of a diplomat was being kept against his will by Russian criminals. And he, his father, couldn't do a bloody thing about it.

Boris was given a quarter of an hour to get to the hotel.

'I won't wait,' Glyeb said menacingly. 'So you'd better hurry. And no talking to anyone. We don't want others to spoil the father-and-son reunion.'

Boris's initial reaction was to call the police, but then he decided that it was too risky, especially as he couldn't really say that his son had been kidnapped. He was desperately trying to think whom he could call. And then he remembered that he gave Pavel Batalov his mobile phone. He was a cop – well, a former cop anyway. So he must know how to deal with situations like that.

Boris dialled his own mobile number. Pavel answered the phone immediately.

'Pavel, it's me, Boris,' he said in nervous haste. 'I have an emergency. My son has been kidnapped.'

There was a buzzing noise on the line.

'Can you pick me up at the embassy?' Pavel said.

'I don't have time,' Boris said. 'The man who called ordered me to come straight to the Embassy Hotel. He gave me fifteen minutes and said he won't wait if I'm late.'

Pavel thought it over for a couple of seconds.

'Right,' he said, 'give me the address of the hotel and I'll meet you there.'

A quarter of an hour later Boris was at the Embassy Hotel. He waited outside for a few minutes, but Pavel didn't show up. As he walked into the main lobby he could not see Glyeb anywhere. He checked the bar and the restaurant, but couldn't find him there either.

He returned to the lobby and sat on one of the small sofas in the centre. Now he was panicking. Why the hell did I need to call Batalov? he was thinking in despair. I've wasted all that time talking and now I'm late. What if they hurt my boy?

Then, to his great relief, he saw Glyeb coming out of the lift. He stood up so that he could be seen. Glyeb looked around and, noticing Boris, walked towards him.

'For a moment there I thought you weren't coming,' Glyeb said with a nasty smirk, coming up to him. 'I've been down once already and you were not here.'

Boris could hardly control himself. There were all those people around them in the lobby and he could have easily grabbed Glyeb and called for help. But what would happen to Ivan then?

'Can I see my son, please,' Boris pleaded.

Glyeb grinned.

'Of course you can see him,' he said. 'But unfortunately he is not staying in this hotel. I'll take you there once we've had a brief chat upstairs. There are several things that I want to clear with you.'

They went to the lift. Boris twice looked over his shoulder, hoping to see a glimpse of Pavel in the lobby, but could not see him anywhere.

At the fifth floor they got out and walked down the hallway right to the very end. Glyeb opened the door and gestured to Boris to go in. As he stepped into the room he saw a man standing by the window. It was Shamil. Boris recognised him from their meeting in the pub. Glyeb closed the door behind him.

'I don't think I need to introduce you two to each other,' Glyeb said. 'We might as well get down to business. There are several things I need you to tell me about the properties at Kensington Palace Gardens.'

Boris noticed a map laid out on the table and several files lying on the beds. He recognised some of the files. They were the architectural plans of the buildings neighbouring the Russian embassy. He'd seen them before when he was negotiating the embassy move. But where had these people got them?

He looked inquiringly at Glyeb.

'As you can see, we are looking at some properties that Volkov was interested in,' Glyeb explained. 'We're trying to figure out what he wanted to know and why. I hope that you can provide us with some details that might help us understand what it was that the criminals were after.'

Boris wanted to shout that he knew who they were and that there was no point in playing this bloody game with him. But he managed to control himself. He was desperate to find out where Ivan was, but he was also afraid to make these people angry and risk putting his son's life in even greater danger.

'What do you want to know?' he said in a businesslike tone.

'That's the spirit,' Glyeb said. 'Let's have a look at the map we've made and compare it to the documents that you have brought us.'

Suddenly there was a knock on the door. Both Glyeb and Shamil looked at each other. Then Glyeb walked to the door.

'Who is it?' he asked in English, pressing his ear to the door as if he could hear much better that way.

'Room service, come to fill the minibar,' a man's muffled voice replied.

Glyeb turned round.

'Shamil, check the bar,' he whispered.

Shamil opened the minibar. It was practically empty.

'I'd better let him in, or he'll pester us for ages,' Glyeb said. 'These idiots are hopeless when you tell them to bugger off.'

He opened the door. The man from room service was standing outside holding a cardboard box in his hands. Boris couldn't see his face.

'Come in, come in,' Glyeb said impatiently, stepping aside. 'But hurry up, we're very busy.'

Once Boris saw the man's face he could barely hide his amazement. It was Pavel. He stepped into the room and, glancing around quickly, established how many people were inside. But then he hesitated for a brief moment, not knowing where the minibar was. Glyeb immediately sensed that something was not right, but he was too late. Pavel took a gun out of the box and hit him on the head with it. Glyeb fell on the floor with a loud grunt.

Shamil tried to reach for his gun in a holster under his jacket, but Pavel beat him to it. He dashed forwards and hit him in the stomach with his fist. Shamil fell down.

'Is Ivan here?' Pavel asked Boris, catching his breath.

Boris was standing at the window, paralysed. Then he snapped out his trance and shook his head.

'They're holding him somewhere else,' he said. 'They promised to take me to him later.'

Glyeb started to move on the floor.

'Boris,' Pavel said without turning his gaze from Shamil, 'close the door, turn the key and feel free to sit on our friend here.'

Boris slammed the door and pinned Glyeb down to the floor. For once I can't complain that I'm overweight, he thought, immediately realising that only he could have had such a stupid thought at such a dramatic moment.

Pavel pulled the cover off from the bed and then tugged the bed sheet off. He tore the sheet into several strips and tied up both men's hands and feet. He took the gun off Shamil and threw it into the cardboard box he had brought with him. Then he went to the table and studied the map and the documents. There were different markings on the map and several buildings had been circled in ink. The Russian ambassador's residence was included on the map, but there were no markings near it, nor was it encircled. These creeps are definitely planning to hit the properties at Kensington Palace Gardens, Pavel thought. But when and which ones?

Meanwhile Boris was more interested in the fate of Ivan. He came up to Glyeb who lay on the floor.

'What have you done to my son?' he said menacingly. 'Where is he now?'

Glyeb looked up at him from the floor.

'How the hell should I know where your son is?' he said. 'He didn't tell me about his plans when he arrived here. He's on a business trip, that much I know.'

Pavel came up to them.

'Why would you need a map of a private road in London?' he said. 'And what do all these markings mean?'

Glyeb shook his head.

'I don't have to tell you anything,' he said. 'You burst into my room with a gun and nearly killed me. You'll have some explaining to do when the cops ask you what the hell you're doing here brandishing a piece.'

Pavel grinned.

'Well, look who's a law-abiding citizen all of a sudden,' he said. 'And how about kidnapping, extortion, blackmail and robbery? Not to mention carrying a firearm? How do you think the British authorities will look at such crimes?'

Glyeb was unmoved.

'I don't know what you're talking about,' he said. 'All I know is that you burst into my room and attacked us.'

Pavel signalled to Boris to go with him to the other end of the room.

'I think you'd better leave,' he whispered to him. 'I'll deal with them myself. I'll see you at the embassy later.'

'But what about my son?' Boris protested.

'Don't worry, we'll find him,' Pavel said.

After Boris had left, Pavel called George on the mobile and asked him to come to the hotel to help sort out 'a problem', as he called it.

When George arrived and learnt what had happened he was furious.

'You'd better tell us where the lad is,' he said to Glyeb. 'And God help you if any harm comes to him. Because if that happens I'll deal with personally.'

He then called Jeremy and told him that Ivan Ossinski was definitely in London.

'Just as I thought,' Jeremy said. 'They must be planning to use him as a hostage if things go wrong for them. And they're bound to get rid of him once he serves his purpose.'

★

London was bracing itself for some serious violence on May Day.

The authorities were taking no chances. If previous years were anything to go by they could expect no less than twenty to thirty thousand people to gather in central London to take part in the anti-capitalist march, with about two or three thousand of them being hard-core troublemakers bent on violence.

Police intelligence suggested that the rioting would be even worse than in the past. According to informers, the leadership of the British Real Socialist Party, an extreme left-wing group, had unexpectedly received a large cash donation from an anonymous contributor several weeks before May Day. The group had been responsible for most of the violence during the previous demonstrations and was hoping to make an even bigger impact this time.

There was word that some members of the BRSP had received training in close combat from former military instructors and – what was even more worrying – had bought handguns and stun grenades on the black market. All attempts to establish who actually provided the group with the money failed. It turned out that someone had simply left a suitcase with cash at the headquarters of the BRSP in East London with a note saying 'Good luck on May Day'.

The police came out in full force on that day. All leave had been cancelled and police forces outside the Metropolitan area had been asked to contribute to the effort. The public was warned to stay away from the centre of London and traffic was diverted from the West End. Drivers were strongly advised not to leave their cars anywhere near Trafalgar Square as on previous occasions many parked cars had been smashed up by 'angry protesters', as some journalists called the thugs who hijacked rallies just to have a go at the police.

On the morning of May Day an uneasy calm settled over central London. The battle lines had been drawn and the time for a showdown was approaching...

★

At 10 Kensington Palace Gardens they were ready to begin.

Around a hundred men were waiting for the order to move out. All of them were armed with either sub-machine guns or handguns with silencers. They all had radio transmitters so that they could get in touch with each other and HQ at any time.

Three men were sitting at the computers in a large room on

the first floor of number 10, ready to take over the security systems and telephone lines in the buildings in Kensington Palace Gardens. During the previous night they had connected their system to communications cables beneath the road which had been dug up and left unattended.

The timing for committing the crime of the century was perfect. Most of the inhabitants of Kensington Palace Gardens were away. Security in central London was concentrated around Whitehall and Trafalgar Square. Seraphim had not only picked the best possible distraction to pull off the job, he had even financed the rioters so as to create as much mayhem as possible. It was his money that had been passed to the BRSP and he intended to get the most out of it.

The man in charge of the operation Ruslan Sultanov, who had initially arrived from Moscow with the 'communications equipment', looked at his watch and nodded to the three men at the computers. The system was then logged onto the local network. There was a split-second blink on the monitors in the buildings down the road. And then the picture was restored, showing an empty Kensington Palace Gardens. From that moment all the closed-circuit television cameras, security alarms and phones were immobilised.

Several men dressed as security guards left number 10 and got into two vans. They were going to replace the guards at the gates and see to it that no one wandered into the area. Although the road was usually open to the public, on that particular day it would have been easy to explain that access was closed for 'security reasons'.

For nearly a week the whole team had been going through every detail of the plan. Computer graphics were used to create interior layouts of the buildings targeted by the gang. It was possible to plan every move using these three-dimensional models created on the basis of the drawings and documents provided by the late Vadim Mironov.

The men who gathered at 10 Kensington Palace Gardens were not planning to return to Russia. They had been promised a million dollars each for their part and intended to settle down in the West. What they didn't know was that most of them were not going to get their money. On Seraphim's orders, once the job was done Igor Kislov and his men, who had arrived separately from all the others, were going to 'cut down the costs'. Literally.

The men were divided into groups of eight to ten with each team given a specific building as a target. All of them had been jogging up and down the road, studying the buildings they were supposed to rob. The idea was not to try to get inside through the back entrances or windows, as they could have triggered some secondary alarm system. They were supposed to go in from the front, either simply knocking on the door and overpowering the people inside or letting themselves in. Afterwards it would only be a matter of collecting the works of art and any other valuables and bringing them down to the entrance. All the groups were given an hour to finish the job. As the transport was due to arrive at eleven o'clock, they were supposed to be waiting at the front doors by 10.50 for the pick-up.

★

Transport for the heist had been arranged by Seraphim himself.

Two days earlier, together with Kislov who acted as his translator, he had met the people who were providing the trucks. They were members of one of the Chinese Triads who had left Hong Kong after its takeover by communist China. They were supposed to provide ten postal trucks to the Russians for two days. These trucks were 'chameleon vehicles' – the special paint on them could be easily peeled off, turning them into ordinary delivery trucks. Each had two sets of licence plates that could be changed quickly once they had shed their postal colours.

Seraphim was hiring the trucks for two days for $200,000 each. But the Chinese were curious, as they always are. They wanted to know why the big important Russian man would need so many postal trucks that could be turned into ordinary vehicles. At the meeting in a small Chinese restaurant in Swiss Cottage the Triad people suddenly raised the price for each truck by another $20,000.

Seraphim rejected their demand straight away. He knew that the Chinese were playing their usual games, trying to find out as much as possible about his plans. He also suspected that if they found out what he was up to and how much money was at stake they might be tempted to wait until the job was done and then kill his people and take everything. At least that's what he would do if he were in their shoes.

Seraphim had been dealing with some of the Triad gangs in the past and knew about their ways: always smiling and bowing and patting on the shoulder, yet ready to stick the knife in their partner's back. So he sold them a story which he knew they'd buy.

'I'm moving some computers to Russia that are still banned from sale to Eastern Europe,' he said. 'The stuff is kept in the Russian embassy and I need the trucks to take it out of there. It's a government thing and I'm doing it for future favours. Big favours, as a matter of fact.'

The Chinese were nodding and smiling. They knew all about the illegal trade in new technologies. They had themselves in the past operated a network that was stealing new Western technologies and state-of-the-art computers. Hong Kong existed for decades as a British colony with China's blessing simply because it was a major black market for new Western technologies. Communist China received most of the new technologies via Hong Kong. Several Triads had made their fortunes in industrial espionage.

Having made his 'confession', Seraphim was watching the Chinese. But he couldn't really tell what they were thinking behind their constant grins. Were they happy or unhappy?

In the end it didn't really matter. The trucks would be driven by his men and once the job was done the Chinese could go to hell as far as he was concerned. In any event, he had made other arrangements for transporting the most precious items, so he wasn't all that worried about the rest.

They agreed that the trucks would be brought to a square not far from Kensington Palace Gardens at 10.30 in two days' time and from then onwards Seraphim's men would take over.

Kislov went to the car and brought two suitcases with a million dollars in cash in each of them.

The Chinese were smiling. They were happy.

★

The President arrived at the Kremlin in the morning to prepare for yet another government shake-up.

He wanted to complete this before parliament returned from the May holiday break. Everyone was expecting him to sack the chairman of the government and cut down the number of vice-premiers from seven to three.

He was also planning to announce the appointment of his advisor, Valentin Ashev, as the new Vice-President, the man who would be his chosen successor when he stepped down. He recalled the conversation they had at his country retreat when they finally decided to go ahead with their plan.

'You'll be able to take over from me as head of state in about six months,' the President told Valentin. 'Once I win the election, and things settle down I'll step down in your favour. And believe me, the people will buy it. Sure, there'll be a few grumbles here and there. But on the whole no one will dare to oppose us. And once you become president, you'll be able to protect all of us, including Vassili.'

Valentin nodded.

'I only hope that your people don't go for my throat the moment they find out that you've decided to ignore all their proposals and appoint me,' he said. 'The bastards in the Kremlin didn't like me from the start. And once news about our family connection becomes public who knows what they might do.'

The President nodded.

'It's always a risk, I know,' he said. 'But don't forget, I have powerful friends who will support me. They promised to back me if I don't interfere with their business affairs. Well, I didn't interfere, as you know, so now it's payback time and they'll have to fund my election campaign. So don't you worry, I'll win the next presidential election for you. And afterwards Russia is yours to rule for the next four years. But you must promise me to protect Vassili. He has a curse hanging over him, so don't be too hard on him.'

Valentin never believed in all that nonsense about the curse. He considered his half-brother to be a drunkard and a thug who constantly manipulated his father. But he decided not to say anything at that point. He would deal with Vassili in due time, he thought.

'Sure, I'll look after him,' Valentin said. 'He is my half-brother.'

The President was happy to hear that. He was looking at his son with pride. An honest, intelligent, hard-working young man, who understood the advantages of a free market. Most of the oligarchs would throw their weight behind him, he thought. They were terrified at the thought of the communists coming back to power. They were bound to support him, if only to save their own arses and the billions they had stolen.

★

The President was going through the list of cabinet ministers when Anatoli, his personal assistant, called him on the internal phone and informed him that the FSB Director, Benedikt Vladimirov, had asked for an urgent meeting. Although the President was not in the mood to see anyone, he decided that in this case he could make the effort, especially as he was planning to meet the man anyway to tell him about the forthcoming appointment of the new vice-president.

He told Anatoli that he would see Vladimirov in an hour. He liked the man; he trusted him. Otherwise he would never have appointed him to be the head of the former KGB. It was still a powerful position, even in the new, supposedly democratic Russia, and it was very dangerous to choose the wrong man for the job. The President was even toying with the idea of appointing him chairman of the government to act as back-up for his son Valentin once he became Vice-President.

Vladimirov arrived at the Kremlin at ten o'clock and ten minutes later he was sitting in the office of the President. Exactly an hour and twenty-eight minutes after that, Vladimirov came out, according to the personal assistant to the President, looking 'rather cheerful'. Then the President asked for one of the secretaries to come in to write down an important document. Fifteen minutes later a decree was prepared appointing Benedikt Vladimirov as the new Vice-President of Russia.

Afterwards many people wondered what actually happened during the time Vladimirov spent with the President. Why did the head of state suddenly decide to pluck this man from relative obscurity and make him the second most powerful politician in the country? they were asking. And what could Vladimirov have said to impress the President so much? Did he by any chance have an ace up his sleeve which he used against the old man?

Only one man who was not present at that meeting had a rough idea of what might have happened. He was General Andrei Kapoustin, the head of the Presidential Protection Service who by that time was being kept under house arrest at his home, charged with misuse of his official position and anti-constitutional activity.

★

One by one the groups sent out to break into the buildings in Kensington Palace Gardens reported back to headquarters that they had managed to get inside. Not a single alarm had gone off. The computer system set up to disarm the whole security network in the area had worked perfectly.

On strict instructions from Seraphim, the residence of the Russian ambassador was not to be approached by anyone. Before the operation started Sultanov was told that a separate squad was going to enter 13 Kensington Palace Gardens. But there was no word of when the group was going to arrive.

As the May Day demonstrators were gathering in Trafalgar Square, and the first scuffles with the police took place, the Russian criminals were taking advantage of the situation and committing a daring robbery in one of the most exclusive areas in London. The men inside the buildings were searching through the rooms and bringing paintings, antiques, silverware and jewellery to the lobbies downstairs. Meanwhile the people at number 10 were watching the entrances to the road at both ends on their computer screens.

At approximately twenty past ten, a coach with darkened windows drove through the gates at the Notting Hill end of the road and stopped at the checkpoint. It could have been the team that was supposed to take care of the ambassador's residence, but Sultanov was taking no chances. He was watching everything on his monitor.

'It's red alert, boys,' he told the 'guards' at the gate over a radio transmitter. 'Don't hesitate to use your weapons if need be.'

The two men could be seen coming out and talking to the driver. Then one of the guards came back on the radio.

'It's okay,' he said, 'it's our guys.'

There was a collective sigh of relief in the control room.

The coach drove down the road and stopped outside the Russian ambassador's residence. Four men got out of it. Three of them were wearing black leather jackets and jeans. The fourth wore a dark suit, white shirt and formal tie.

They made straight for the gate of the ambassador's residence.

★

Tension was building in 13 Kensington Palace Gardens.

Earlier the ambassador had called Vice-Premier Vitalli Tenko and told him that he could not have a meeting with him that day. He did offer to send his official Jaguar to pick up the Vice-Premier at his hotel and take him on a sightseeing trip around the capital. But Tenko, who was already very unhappy with the way he was being treated, told him that he did not need any assistance as, in his words, he was 'being looked after by some friends of his'.

The ambassador was unable to think of any 'friends' that the Vice-Premier might have in London, since he'd been there only once before and stayed at the embassy all the time. But in any case he thought it was for the best, considering the situation.

'We will have to meet at some point,' Tenko said with scorn in his voice. 'I have a very important letter from the Kremlin to show you. I hope you'll find the time for me soon.'

The ambassador assured him that he would do his best.

'It's one of those things,' he said, thinking that actually it was not 'one of those things' at all. 'I'm besieged by problems and people.'

Tenko mumbled something incoherent and hung up.

Earlier in the morning several people in the embassy, including Colonel Kotov, the chief of security, had tried to persuade the ambassador to leave for the embassy's country retreat in Kent saying that it was too dangerous for him to remain in London considering the circumstances. But he flatly refused.

'The captain does not leave his ship in times of danger,' he said. 'I'm staying.'

The men in the building were positioned in such a way as to cover all possible access routes to the residence, including the back garden. There were six people guarding the garages where the crates with the exhibits for the forthcoming Russian folk art exhibition were stored.

All the paintings from the main hall on the ground floor and from all the other rooms had been stored in the basement under lock and key, so that in case of an attack the criminals would have to spend a lot of time finding them. All the other valuables were put into the communications room on the second floor and also locked up.

Pavel stayed with the guard on duty at reception, watching all the screens which were showing the front entrance and the garden at the back. They also had a small TV set switched on and could see from the news reports that trouble had already started in and around Trafalgar Square. Several shops were being smashed and looted and cars were being overturned. The police were attempting to push the demonstrators into side streets to split them up into small groups. But more and more people kept arriving.

The British Real Socialist Party was very visible among the demonstrators. There were red banners and posters with the name of the party all over the place.

Pavel was shaking his head in disbelief. This was not the Britain he remembered from his younger days. And yet he had a strange feeling that something was not right about the unfolding events. Something was not right at all...

★

Alex and Clay were sitting in a small room on the ground floor of a two-storey building in the grounds of the ambassador's residence. The room was normally used by the drivers and mechanics for tea breaks, but on that day it was empty.

From the window they could see only the doors of the embassy garages where the exhibits for the forthcoming exhibition of Russian folk art were stored. Alex was sitting in an old leather chair holding a sub-machine gun in his hands. Clay was sitting on top of a desk, his sub-machine gun beside him. They were both wearing jeans and casual shirts. Alex had a bullet-proof vest on top of his shirt.

He was sipping coffee from a plastic cup.

'Why is it,' he said rhetorically, 'that most of the "Best of..." albums usually contain some of the crappiest songs ever? I mean, they should have all the hits and all. But every time I buy those compilations half of the bloody songs are rubbish.'

Clay looked at him, caught off guard by the question.

'It's 'cos yar music's gone down the shithole,' he said after a while. 'There ain't any more Beatles or Stones.'

Alex thought about it for a moment.

'You can say that again,' he agreed finally. 'The old bands were the best. Them guys had no problems filling their "Best of..." albums with great stuff.'

They sat in silence for several minutes.

'So how many d'ya think there'll be of 'em?' Clay asked.

Alex felt that his partner was getting anxious. He was feeling the pressure himself. The waiting was getting on their nerves.

'I don't know how many there'll be,' Alex said, 'but I bet you they'll be more professional than our crowd. I wish we had more people on our side who knew how to use guns. I only hope George gets his people here soon.'

Before they had taken their position George had promised to get some back-up and Alex was wondering who it might be and when they would arrive.

★

Boris and the ambassador were watching the May Day chaos on television.

The levels of violence were getting worse by the minute. The anti-capitalist protesters were smashing everything in their sights and pelting police with stones. A McDonald's outlet on Whitehall was trashed by the crowd in a matter of minutes: windows were smashed, chairs and tables torn out and thrown on the street. Several smoke grenades were hurled by the protesters and, according to unconfirmed reports, two policemen received gunshot wounds.

'Do you think that someone might have financed these protests?' the ambassador suddenly said.

Boris was taken aback by the question. He was thinking about the whereabouts of his son. It took him a while to respond.

'I really can't imagine anyone funding hoodlums to smash up shops and attack the police,' he said. 'What would be the point?'

The ambassador looked at him.

'Someone always benefits from chaos and confusion,' he said. 'Just look at the posters and banners the protesters are carrying. They all seem brand new and factory-made. And the rioters are very well organised, I'd even say too well organised. Look how they attack the police as if they've been taught how to stage a violent street protest. They operate in small groups and once they strike they immediately disperse and mix with the crowd. It all seems choreographed, stage-managed, so to speak.'

Boris was nodding but said nothing.

'How about a crazy hunch?' the ambassador said. 'What would you say to a wild guess that the people who financed these violent protests are the very same people who are planning to attack us? This would be a great distraction for them, wouldn't it?'

Boris stared at the ambassador in disbelief. What he just said sounded absurd. Russian criminals funding a mass protest in London to cover up a heist? This was way over the top.

Luckily the internal phone rang just then, and he didn't have to respond to the ambassador's question.

It was the guard downstairs. He informed him that Vice-Premier Vitalli Tenko was calling from the entrance gate.

'Should I let him in, sir?' he asked.

'Of course you bloody well should,' the ambassador said. 'He's the Deputy Prime Minister of Russia!'

He got up from his chair.

'Why on earth did he come here?' he said. 'I thought he'd be with his friends. And how am I going to explain to him that our embassy is under siege and that he'll have to leave as soon as possible?'

Boris didn't have an answer to that. He had an uneasy feeling that the visit did not bode well.

★

After appointing Benedikt Vladimirov as the new Vice-President, the President retreated to his country residence.

He had absolutely no desire to discuss the new appointment with anyone, especially not with Valentin Ashev, for whom the outcome must have been a much bigger shock than for anyone else.

Yes, he did make an unexpected decision, he imagined himself answering journalists. Yes, he had full faith in Benedikt Vladimirov. No, he was not worried that a former KGB agent could become the next head of state. No, he was not running for another term.

The President was himself surprised at the speed with which he had made his decision. What was it? An hour, an hour and a half that the conversation with Vladimirov had lasted? He wasn't really watching the time. For him the whole meeting went by in a flash, although he could remember every detail.

When Vladimirov had walked into his office and sat down across from his desk he was a bit fidgety. The President had shuffled his papers for a few seconds to make it look as if he had still been working only a moment before the visitor walked in. He had learnt the trick from aides who'd worked as television presenters before coming to the Kremlin. Every time the cameras started rolling they would take a pen and pretend that they were making final corrections to their texts before going on air. It was supposed to make them look sharp and professional.

The President closed the file and looked at Vladimirov. The FSB Director smiled faintly and bowed his small balding head slightly. He does look remarkably like a rodent, the President thought. How on earth did he ever get into the KGB?

'What brings you to our corridors, Benedikt Vladimirovich?' the President said.

Vladimirov moved slightly in his chair, clenching his buttocks tightly several times and then relaxing them. That was how he usually released the tension in his body.

'I really don't know how to tell you this, sir,' he said, 'but we have uncovered some very disturbing information during an undercover operation that we've been conducting.'

He stopped for a moment to check how the President was reacting to his opening statement. The old man was looking at him without any hint of anxiety in his face.

'This information,' Vladimirov continued, 'concerns, among other things, the activities of General Andrei Kapoustin, the head of your security service, and, in part, relates to your son... sorry, your special advisor. It seems that he has had the misfortune to get mixed up with certain individuals who are suspected of committing serious offences...'

The President did not let him finish. It was as if the meeting was a repeat of his previous conversation with the late General Mikhailov.

'I always thought, Benedikt Vladimirovich, that you were above the petty political games that are played around the Kremlin by some people,' he said. 'But now I see that I was wrong. What on earth are you mumbling about?'

Vladimirov's face reddened. He was trying hard to pick the right words. For a moment he even thought that he shouldn't have acted on the information he received without first talking to the head of state. He never did anything without consulting the President in the past. But on this occasion he really had no choice. He had to act quickly to protect the top man and prevent any fallout from the revelations that were about to be unravelled. He had already ordered General Kapoustin to be placed under arrest. In addition, also on his orders, FSB commandos stormed the military base outside Moscow where Kapoustin's people, members of the secret 'hit squad', were all arrested. Vassili, the special advisor to the President, was being kept under guard at a secret location. For his own safety.

And now Vladimirov had to tell the President of Russia what he'd done.

★

The President was looking at Vladimirov, waiting for him to explain himself.

Here goes, Vladimirov thought, clinching and relaxing his buttocks again. I only hope he doesn't sack me on the spot.

'We have established, sir, that General Kapoustin created his own team which had been carrying out killings of known criminals on his orders,' Vladimirov said. 'By our preliminary estimates, at least several hundred people have been murdered by the squad, including, I'm sorry to say, my deputy, General Aleksei Mikhailov. It also appears that your son – sorry, your special advisor – knew about the hit squad and was even in direct contact with some of its members. We now know for a fact that on his request two gang leaders had been eliminated, sparking the recent massive gangland war in the capital.'

Vladimirov stopped for a moment. The President was now looking pale and his left hand was visibly trembling. Things were not looking good for the FSB Director, but he had no choice but to continue.

'Your special advisor,' he said, 'has also been in close contact with a criminal known as the Crow. It appears that, through this criminal, sensitive information about our operation in Chechnya might have been passed to the bandits, resulting in the murder of our agents on the ground. On my orders your son has been temporarily put in protective custody, for his own safety…'

'Stop!' the President said looking up at Vladimirov. 'That's enough. I don't want to hear any more about it!'

Silence fell in the room, lasting for several minutes. The President was coming to terms with what he had just heard. General Kapoustin, his trusted friend and ally, was conducting an illegal war behind his back against people he perceived as posing a danger to the state. He always suspected the General of meddling in politics, but this was way, way out of line. And his son Vassili was now directly implicated in corruption and treason. The situation was desperate. Something drastic had to be done. Something that no one would expect him to do…

The President looked at Vladimirov.

'So what do you suggest we do?' he asked.

Vladimirov was relieved to see that the President wasn't angry with him. But he was rather hoping to receive orders rather than come up with solutions. He was a man who rarely took decisions himself.

'In the light of the facts that have emerged,' Vladimirov said, 'I suggest, sir, that we act swiftly to protect you and your family from any potential danger that might arise from possible accusations of treason and misuse of official position. I can assure you, sir, that I will do everything in my power to shield you and your family from your enemies.'

The President was watching the FSB Director in silence. He had not really expected him to come up with an answer. After all, he had personally picked him for the job, out of several candidates, knowing perfectly well that Vladimirov was a grey non-entity, a man with no particular talents and no character. But he also knew that he was fiercely loyal to him and would come down like a ton of bricks on anyone who dared oppose him. There was a reason for this loyalty of course. Vladimirov was no angel and could have paid heavily for his financial 'indiscretions' during his time in the Moscow mayor's office. But the President had personally ordered his file to be taken out of the FSB archives and passed over to him. And Vladimirov knew about this.

It was then that the President suddenly had a crazy idea. Why not appoint Vladimirov as the new Vice-President? he thought. Why not make him the next President? No one would ever dare go against the FSB Director. Everyone knew that the FSB kept files on most politicians and businessmen. But most important of all, Vladimirov would not allow the President and his family to be prosecuted. He would never allow that, if only because he would go down with him!

The President stood up and started pacing about the room. For a brief moment he completely ignored Vladimirov, who was sitting in silence, tightening his buttocks from time to time.

The most important thing is the safety of my family and myself, the President was thinking. Once I appoint Vladimirov as my successor no one will care what General Kapoustin was doing behind my back. And Vassili's antics would eventually be forgotten. Everyone will be busy kissing the new President's arse.

The President got back behind his desk. Vladimirov was

watching him closely. He was still terrified at the idea that he could be arrested himself for going after General Kapoustin and the President's son.

'How would you feel if I offered you the post of Vice-President with the prospect of replacing me as head of state?' the President said, looking Vladimirov straight in the eyes. 'Do you think you could handle that?'

Vladimirov sat there not really knowing how to respond. Initially he became even more terrified. He thought that the President was testing him, checking his loyalty.

'I don't know what to say, sir,' he mumbled. 'I wasn't ready for such a turn of events. Are you sure I'm suitable for the post? I mean, you are a world statesman, a man respected by the nation and I'm a humble…'

Perfect, the President thought, studying Vladimirov's confused, slightly reddened face. A devoted, loyal non-entity with enough power to keep all my enemies at bay. He's perfect for the job.

The President pretended not to notice Vladimirov's anxiety.

'Well, that's settled then,' he said as if the FSB Director had just agreed to his proposal. 'I will sign the decree immediately appointing you the new Vice-President. And I will step down and appoint you my successor. Congratulations, Benedikt Vladimirovich!'

Vladimirov smiled faintly. He was still coming to terms with what had just happened. He still had a feeling that it was some sort of a game.

The President had one last thing to clear with his new chosen successor.

'I want you to promise me something, Benedikt Vladimirovich,' he said. 'I want you to give me your word that you'll provide full protection for my family once I step down.'

At that moment Vladimirov suddenly realised that it was no game. He was going to become the new president of Russia.

'I give you the word of an officer, sir,' he said standing up. 'You can count on me to uphold the interests of you and your family, whatever the situation.'

★

Ivan could not understand what was happening. He had arrived in London to be met at the airport by two men who took him to a room in a shabby hotel and told him to sit tight and not call anyone. He spent a whole day there watching television.

The next morning the two men came to his hotel. They told him that there had been a change of plan, and that they were moving him to a 'company flat'. He was taken to a flat somewhere in North London. The two men told him to wait for further instructions and left. Ivan heard the turning of a key in the lock and when he tried to open the front door he couldn't.

He tried to find a telephone but there was none. When he checked the windows he discovered that they all had steel bars on the outside.

Ivan found himself imprisoned in London.

★

Pavel was trying to figure out why the security monitor did not show the Vice-Premier walking up the driveway to the building. There was nobody on the screen and yet, just a moment before, he had heard Tenko's voice on the intercom, the guard pressed the button to open the gate and let the Vice-Premier on the compound. Something was not right. Pavel reached inside his jacket and touched the handle of the gun that George had given him. He was ready for anything.

The two 'SVR agents' had not told them much. They kept talking about plans to purchase properties in Kensington Palace Gardens and insisted that the information they were gathering was needed solely for the potential buyers. Both men said that they knew nothing about any possible plans to burgle the properties in the area.

The guard pressed the button and the lock in the big oak entrance door started to buzz.

Four men entered the lobby. Pavel glanced at the visitors. Three of them looked more like some heavies from a Moscow suburb. He reckoned they must have been Tenko's bodyguards.

The Vice-Premier came up to them.

'I would like to see the ambassador,' he said. 'Is he in?'

He looked tense. Pavel suddenly felt the tension spreading to him as well. And then it hit him. Of course, they have tampered with the security system! That's why the 'SVR agents' had maps of the communications networks in the area. How could he have been so stupid! The attack on the embassy had begun!

'He's on his way down to greet you, sir,' the guard said.

One of the men accompanying the Vice-Premier stepped forward.

'Are there any more people in the building apart from you two and the ambassador?' he asked.

If Pavel needed any more proof that these were the attackers the question was a giveaway. The guard opened his mouth to speak, but Pavel kicked him with his left foot.

'There are only us two and the ambassador,' he said in a loud voice. 'There's no one else here.'

He was hoping that the others would hear them talking to the visitors and come to their rescue.

The man nodded and turned around to his two companions. The next moment all three produced guns fitted with silencers from under their leather jackets and opened fire. The guard fell from his chair, shot in the chest several times. Pavel was thrown back to the wall. The force of the bullets hitting him made him lose consciousness.

'There was no need for that!' the Vice-Premier screamed. 'There was no need to kill them! I'm doing everything you asked me to do!'

'Shut the fuck up!' one of the men shouted. 'Or you'll be joining those two!'

He leaned over the counter and pressed the button which opened the outside gates. The coach with the rest of the team drove through and stopped on the driveway outside the entrance to the building.

Tenko watched in silent horror. How could I have let these people to trick me into helping them? he thought. How could I not see that Voronov was up to no good?

But an inner voice was telling him that he had no choice. That it was at the request of the son of the President of Russia that he had agreed to take Seraphim Voronov with him. How was he supposed to know that there was a plot to steal the national treasures and that the embassy in London was involved in it? He remembered the brief conversation with Seraphim earlier. Voronov had arrived at his hotel and met him downstairs in the lobby.

Seraphim was accompanied by two men.

'Mr Tenko, Vitalli Abramovitch, we have a very important job to do,' he said. 'We have to save the national treasures of Russia before they are taken out of the country and disappear for ever.'

Tenko had absolutely no idea what the man was talking about. But Seraphim paid no attention to the bewildered expression on the Vice-Premier's face.

'We have no time left,' he said. 'The criminals are planning to strike this morning. They are using the May Day demonstration as a distraction to commit the crime of the century. You, as the Vice-Premier of the Russian government, have a duty to protect your country's national interests. You have to talk to the ambassador and convince him that a conspiracy exists within his embassy to steal the national treasures. You must tell him to let us move the treasures from the embassy and hide them somewhere safe. Like on your plane, for example.'

Tenko was lost for words. He desperately needed to talk to someone, anyone, in the Kremlin. He had to get an authorisation to act.

'I have to get in touch with Moscow,' he said hoarsely. 'I have to tell them what's happening here.'

Seraphim looked at him in disgust.

'You do no such thing!' he said in a voice so loud that even the hotel reception staff turned to look at them. 'What the hell's wrong with you? Why can't you act on your own? Where's your initiative? We're leaving straight away. The special group that has been assembled to prevent the crime is already here. They are all special agents of the Russian intelligence who are ready to sacrifice their lives for their country. And all you can think about is calling Moscow. Shame on you, Mr Vice-Premier!'

Tenko hesitated for a moment. But Seraphim was not prepared to wait.

'Let's go,' he commanded. 'On the way I'll let you talk to our mutual friend Vassili on the phone and he'll give you all the clearances in the world.'

They left the hotel and got into a coach. There were at least twenty passengers inside. Soon they were outside the residence of the Russian ambassador.

'My men will accompany you to the building,' Seraphim said. 'The rest of the team will join you very soon.'

★

Boris was following the ambassador down the stairs when they heard several loud thumps and then the loud voice of the Vice-Premier. Boris reacted immediately.

'Mr Ambassador,' he said, 'I have to ask you to get back to your office.'

The ambassador turned round to face him. His face was distorted with anger.

'Do you really expect me to sit it out in the office while my men die down there?' he thundered. 'Go and fetch the others! We're under attack!'

The ambassador then ran up the stairs to his office and went straight to the fireplace. He moved the painting above it, behind which was a small safe. He opened the safe and took out a gun.

'At least we're not going down without a fight,' he said out loud and hurried downstairs to the main hall.

Before running for help, Boris bolted the door separating the main hall from the lobby. It was a big oak door reinforced with steel plates, which would take some time to break down. Then he ran to the Winter Garden Hall where three diplomats were positioned at the windows, all armed with AK rifles.

'We've got a problem in the entrance lobby,' Boris said. 'I think the attackers have already killed some of our people.'

They decided to surprise the intruders by storming the entrance lobby. It was possible to reach it through the office of the deputy ambassador, which had doors leading both to the main hall and to the lobby.

Boris and two of the men got into the office and quietly approached the door. Boris looked through the spyhole. He could see three men talking to each other. The Vice-Premier was standing alone, looking terrified. Boris could not see the whole reception area and could only guess that the guard and Pavel had probably been shot.

He whispered to the two men, 'On the count of three I open the door and we go in. Try to shoot them in the legs and at all cost avoid the Vice-Premier. We don't need to have a senior member of the government shot in the embassy.'

He came up to the door and turned the key as quietly as possible.

Before opening the door he looked back at the two diplomats who were holding the Kalashnikov rifles, ready to go into battle. Both men were visibly tense.

Boris felt his heart beat faster. He was about to confront criminals who would not hesitate to kill him and all the other people in the building.

'Let's do it,' he said and swung the door open.

★

Pavel regained consciousness. He was lying on the floor. The bullet-proof vest that he had so reluctantly accepted from Clay had saved his life. Somehow he managed not to groan or make any other noises that could have alerted the men in the lobby. He turned his head slightly and saw the dead guard lying close to him. There was blood all over the floor. That had probably saved him when one of the men looked over the counter. He must have seen the blood and decided that both men were dead.

Where the hell is everyone? Pavel thought. He glanced at the monitor but it was showing an empty driveway although there was definite movement outside.

Slowly he moved his hand to his breast pocket, got out the mobile phone and pressed the memory button with Alex's phone number. They agreed that if things went seriously wrong he would make two rings and then disconnect. But the phone would not access the network. There was some interference with the signal.

'I demand to know what is going on here!' he heard the Vice-Premier asking in a loud voice.

'Shut the fuck up!' one of the men yelled. 'Don't interfere...'

He did not have time to finish. Boris and the two diplomats stormed into the lobby. Pavel could see them coming in from where he was lying.

Several shots were fired. Pavel saw one of the diplomats hit. Summoning all his strength together, he got up. The second diplomat ran back through the open door. Boris took cover behind a desk. From where Pavel was standing, he could clearly see the attackers. He fired several shots and hit two of the men. The third grabbed the Vice-Premier by the arm and, hiding behind him, moved quickly to the front door, opened it, and got out.

Seeing that the coast was clear, Boris rushed to the diplomat who was lying on the floor, but to his horror he saw that the man was dead. A bullet had gone through his eye. He stood up.

'We've got to call the police!' he shouted to Pavel. 'We need help; there might be more of them on the way.'

Pavel grabbed the phone. The line was dead.

★

As soon as Alex and Clay heard shots coming from the main building they knew that there was no point waiting for back-up.

They picked up their machine guns and ran out. They made their way up the driveway leading from the garages to the main building and, as they turned a corner, they saw a group of men, all armed, getting out of the coach parked outside the main entrance. As soon as the intruders noticed them they immediately opened fire. Alex dived behind some thick bushes. Clay crouched on the ground and returned fire.

Two of the men by the coach went down.

Alex ran back to the garages. Clay had to roll over several times to get out of the line of fire. Then he got up and ran.

The men who were assigned to protect the exhibits took cover behind cars that were parked outside the garages. Colonel Kotov, the embassy's head of security, ran down the steps leading from the tennis court situated above the garages, and joined them. He held an Uzi in his right hand.

'What the hell is happening?' he asked.

'We are under attack!' Alex said. 'I hope George arrives with the back-up soon!'

★

Pavel had managed to shut the main entrance doors of the ambassador's residence and bolt them.

He quickly checked the two men that he shot. They were both dead. He then looked out through a small window and saw the Vice-Premier being pushed into the coach. The Crow also got in and shut the door behind him. The coach drove off. The gates opened automatically as if someone had a remote control to operate them. Several armed men were watching the building's entrance.

'It's all clear down here!' Pavel shouted, and the ambassador unlocked the door to the main hall and came out. He was holding a gun in his hand.

'What happened here?' he asked, looking around the entrance lobby.

'We've lost two men, the guard and one diplomat,' Pavel said. 'But it seems the attackers are not showing any interest in the main building. Judging by the gunfire I hear they are trying to get to the area of the garages. They do have the entrance to this building covered though and if we attempt to get out they'll finish us off.'

The ambassador shook his head in disbelief.

'What about mobile phones?' he said. 'Can we use them to call for outside help?'

'I don't think so,' Pavel said gloomily. 'They seem to have blocked the local mobile network.'

★

Outside the garages a gun battle was raging...

The attackers were attempting to get through to the garages, but met fierce resistance from the defenders. From the coach parked outside the ambassador's residence Seraphim got in touch with Sultanov using a short-wave radio.

'Our people are stuck at number 13,' he said. 'Start moving the trucks out. And send all available men over to the ambassador's residence. We need to wind this up as quickly as possible. I'm getting out of here.'

The fighting continued. The Russian diplomats, along with Alex and Clay, were defending their positions. But when more than thirty armed men joined the attackers, they had no choice but to retreat deeper into the compound.

Seraphim's people opened the garage doors, carried out the crates that were stored there and linked them together with chains and ropes. Then came the sound of an approaching helicopter. It looked like an air ambulance, one of several circling over the centre of London on that day. This one came to hover over the ambassador's residence. A metal cable was lowered with a steel hook on its end and the next moment the first batch of crates that had been tied together was lifted from the ground and the helicopter flew off. Several minutes later a second 'air ambulance' arrived, picked up another stack of crates and disappeared from sight just like the previous one.

Then, just as Seraphim's men were about to retreat, about ten diplomats, headed by the ambassador himself, suddenly attacked them. They ran out of the main building, shooting in every direction, and about four attackers went down. Alex and Clay immediately responded, making a desperate dash from the inner yard. For a brief moment Alex even thought that they were going to gain the upper hand. But suddenly more of the Crow's men stormed through the gates of the compound and soon the defenders were once again pinned down by gunfire.

The ambassador was wounded, lying on the grass. Several of the diplomats were killed.

'Where the hell's the back-up?' Alex roared.

And that was when Clay went down, having been hit by two bullets. Earlier he gave his bullet-proof vest to Pavel and now he paid the price. Alex ran up to him. He knelt to check whether he was alive, but there was only a very slight pulse.

He got up. He saw three men running towards him. He pulled the trigger, but there was only a loud click. He was out of bullets.

'Die, you bastards!' Alex shouted. With a quick move of his hand, he took out three rounded razor-sharp disks out of a leather case on his belt and threw them one by one with all his strength at the approaching men. Two of the disks hit their targets, striking one of the men in the forehead and the other in the neck, killing them instantly. But the third disk missed its target. The man shot Alex at close range in the neck, sending him crashing down to the ground. But as he ran up to him to finish him off, one of the diplomats cut him down with a burst of machine-gun fire.

Alex could hear shouting and gunfire all around him, but it was as if the noises were distant, coming from afar. He could not feel his body.

I'm done, he thought. This is the end.

It was then that a group of men led by George arrived on the scene. They were top professionals, security people from the Israeli embassy down the road. And they all agreed to help the Russians.

★

The trucks with the valuables stolen from the buildings in Kensington Palace Gardens were speeding along the motorway. They were heading for different ports on their way to Holland where a team of 'experts' assembled by Yeffim Kaltzman was supposed to evaluate them and arrange their sale. All the trucks were by now transformed from postal vehicles into ordinary delivery trucks.

Meanwhile the two helicopters had offloaded their precious cargo at a farm three miles from a major motorway and the crates were loaded onto a big truck with diplomatic licence plates that left for Heathrow.

The coach carrying Seraphim, Vice-Premier Vitalli Tenko, Ivan Ossinski, Yeffim Kaltzman and several of the men who took part in the attack on the Russian embassy, was also heading for Heathrow.

The Russian government plane, which had brought Vice-Premier Tenko to Britain, was on standby, waiting to take the passengers and an unspecified 'diplomatic cargo' to Columbia.

★

Once the Israelis stepped in, the fighting quickly subsided.

George came up to Pavel.

'The police are on their way here,' he said. 'But we have to do something quick. Otherwise they'll get away.'

'I'll go after them,' Pavel said. 'I'll try to stop them somehow.'

George nodded.

'It's no longer about Operation Saving Ivan, you know,' he said. 'It's now about helping Russia.'

Pavel said nothing. At that moment he realised that if he could find the Crow and bring him back, he could strike a deal with the FSB and the Prosecutor General's office back in Moscow.

He had a hunch that Seraphim would try to escape in the plane that brought him to Britain along with the Vice-Premier.

'I have an idea,' he said to George. 'I think the Crow might try to slip away using the Vice-Premier as cover. Get me a car and I'll drive to Heathrow.'

Several minutes later he was speeding down the road in a diplomatic BMW.

★

Pavel drove like a madman. But when he reached the VIP suite at Heathrow Terminal 4 the plane was already moving to the runway. A big truck and a coach were parked at the car park of the VIP suite. There were no people in the area.

Pavel got out of the car and ran to the building. It was closed. He looked around. He could see the plane, an Illyushin-86, moving slowly away. They were getting ready for take-off.

Pavel dialled George on his mobile.

'They're ready to take off,' he said. 'I need to get on the plane. Can you do something?'

'I'll do my best,' George said.

Pavel could hardly control his nerves. It had all been too much for one day. Now, if George could manage to get through to his friends Pavel would be confronting the Crow once again. This time in London.

★

Seraphim was sitting with Yeffim Kaltzman in the first class section of the plane. Ivan Ossinski was sitting separately in the front row. The Vice-Premier and one of the Crow's men were in business class. The rest of the men were drinking in the economy section.

There were two air stewardesses, who attended only to the first class passengers. The rest of the people on board looked after themselves.

Yeffim was explaining the arrangements he had made with private collectors. It was only a week since he found out what was being offered for sale. Seraphim told him that, on instructions of the Kremlin itself, he was supposed to organise the secret sale of a large part of the Russian national treasures. He said that there was a plot to steal them and that was why he had to send in his men to get them out of the embassy. But he did not even bother to explain why valuable items from other buildings had been taken, and Yeffim decided not to ask. He did not really care who had instructed whom to do what. The only thing that interested him was the size of his commission. It was promising to be even bigger than he had been hoping for.

'We're going to sell the stuff in several lots,' he was saying to Seraphim. 'I've quoted the prices to the buyers at a forty per cent discount, compared to similar items from the catalogues. It's a bluff, of course, as hardly anything can be compared to the stuff we're offering. I figure the overall profit will be in the region of three billion US dollars! Three fucking billion! That would mean that the smallest cut of the profit for your men could be several million each.'

Seraphim grinned. There would be no cuts, he thought. Not in the traditional sense, that is. He would be getting most of the money. Kislov and his men would see to it.

The captain came over to Seraphim.

'The British authorities are requesting to board the plane,' he said. 'Some papers have not been stamped properly.'

Seraphim immediately flew into a rage.

'What bloody papers!' he yelled. 'This plane belongs to the

Russian government! No one has the right to inspect us!'

The pilot shrugged his shoulders as if saying, 'I'm just the pilot, what can I do?'

'Relax,' Yeffim said. 'These things happen. They'll come on board, stamp the documents and be off in a few minutes. We won't even need to switch off the engines.'

Seraphim calmed down.

'Open the exit at the rear of the plane,' he said, 'and don't allow them into this section. And get the Vice-Premier to join us here.'

The customs people arrived ten minutes later. There were six of them. They asked for the paperwork for the diplomatic cargo and stamped all of the pages.

They then left the plane and bade everyone a safe journey.

But one of them remained on board. He managed to slip unnoticed into the special baggage compartment at the back where some of the crates with the diplomatic cargo were stored.

It was Pavel Batalov.

★

The British ambassador in Moscow was compiling an urgent report for the Foreign Office in London.

Embassy sources were reporting that a 'sudden transition of power' had taken place in the Kremlin and that a new leader was about to emerge as a result. According to information that was slowly filtering through, the President had taken an unusual decision to appoint FSB Director, Benedikt Vladimirov, as the new Vice-President. The official announcement was expected on Monday morning. The ambassador had summoned the head of the embassy political department, Richard Atley, to prepare a background report on the new Vice-President. Atley was busy going through the computer archives assembling all the available data on the new man.

According to the files, Vladimirov had served in the KGB, initially in the Second Directorate that dealt with counter-intelligence matters. Later he was rewarded for his 'dedication to duty', whatever that meant, with a posting to Vienna as an agent of the First Directorate, dealing with matters relating to international organisations based in Austria.

After four years he returned to Moscow and briefly worked in the secretariat of the chairman of the KGB. He held the rank of Colonel when communism collapsed in the Soviet Union and he was one of the first people to leave the force. It was unclear from the files whether he jumped or was pushed.

Later he went into politics and became an advisor to one of the leaders of the democratic movement in Russia, eventually becoming his deputy. At some point he must have rejoined the KGB, which by then had changed its name to FSB, apparently without his boss's knowledge. From 1992 to 1993 Vladimirov worked in the Moscow mayor's office, heading the external affairs department.

It was a surprise to everyone that after Yeltsin's downfall the new President appointed Vladimirov as FSB Director. He was never seen as a close ally of the new Russian leader and was not even involved in the coup that led to Yeltsin's demise.

In fact, as Atley found out, there was not much information about the new potential head of state anywhere. He seemed to have existed on the backstage of Russian politics. He was not linked to any of the interest groups, nor to any of the power brokers that had influence over members of the government. In fact, even his physical appearance was instantly forgettable, as Atley found out for himself. For as soon as he closed the file with Vladimirov's photograph in it, he couldn't really remember what the man looked like. His facial features were so unremarkable, so colourless, that they left no imprint in other people's memories.

When Atley finished his report he went to see the ambassador. He placed the report in front of him and sat down to wait while he read it.

'So, what do you think it all means?' the ambassador asked after glancing through the two pages that Atley had managed to scribble.

'I suspect the initial reaction of any outsider would be that of anxiety, sir,' Atley said. 'A KGB operative becomes the second most powerful man in Russia, with a view of replacing the head of state. And yet it could have been much worse.'

The ambassador opened the drawer of his desk and took out a pack of Marlboro Lights. Atley immediately realised that Sir Brian was getting nervous. He usually smoked a pipe.

'Go on,' the ambassador said lighting up the cigarette.

'Well, sir, the new man is not linked to any of the unpleasant characters that are circling around the Kremlin and he hasn't been involved in any past scandals. At least not that I'm aware of.'

He looked at the ambassador, who had smoked half of the cigarette in a matter of seconds.

'Not that London will be pleased at the news of course,' Atley added. 'It's not exactly what we've been expecting to happen.'

The ambassador got up from his chair and walked to the window.

'No one in the world could have predicted a scenario like this,' he said looking out of the window. 'Any more than one could have foreseen that communism would collapse in Russia in a matter of days or that Yeltsin, the first democratically elected Russian leader in 1,000 years, would order the shelling of the country's parliament. And again, no one expected him to be ousted without a fight.'

The ambassador turned round to face Atley.

'Russia is an enigma and we will see many more surprises in the years to come,' he said. 'So don't blame yourself for not getting it right this time. And now let's explain to London that things are not as bad as they look.'

★

Pavel was thinking about his next move.

They had been airborne for about half an hour and luckily for him no one had yet come to check the crates at the back. They all had special seals on them and were marked 'Diplomatic cargo! Handle with care!'

He was wondering why the Crow had gone to such trouble to get these crates out of the embassy. They were supposed to contain contemporary Russian folk artefacts destined for some exhibition. And yet the Crow had arranged for the two helicopters to pick them up and had sacrificed many of his men for these crates.

Pavel decided to try and open one of the crates to see what was inside. He picked the one which seemed to have been slightly damaged during loading. A crack had developed along the wooden frame. Using a souvenir pocket knife that he had bought in London Pavel widened the crack and then gradually lifted the top of the crate. The artefacts were all wrapped in paper. He took out one of the items and unwrapped it. It was a diamond necklace and the small label attached to it read: 'Empress Catherine the Great necklace. Gift from Prince Potyemkin.'

Pavel could not believe his eyes: the Crow had stolen the Russian national treasures from the Kremlin's Armoury!

★

Vice-Premier Vitalli Tenko finally realised the real scale of the disaster that had happened to him.

He had been set up by Vassili, that double-dealing bastard, who had forced him – and there was no other word for it – to take on board his plane a dangerous criminal, who had then tricked him into assisting him in his evil schemes.

The Vice-Premier could not yet understand exactly what had taken place in the embassy in London. But he sensed that something extraordinary was happening around him and that his future was – to put it mildly – not looking good at all. He was a virtual prisoner on a plane destined for Columbia with no possibility of contacting Moscow.

The man who was guarding him in business class was obviously eager to join his friends back in the economy section. He kept turning his head every time a roar of laughter came from the rear of the plane. Finally, he could resist no longer. He stood up and simply walked out to join his friends.

The Vice-Premier noticed him leave, but did not react in any way. He was thinking about his life and the efforts he had made to achieve his rise to power. He recalled the many occasions he had had to make compromises and reject his friends in order to become part of an emerging new political team. For the first time in his life he was ashamed of betraying the ones who had trusted him.

And now he found himself in a situation where not only his career but his life was on the line. He had two options left: either sit and wait for his fate or put up a fight.

He chose the latter…

★

Ivan Ossinski could hear the murmur of voices from the row behind him. Seraphim Voronov, whom he had met for the first time earlier that day, was taking him to Columbia 'on business'.

From the moment Ivan arrived in London he couldn't understand what was happening around him. He spent the first night in a hotel with orders not to call anyone and then the next day they practically imprisoned him in a flat where there was not even a telephone. And when the two men came to pick him up the next day and he started to protest about his imprisonment, one of them said, 'You should be grateful that you're not in prison sucking some dick just to stay alive. If not for Mr Voronov you'd be banged up in some shithole in Russia.'

It sounded so threatening that Ivan fell silent. He followed the men downstairs and they all got into a car that was waiting for them. They drove to a hotel where they spent a good hour sitting in the car waiting for something to happen. Then a coach stopped at the hotel and Ivan was taken on board. Most of the seats were occupied and Ivan was told to go to the rear of the coach. As he passed between the seats he couldn't help noticing a big man who was smoking a cigarette.

The man nodded to him. Later, at the airport, he approached Ivan.

'Let's get to know each other better,' he said. 'My name is Seraphim Voronov.'

★

Pavel was desperately trying to come up with some sort of plan.

He knew that once the plane landed he would be found and probably killed immediately. Somehow he had to take control of the plane and divert it back to London.

But what could he do?

There were at least a dozen men in the economy-class compartment, all armed. He would have to deal with them before he could get to the cockpit. Pavel had a gun with him but he was up against a group of trained men with machine guns. He would have to come up with something very unusual to get past them. If only he could get someone to help him, he thought.

Then, when he was least expecting it, help arrived – in the unlikely form of the Vice-Premier Vitalli Tenko. He needed to go to the toilet and, not wanting to face Voronov, went to the one at the rear. Pavel saw him walk down the aisle passing the men in economy class. He waited till he approached the rear of the plane. Tenko was shocked to see a man appearing out of nowhere.

'Mr Vice-Premier,' Pavel whispered, 'my name is Batalov; I'm a former undercover agent for the central Moscow CID. I have no time to explain the details, but we need to divert this plane back to London. I need your help.'

He quickly described what he was trying to do. There were two of them already, plus Ivan Ossinski who could help them. And there were three pilots and two stewardesses. It didn't amount to much but it was something.

They decided that the Vice-Premier would try to pass a message to Ivan, who would pass the word to the pilots that the plane was hijacked and that they had to do everything in their power to get back to London.

The next few minutes turned into a test of nerves. The Vice-Premier managed to get into first class and strike up a seemingly innocent conversation with Ivan Ossinski. Seraphim was relaxing his guard. There was a still a long way to fly and he reasoned that he might as well enjoy himself.

The Vice-Premier managed to pass the message to Ivan from Pavel about the need to take control of the plane. From his seat near the cockpit Ivan had to get inside it and persuade the captain to turn the plane round and go back to London.

At that moment everything depended on Ivan's ability to convince the crew to take their side.

★

Pavel reckoned that he could get his hands on one of the sub-machine guns that were lying on the seats in the economy class. But he needed a distraction, to ensure that the men would be facing the other way.

He could not think of anything. And then the Vice-Premier appeared at the front of the section. He was looking pale and nervous.

'I want to make an announcement,' he said. 'The cargo that you are taking to South America consists of Russian national treasures that have been stolen and are going to be sold off. If you have any decency left in you, you will stop this crime taking place. And I promise that if you help me I will do my best to negotiate a full pardon for you all.'

The men were so taken aback by what they had just heard that it was not immediately clear what their reaction would be. But then one of them grinned and said, 'A full pardon, sure. And will they also pay us to go straight?'

Everyone laughed. The remark killed off the impact of the passionate address made by the Vice-Premier. But the confusion had lasted long enough for Pavel to sneak between the rows of seats and grab a machine gun.

'Get back to your seat before you get hurt!' somebody shouted to the Vice-Premier.

But there was no stopping Tenko, especially after he noticed Pavel getting hold of the weapon.

'I can only tell you that all the law-enforcement agencies throughout the world will be looking for you from now on,' he said in a loud voice. 'There won't be a day when someone will not be asking questions about you.'

The men seemed unimpressed. Then one of them yelled, 'Let's send the important son of a bitch down without a para-chute! That'll teach him a lesson!'

Several of the men got up from their seats.

It was then that the Vice-Premier took what looked like a grenade out of his jacket pocket and held it high. Pavel was watching him closely. The grenade was in reality a lighter but by using it to threaten the occupants of economy class Tenko provided him with valuable time to hide some of the weapons.

Having pushed the machine guns under the seats, Pavel straightened up and announced, 'You'd better listen to what the man says!'

Everyone turned in his direction. There was genuine shock on the faces of all the passengers. But Pavel knew that it would only be a matter of seconds before they regained their senses. He walked to the man closest to him, who was reaching for a machine gun, and hit him with the butt of his automatic rifle. Another man tried to jump him but he managed to evade him and knock him down.

The Vice-Premier froze for a moment, still holding the 'grenade' in his hand. But after the second man went down he shouted, 'If anyone makes another move I blow the whole fucking plane to bits!'

Attention once again switched from Pavel to the Vice-Premier. Pavel grabbed a machine gun from the seat and threw it to the Vice-Premier, who caught it with his left hand like an experienced soldier. They could now control the situation in the economy class section.

From here on everything depended on Ivan being able to deal with the crew.

★

Ivan could not hear what was happening in the back of the plane, but he was thinking hard how he could get into the cockpit.

By then Seraphim and Yeffim had drunk a few large vodkas and were oblivious to what was going on. Ivan decided to make a move. He rose from his seat and walked directly to the cockpit. He moved so quickly that Seraphim and Yeffim did not at first realise what he was doing. Before they could even open their mouths Ivan had entered the cabin, shut and locked the door behind him.

All the pilots inside turned around and were staring at him.

'I have a very important message from the Vice-Premier,' Ivan said in a loud voice. 'This plane has been taken over by criminals. We have to stop them. You must turn the plane back to London right now!'

There was banging from the other side of the door. Seraphim was furious. The young punk had managed to get into the cockpit! He signalled to Yeffim to go and get some of his men. When Yeffim reached the economy section he saw Pavel and the Vice-Premier standing there, pointing machine guns at the 'passengers'. He couldn't figure out what was happening.

'What's going on?' he shouted.

The Vice-Premier instinctively turned round to see who it was. That was enough for one of the Crow's men to attempt to grab a machine gun that was lying on the seat across the aisle. Pavel blocked his way and hit him in the stomach with his fist, sending him down. A second man tried to jump him and Pavel hit him with the butt of his automatic rifle. The rest got the message and stayed put.

'Are you okay, sir?' Pavel asked the Vice-Premier.

'I'm fine,' he said.

He then raised the machine gun and pointed it at Yeffim.

'You make one move and I'll shoot you,' he said.

The look in his eyes proved that he was not joking.

Yeffim joined the rest of the men.

'Hold them while I get the Crow,' Pavel said as he ran past him down the aisle.

When he entered the first class salon he saw the Crow kicking hysterically at the cockpit door. Pavel quickly walked up to him and spun him around. Seraphim recognised him immediately. A look of shock and amazement distorted his face.

'You? It's you?' he uttered.

Pavel pointed the barrel of the machine gun at his face.

'Yes, it's me, Crow. And it's all over for you,' he said.

★

Alex was recovering in hospital. The operation had gone well and the bullet had been removed from his neck.

George came to see him. He entered the room and stood by the bedside. He looked pale and thin. He was unshaven, wearing a worn-out casual jacket and slacks.

Alex opened his eyes and looked up at him.

'How are you feeling?' George asked.

'I'll pull through,' Alex said quietly.

He kept on looking at George. There was a silent question in his eyes.

'He is still in a coma,' George said.

Alex started to cry. Tears ran down his cheeks.

George stood motionless.

The door opened and Jeremy came in. He came up to the bed and stood silently for several moments.

Alex turned his head to face Jeremy.

'I am very sorry about your partner,' Jeremy said. 'I have asked the doctors to do everything possible to save him. He is a brave man and he fought like a hero.'

Alex said nothing. He was still crying.

Boris was having a drink with Ivan. It was the first time that they had actually had a drink together like two men. Boris was proud of his son. Ivan was a real hero. Jeremy had told Boris what happened on the plane and how Ivan had managed to convince the crew that the plane had been hijacked. The pilots had turned round and landed at Heathrow where the cops, alerted by George, were waiting for them.

Boris stayed behind with the ambassador at the hospital where he was being treated for his wounds, and did not go to the airport. The head of the embassy visa section represented the Russian authorities and oversaw the search of the plane. The crates with the diplomatic markings were then taken away and stored in a bonded warehouse under armed guard.

Vice-Premier Vitalli Tenko was on his way back to Russia on the first available Aeroflot flight.

Pavel Batalov stayed behind in London to arrange extradition papers for Seraphim Voronov on charges of being accessory to murder, kidnapping and armed robbery. On instructions from the

Prosecutor General's office in Moscow, Pavel was reinstated as special investigator of the Moscow central CID and given authority to negotiate on behalf of the Russian side on all matters relating to the attempted hijacking of the Russian government plane and its priceless cargo.

★

In Holland a shipment of stolen valuables and large amounts of cash were intercepted by the police acting on a tip-off from their British counterparts. The goods were hidden in a warehouse and the cash was stored on a yacht ready to be moved to Eastern Europe.

About thirty people were arrested, some of whom turned out to be connected to very big international art collectors. All of them named a Russian, Yeffim Kaltzman, as their contact who had informed them of the 'private sale of the century'. Kaltzman was under arrest in Britain for dealing in stolen goods and being an accessory to the hijacking of a plane.

A Russian colonel, Igor Kislov, was among those arrested. He refused to give any evidence, but once his name was traced to an Interpol wanted list, he asked for political asylum.

One of the arrested men told the police that Kislov had carried out a mass execution of twelve people who they later buried at a disused industrial site. He said that the orders to kill the men came from a Russian criminal known as the Crow.

★

Seraphim was brought into the Lubyanka jail and put into one of interrogation rooms. He waited there for a good hour. He seemed to be indifferent to everything that was happening around him.

What next? he thought. They'll probably send me to jail for tax evasion and fraud, but I'll appeal and come out in about two or three years. I still have enough money hidden to last me a while.

The door of the interrogation room opened. An FSB major and two wardens walked in.

'Citizen Voronov, we are taking you to your cell,' the major said. 'There'll be no interrogation today.'

The Crow got up.

Well, at least I'll have a rest after the flight from London, he thought.

He was led down a long corridor with no windows and then down several flights of stairs into the basement. They brought him to a steel door and took off the handcuffs. One of the wardens opened the door and signalled to Seraphim to step in.

'You will be sharing the cell with another convict,' he said.

Seraphim walked in. It was dark inside and he couldn't see the man on the lower bunk.

The door behind him slammed with a loud bang.

Seraphim came up to the bunk.

'How you been doing, Crow?' he heard a familiar voice.

It was Shark. He'd come back from the dead.

★

The first issue of the newspaper *The Daily News* came out with a world exclusive front-page story entitled 'Russian National Treasures Saved'. It was all about a daring attempt by the Russian mob to steal priceless artefacts from the Kremlin collection and about a covert operation by an international team that foiled the robbery…

Printed in the United Kingdom
by Lightning Source UK Ltd.
119895UK00001B/10-39